ALL THIS AND SOAPSUDS, TOO

Jasmine was reaching behind her, intent on soaping her back, when his voice interrupted her thoughts. "Would you like me to do that for you?"

Her eyes widened with surprise. But for the one morning after their wedding, he hadn't touched her in four months. She couldn't believe she was hearing him right.

But when he came suddenly to the tub and knelt at her side, he repeated, "Would you?"

Jasmine could only nod her head.

His voice was husky, sending chills down her spine when he whispered, "You are so pretty, Jasmine." Silently he cursed the idiotic remark. To say she was pretty was like comparing the Atlantic to a puddle. The cloth slipped from shaking fingers. His hands smoothed over her soapy skin, bringing her to a state of near delirium.

Her eager sigh of delight mingled erotically with the silkiness of her flesh and the sweet clean scent of her bath crystals. Her head fell back against the rim of the tub. Her eyes half closed with passion, while a strangled, "Oh, Anthony," whispered past her soft lips.

He felt himself drowning in her, knowing only that he had to have more of this delight or risk his very sanity. It had been so long, so terribly long.

CREOLE CAPTIVE

PATRICIA PELLIGANE

ZEBRA BOOKS
KENSINGTON PUBLISHING CORP.

ZEBRA BOOKS

are published by

Kensington Publishing Corp.
475 Park Avenue South
New York, NY 10016

First printing: September, 1989

Printed in the United States of America

Prologue

It was finished. Before this day was over he'd know where to find her. Elizabeth, his beautiful Elizabeth, the only woman he had ever truly loved would be his at last. Please God, he silently prayed, it's not too late. Don't let it be too late.

Some might think it ridiculous, nay impossible, to have loved her for nearly twenty years. They'd accuse him of loving a memory, no more, but in his heart he knew the truth. There had been women since. He was a man, after all, with all the normal needs that would come to assault in the loneliness of night. But the women had been naught but warm bodies, needed for physical relief and then forgotten, for none could compare to this love.

She'd had a daughter, he'd heard, and then cursed at the jealousy that raged. It was selfish to hope she had remained celibate while he had not. Was her man important to her, he wondered, or was she, too, seeking comfort and ease from her loneliness? The pictures his thoughts brought to mind tormented and yet he had to know.

Lord Richard Townsend thought back over the last hectic year. The moment he was free he had come for her, only to find her home abandoned and in a sad state of disrepair. The townspeople knew only that she had gone away four years ago. Not a soul knew of her present whereabouts.

Despite the danger, for war raged still between the Colonies and her motherland, he had left then for New Orleans, hoping she might have returned to the place of her birth, only to find her family had long since died. Desperate now, he returned to London and searched out the man she called, by law, husband.

Now, positioned opposite him at the gaming table in one of London's more disreputable clubs, Richard Townsend watched Lord Huntington dab at the nervous sweat that coated his forehead and upper lip as he calmly gathered the assortment of bills, bank drafts, and personal notes of debt taken from the center of the table.

"You've got to give me another go at it," Lord Huntington almost whined in his desperation, dabbing again at his lip. "I must have a chance to get even."

"I'm afraid that is quite impossible," Richard Townsend returned as he held up the deed to Huntington Hall, folded it neatly in half, and placed it in the inside pocket of his black velvet coat. "Am I mistaken, sir? Have you anything left with which to wager?"

"Good God, man! That deed alone is worth four times my wager."

"Actually, Huntington, I've recently had cause to visit the countryside and seen the manor. The walls are crumbling, the windows broken. No doubt the roof leaks. I'd say it's worth less than half."

Huntington turned eyes filled with hate upon the man who twenty years ago had, for a short time, been his neighbor. Even back then he was reputed to be a ruthless bastard. Word had it that he had put his wife away merely because another had interested him more.

6

For a time, Huntington had wondered if he wasn't Elizabeth's lover. Someone certainly had been. But when Townsend had moved away, he'd discarded the notion. Not that he cared, in any case. He'd hated the Creole bitch from the first moment he'd laid eyes on her. And hated even more the bastard daughter he'd had no choice but to claim. He'd been forced by his family to marry. The Huntington coffers had been in desperate need of replenishment. A marriage of convenience was arranged. He hadn't argued when his father had chosen his bride, but he put his foot down when his father had hinted at, nay demanded, heirs. Huntington repressed a shiver of disgust. Just the thought of touching that soft body was enough to make him physically ill.

"I know what you want, Townsend. I've known from the first."

Lord Townsend's cold gray eyes grew to the color of pewter and glittered with imminent victory, a victory, to his way of thinking, all too long in coming. His mouth twisted into a goading smile. Huntington believed him desirous of his most eligible daughter and that was exactly what Townsend wanted him to think. Had he not, in fact, started the rumor himself? How else to find the mother? "Would you wager your own blood, Huntington?"

Lord Jamison Huntington forced back the retort that almost burst forth. He'd known, of course, from the first, that Jasmine wasn't his daughter, but Townsend didn't have to know. Indeed, if Townsend suspected the truth of Jasmine's unknown parentage, it would lower her worth considerably, perhaps leaving Huntington with no hand to play.

Lord Huntington laughed with growing confidence as his wily mind conjured up a solution to his dilemma. "Nay, I'd have to be daft to wager further against your incredible luck tonight." And indeed

7

Townsend's luck had been incredible. If he didn't know better, he just might think the man a little too lucky. Huntington shrugged aside the thought. He'd have a time of it trying to prove any quick of hand on Townsend's part. "I think," he began confidently, "a gentleman's agreement might be in order. In truth, I expected to gain . . ." He shrugged as if the matter were of little importance, when, in fact, the outcome of his proposition posed nothing short of life or death. Were his offer to fail, he'd be forced to flee the country or face debtor's prison, for he hadn't a farthing to share among his many creditors. And that bitch of a wife of his ignored his every plea, likewise his threats. He had long since gone through the huge sum she had brought to their marriage. The rest was in trust, held in her name, and no matter his desperate correspondence, she wouldn't part with a shilling. "Shall we say the girl for everything that is on this table?"

Lord Townsend laughed with all the confidence of a man in complete control of any given situation and leaned comfortably back in his chair. One dark brow rose above piercing silver eyes that pinned the man across from him. "I'd say you prize her overly high."

"No higher than her worth, surely."

Townsend gave a secret smile. No doubt he could have held out for less—Huntington was plainly desperate—but Townsend cared nothing for money and, knowing his search was nearly at an end, felt particularly magnanimous. No, he wouldn't squabble over a farthing or two. He didn't need the man's money. There was but one thing on earth he needed and that was to find Elizabeth. He felt a wave of relief assault and knew had he been standing his knees would have had a time supporting his weight.

Aye, it was finished. He'd know now where to find her. Idly he asked the seemingly innocent question, "Where is she?"

Chapter One

Anthony Montgomery grinned as he rolled off the soft, plump body beneath him and listened to the huskily murmured whisper. "God," she gasped in breathless wonder, "you're apt to ruin me for the other blokes if you keep that up."

Smiling at her compliment, Anthony pulled her warm, pliant body close against his. He hadn't a doubt she said as much to all who serviced her, but there wasn't a man alive whose ego couldn't stand her obvious pleasure, be her words truth or not.

He mumbled something unintelligible as his hand cupped her lush backside, and he waited for the inevitable moment when conversation would begin. Anthony hadn't visited this tavern wench by chance. Nay, he'd planned these encounters for some time, for little was known to stay secret when a soldier was deep in his cups, and who else was apt to hear these tasty tidbits but the wench who served the brew.

Anthony forced aside the smile that threatened as he mused over the arrogance of his former countrymen. Simply because the colonists were forced to sign pledges of loyalty to the Crown, it was assumed all problems regarding subterfuge would then cease to exist. Indeed, their attitude defied all good sense and often allowed the most secret of information to be passed on to eager ears in idle conversation.

Unbeknownst to her, Sally was better by far than most would-be informers, for she was the possessor of many excellent attributes, including an extraordinary memory for the smallest of details and the loosest tongue he'd ever come across. Nothing remained a secret once it reached her ears and for that he was extremely thankful, for he never once found the need to coerce her into telling him just what he wanted to know.

"How was your day, sweet?" he asked conversationally and then smiled into her harshly dyed red hair as she began her long rendition of the exact happenings of the day.

Jesus God, when had he ever been so wet and cold? Thank the good Lord he no longer had to make the trip all the way to Connecticut. A short ride to Long Island was all that was needed nowadays, thanks to Caleb Brewster and his swift longboats. Anthony imagined the information imparted, hardly two hours past, was already in Washington's hands. He gave a great shiver from the cold, thankful his work was done for the night. He was looking forward to stabling his horse and from there, the short walk to his rooms, to find awaiting him a stout tankard of mulled wine and a roaring fire to warm his bones.

Anthony gave an unconscious curse as he pulled his horse to a stop at the stable door. The place was dark and looked to be deserted. Anthony called out, only to be greeted by a short, whinnying sound. Where the hell had the boy gone off to? He sighed with disgust. He should have known, on a night such as this, he'd be forced to take care of the horse himself.

Wearily Anthony dismounted and brought the animal to his stall. He was bone-tired, but the horse couldn't be left wet and cold. No, there was no help for it. He'd have to do the chore himself.

Anthony shivered again and pulled off his heavy, thoroughly soaked coat, clearly more comfortable without it, since the stable gave off its own warmth, filled as it was with the heat of horseflesh. And if the warm, moist air was a bit too pungent, it was nevertheless preferable to the bone-chilling dampness outside.

Anthony had stripped down to his trousers when the soft sounds of feminine laughter filled the stable's roughly hewn interior.

"She's going to be furious, Jasmine. I'll wager she never allows us to ride outside the coach again."

"Nonsense" came a deep, sultry, feminine voice. "Mother is never furious." A low, delicious chuckle. "Well, at least, not for long."

The softly spoken words caught Anthony's attention. He smiled as he listened to the two ladies chatter while continuing on with the care of his horse.

"It was almost a month before you left your room after she found you with Justin. I'd say that was long enough."

"I can't imagine why all the fuss. Lord, you'd think she found us naked and in bed, for all the ranting that went on."

"Jasmine!"

"No need to sound so shocked, Deborah. We both know what goes on behind bedroom doors. Besides, I only let him kiss me. Was that so dastardly a deed?"

"Jasmine, you know very well your mother was only worried of your reputation. What decent man would want you if—"

A low, dramatic groan interrupted. "Lord, I can't think of a more boring prospect than a decent man."

"Jasmine!" The voice was clearly aghast.

"Well, I *can't*" came the sullen, almost childish response. Anthony found himself hard put to hold back the laugh that threatened. A short moment of silence ensued and then, "Besides, when have I ever given her cause to worry?"

"I can't imagine" came the softly spoken, if slightly sarcastic response. "Except for the time you went off with Tommy at the church picnic and then danced three times with Mr. Howlster at Rachel's coming-out. God, that caused quite a stir, him being a married man and all."

"The man was an excellent dancer," the one called Jasmine returned with no little annoyance, obviously remembering the problems that little indiscretion had caused. "And we did nothing but dance!" she insisted. "Why anyone would care is beyond me. Those muckraking old biddies have nothing better to do than gossip."

Anthony grinned. Apparently it was the one called Deborah who sighed, "And then there was the time John—"

"Enough! If you want to remain my friend, you'll say not another word. You know as well as I that absolutely nothing happened! The man fairly reeked of garlic."

Intrigued, Anthony peered out of the darkened stall, curious to discover the owner of the voice and the culprit behind these many hideous crimes against polite society.

"Where is everybody? I've never known the place to be so quiet."

Anthony walked toward the dim light at the barn's entrance. There, in the center of the hay-strewn dirt floor, stood the two young women, holding the reins of their horse.

Jasmine turned as she heard the slight sound of Anthony's boot scraping across the flat rocks that dotted the dirt floor. "Oh, there you are. I was beginning to think the place had been abandoned."

"Did we wake you?"

Anthony nearly gasped aloud as he realized that honey-sweet voice was coming from the most beautiful woman he'd ever seen. His eyes widened as he took in the sight of her. The dim light of a lantern lent a warm, golden glow to her skin, while eyes the color of polished silver invited a man closer and then dared him to try.

Her mouth, pouty and naturally pink, was as devoid of artificial coloring as her creamy, golden skin. And surrounding that marvelous face was a glorious cloud of black curls even the rain hadn't managed to subdue. She was taller than most women; he guessed the top of her head would reach his jaw. *He wouldn't have to bend far to kiss this one* came a wild thought. Suddenly he felt an unreasonable hatred for this Justin fellow as well as a growing sense of anger toward this woman that she should have allowed such liberties. The notion was ridiculous, of course, yet Anthony couldn't imagine a man not being intrigued by that mouth and he made a determined, silent vow that he was going to sample her favors himself.

It was apparent that she believed him to be the stablehand. Anthony grinned and moved closer. For some reason he couldn't fathom, he allowed her first impression to stand. He shook his head. "I was workin' out back," he remarked, his cultured manner of speech gone and replaced with a Cockney accent he'd learned as a lad aboard ship and until this minute thought long forgotten.

"Where is Mr. Cramby?"

"Out."

Jasmine raised a fine, feminine brow at his arrogant stance and manner. She'd never seen a stablehand stare so rudely, nor for that matter stand—no, that wasn't quite correct, *lounge* was

13

more like it—against a wall with a decided insolence as he spoke to his betters. And the worst of it was the man stood there half naked and seemed not to care in the least.

Jasmine felt a tremor not unlike fear slither down her spine as she took in the sight of him. Even now, in the dimness of the stable, she could clearly see the dark bronze of his skin, proof, she imagined, of a great amount of outdoor activity. Her mind refused to accept her notice of the golden mass of hair upon his chest and the intriguing way it darkened as it wove its way down his body to form a thin line that disappeared into the waistband of tight trousers. His brown hair, tied neatly at the nape of his neck, was liberally laced with blond streaks, and because of a lantern lit some distance behind him, gave the ethereal impression of a halo. Jasmine almost laughed as the absurd notion came to mind, for the saintly effect of his coloring was easily belied by the devilish glitter in eyes that were either black or so darkly blue they appeared to be black, a glitter that both intrigued her and sent a tingling of fear down her spine. Jasmine knew a moment's trepidation, for as sure as she breathed, this man posed a danger, though exactly what kind of danger she couldn't begin to fathom. Annoyed, she gave an imperceptible shrug, mentally denying the fact that he had made so great an impression. He was a stable boy, for God's sake, and if he appeared a bit too sure of himself, it was, no doubt, that stupid notion of Jefferson's that caused this misjudgment of his. Created equal, indeed! What utter rubbish. What was needed here was a good setting down. And she was just the one to do it. "Your name, boy."

Anthony's grin flashed white, even teeth. Boy? She called him "boy," when she was easily ten years his junior? And to top it off, she wasn't asking, she was *ordering* him to tell her.

14

Anthony's gaze glittered from the murky shadow. She had a nasty mouth, this one, and her attitude, toward those whom she believed of a lesser station than she could stand a bit of improving. And if the lady at her side didn't look as if she was about ready to faint from the shock of seeing a man half dressed, he would have been more than happy to show her the best use of that mouth, and what would naturally follow would go far toward improving her overall attitude.

"Is something wrong with your hearing, boy? I asked your name."

Anthony forced aside his grin and lowered his eyes in a more subservient manner. "Sorry, miss. Guess I was thinkin' on my work out back. Name's Monty."

Anthony almost grinned at the low sounds of obvious relief when both women gave breathless sighs. He hadn't realized till then that they were both frightened half out of their wits. And right they should be. What kind of fools wandered about alone at night? They were lucky one of the gangs of ruffians that often ran the streets of this city had not accosted them. What in damnation were they up to anyway, and who was fool enough to allow them this much freedom?

"I'll get me shirt and see to your 'orses directly," he murmured as he backed away into the darkness.

"Lord, he gave me a scare," Deborah whispered to her friend. "His eyes glittered so, I half expected to see him pounce upon us at any second."

"Nonsense," Jasmine returned as she raised her jaw a fraction, the action adding much-needed strength to her wavering confidence. Purposely, she pushed aside the fact that her heart had yet to calm itself. "It was a trick of the light, is all."

"If I might, a moment of your time, Mr. Cramby?"

15

"Aye, governor." Mr. Cramby brought his attention from the horse he was readying for a customer's afternoon ride. He smiled as his gaze took in the finely dressed gentleman. "Somethin' you be needin', sir?"

"Well, two matters in fact, Mr. Cramby. First, I couldn't help but notice that gray roan." Anthony nodded toward the stall that held the horse in question. "An exquisite piece of horseflesh, wouldn't you agree?"

Mr. Cramby nodded his head. "Spirited, too. But as sweet and gentle as a kitten when Lady Huntington mounts him."

Anthony smiled at how easily he had gained the lady's name. "You don't imagine Lady Huntington would be willing to sell him?"

"Hercules?" He shook his head. "If'n you'd ever heard her talking to the beast, you'd know he was her pet."

Anthony nodded. Now for perhaps the most idiotic request he was ever likely to make. Indeed, once he voiced the words, poor Mr. Cramby simply looked up at him as if he'd lost his senses.

After a few moments of stunned silence, Mr. Cramby ventured with as casual a shrug as he could manage, "Can always use a good hand. If'n you're sure that's what you want."

Anthony grinned at the man's obvious bewilderment. "Oh, I'm sure, Mr. Cramby. I'm quite sure."

Just before Anthony turned on his heel, he remarked, "One more thing. It might be better, for the time being, if you forget the 'sir.' I'd be obliged if you'd call me Monty."

"Monty?" Mr. Cramby croaked, eyes wide with disbelief.

"It would look a bit odd, wouldn't you say, if you addressed me as sir while I'm working for you?" A long moment of stunned silence came before Anthony

16

coaxed, "Don't you agree?"

Cramby didn't know what to say. He'd never in his life heard of such a thing. Finally he realized the man was waiting for his answer and he mumbled, "I imagine."

Anthony nodded, apparently satisfied with the outcome of this bizarre meeting and left a gaping Mr. Cramby to stare incredulously at his retreating back. "No doubt about it," the man mumbled as he returned to his chore, "the richer they get, the odder they grow." Cramby shrugged a thick shoulder. "Must be a problem with their breeding."

"Don't you ever wear a shirt?"

Anthony turned from his chore toward the low, breathless sound, while forcing aside his grin and maintaining a look of complete innocence. He knew well enough how his half-naked state bothered her, knew how she shivered every time he *accidentally* rubbed against her. Even now she was having a time of it keeping her eyes from his chest. "I was cleaning out the stall, miss. It's a messy job."

Sweat glistened over the smooth, muscled flesh of his shoulders. Jasmine felt decidedly light-headed as he moved closer and she saw clearly the moisture holding to the crisp golden hairs upon his chest. At least she imagined them crisp. Suddenly she shook her head, forcing aside her wayward thoughts. Her lips tightened with annoyance. It was indecent that he should so carelessly flaunt his near-naked state in the presence of a lady. Firmly she refused to listen to the nagging thought that it was perhaps the feelings he instilled in her breast that were indecent. She took a deep, steadying breath. Good God, she could smell him! The fact he smelled wonderful she would not even contemplate. Surely her weakness was due to the fact that she had not as yet eaten. She didn't like

17

this man. She didn't like his arrogance, his handsome looks, his long, muscular body, or the oddly hungry look that frequently came to his eyes. Her lips tightened further with disapproval. "Odd, but I manage the chore without disrobing."

"A shame," Anthony instantly returned, for he couldn't imagine a more lovely sight than this woman about any chore without a stitch.

"What?!" she exclaimed, unable to believe a stablehand would have the audacity to make such a remark.

Anthony gave her a carefully blank look. "I said I'll rub Hercules down for you."

Jasmine didn't for a minute believe she had imagined his first remark. Still, it would have been most uncharitable to call the man an out-and-out liar, though she had no doubt he was. Breaking eye contact, Jasmine ignored the slow, vaguely taunting smile she saw forming on his lips. "There is no need. I enjoy seeing to his care."

"It's my job, miss."

"And it's my pleasure, Monty. Surely you have other more pressing chores to occupy?"

He was tempted to argue, but at her glare, he wisely decided to allow her to win this point.

But if Jasmine believed her sharp words to have ended the matter, she soon realized she was doomed to disappointment. He was back in a few minutes, her words apparently forgotten. In his hand he held a sack of oats. It took him some time, and much supposed fumbling, before he pulled the feeding sack over Hercules's head. With only the slightest of grins and a silent sigh of satisfaction, Anthony finally managed to position himself close enough to Jasmine. Patiently, he waited.

Jasmine sent the oaf more than one meaningful glare. Did he have to stand that near? In fact, did he have to come in here at all? Hadn't she told him she'd take care of this? What was the matter with him?

Perhaps he was feeble-minded. Of course! She almost sighed aloud with relief. That would account for the unlikelihood of someone of his size and looks working in a stable. Jasmine silently berated her thoughts. What difference did it make what the man looked like? It was obvious there was something wrong with him, but maybe it was more than just feeble-mindedness. Maybe he was dangerous. Certainly he aroused in her the most peculiar feelings. Jasmine looked at him again. He wasn't saying or doing anything, just watching Hercules eat. Surely there was nothing wrong with that. No, instinctively she knew the man posed no danger to her, but obviously her assumption on his mental capabilities was close to the mark, for he couldn't seem to tear his eyes from the horse.

Jasmine inched away form him. God, he took up so much room. She had realized from the first, of course, his unusual size, but here in the small confines of the stall, he appeared enormous.

Jasmine very much wanted him gone but hesitated to tell him so. Having finally come to the conclusion that the man had not all the usual mental faculties, she didn't want to hurt his feelings. Still, his nearness bothered her more than she could have imagined.

Finally, Anthony almost groaned aloud as Hercules pushed back against his weight. It had taken the stupid beast long enough to grow annoyed. Anthony took the opportunity he was waiting for and stumbled back, but not before allowing a sharp exclamation of surprise and grabbing on to the lady at his side, ostensibly for support.

Anthony knew this was a shabby trick, but he also knew she didn't deserve much better. This woman was arrogant beyond belief. What she needed was a little lesson in manners. He didn't care who she was, there was no way he was going to let her act the

19

spoiled brat in his presence.

Jasmine landed with a grunt of surprise. She never realized that Anthony's knees had taken most of his weight. Had he honestly fallen upon her, his size and weight would have knocked her senseless. As it was, they landed on a pile of clean hay, Anthony's body sprawled, "by accident," over her.

Jasmine's mouth opened with astonishment, while Anthony desperately tried to contain the laughter that threatened.

Suddenly his merriment dissolved as she nervously licked her lips and his gaze caught the sight of her pink tongue. He lay still half over her, eye to eye, almost mouth to mouth. Her warm breath hit him full in the face and Anthony had to force down the urge to touch his lips to hers. He breathed in the heady scent of her and almost smiled as fields of wildflowers came to mind.

His little ploy was intended to tease, to annoy, but what he hadn't realized was how it would entrap him. He'd never suspected what the touch of her might do to his equilibrium. God, he felt his stomach tighten as if it had taken a blunt blow. The air left his lungs and he began to gasp, his whole being hungry for a greater, more explicit sampling of the softness that lay beneath him.

After her initial gasp of surprise, Jasmine simply stared at the man above her. An unfamiliar trembling began deep within her and a definite shallowness constricted her breathing. Above the scent of horse-flesh, leather, even over the sweetly clean hay upon which she now lay, there was him. How could a man work in a stable all day and smell so wonderfully clean? She denied that the erratic flutter in her chest meant anything. To imagine more here than mere surprise was absurd. The poor man had fallen and dragged her down in an effort to save himself. If anything, it only convinced her further of his mental disability.

"Get up, Monty," she managed at last in a voice that was oddly shaken and breathless.

"Sorry, miss, Hercules knocked me back," Anthony offered.

"That's quite all right. I understand," she said gently.

Anthony shot her a look of confusion. To say he was surprised at her reaction was to put it mildly. He had thought she might rage at his clumsiness, order him out, perhaps threaten to report him to his employer. But no, she did none of those things. Instead, she grew gentle. Why?

Anthony rolled to his feet and held out his hand. It was easily the most obnoxious thing he was ever likely to do, but Anthony just couldn't resist. She was simply too lovely, too spirited, and too damn adorable.

When Jasmine extended her hand to his, he pulled back with more strength than was necessary and she was yanked to her feet and flung up against him with startling force. On the pretense of steadying her, Anthony reached around her tiny waist and held her against him.

"Are you all right?" he asked, his mouth only inches from her parted lips. Again he caught the scent of wildflowers and easily imagined sunshine and sweet meadows and most definitely what he'd like to do to this lady if he ever got her truly alone.

Odd, but what he believed to be the greatest of jokes didn't seem at all funny right now. Right now he couldn't imagine anything more delightful than the delicious scent of her and the softness of her slender form in his arms.

"I will be, Monty," she answered, trying to disengage herself from him. Unthinking, small hands came to his chest meaning to push away. Instantly she dropped them back to her sides, her palms tingling almost as if his skin were fire and she had been burned. She struggled just a bit, but the arms that held her might have been forged from steel for all the give in them. "I understand you can't always help this, but you must be careful. Many ladies would be quite upset if you touched them like this."

Anthony blinked his surprise, his obvious confusion only adding to Jasmine's conviction. "What?"

Jasmine breathed a long, patient sigh. She wasn't doing this at all well. The trouble was she'd never before had a conversation with someone so obviously disabled and she didn't know how to go about telling him the error of his ways. "I don't want you to get in trouble. Do you understand that?"

She was talking to him as if she might speak to a child or someone feeble in mind. Anthony stared at her, wondering at her manner. Finally he nodded his answer.

"But you will get in trouble if you touch the ladies that come here."

At last Anthony realized she believed him to be simple-minded. He didn't know whether to laugh or play along with her supposition. If he laughed, she'd be outraged, he reasoned correctly. No, it might be safer and prove much more interesting if he played along, at least for the time being.

"Why? I like to touch ladies." He pulled her more tightly against him and smiled with an innocence he could only hope she'd believe. "They are soft and cuddly. Besides, they smell good."

Jasmine gave a silent groan. He was running his hand over her back and it was obvious he didn't see anything wrong with it. What was she supposed to do now? "I realize that, but we can't always do everything we want, can we?"

"Why not?" he asked petulantly.

Having no answer, at least none he'd understand,

she merely repeated, "Because we just can't, Monty. You must let me go now."

"Sally lets me touch her. She likes it when I touch her here." Boldly he ran his fingers over her breast.

Jasmine stiffened with shock, emphatically denying the tingle that ran down her spine at his touch. Anthony wondered if perhaps he hadn't gone too far and quickly pressed on, giving her little time to think about his outrageous actions. "She taught me how to kiss, too."

"Did she?" Her voice was strained. "How nice for you. Now, let me *go!*" Her voice was clearly tinged with panic and Anthony knew he'd pushed her as far as he was able. In another minute she'd be screaming for help.

Jasmine backed up against the wall of the stall and inched her way toward the door. "You can finish rubbing Hercules down, Monty. I have to go. I'll see you tomorrow." She was gone before he had a chance to nod his answer.

Chapter Two

She didn't see him at first, for he was bent at the waist spreading a clean layer of hay upon the dirt floor in the far corner of the stall. Jasmine muttered a cooing sound as she moved inside and patted Hercules's side, nuzzling her face to his smooth neck. "How are you today," she asked, certainly expecting no answer.

"I'm very well, thank you" came a startling sound from behind the horse.

With a short cry, Jasmine lurched away from the animal, thinking the terrible confusion that had granted her not a moment's peace these last few days had gotten the best of her. She denied the fluttering sensation in her chest as Anthony's face came into view, denied as well the warmth she felt at his wide, welcoming smile. He had turned to face her, but not before she caught a glimpse of his back, glistening with sweat and bronzed from hours spent in the sun. Damn, again he wore no shirt, and that fact seemed to bring again the slight constriction to her breathing.

It wasn't that he appealed to her, of course. The truth was, she was simply unused to seeing a man, any man, partially disrobed. It mattered little what the man looked like. No doubt she would have been equally shaken had he been less agreeable to the eye.

"Good morning, Monty," she said, forcing a lightness she didn't feel to her voice.

Anthony's lips lifted in a teasing smile. He never answered her breathless salutation but allowed her a long, lazy look that held her helplessly trapped against the low wall. For a fleeting moment she thought he might move toward her, perhaps trap her in place with his body. Maybe lean that hard, half-naked body against her. Maybe rub . . .

Jasmine's eyes widened with shock at her errant thoughts. What in the world had come over her? How was it this man, this poor, disabled man could cause her such lurid, sinful imaginings? Her voice was low, husky with the results of these thoughts when she asked, "Would you saddle Hercules for me?"

He nodded, his eyes holding still to hers as he moved past her, heading for the tack room.

Jasmine's thoughts were on his chest, as were her eyes, and she never thought to move aside. Anthony had no choice but to rub against her if he was to leave the stall, for she almost completely blocked the door.

Anthony, not wishing to pass up the opportunity to touch her, did not hesitate to do just that. His chest brushed against the softness of her breasts and he found his hands balled into fists with the effort it took not to reach out and bring her against him in an embrace.

He was no more than six feet from the stall when he heard her sharp cry. He raced back, his heart thudding with fear, to find her face white with pain, her body leaning weakly against the wall. "What happened?"

"I wasn't watching. Hercules stepped on my foot."

Effortlessly Anthony picked her up and held her against his chest as he hurried to the back of the barn. His heart thundered with fear, for he knew the horse could have crushed every bone in her foot. He sat her before him on a table in the tack room, knocking pieces of leather and tools to the floor with one sweep of his arm. Gently he removed her boot.

A moment later, to her stunned surprise, his hands reached beneath her skirt and rolled her black stocking down her leg. His hands had moved without thinking and had accomplished their purpose before she thought to thwart his intimate handling of her.

Anthony breathed an unconscious sigh of relief, for although her foot was already showing the purple hint of a bruise, there was almost no swelling.

Jasmine's eyes were wide with shock, her cheeks pink at his daring. But even now as he held her bare foot in the palm of his hand, she offered no recriminations, for she knew, no matter the intimacies involved, he was examining the injury with a purely clinical eye.

She didn't know the exact moment when that clinical look had turned to something far more potent and dangerous. All she realized was that her pain had suddenly disappeared and the whole experience seemed to have left her slightly dizzy. Her eyes widened with some surprise, for she could only attribute this sudden absence of pain to him. Did he, in fact, possess the power for miraculous healings in the touch of his hands? She doubted the possibility, but how else to explain this amazing happening? In her innocence, Jasmine had yet to realize his touch had brought about the throbbing sensation of desire. And it was the strength of this desire that blocked from her mind any previous discomfort.

He stood close, filling her field of vision and causing all else around them to blur out of focus. Had she ever known a man so tall, with shoulders so wide that she, who stood equal in height to most men, felt dwarfed when in his company?

26

"It's all right now," she said, surprised to find her voice shaken and husky as she strove to bring a sense of normalcy to the moment—not an easy task to be sure, since his fingers were rubbing the arch of her foot, causing tingling sensations to race up her leg.

Anthony's blue gaze rose to her obvious confusion. For a long moment he studied her face, his hands still holding her foot. "Are you sure?"

She nodded, not daring to speak again, for she doubted she had the ability.

"You have beautiful feet," he said.

Lord, she had to think of something to break this strange, almost strangling sensation that threatened to rob her of her breath. He moved closer. He stood boldly between her legs now and her heart pumped wildly as his head began to lower, their mouths seeming to draw closer. "Foot," she corrected.

Anthony hid his grin, knowing full well the effect he was having on her. He could see the flush that covered her cheeks, the beating of a pulse in her throat. He heard the huskiness in her voice, her labored breathing, saw the heaviness of her eyes as they threatened to close in submission. "You don't have two?"

"The other one is wooden." Jasmine almost choked with relief to see his eyes widen with surprise. But if she thought to lighten the smoldering mood of desire, her humor was apparently lost on this man. How was it she kept forgetting his mental capabilities?

"You have a beautiful foot then."

"Thank you. You can let it go now."

"Is anything else wooden?" he drawled, his voice low and sensual, in direct contrast to the look of innocence in his eyes.

"Just my teeth," she remarked in a quivering voice, for her full concentration was on his hand as it slid slowly up her leg.

27

Anthony forced aside the urge to laugh, his tongue licking at his bottom lip as his gaze centered on her mouth, her teeth. "They look real enough."

"My eyes do, too."

"They're not?" he asked, forcing a look of amazement as a chuckle threatened to escape his throat.

"Not this one," she returned as she pointed to her left eye.

Anthony's shoulders were shaking with silent mirth and the look he bestowed upon her was filled with tender admiration at her jesting. "In that case, I'd best lend you a hand."

In an instant he had her stocking over her foot and was rolling the thin fabric up her leg. "No!" Jasmine gasped. She would have shot him a fierce look but had somehow lost the ability to do anything but allow this outrageous intimacy.

Jasmine blinked, her mind now filled with pure sensation as his fingers slid under her skirt to graze and linger at the naked flesh above her stockings. Her head tipped back as if she suddenly hadn't the strength to hold it up. Her eyes half closed, her breathing grew even more erratic.

"I'll saddle Hercules," he said, his mouth so close to hers she could feel his breath against her lips.

It was with an almost mournful sigh of loss that Jasmine suddenly found herself alone. A moment later, her cheeks suffused with color, for she realized sounds she had not previously heard. People were talking as they readied their horses for their morning ride and she had not heard anything but the thumping of her own heart.

It was almost a week before Jasmine found the courage to return to the stable. She had missed her morning rides, but the fear of encountering Monty again proved just too great a risk. The worst of it was it almost didn't matter. No matter her forced absence, he was always on her mind. If she was honest, she'd have to admit he was one of the most handsome men she'd ever known. What a shame his intelligence didn't halfway match his looks. And if it had . . . ?

Jasmine was, in truth, a kind, sweet young lady and would no more look down her nose at those born of a lesser station than she would have thought to treat such a person with cruelty. Still, even though she might have denied it, did in fact not even know it, she was a snob. Having lived with it all her life, she saw no evil in class distinction. In truth, she never thought of it at all, for it seemed natural and right to her way of thinking as it no doubt did to most of those fortunate enough to be born of means.

He was, to her mind, no matter the unreasonable attraction she felt, a stable boy and she the daughter of an English lord. Of course she had heard stories of women taking sport with those of lesser standings in their community, but her morals clearly forbade such action. Indeed, it was impossible for her to imagine herself indulging in an afternoon of illicit pleasure with anyone.

Jasmine didn't know how to handle this situation. Terrified that he might touch her again, and, worst of all, that she might want him to, she had simply stayed away.

"Are you angry with me?" Anthony breathed a sigh of relief to find her back at last. Every day for the last week he had waited for her return, praying she would come, but the niggling fear that she might stable her horse elsewhere wouldn't desist.

Jasmine spun around. When she'd arrived, the stables had appeared to be empty. She'd thought she might take Hercules and be gone before seeing anyone, most especially the man who wouldn't leave her thoughts in peace. Jasmine forced a smile she

29

didn't feel. "Of course not, Monty."

Anthony leaned against the stall and gave a slight shrug of his shoulder. His eyes downcast, he continued his charade. "I want to be your friend."

Jasmine smiled at his childish innocence. Surely the man had not a mean bone in his body. She couldn't imagine anyone sweeter or more gentle. She had no doubt that his arrogance and the hungry look that had come to his dark blue eyes were figments of her imagination. Now she wondered what in the world had kept her away from him? In his company once again, she knew she had nothing to fear and that she had greatly exaggerated this situation. "Of course you are my friend."

Anthony allowed a tentative smile. "Then you'll talk to me?"

"Monty," she admonished gently, "Why would you think I would not?"

"I thought you were angry. You didn't come back for so long."

"I was busy."

Anthony watched her from across the small stall. Again she wore her royal blue riding habit. A velvet bowler hat to match sat at a jaunty angle upon thick black curls. Her veil came over her face and around the back of her head to tie upon the hat, leaving long whispery trails of netting to fall upon her slender back, almost to her tiny waist. God but she was beautiful. He hadn't quite remembered just how beautiful until he'd seen her again. His heart pounded painfully in his chest, the pulse at his throat almost closing off his breathing. How could this be? They had met but a few short times and yet he couldn't shake the spell she seemed to have cast over him. Nightly he dreamed of full pink lips and silver eyes glowing in the half dark, dazed with a passion he instinctively knew was hidden beneath her cool exterior. He was being slowly driven out of his mind and wondered at such a need as to nearly render him the fool she thought him to be.

Lord but he wanted to touch her again. He hadn't been able to think of anything else since the day his fingers had grazed her thigh. Why had he stopped there? Why hadn't he inched his fingers higher? Why hadn't he sought out the heat that awaited his touch?

Anthony almost trembled with the overwhelming need to go to her now. It took every ounce of willpower he possessed not to stalk her into the corner and taste those softly curved lips. "I made you angry."

"Nonsense." Jasmine turned from Hercules and moved toward the man. "If you had, I would have told you."

Anthony watched her eyes, the color of spun silver, glow in the dim light of the stall as she tenderly surveyed his face. His voice was none too steady when he finally asked, "Then why did you run away? Why didn't you come back?"

"I'm back now."

"And we can be friends?" he asked, pretending innocent enthusiasm.

"We are friends, Monty."

"Can I hug you? Friends sometimes hug, don't they?"

Jasmine swallowed. This was dangerous. Still, there was little he could do without her permission. Surely there were others about who could hear if there came a need to call out. Jasmine gave a silent laugh of self-mockery. If the truth be known, the trouble wasn't that she was afraid of him but that she was afraid of her own response when this close to him.

She hadn't enough experience along these lines, that was it. If she had responded so violently to this man's touch, it was obvious it mattered little who held her. She was apparently one of those women

31

who enjoyed being held. The idea was most unsettling. She couldn't help but wonder what else she might enjoy. Jasmine determinedly forced the disgraceful thought away. "Will you let me go when I say?"

Anthony nodded and then groaned when Jasmine stepped into his arms. He closed his eyes, savoring the feel of her against him. God, he hadn't imagined it. She was just as luscious as he'd remembered. Just as soft, just as sweet.

He murmured an unintelligible sound into the sweetness of her throat exposed just below her veil and breathed the intoxication of clean, lightly scented flesh.

Jasmine's heart pounded in her chest. How could this be? He wasn't the man he appeared. She knew he was different. Why then did his nearness so greatly affect her?

It was awful of her. Jasmine felt shamed at the emotion that assailed her. She wanted this man to hold her and perhaps touch her in a way that was anything but friendly.

Finally she stepped away from his embrace. Gently she touched her lips to his cheek and forced a smile. "Do you believe me now?"

Anthony couldn't speak, so filled was he with lust. His hands shook, his body trembled with the need to take her. God, she had haunted his thoughts since he'd first laid eyes on her. He couldn't remember when a woman had so greatly affected him. There was nothing he wanted more than to take her here and now. But he couldn't. Even were she willing, he couldn't do as he wished, here in a stable, and if she weren't willing and read his thoughts correctly, she'd no doubt flee in terror.

It had gone on long enough. He couldn't take much more of it. He knew he had made a disastrous error. Never should he have allowed her to believe her mistaken impression of him. He should have corrected her from the first, for her embarrassment would have been nothing compared to the anger she was sure to know once she found out the truth. Damn it, how in hell was he going to get out of this mess without losing any chance he might have had with her?

He didn't want her to feel friendship or pity for him. He wanted her to feel what he felt. He wanted to touch her the way a man was supposed to touch a woman and he wanted her to love it.

There was no hope for it. He had to tell her the truth and pray he could convince her to eventually forgive him. Anthony sighed morosely. "May we talk?"

Jasmine nodded. "After I get back from my ride."

He would have insisted that their talk be now, but others were in the stables. He could hear them moving about, muttering to their animals, and he knew this wasn't the time to press her. Anthony nodded, took Hercules's reins, and led the roan to the stable's doors.

It should have been an effortless accomplishment to lift her into her saddle, but once his hands settled at her sides, Anthony couldn't resist the temptation to slide her body along the length of his. Their eyes held, silver flashing with surprise as heated blue turned almost black with need. Their breathing ceased as she was slowly taken from the ground and Jasmine bit back a soft, startled cry as her breasts rubbed against his chest, her belly against his stomach, her legs along the hardness of his thighs.

Muscles bulged as he held her high above him. For a long, silent moment she watched, entranced by the play of bronzed, muscled flesh and the short, golden hairs that seemed to call out for her touch. She closed her eyes, her cheeks reddened, ashamed of the unreasonable urge that had suddenly come over her.

God but he was so appealing. The warm rays of the morning sun brought to life the thick golden streaks in his brown hair. For an insane moment she wondered what it would feel like if she dared run her fingers through its shining length. She bit at her bottom lip as she fought against an urge that could only bring about disgrace.

He watched as, chest heaving, she silently adjusted her seat and leg upon the sidesaddle. A moment later she gathered her reins and trotted off toward the park.

It was the most ridiculous thing. Surely she had imagined the sensation and the need to touch him. Jasmine shook her head. It was only because the man was so good to look at. No, she didn't really feel attraction for him. It was a new experience for her, this type of friendship. She simply didn't know how to handle it yet, but she would learn. Yes, someday they would be good friends, Jasmine was sure of that.

Jasmine pushed aside her confusion. She was going to enjoy her ride this morning. Nothing and no one was going to take this pleasure from her, not even the note that had arrived yesterday. No, she wouldn't think of that now. If her father thought he was going to marry her off to one of his licentious friends, he could think again. Idly she wondered how much her proposed fiancé was paying, for surely money was the only reason Lord Huntington could be enticed away from his life of debauchery in London.

Jasmine gave a hard laugh. She'd die before she'd allow herself to be sold off like some unneeded possession. Idly she wondered what was the matter with her? Why didn't her father love her? Jasmine had known for a long time he cared nothing for her. Why, not once in all her twenty years had the man hugged or kissed her. It was almost as if the very sight of her disgusted him. Jasmine shrugged away the hurt the thought brought to the surface. Just as well, she reasoned, and in self-protection insisted she felt very much the same.

Oh, why hadn't her mother left him years sooner? Why had she believed, no matter the obstacles, she must honor her marriage vows? Jasmine shivered. She couldn't go back. She couldn't bear the snickering, the whispers. All of London knew. And yet, as horrible as his life-style was, she could have forgiven him even that if only he could have loved her.

And now he wanted her to accept the kind of life her mother had endured. Never! Never would she marry a man whose intentions were to use her for her money. If the truth be told, she was very marriageable material indeed. Her mother's family were, to the shame of the aristocratic Huntingtons, people of business and so her father, an impoverished lord, had married her mother solely for her money.

Jasmine hadn't a doubt that if her mother had known the truth of Jamison Huntington's sexual preferences, she would not have acceded to her family's wishes. Elizabeth Huntington had suffered much during the years of living with her husband. Shunned at first from polite society because of her merchant class background, she might have one day been accepted if it hadn't been for her father and his well-known sexual aberration.

No, she would never permit herself to be the object of gossip, of pity. And Jasmine had no doubt the man she was promised to would be no different from her father.

She and her mother had decided last night that she would go to Canada. She was taking Essie, her childhood nurse, and leaving two nights hence on the merchant ship *Star*. The arrangements were already made. Nothing was going to stop her from getting away. Nothing!

It was nearing the noon hour before Jasmine finally returned to the stables, for she had encountered a group of friends and had spent her morning racing and laughing, happily oblivious to the problem that awaited her.

Jasmine's eyes rounded with surprise to find her one-time nurse and now companion, Essie, pacing the area directly before the barn. A worried look etched upon the old woman's soft features gave her the first clue that something was wrong.

"What is it?" Jasmine asked, reading correctly Essie's worried expression. She slid quickly from her horse, never noticing the helpful hands that were ready to assist. "What happened?"

Wordlessly, Essie handed her mistress a small packet.

Jasmine's honey-tinted skin paled to a sickly gray hue as her silver eyes scanned the small piece of paper, while the accompanying bills drifted unseen to the ground.

Lady Elizabeth Huntington sat at the delicate lady's desk in her spacious suite of rooms high atop the huge mansion she had taken in the heart of New York City. Elizabeth was penning polite excuses to the many parties her daughter had already promised to attend, when a soft knock sounded at her door.

Without looking up from her morning's chore, she called out, "Enter."

"What is it, Manning?" she asked, knowing by the starch swish of skirts and petticoats that her housekeeper had entered.

"You have visitors, ma'am."

Elizabeth glanced at the small timepiece attached

to the bodice of her dress and gave a small frown. The chimes had yet to ring nine. Who would be calling at such an hour? "Who is it?"

Manning shrugged a large, rounded shoulder. "Two gentlemen. They wouldn't give their names."

Elizabeth bristled at their lack of manners. "Tell them I'm unavailable then."

"The one said you'd see him all right."

"He did, did he?" Elizabeth's mouth tightened with annoyance. "Well, inform the gentlemen your mistress is out for the day. You might add that you have no idea when I will be returning."

"He said to give you this."

Manning held out her hand and slowly opened meaty fingers. In the work-roughened palm sat a diamond wedding band, the very same ring she had left in England on the night she'd left her husband. Elizabeth felt the room sway. It couldn't be! Not so soon! They had only received the note yesterday. Jamison must have followed on the very next ship. Lord, he must be desperate, for she imagined nothing short of desperation could bring him from the gambling and whoring found and gleefully practiced in London.

Elizabeth's mind raced on. She had to find Jasmine. She had to tell her to hide, hide until the ship was ready to leave.

"Get Essie in here right away," she ordered, not realizing the unusual sharpness of her voice. Manning left to do her mistress's bidding while Elizabeth quickly penned another note. Adding a stack of bills to the paper, she wrapped and sealed her letter.

It took a few moments, but Elizabeth finally managed to calm her shaking hands. Jasmine would be all right. She had enough money to take a room for the two days she would be forced to wait. Once the *Star* left port, Jamison would never find her.

Elizabeth waited until Essie had gone before she

descended the long stairway to the first floor. Outside the day room, she hesitated for just a second. Taking a deep breath, she prayed for courage and pushed open the double doors. The soft smile on her lovely lips froze as her deep blue eyes took in the two men impatiently awaiting her arrival.

She never heard her husband's annoyed remark, "It took you long enough," as she fainted dead away at the sight of the second man.

Strong arms circled her waist and from somewhere far off she heard, "Are you all right?"

Anthony ignored Essie's scowl as he pressed Jasmine closer into a comforting embrace.

Jasmine never noticed his touch, so feverishly did her mind work. She had to make a decision. If he came this far, this soon, it was clear he'd follow her anywhere. Canada would be no safe haven, for no doubt he'd show up on her doorstep, fiancé and preacher in hand.

No, her mother was wrong in this case. Running would only delay the inevitable. What she needed was a means to escape him forever. What she needed was a husband, at least a supposed husband. But who?

Edward! No. Jasmine gave a soft, negative sound. He was gone to Philadelphia to see to his holdings. He wouldn't be returning for a fortnight.

Samuel! No again. The man was an officer in the king's dragoons. He had left two days past with his regiment for upstate New York.

Jonathan. Oh, God, she doubted Jonathan had it in him to carry through a charade of this magnitude. He was too obviously weak. No, she needed someone who wouldn't fear going up against a man like her father. Jonathan would definitely crumble before the man's anger. Jasmine almost smiled. And that he would be angry, she hadn't a doubt. Enraged would be closer to the truth.

"Was it bad news?"

"What?" Jasmine asked, looking up to Anthony's worried gaze.

"The note. Was it bad news?"

Oh, God, why couldn't she find someone like this man to be her husband? He gave off an aura of power and strength, no matter that it was false, yet he was amicable enough for her to bend him to her will. If she could find someone like Monty.

Jasmine gasped and turned to face him. For a long moment she studied his face and form in the most clinical sense. He was big enough. His features were good. Actually, they were better than good, but that didn't matter. What mattered was with the right clothes, he could easily pass for a man of breeding. His speech! Oh, God, she almost groaned aloud her disappointment. It wouldn't work. The moment he opened his mouth they'd know.

Jasmine blinked as she sought a solution to this obstacle. Need he open his mouth? Suppose he had suffered some injury to his throat. Suppose he was unable to speak?

Anthony's eyes widened with surprise and worry as he watched Jasmine's color return and then some. She was cherry red before she finally found the courage to ask. For the life of him he couldn't imagine what had come over her. And when she did finally speak, the shock he felt left him speechless.

"Monty, I have an enormous favor to ask of you."

Eyes wide, Anthony nodded, knowing already there was little within his power he wouldn't grant this woman.

"I need a husband. Immediately."

Anthony almost laughed. He thought she had said she needed a husband. Of course, he hadn't heard correctly. "What?" he asked, the tiniest of grins touching the corner of his lips.

"I haven't the time to go into it right now. I need someone to act as my husband for a short time."

There was no playacting on his part. If he looked stunned, it was because he was. If he appeared suddenly unable to comprehend, it was because he couldn't believe what he'd just heard. "Act?" Anthony finally managed through a throat almost closed down with shock.

"It wouldn't be for long."

Anthony's eyes were glassy with amazement. "Monty, pay attention! I need you to make believe we're married. That we just got married today. Can you understand?"

"Why?"

"That's not important." Jasmine shrugged, as if it were the least important thing she might ever know. Her eyes glittered polished silver as she pleaded. "Would you do me this favor?"

Now Anthony couldn't deny that he'd wanted this woman from the first moment he'd seen her. Wasn't he running himself ragged getting up at the crack of dawn every morning, sometimes never even getting to sleep the night before, just to see her? But wanting to bed a beautiful woman and marrying her were definitely two separate things. Never for a moment did he take into consideration the charade she proposed. No, if he gave in to her pleading, it would be for real. The question was, did he want her enough?

Playing for time, while he thought out this question, he asked, "You want me to make believe? Like a game?"

"Yes! That's it. Just like a game. I want this man to believe we're married. Do you think you could make him believe that?"

"Miss Jasmine, I don't think . . ."

"Essie!" Jasmine returned as if she'd suddenly

40

remembered her companion was still present. "Don't scold me. What shall I do? Run for the next year or so? Suppose he finds me in Canada? I can't live under a threat like this. I have to make a stand."

"With him?" Essie's look clearly bespoke the idiocy of the younger woman's plan.

"Give me the money," Jasmine ordered, referring to the bills that had fallen from the note.

"No one's goin' to believe it," Essie warned.

"They'll believe it." Jasmine spoke as if Anthony weren't present. Her silver eyes scanned his form. "Can't you imagine him in proper clothes? Why, I daresay he'd cut quite a dashing figure."

"But when he speaks?"

Jasmine bit at the inside of her cheek and concentrated. "I know, I know. We'll correct that."

Anthony was beginning to feel decidedly uneasy. What the hell was she talking about? Was she planning to do him some bodily harm?

Apparently his thoughts showed clearly in the narrowing of his eyes, for Jasmine suddenly smiled. "No need to worry, Monty. We will make believe. No one will hurt you."

And when nothing more was said, she asked softly, "Will you do this for me?"

"You want me to make believe. Why?"

Jasmine pushed aside the annoyance she felt. Perhaps it was only fair that she explain. "My father is here from England. He wants me to marry one of his friends."

"And you don't want to marry him?"

Jasmine never realized the slight shudder that shook her slender frame. "No. I definitely do not want to marry him."

"Won't they ask to see the paper?"

"What pa—" Oh, God!" Jasmine shot Essie a pleading look of help. Why hadn't she thought of it? Of course they'd insist on seeing the marriage

41

certificate. They'd belive nothing less.

Anthony came to a decision. Damnation, he couldn't remain unmarried forever. Sooner or later he'd want children. He could do a lot worse than marrying this one. "I have a friend. He could get you one," Anthony remarked, instantly relieving her mind.

"Would he?" Jasmine lunged into Anthony's arms, almost weak with relief. "Oh, Monty, I'll never be able to thank you for this."

Anthony's grin was hidden against her veiled hair. *I'm sure we'll think of some means of showing gratitude.*

The plan was exceedingly simple. All he had to do was go to the men's store to which she had directed him and ask Mr. Cassey for his best suit of clothes. Then, once dressed, he was to meet her back at the stable.

Jasmine paced the small area in front of the stable. What was taking him so long? Good grief, he could have been dressed three times in the hour since he'd been gone. Had he forgotten their plan? Had he taken the money and gone home, never thinking about how she was anxiously awaiting his return?

In her pacing, Jasmine walked right by the man in the white satin breeches, embroidered short coat, and emerald-green jacket.

Anthony grinned as he watched her turn and walk right by him again. "Where is he?" Jasmine asked a suddenly flabbergasted Essie. Jasmine slowly turned her head and followed the direction of Essie's gaze. Her eyes widened with shock.

"Monty?" Jasmine asked, not at all sure that the powdered, bewigged gentleman smiling down at her was the same man she had sent off nearly an hour ago.

Anthony nodded.

"Good God!" Jasmine breathed her astonishment on a sigh. "This is going to be easier than I imagined."

She stared at him for another long moment before she thought to ask, "Did you get the paper?"

Anthony shook his head. "Trevor says he wants to play, too."

A puzzled frown creased her smooth brow. "What do you mean?"

"He sweeps out the church. He says he always wanted to be a preacher."

Oh, God, this was too much. As if her nerves weren't bad enough, now she had to play yet another game. Jasmine breathed a sigh. "All right. Where is this church?"

Anthony helped the two ladies inside the hackney carriage that awaited and if he was a bit clumsy while helping Jasmine, she seemed to understand. She never remarked at how his hands had somehow missed her waist completely and landed over her breasts before sliding into place. And when he cupped her bottom to give her a lift up, Jasmine did little more than stiffen, while bravely keeping her smile in place.

"You're crushing my dress, Monty," Jasmine remarked, never mentioning the fact that the back of his arm touched her breast every time the carriage hit a bump. She tried to move away, but the man was so big he took up nearly all the space on the seat, leaving Jasmine all but squashed in the corner. "I'll sit across from you."

Essie moved to one side and Anthony allowed Jasmine to stand unassisted. But when the carriage took an unexpected swerve, he caught her before she fell at his feet. She never said a word but shot him a suspicious glance as his thumbs rubbed twice across her nipples.

43

Satisfied by his innocent expression that proved to her he had never even noticed where he had touched her, she thanked him politely.

Anthony almost burst out laughing. He hadn't a doubt that once she found him out, her one and only thought would be to kill him. But once this little trip to the preacher was done, she'd have little to say about it, wouldn't she?

Wisely and with some effort, he gained control over the merriment that threatened.

Jasmine's head was spinning. No doubt this had been not only the oddest but possibly the shortest experience of her life. She and Monty were in and out of the church with dizzying speed.

Settled once again in the carriage, Jasmine gasped, "Lord, that was quick, wasn't it? And the preacher. Trevor, you said his name was? He was perfect. If I didn't know better, I would have believed him to be real. Wouldn't you?"

Jasmine sighed, a bit disappointed at Anthony's shrug and carefully blank expression. Thank God she wasn't really married to him. He might be sweet, but there was definitely more than sweetness needed in a relationship. Why, there had to be some sort of conversation, something.

Jasmine barely had the time to smooth her skirts when Anthony gave the order for them to move on. She uttered a small cry of alarm. "No! Stop! You've forgotten someone!" The driver had stupidly gone off while Essie was signing those silly papers.

The driver seemed to be having a problem with his hearing, for the vehicle never hesitated. If anything, it only gained in momentum at the sound of her voice. Jasmine spun in her seat to see Essie's lone figure standing on the steps of the church.

"She'll find some other means of transport,"

44

Anthony remarked, apparently unconcerned that they'd left Essie behind.

Jasmine tried to smile, but her expression was more of a grimace. She had never been alone with this man, not truly alone, and for the first time she felt a premonition of fear.

In order to relieve the tension between them, she tried to initiate some conversation, but Monty seemed to suddenly have trouble concentrating, for she received little but yes and no for answers to her questions. Jasmine frowned at the man beside her. He might be a dear and all, but a few weeks of such stilted conversations would destroy her mind. If her luck held, though, she wouldn't have to wait that long to be finished with this masquerade.

She shot him another glance. What in the world was the matter with him? Why was he looking at her so strangely?

Jasmine felt another glimmer of fear. Had she made a terrible error in judgment? Was there more to the man than she had thought? Was he perhaps stranger than she had first imagined?

Anthony broke into her thoughts. "How old are you?"

"Twenty," she answered automatically.

Anthony nodded, seeming to be satisfied with her answer. This was the old Monty, the one she knew she could control.

Suddenly he blurted out, "Shouldn't we be kissing? That's what people do when they get married, don't they?"

Jasmine smiled sweetly and reminded, "But we're not really married."

"Oh," he remarked vacantly.

"Monty, you're not going to forget about speaking, are you?"

"I'm not allowed to talk."

Jasmine nodded. "But you mustn't tell anyone

45

that. It will be our secret.

"If anyone asks you a question, simply point to your throat and shake your head."

"Like this?" He mimicked her actions.

"Exactly," Anthony smiled. This was probably the most ridiculous of ploys and yet what could her father do about it? If Monty remembered his role, Lord Huntington might never know the truth.

A smile teased her lips. For all intents and purposes, she'd married the stable boy. If her father knew the truth of Monty's humble status, she didn't doubt an attack of apoplexy from the man. Jasmine grinned, silently applauding her actions, for she liked nothing better than to ridicule the aristocratic Lord Huntington and his snobbish family. Jasmine never realized her own snobbery and would have been shocked had it been pointed out to her.

"Sally knows a real good way to stop people from talking."

Jasmine gave a slight frown. Sally again. Damn the woman. Just how much of an education had she given this man? Instantly Jasmine shrugged away the thought. It was no concern of hers. "No doubt."

"Want me to show you?"

"No Monty, I do not." A long moment of silence ensued before Jasmine suddenly offered, "If you are a good boy and remember everything I've told you, you can see Sally tonight." Odd. Why did the thought of him visiting the woman send discomfort to her chest? Jasmine shook her head. It wasn't that at all. It was the confrontation looming ahead that caused this unusual sensation, nothing more.

"Really?" Anthony asked, his amazement apparent. "I thought when people got married, they weren't supposed to . . ." He let the sentence falter.

Jasmine was about to remind him again that they weren't really married but instantly thought better of the notion. Perhaps it was best that he forgot. If he

46

believed them married, he was apt to act the part.

Jasmine could feel him watching her from the side of her eye. He had followed her into the cab and sat at her side; this time there seemed to be more than enough room. Jasmine turned to look him in the eye. She could see something was troubling him. "Is something wrong?"

"How can I be married to you? You never kissed me but for once on my cheek."

Jasmine gave him a tender smile. He was really so sweet. No matter his size, he was a child at heart. Surely there was no harm. "Will it make you feel better if I kiss you?"

Anthony shrugged, knowing it would do anything but, for he wanted far more than one kiss from this woman.

Jasmine leaned over, lifted the veil that covered her mouth, and planted a chaste kiss on his lips. "Better?"

"Not quite," he said as his arm snaked around her tiny waist and he pulled her to lean completely off balance across his lap. "This is closer to what I had in mind."

Jasmine stared in shock as his mouth came down to brush enticingly over hers. It wasn't so much the kiss that so startled but his manner of speech. He had lost his accent and spoke in clear, crisp king's English!

But Jasmine soon forgot her momentary surprise as his mouth took hers in a masterful kiss. Jasmine wasn't at all positive the kiss was masterful, having limited experience along these lines, but her stomach and thighs seemed to approve immensely.

Her head grew dizzy, but she supposed that was from lack of air rather than this oddly delicious contact of mouths. What was he doing? It seemed to her he wanted her to open her lips. Why?

Jasmine tried to turn her face away, but long

fingers held firmly to her jaw, securing her in place. She pushed against his shoulders.

"Relax," he whispered against her lips.

Jasmine gave a low laugh. Relax? Here? Now? Impossible!

But the inadvertently sultry sound brought an answering growl from Anthony as he gathered her closer to his chest and insisted on entrance to her mouth.

Jasmine imagined it was the laugh that did it, for one could hardly laugh with her mouth closed. And Anthony, not one to hesitate when an agreeable opportunity showed itself, took swift, sure advantage of the moment. The instant her lips relaxed in a smile, his tongue plunged deep into her mouth.

Jasmine, truly a novice in the ways of men and their lovemaking, was deeply shocked at this happening. Thinking about it later, she thought she should have felt a measure of disgust. At the time, however, she felt nothing but surprise, for never in her life had she imagined one might kiss like that.

Actually, she was so astonished that she never felt his hand reach unerringly beneath her skirt. His fingers smoothed over shapely stockinged legs and Jasmine never noticed the movement at all until they reached her garters and the smoother span of naked flesh above.

She stiffened all the way to her toes and gasped her outrage, but the reaction only brought the warm, clean scent of him deep into her lungs and allowed him even further liberties with her mouth.

What did he think he was doing? Did he imagine she would actually enjoy this dreadful act? The man was obviously more simple than she had once supposed, for not only didn't she enjoy it, she *abhorred* it. Jasmine tried to pull away as a wave of dizziness threatened the last of rational thought. Damn the man. How did he expect her to breathe, when he wouldn't for a minute release her mouth? Jasmine struggled against his hold, but the fingers that had held so firmly to her chin had somehow disposed of her hat and veil and were now threading through her hair, pressing at the back of her head so that she was helpless but to lean into his mouth.

"Monty," she gasped into lips wet and hot with a hunger she could only imagine. "You mustn't."

"Hmm," he moaned, enjoying the movement of her mouth as she tried to speak. "Call me Anthony."

Chapter Three

Never for the rest of her life would Jasmine again come to know so great a degree of mortification, for this rascally fellow had somehow convinced her she did indeed enjoy this particularly odd form of kissing, enjoyed it very much, in fact, so much that all conscious reasoning had fled to the back of her mind and she was left in a floating state of euphoric mindlessness.

She never noticed that his hand was still beneath the full skirt of her dress. If the truth be told, however, she *did* notice, but in her dreamy state of sweet pleasure she simply forgot to stop him. What she *didn't* notice was that the carriage had come to a stop. And she never heard the discreet clearing of someone's throat.

Jasmine moaned her obvious disappointment when Anthony, realizing at last that they were not alone, released her mouth and smoothed down her rumpled skirt. Her mouth, free of his, was still under his spell as it nuzzled the flesh of his neck.

Anthony grinned at the astonished expression of the doorman. "Jasmine," he whispered gently. "We're here."

But Jasmine never heard his words. She grumbled a sound of annoyance, her mouth obviously hungry for more as her lips moved over his throat and jaw. Her arms at his neck pulled his face lower so she might sample again the sweet deliciousness he had shown her.

"Jasmine! What are you doing?!"

Jasmine jumped at the sound of her mother's voice, jumped so hard and moved so fast that she fell off Anthony's lap and landed on the floor with a hard bounce, amid yards of lace and ruffled petticoats.

To add to her horror, her legs didn't actually fall with her body, but were, in fact, still on the seat.

Anthony fought and won a brilliant battle with the laugh that threatened as her legs realized they should have joined her body and floundered for a moment in the air. The movement offered him a view of lusciously smooth shapely legs and the lacy drawers he had so recently tried to push aside.

Elizabeth Huntington had suffered a great shock. It was because of this morning's happenings that she happened to be outside. Unable to face her husband, especially unable to face the man who had accompanied him to the colonies, Elizabeth had left the house only moments after coming from her faint.

She was just now returning from a long, thought-filled walk when a hansom cab came to a stop before her home. No doubt Elizabeth would have ignored the carriage's presence and proceeded into the mansion had not her manservant's astonished expression caught her eye. Jenson, so usually placid and unshakable, was gaping, wide-eyed and open-mouthed into the cab.

Elizabeth never thought but to glance inside and see why the man should appear so astounded. Right now her lips were thinned in anger and she glared at her daughter, who seemed to have forgotten every ounce of proper behavior she had for years drummed

51

into her head.

Jasmine had always been a bit on the wild side, and Elizabeth had had her hands full guarding against the young woman's impulsive nature. But *this!* This was the most outrageous thing she'd ever witnessed.

"Would you mind telling me just what you think you're doing with this man?" Elizabeth shot Anthony a quelling look, that dared him to offer a word of excuse. "And where is Essie? Did you not get my message?"

"Mother, I . . ."

Anthony's eyes widened with surprise. Mother?! This was Jasmine's mother? Why, the woman looked barely of age, never mind the mother of a twenty-year-old daughter.

"Perhaps we might speak inside, Mrs. Huntington," Anthony interrupted Jasmine's obvious stuttering.

Elizabeth, remembering at last the very public spectacle they were about to make, gave him a stiff nod and turned her back. "Inside," she said, her tone less an invitation than an order.

It was easy enough for Anthony to see from whom Jasmine had gotten her beauty. Except for their coloring, Jasmine being dark and her mother blond, they might have been identical. No doubt, Jasmine would, for some years to come, remain the beauty she was today.

Anthony watched the older woman for a long moment. She was astonishingly lovely. Even angry, as now, she was the epitome of graceful style and beauty.

Anthony glanced at the lady who still occupied most of the space on the carriage floor. He couldn't move, lest he chance stepping on her, for ruffles and lacy petticoats spread over the floor and hid the exact location of her legs from his view. It took him a full minute to find her waist amid all her fluff and finery and maneuver her to the seat opposite him.

"Oh, my God!" Jasmine groaned, her face hidden behind her hands. She couldn't face the man across from her, and dreaded even more facing her mother.

"Are you all right?"

"I'll never be all right again," she moaned.

Anthony chuckled at her overstatement as he jumped from the carriage and reached for his bride. Jasmine gave him a sharp glance as he helped her to the street. Her sneering comment was out before she realized she'd spoken. "At least you managed that without giving my entire body a massage."

Anthony's lips twitched. It was easy enough to see he was having a time of controlling his merriment. Jasmine caught his smile from the corner of her eye. She did a double take and studied the man more closely. "I'm pleased to see one of us is enjoying this."

"Shall we?" he asked as he offered her his arm.

Jasmine eyed him for a long moment before a wild thought made itself known. It couldn't be, of course. She must be mistaken. He wouldn't have . . . He couldn't . . . Jasmine ignored his offered arm and spun away from him, terrified her suspicions just might be true and unable to face the horror of that possibility.

Her mother was waiting for them at the steps to her home. "Why did you come back?" she asked her daughter.

"It might relieve your mind if Jasmine introduced me, Mrs. Huntington." It was easy enough to see the woman was extremely upset.

"Why?" Jasmine grated between clenched teeth. "It definitely does not relieve mine."

Jasmine ignored his grin and silently berated herself. She thought she was so clever, thought with a little luck and a bit of daring, she could defy her father and live her life without his interference.

Instead, what had she done? She'd gotten herself into a situation, the possible consequences of which were so horrible she dared not allow them a thought.

Her eyes narrowed as she watched the merriment in his eyes. She was dying to know what he thought so hilarious, and yet the niggling fear that wouldn't dissipate prevented her from asking straight out.

Finally, unable to stand it any longer, she asked the one question that had nearly choked her since it first came to mind. In her heart she already knew the answer, but she had to ask, "That man really was a preacher, wasn't he?"

"I'm afraid so."

Jasmine closed her eyes and gave a long, weary sound that bordered on pain, realizing the truth of her dilemma.

"Would someone mind telling me what is going on?"

Jasmine stood a good head taller than her mother, yet the older woman's presence was not easy to ignore. To Anthony's amazement, however, Jasmine did just that. "And you are not feeble-minded, are you?"

"Not so I've noticed."

"Oh, God."

"Please! What's happening?"

So caught up in her own misery, Jasmine never noticed her mother's plea and asked the man who was her husband, "Why did you do it?"

"What did I do?"

"You allowed me to believe you hadn't all your senses, that's what!" Her voice rose in outrage. "What I want to know is why?"

Anthony grinned and gave a shrug. "You seemed to so enjoy the idea. I didn't want to disappoint you."

Jasmine's slender hands closed into fists. Never in her life had she known this need for violence. Her lips never moved as she grated out, "It was the only excuse I could come up with. How else to explain

54

your clumsiness? How else could I condone your actions?"

During this confrontation, Elizabeth's blond head was snapping back and forth between the two. Finally her eyes narrowed with suspicion as she faced the handsome man at her side. "Exactly what were his actions?"

Jasmine gave him a smug smile, her eyes never leaving his as she nodded toward her mother. "Why don't you tell her?"

Anthony grinned, obviously unafraid of any possible consequences. "Why don't you?"

Elizabeth couldn't follow anything either one of them said and was tired of the confusion. "Tell me what?"

Anthony faced his new mother-in-law. "We're married."

"What?" she asked, clearly astounded. Her hand reached for her throat, and her legs wobbled noticeably, as she stumbled back so she leaned heavily upon the solid oak door. She glared at her daughter, waiting for her answer, praying this was some sort of joke.

Jasmine nodded as she met her mother's pleading expression. Her voice was little more than a childish sulk. "We're married."

"Oh, God." Elizabeth closed her eyes with despair. She knew without asking why Jasmine had done it. But what Jasmine didn't know was that it was all for nothing. She hadn't spoken a word to Richard, but there was no doubt in her mind why the man had come and it had nothing at all to do with marrying her daughter.

"Oh, Jasmine, why do you never listen?"

Jasmine shrugged at her mother while doing her best to ignore this most annoying man who was now her husband—not an easy feat considering the fury that was building in her breast at the growing

55

smugness of his grin. Well, she'd show him a thing or two.

What bothered her the most was the ease with which he accepted the idea of marriage. Why? Didn't the man value his freedom? Why would he have taken her mere suggestion and allowed it to become reality? Why indeed, she realized with no little disgust. Obviously he wasn't so very different from all the rest. He was after her money, just like so many others, her father included.

There would be an annulment of course. It was out of the question that the law would hold her to vows she believed taken in jest. Jasmine sighed wearily, wishing she could take in stride the happenings of today as easily as did he. And perhaps she might have if she didn't feel such a fool for being tricked. A moment later she left him and her mother on the steps and entered the house, defending her actions with feeble, final words, "At least I won't have to marry the one father brought."

"Married! What the hell do you mean you're married?" Jamison Huntington snarled into his daughter's face. The bitch! The goddamned whoring little bitch had done him in. Because of her he'd lost everything. Everything! Now what the devil was he to do?

Jamison Huntington had conveniently forgotten it was his gambling that had placed him in this awkward position. It was easier to shift the blame, and especially to someone incapable of defending herself. Before she had left him, it was Elizabeth who usually bore the brunt of his anger. Damn her as well as her daughter. Damn all women to hell. The world would be a better place without them.

Anthony flicked an imaginary piece of lint from his sleeve while holding tight to his growing anger.

Surely the man had no call to take on so. He especially disliked the disgust with which he addressed his daughter. "I'd take it as a personal favor, sir, if you wouldn't speak to my wife in that tone."

Jamison laughed incredulously. "Would you? What did the bitch give you to ensure your protection?"

Anthony started, his eyes widened with surprise. His muscles bunched beneath his coat, but he instantly gained control of the urge for violence. His arm came around his wife, a human loop of steel, and pulled her closer to his side. "I'm afraid you didn't understand. As long as I'm married to Jasmine, no one will speak to her thus." His words were cut from ice.

Jasmine felt a shiver run down her back. Vaguely she wondered if her father would heed the out and out threat.

"Easy enough to correct. The marriage will be annulled. I shall, this very night, contact my solicitors."

"I'm afraid it's a bit late for that, sir. Jasmine and I were married this morning. We've spent the entire day together."

Jasmine blinked as she listened to the exchange, amazed how the man could lie so smoothly.

"What do you mean together?" Huntington asked suspiciously.

"I mean *together*. Shall we say, in the biblical sense?" Anthony watched his father-in-law's eyes widen with shock. "I presume you understand my meaning. I wouldn't embarrass my wife by being more explicit than that."

Jasmine gasped.

Elizabeth moaned.

Richard grinned.

And Jamison, had he the nerve, would have punched his new son-in-law in his smirking mouth.

"No matter. Jasmine is not of age. There will be an annulment," he insisted.

"I'm afraid I must once again disagree. I'd hoped to keep this little secret between us," he shrugged as if it were in truth of no importance. "You see, Jasmine and I have been, shall we say, the closest of friends for some time. There is more than a distinct possibility that a child is in the offing," he lied blatantly.

Huntington gave a long sigh and desperately tried to ignore the sense of doom that was slowly creeping over him. He chanced a glance at the man who stood at the opposite end of the room. Would Townsend want her still? Would it matter to him the chit was no longer a virgin? And very possibly an expectant mother? There had to be a way. He was losing everything! "I presume you knew my daughter's worth when you married her?"

Anthony forced a laugh, disguising the rage that suddenly filled his being. Of course the insult was two-sided. Huntington had hinted that he was a fortune hunter and that Jasmine had no redeeming qualities but for her money. Had this man not eyes in his head? Didn't he realize the worth of his daughter far exceeded monetary value? Anthony felt the most irresistible urge to deliver a blow that would lay this man low. He didn't understand this need he felt to protect his bride, but he was damn near ready to kill this pantywaist, sorry excuse for a father.

Anthony's arm held her tighter than ever. "I have no need for your daughter's money. I am most fortunate on that score."

Jamison gave a grunt of disbelief. "Of course we have only your word for it, Montgomery."

"I shall have my man of business deliver my dossier tomorrow." He looked down to Jasmine's wide-eyed stare of astonishment with a tender smile. "Perhaps you might like to rest, my dear. I presume you would prefer to stay with your mother for the

58

time being? I'll need to send word to my man for my things.

"What time is dinner served, Mrs. Huntington?"

"Seven," Elizabeth returned with the beginnings of a smile while wondering if she hadn't been a bit too hasty in judging this young man.

"I'll see you at seven then, darling," Anthony promised, and then to Jasmine's utter astonishment and mortification, turned her more fully into his arms and delivered a kiss that rocked her to her heels.

He was laughing and she blushing red when he released her at last and made his cheerful way to the door.

Richard stood in the back of the large drawing room, a smile lingering on his well-shaped lips as he watched the confrontation. Jasmine had chosen well, he thought. This man would take no nonsense. He might not love her as yet, but he would. Ah yes, he would. And when he did, stars would shine in eyes where innocence now lurked, for Richard hadn't a doubt that the time spent together so far was a bit less satisfying than Anthony had hinted.

"She's beautiful, Elizabeh. You've done well."

Elizabeth's heart began to pound with a mixture of dread and excitement. Lord, you'd think she was but a young girl the way she was acting. She hadn't known he was in here when she entered the library. Now, if she turned on her heel and left, without a word as she was greatly tempted to do, she'd look the complete fool.

"Thank you," she replied softly, while forcing herself to act nonchalant at this unexpected meeting. It was bad enough she had fainted at the sight of him. She couldn't, wouldn't allow his presence to bring further disgrace. No, she'd show no emotion other than cool control.

"I trust you are feeling more yourself?"

Elizabeth colored slightly. "I'm fine. It was the shock of seeing him again," she lied.

Richard chuckled softly, the same sound that had brought chills down her spine more than twenty years ago. "Why do I get the impression that's not entirely true?"

"I'm sure I couldn't say."

"But you would if you could, is that it?"

"Lord Townsend, I'm afraid I haven't the slightest idea of what you're talking about."

"Don't you, Elizabeth?"

She shook her head, unwilling to meet the silver gaze that had haunted her asleep and awake for most of her life. Determined to show him no lack of bravery, she sat in the chair opposite him. "How is Emily?"

"She died. Nearly a year ago."

Elizabeth looked up at him then, her surprise couldn't have been more obvious. "I didn't know. I'm sorry."

"Don't be," he sighed as he leaned back in the thickly cushioned leather armchair. "She suffered terribly. Her death was a blessing."

"How horrible to think of death as a blessing. How can you say that?"

"She was quite insane. That's how I can say it. She didn't know where she was. She didn't know who she was. All she knew was torment."

Elizabeth's heart twisted at the sight of his pain. For years she had fought against the memory that refused to abate. She wouldn't now allow this weakness to control her. She couldn't, wouldn't allow the pain again.

She did not love him still. The young virgin bride who lived on the property adjoining his was no more. Despite her efforts, memories of the first days of her marriage came to plague: her confusion at

Huntington's disgust of her person and her inevitable despair of the brilliant marriage she was supposed to be enjoying. And the young, handsome neighbor, whose wife was so terribly ill. How often had they met in the woods that joined their properties?

Elizabeth smiled as she remembered how innocent their meetings were at first. All they had done was talk, and how desperately had she needed that contact!

It might have stayed that way indefinitely but for the day Emily had tried to take her own life. The shock of it had brought him trembling to the glen. He needed her then, but, God, not as much as she needed him. Two desperately unhappy souls reached out for comfort, searching for and finding a few hours of happiness in each other's arms. How sweetly tender, how heart-wrenching was their love and how pitiful their parting.

She was married, as was he. There could never be a future for them, not while their spouses lived. And yet he was here. Why had he come?

Richard nodded. "It's taken me almost that long to find you."

"Find me?" Her voice faltered, her hands trembled. "Why on earth would you have tried?"

"I'd heard you left him years ago, but no one knew where you'd gone."

"Honestly, I cannot imagine why you would bother."

"Can't you? Have you forgotten then our meetings?"

Elizabeth laughed nervously and came to her feet. She began to prowl the room. "Richard, you must not think of such things. It matters not the indiscretion of our youth."

"Is that what you call it? An indiscretion?"

"I'm not free," she snapped almost desperately.

"You were free from the first. Huntington can

hold no claim to you. You were never his wife. Were you?" And when she refused to answer, refused in fact to look at him, he came to his feet and stepped before her. Gently he caught her chin between long fingers and insisted, his voice growing in volume, "Were you?"

Elizabeth wrenched herself from his light hold. "Amazing how you can remember that now. You knew the truth of it then but did nothing. Child that I was, I would have given my life for you. Anything! Anything you wanted would have served me as well. Anything but to part from you."

Elizabeth felt dangerously close to tears. She felt trapped, and with the emotion came anger. He had no right to do this to her. He had no right to come into her peaceful existence, not now. Not ever again. "It's too late, Richard. You made your choice."

Richard's lips tightened with sorrow at her obvious suffering. He knew he had hurt her deeply. He remembered clearly the last time they had met. Fool that he was he had worried about her reputation when she had begged him to take her away. God, he had loved her so much. How had he found the strength to part from her? Richard shook his head. What nonsense to worry over gossip when two lives were held in the balance.

But the past was gone, over and done. He gained nothing by wallowing in remorse. They were still young. It had taken years for him to realize what a fool he had been and find her again. It wasn't too late. It couldn't be too late.

She tried to push by him, but he continued to block the path she had made around the desk and chair. "Elizabeth, we are not children any longer. We harm no one if we love."

She gave a sputtering sound of disbelief. "How can you speak of love? We haven't seen each other in twenty years."

Richard smiled, his eyes promising all the patience she'd need. "I will not press you now. This has been a shock. Come ride with me tomorrow?"

Elizabeth shook her head. "You're wrong. There is someone . . . I'm her mother, what would she think if . . ."

"If her mother and father found each other at last?" Richard smiled at her shocked expression. He shook his head. "Do not deny it. I knew the moment I saw her."

"She's mine." He didn't miss the stubborn look in her eyes. "You might deny it, but your words will not suffice. She is mine," he repeated with finality.

Elizabeth felt her anger grow in leaps and bounds. She couldn't stop herself from lashing out at this man. "I deny nothing, and tell you less. You need only know she's mine, Richard. She may not know it but she's a du Maurier. You had your wife. I had Jasmine."

"Was it so hard?"

Elizabeth gave a low, humorless laugh. "Hard? It was torture. He knew the child wasn't his, couldn't be his." Elizabeth shivered at the remembered horror, her anger at this man coming into full bloom. How dare he show himself now? How dare he assume Jasmine to be his daughter? How dare he assume anything after what she had suffered?

To all the world she and Jamison appeared the happy couple. It wasn't until the last of his friends or the servants were gone that he turned his fury and hatred upon her. He ridiculed her accent, ridiculed anything French. Shamed her until she sounded and acted no different from any of their acquaintances. And still it made no difference. He hated her, had always hated her. He'd married her for her money and threw the fact in her face and laughed at her shame.

"When I found out I was pregnant I went home to

my family. But once Jasmine was born, they forced me to return." Her eyes took on a hard glitter. "It wasn't right, you see. A father has a right to his child. And I couldn't bear to tell them the truth."

It wasn't until Jasmine had grown old enough to notice the strange men who visited the house at night that Elizabeth finally found the courage to leave again. It was four years since she'd seen him last, four years of peace.

And now, after almost twenty years, Richard had come for her. So he had taken care of his responsibilities and now expected to continue as if twenty years and two spouses had never come between them. Well, it was too late. She didn't love him anymore. The dreams of a young woman were dead and buried, never to rise from their grave again.

Chapter Four

The dinner shared with Jasmine's family had been ghastly. Anthony had sat helplessly by and watched Jasmine come close to tears a number of times before it was finally over. Anthony felt a moment's dread. He hadn't a doubt that the day was fast approaching when he'd be forced to resort to violence, for Jamison Huntington seemed unable to control the hideous remarks and obvious contempt directed at his daughter. Idly he wondered how his wife would react if he delivered her father a badly needed punishing blow.

The collective sigh of relief was almost audible when Jamison had finally remarked he was going out to see what New York's night life had to offer.

Anthony felt his anger begin anew as he watched this delicate creature settle herself in a library chair where Elizabeth, Richard and himself had gathered to share a few peaceful moments along with a glass or two of port and sherry. He wondered how a man as diabolical as Huntington could have fathered this lovely woman. Damn the man, but he never let an opportunity pass to show his distaste of her. Actually, Anthony imagined *disgust* to be closer to the truth. What he couldn't understand was why a father, especially *her* father, could feel such enmity toward her. Anthony knew were she his child he'd feel nothing but pride and love for her. What in damnation was wrong with the man?

They were silent for a long moment, no doubt each lost in their own thoughts of the disastrous meal shared. After one glass of spirits, they seemed to relax and soon they were conversing almost happily when the conversation turned to the conflict that raged throughout the Colonies.

"It's merely a rebellion," Jasmine remarked in an agitated tone, for she had wanted to get Anthony alone since he'd returned an hour before dinner with a dozen or more boxes of his personal belongings. She found his inclination to linger in the company of her mother and Richard most annoying, filled with the yearning as she was to rail at the man and his daring of this afternoon. "I'm sure the king's forces will soon have it all under control."

"I'm afraid you're mistaken there," Anthony remarked as he stood, his arm coming to rest upon the mantel, while he absorbed the warmth of the low, burning fire.

"How so?" Her eyes sent daggers from across the room.

"The patriots, as they prefer to call themselves, are besieged with this need for freedom. They profess, as they put it, that the strangling hold of English tyranny can no longer be borne."

"Certainly you don't agree with them?"

"Indeed not! I'm merely relating their beliefs." Anthony smiled as he listened to her sigh of relief. Had she for a minute imagined his loyalties lay in the rebel cause? Idly he wondered what she would do if she knew the truth of the matter? "And since these beliefs are so strongly felt, I doubt the king will have them under control anytime soon. Perhaps never."

"Do you contend there's a possibility that they might win?"

"Anything is possible, darling. Especially when

66

one wants so dearly."

"Freedom," she repeated, her disgust obvious. "Nonsense spouted by that fool Jefferson. I suspect these colonists would know not what to do with it if gained."

"Don't you? I wonder why? Some believe the state to border on Utopia."

Jasmine laughed at the nonsensical notion. "No doubt. In truth of fact, freedom can mean little to most women, whether in England or the Colonies."

"Why?"

"Because they are all subject to their parents until they marry and then their husbands take over the role of master." She gave a small shrug. "How do you suppose a woman would enjoy the freedom so longed for by these rebels?" Jasmine smiled tightly. "What, for instance, would I gain by seeing these rebels win out against a king I love?"

Anthony shot her a look that bordered on incredulity. "What kind of questions are these? You are a woman. A woman belongs to her husband. She always has. Would you change this fact?"

Jasmine shot him a grin that had nothing to do with humor. She most certainly would change it, but she dared not say her thoughts aloud. In truth, these thoughts were as new and radical to her way of thinking as to his. No doubt they never would have come to mind had Anthony not chosen to play devil's advocate for the rebel cause. Who was he? she silently mused. Who was this man she had so foolishly married and why had he seen fit to play such a devious trick on her?

Jasmine forced her mind from her own problems and back to the conversation at hand. She sighed aloud, knowing a sadness she hadn't dreamed possible, for no matter her brave words she hadn't a doubt the rebel cause would win out. Anthony was right on that score, for England couldn't hope to extinguish the fire that lurked in the hearts of these rebels. She wondered if the country would survive the victory and gave a small shrug as answer to his question. "No matter who wins this conflict, things will stay much the same."

Anthony shot her a puzzled look. "How?"

"They fight against the king and the laws of parliament, but there will always be law, lest anarchy result."

"So?"

"So they'd replace one king for another."

"They say America will never have a king," Elizabeth responded.

"Well, someone must lead," Jasmine returned with a logic, Anthony realized with no little discomfort, he hadn't suspected in a woman. "They hide from the truth if they believe so much will change."

For a long moment he watched her with dawning respect. He knew the truth of her words and had often pondered the notion himself. Already, there was a group of men in Philadelphia led by Joseph Reed who saw, as best they could, to the running of this war. He had every confidence many of them would continue on after the current conflict, creating a new set of laws for this young nation. What surprised him was that this woman would have the foresight and intelligence to realize the need.

Feeling an almost overwhelming tenderness, his voice softened measurably. "My darling little Tory. I, too, doubt that things will change, but they believe it to be so. In their words, men will be free. I suspect their hopes to be not far from every man's dream, although they might have taken it to some extreme here."

"Might have?" Jasmine laughed. "An understatement to be sure."

Anthony shrugged. "There are times when the

need is so great the means matter little."

"And if the impossible happens and they win? Do you imagine perfection?"

Anthony shook his head. "I think only God is perfect and only from him can we expect this trait. I imagine the future holds many mistakes in store."

Jasmine nodded. "Indeed the words they spout are pretty. Even I, who consider his speeches drivel, at times enjoy reading Jefferson and even Paine, but the fact remains that the freedom they long for, fight for, is meant for only a few."

Richard asked, "Do you think so? What then would you do, if you could?"

Jasmine laughed and skimmed her gaze over the three. "If I ruled the world?"

Anthony grinned. "Let's just say our part of it."

Jasmine chuckled, her eyes taking on a vivid light of enthusiasm. "The idea is intriguing, but impossible, of course."

"Why?" Elizabeth injected. "England has had its share of queens."

"And to their disgrace they did nothing to help their own," Jasmine blurted out before thinking.

Elizabeth's eyes widened. "What would you have done?"

"I'd have made them, by law, equal to men." Jasmine almost gasped at her own words, for she had never suspected herself capable of believing such a thing.

Anthony's mouth hung open with surprise. A woman equal to a man? He'd never heard such an outrageous notion. "Would you? But who then would take care of them?"

"Why couldn't they take care of themselves?" she remarked almost offhandedly. She had spoken without thought, but oddly enough the subject was taking on a goodly amount of appeal.

"Who would protect them?" Richard asked.

"Who protects men?"

"Their own strength, I think," Richard again answered.

Jasmine bit at the inside of her lip, pondering the solution. Suddenly she graced all three with a smile. "Well then the law should protect those who are weaker."

"Meaning women?" Anthony asked.

Jasmine shrugged. "Meaning anyone."

Anthony and Richard chuckled at this unorthodox reasoning, while Elizabeth's smooth brow grew creased as she thought further on her daughter's remarks. "I'm inclined to agree with you, Jasmine. Where did you come by such thoughts?"

"Till this moment, I hadn't known I had them," she answered honestly.

"Do you wish to be equal to your husband?" Anthony asked.

Jasmine chose to ignore the fact that his eyes were a bit brighter than before, no doubt from suppressed laughter. She replied in all seriousness and complete conviction, "I am equal to him."

Anthony looked deep into her eyes and knew she meant every word she said. To his surprise he found himself silently agreeing, for this woman was at the very least his equal. He wondered if she wasn't even superior in many ways. Surely she was every bit as loyal to her cause as he was to his. He had to respect that loyalty, even if their objectives differed. He shrugged, "In some ways, perhaps."

"In all, but for the law."

"But without law there is anarchy," Anthony returned, a smile teasing his lips as he reminded her of her own words.

Richard hid his laugh behind a cough as Jasmine grinned. "I'll have to give this subject some further thought. It wouldn't do for you to have the last word."

Anthony laughed. "No indeed, as my wife that wouldn't do at all."

She didn't hesitate. The moment the door to her room closed behind them, she railed at him with fury. "Are you stark raving mad, or as simple as I once believed? Why in the world would you marry someone you do not know?"

A good question, Anthony silently reasoned. Too bad he hadn't an answer. He looked down at his wife's flashing silver eyes, midnight hair, and honey-golden complexion, amazed yet again as he was at every sighting, at her startling beauty. In truth, she wouldn't rank high on the current fashion mode. She was too natural, too robust, too earthy. Today it was paper-thin, almost translucent-white complexions and coarse, powdered hair that were considered the height of beauty. Anthony's lips curved into an appreciative smile. For his taste, not another on the face of this earth held such sparkle, such fury, such passion.

"Well?" She faced him impatiently, her fists pressed to her hips, eyes aglow with anger, cheeks rosy with emotion, her stance all belligerence. "Are you going to answer me?"

Anthony smiled at his hot-tempered wife, feeling a moment of great tenderness. "Why in the world would you ask me?"

Jasmine bared her teeth in a sneer, barely in control of her temper. "You know why. It wasn't supposed to be real! You knew it wasn't!"

Anthony shrugged out of his coat. "What difference does it make? You had to marry eventually. I promise you there could have been worse choices."

"What difference?!" she sputtered, obviously aghast at his nonchalant attitude. "My God, I cannot believe I'm hearing this. Do you make it a habit of

marrying anyone who asks?"

Anthony grinned. "Hard to say, since you are the only one who ever did."

Jasmine wasn't so enraged that she didn't notice his amusement. Her lips curled into a snide semblance of a smile. "I suppose you think this is quite hilarious."

"Actually, I do find it somewhat humorous. I'm sure you will agree, once you've gotten over this snit."

Jasmine laughed without a trace of humor. "I'd hardly call the anger I feel at being duped a snit." Her eyes narrowed with obvious menace. "I want you out of my room."

Anthony shrugged, retrieved his jacket from the chair on which he had thrown it, and sauntered toward the door. "Have it your way, but in my opinion you're making a serious mistake."

He was at the door, his hand on the knob before his warning penetrated her anger. "Wait! What are you talking about?"

Anthony sighed. He was tired. He never got to bed last night and he had to strain for a patience he was far from feeling. "Do you or do you not want your father to believe in this marriage?"

She nodded, her eyes wary. "You know I do."

"Well then, would it not raise an eyebrow or two if the newlyweds maintained separate beds?"

Jasmine said nothing, torn between the knowledge that he was right and the need to throw the beast out on his ear. Her shoulders slumped with defeat and she gave a great sigh, knowing she had little choice in the matter. "I will not share a bed with you," she said with childish sullenness.

Anthony grinned as he moved from the door. "I never assumed you would," he lied quite blatantly.

Mouth agape, Jasmine stared in astonishment. Had he forgotten her presence? Didn't he realize what he was doing? Her eyes widened with surprise as he moved toward the bed, calmly disrobing before her. "What do you think you are doing?"

Anthony shot her a puzzled glance. "I'm readying myself for bed, of course."

"I can see that much," she sneered. "I'm not a total fool." Jasmine gave the room a pointed look and then emphasized the look with a wave of her hand. "As far as I can tell, there is but one bed in this room. Where is it you intend to sleep?"

Anthony grinned at the look of near panic in her eyes. "Did we not just come to the conclusion that separate sleeping chambers would not be the thing?"

"Would you put me out of my bed?"

"Of course not." Anthony gave the bed a deliberate look and then smiled at Jasmine's obviously confused expression. "The bed appears large enough for two, wouldn't you agree?"

"You cannot be serious! You cannot believe I'd lie down with a perfect stranger!"

Obviously unconcerned with Jasmine's dilemma, Anthony shrugged and pulled the light coverlet and top sheet down. "I've been told I snore. If it bothers you, just give me a shove and I'll roll over."

Jasmine spun around, turning her back on him as he casually opened the buttons of his trousers and slid them down his legs. He was in her bed, covered by the sheet, by the time she had the nerve to glance his way again.

"Snuff out the candles, would you, sweet," Anthony muttered with an elaborate yawn.

Jasmine glared her frustration and anger. "Snuff out your own damn candles," she snapped, and then gasped at her use of profanity, which had escaped unbidden from her lips. She moaned as she watched his movement. She knew her words had been a mistake, but she wouldn't take them back. In any case, it was already too late. With a murmur of annoyance, he had thrown the bedclothes aside and was on his feet.

Jasmine's cheeks blazed with mortification. Had the man no shame? How could he calmly walk to the mantel, naked as the day he was born?

Her softly muttered, "No" was lost in the gasp of astonishment as she watched him turn toward her. Jasmine had never seen a naked man before. She knew she should turn away. She knew if she were a properly moral lady, she would have swooned or at the very least made some sort of protest. But she did neither. Amazingly her embarrassment took second place to the sudden need to learn what lay beneath the smart cut of a gentleman's trousers.

Intrigued, Jasmine's gaze moved over the length of him. Her eyes widened with interest. Did all men look like this? Obviously not, for she had often heard her mother's friends snicker at the ugliness they described. Apparently they had not seen a man such as this one. Lord but he was a wonder to behold, and she couldn't tear her gaze from the beautiful sight of him. His shoulders were wide and bronzed from the sun. The tanned skin ran all the way to his waist, where the flesh suddenly grew paler. Her eyes followed the thick mat of dark golden hair beginning at his throat and covering a good portion of his chest, narrowing a bit as it bisected his stomach and then grew darker still and full again as it surrounded his sex.

Jasmine swallowed convulsively and forced her gaze from that mystery to the long line of muscular, hairy thigh and legs.

Despite his weariness, Anthony felt his body respond to her long look of inquiry. Her eyes were as round as saucers. Quickly he snuffed out the candles lest the obvious proof of his desire frighten her unnecessarily.

In the darkened room, lit only by the cool silver light of the moon as it filtered through gauze drapes,

74

he moved toward her. "Are you afraid?"

"Of course not!" Jasmine croaked after a moment or so of throat clearing. "It's just that I've never . . ."

"You've never seen a naked man before," he finished for her, when it grew apparent she couldn't go on.

Jasmine swallowed and shook her head. As he came closer, she took a step back.

Anthony smiled. "I think it only fair that you return the favor."

"You've never seen a naked woman?" she asked, her eyes round with amazement.

Anthony grinned. "I've never seen a naked you." His hands reached for the buttons of her bodice.

"No!" she gasped, her voice wavering as she struggled to rid herself of the violent tremors that had suddenly come over her. She took another step back.

Anthony shrugged as if her reluctance was of little importance, when, in fact, bedding her had suddenly cleared his mind of any inclination to sleep. "No matter. I'm a bit tired, in any case. Tomorrow night will suffice."

"Suffice for what?"

"Why, to bed you, of course."

Jasmine threw her head back and laughed. "Mr. Montgomery, I'd wager a year of tomorrows wouldn't suffice. You will never bed me."

Anthony grinned at her show of bravado as he settled himself comfortably in her bed. God but she was a spunky wench, her spirited denial only adding to her appeal.

His smile turned sly as he listened to her grumblings as she settled herself on the lounge. Silently he promised himself to sample again the passion he had discovered in the hansom cab this afternoon. And if he had his way he wouldn't be waiting overlong. A plan of enticement formed as he lay looking up at the dark ceiling. Anthony grinned, having not a doubt that by the time he was finished, she'd be as crazed for him as he was for her. He was going to drive her wild with frustration and he couldn't wait to begin.

Suddenly he almost groaned aloud at the thought that had just occurred. Good God, what could he have been thinking? It wouldn't do. Anthony shook his head wondering if he had the strength to bear the pain that was sure to come. No, it wouldn't do at all.

Jasmine muttered sleepily as she snuggled her backside closer to the comforting warmth, but what should have been a most delightful position was marred by a definite poking. Something annoyingly hard was pressed against the bottom of her spine.

Jasmine shifted again, snuggling deeper into the feather mattress and sighed contentedly as her heavy breast spilled from her opened bodice and overflowed Anthony's eagerly awaiting hand.

She paid no mind to the grunt of pleasure that penetrated the fog of sleep as a finger passed over her nipple. Something warm and definitely sweet stirred in her belly. Innocent that she was, Jasmine was unaware the rosy tip of her breast had hardened, but Anthony's action did serve to bring her closer to a level of consciousness. She blinked in sleepy confusion and then came instantly awake, her body stiff as she realized she was not alone.

Not only was she not alone, she was apparently in bed with the boldest of men. Jasmine's eyes widened with fear. But what man?

She groaned with disgust as memory returned. She hadn't gone to sleep in her bed. No, the brute must have moved her during the night. But had he done more than move her? Fear slithered down her back causing a shiver to tremble her body. Had he accomplished his threat while she lay unprotesting in sleep? Jasmine knew the basic facts of the act of coupling, but having had no experience along these lines, couldn't be sure if both parties participating needed total consciousness. And she wasn't about to ask.

Her lips tightened with anger. How had he dared touch her? And how had he done so without her awakening? A moment later Jasmine breathed a long sigh of disgust. It accomplished nothing to wonder about last night's happenings now. The first and most important thing she had to do was get out of bed and this room before he awoke.

Jasmine tried to slide away, but instantly realized his other arm was beneath her. Curse the man. Even in sleep he was holding to her waist, preventing her from moving more than an arm's length away.

Jasmine turned to her back and almost jumped with alarm to find him awake, his eyes twinkling with laughter. "Were you trying to sneak away from me?"

"Were you to gain a more intimate knowledge of my character, Mr. Montgomery," Jasmine added quickly at the widening of his eyes, "which you will not, you would know I never sneak. I was merely trying to get up."

"Mmm, I see," he remarked. "And my arm stopped you?"

"It did. Would you kindly remove it?" Jasmine felt an almost hysterical giggle threaten and desperately strove for control lest she give in to the impulse and run screaming from her chamber.

Still, she had to get away from this . . . this . . . man. What truly amazed her was the fact that she could lie here, discussing in the most polite terms the position of his arms when she knew next to nothing about him. Who was he? What kind of man would have done as he? Jasmine slowly shook her head and wondered if anything could be half so bizarre.

"What will you give me if I do?" he teased, referring to his constraining arm.

Innocently she asked, "What do you want?"

Anthony grinned. "I'll settle for a morning kiss. We'll get to what I really want later."

"Kiss!" Jasmine exclaimed with no little astonishment. "Are you mad? I'm not in the habit of kissing strange men."

Anthony's laughter held a lazy, teasing ring that did strange things to her insides. "I'm not all that strange. Besides, you kissed me yesterday. If memory serves, you did quite a bit of kissing and seemed to enjoy it as well."

"I'm afraid you are mistaken there. *You* did the kissing," she insisted. "I merely tolerated your unwanted advances."

Anthony chuckled at the barefaced lie. "Tolerated? Is that what you call it?"

"I do," she answered determinedly, swearing to suffer the ravages of hell before she'd admit to the truth.

He grinned as he came up to lean on his elbow, his eyes darkening with purpose. "If that was mere toleration, it boggles the mind to imagine your full participation. I can hardly wait."

Jasmine answered his grinning leer with a look of disgust. "Were I you, I wouldn't allow the thought all that much consideration. You're bound to suffer a measure of disappointment."

"Do you think so?"

"I'd wager half my worth on it."

"Only half? In that case, perhaps you are not as sure as you profess."

"The whole of it then," she snapped, her anger rising with every passing minute.

Anthony nodded, apparently more than happy to take up her taunt. "Shall we put it to the test then?"

Jasmine, surprised at first with the outrageous

position she found herself in and then engrossed in what she believed to be a most unpleasant subject, hadn't realized till that moment that his hand held still to her naked breast. She was dressed as she was the night before, except for the fact that her bodice had somehow come undone in sleep and the beast had taken full advantage of that odd happening.

In an effort to dislodge his hold, Jasmine's hand came to cover his, but she never got the opportunity to do more than begin a feeble prying of his fingers when his mouth covered hers.

Jasmine, surprised at his unexpected move, did little more than lie there stiffened into immobility.

"Come now," he whispered against her closed lips, "surely you can tolerate a kiss better than that."

"Let me go!" she murmured, the sound muffled against the insistent movement of his mouth.

"Mmm," he returned as his tongue took the opportunity to slide into her mouth.

Jasmine gasped and stiffened. Good God, he was doing it again! Why did he kiss like that? How had he come about learning such a thing? She pulled her head sharply away. "If you find you must kiss me, perhaps you might do it right."

Anthony grinned. He couldn't remember a time when a woman had told him his technique needed improvement. His eyes gleamed with humor and surprise. "Have I been doing it wrong?"

"You use your tongue," she said as if that were explanation in itself.

"And that doesn't please you?"

"It's disgusting."

He laughed again. "Have you never been kissed before?"

"Of course I've been kissed before." Jasmine raised her fingers as if to count off. "There was . . ."

"Spare me the intimate details, sweet," he said, feeling a sudden burst of anger that another should have sampled the taste of her mouth. Oddly enough, the fact that those kisses were less than passion-filled, since she had no knowledge of what a real kiss consisted, did not seem to mollify him. "You didn't seem to think it disgusting yesterday."

"Of course I did." *Well, I did at first,* she silently corrected. "I was just too polite to tell you."

"And today you feel no need for politeness?"

Jasmine lowered her gaze. His grin was maddening and she much preferred not to watch his laughter at her expense. "If you are quite finished . . ."

"Darling, I suspect it will be some time before I'm finished."

Jasmine felt her whole body jerk as Anthony's mouth came to nuzzle her cheek, her ear, and the sensitive flesh just beneath it. She pushed at his shoulders and strained against his arms, desperate to create some distance between them, but her efforts were as nothing compared to the ease with which he held her.

It didn't matter what he did, she silently swore. She wasn't going to allow herself to succumb again. He could kiss her all he wished. She felt nothing. Well, almost nothing. She did feel the tiniest flutter in her chest when his lips grazed her neck like that. And when his mouth lingered on that spot Jasmine unconsciously arched her neck and gave the smallest of sounds. Yes, that spot, it did bring a certain unevenness to her breathing. In truth, this was not the horror she had tried to make herself believe.

Anthony smiled with satisfaction when he heard the softest of murmurs escape her lips. "You like that?"

Jasmine tried to appear uninterested, completely indifferent. She meant to shrug to let him know just how little she did like it, but her muscles had somehow lost their coordination and her head tipped back, allowing him greater access to the skin of her slender throat.

A soft sound whispered past her lips and Anthony growled his own pleasure feeling her soften against him.

Something was clearly wrong here, but Jasmine couldn't quite put her finger on the problem. Then it finally occurred to her that she wasn't fighting his advances. *Why?* she wondered absently. She should be fighting this, shouldn't she? Jasmine tried to keep the thought in mind, but the delicious chills that were spreading down her back were preventing her from thinking very clearly—if at all.

His mouth was working its way up from the almost ticklish spot where her shoulder met her neck to her jaw. He was kissing and then licking her much as he would a sugar treat and seeming to enjoy the taste equally well, were his sighs of satisfaction any evidence.

But the most peculiar thing of all was that Jasmine was enjoying the touch of his mouth easily as much. She should have been amazed at her reaction and she might have been such had her senses not been so wildly affected. But she couldn't think clearly, not with the tingling sensations that were fluttering up and down her spine.

Jasmine felt her breathing growing shallow as she waited in anxious anticipation for his mouth. He was coming closer. She knew he was going to kiss her and the thought of his mouth touching hers did not bring about disgust but rather a secret yearning for his kisses.

Jasmine moaned with building hunger, her lips parting in clear invitation as he covered her mouth at last. This time Jasmine felt no need to pull back but welcomed the shock of his tongue with a groan of hunger appeased.

She never realized her hand reached up to hold to his naked shoulder. The room swam dizzily around her and she needed his solid form to steady her senses lest she be flung from the bed and out of his arms. Jasmine moaned, relishing the sweet, possessive invasion. Her mouth came alive beneath his expertise. Eager and hungry it pressed instinctively closer to the delicious heat, her whole body suddenly matching his for warmth.

An ache began, a piercingly sweet ache somewhere deep in her belly as his fingers grazed the tips of now fully exposed breasts. She didn't realize but to answer the taunting thrusts of his tongue with similar movements of her own and sighed with delight as she heard his low growl of hunger at the exquisitely sweet combat.

Feelings never before experienced surged through her body, bringing heat, burning liquid heat to fill her veins and grow like fire in the pit of her stomach. Her breath left her lungs in a rush as his hand flattened against the juncture of her thighs. Reflexively she arched her back toward the exquisite pressure and his mouth absorbed her soft moans of pleasure.

Anthony shivered as she ran her hand down his back. Good Lord! What in damnation was he doing? Hadn't he realized last night this would be a terrible mistake? Hadn't he warned himself this could never be?

Jasmine felt an almost overwhelming sense of disappointment when he suddenly pulled his head back and almost sadly smiled into her dazed expression. "Good morning, sweet," he said a bit unevenly as he sprang from the bed.

He had already donned his trousers, an immediate and necessary act, lest she see the obvious results of the last few minutes. Anthony knew his wife to be an innocent. No matter her daring, youthful escapades, she had no knowledge of a real kiss, much less he supposed the sight of a man in the midst of passion, and he had no wish to shock her sensibilities—at least, not yet.

Anthony had his shirt on, the long ends trailing over the bulge in his trousers, before Jasmine came fully to her senses. She watched with nothing less than astonishment as he smiled down at her. She reached with shaking fingers to adjust and secure her bodice.

She turned from him and sat on the opposite edge of the bed. How had he done that? How had he made her forget her dislike of kissing? How had he brought such sweet pleasure with the simple touch of his mouth? How had she been so engrossed with the happenings as to have forgotten he was caressing her naked flesh? Jasmine groaned with embarrassment as she remembered how she had pressed herself closer, wanting more.

She should have drawn away. Indeed, she had wanted to draw away, but there was a drumming in her ears and brain, a lassitude that had come over her, a heaviness in her limbs, a weakness in her spirit and she found it impossible but to press closer. God, how was she to bear the shame of it? What was the matter with her to so enjoy his kiss, his touch?

"Are you hungry, my love?"

"Please, Mr. Montgomery," Jasmine croaked between stiff lips, "I'd much prefer for you to bestow your endearments upon another."

"Would you?" he asked with a laugh and then, spying her tormented expression, realized her agony and confusion.

Anthony grinned as he watched her brow furrow in thought. It was obvious she was silently berating her actions while at the same time feeling some astonishment at her response. Anthony wasn't unaware of the passion that lay dormant in his wife. With some gentle coaxing he knew it could be brought to the surface. Indeed, he imagined that the time wasn't far off when she might initiate these delightful moments.

She, like many other young women of her station, had no doubt heard since childhood the nonsense spouted by some as to a wife's duty. Ladies weren't expected to enjoy the marital bed. Anthony realized Jasmine must now be suffering some confusion, realizing the passion within her.

Anthony gave a silent curse at the waste. There was nothing he could do but bemoan the fates that had brought this woman to him. He couldn't act the lusty husband while in bed and then suddenly switch roles in public and become the overly refined, somewhat effeminate gentleman his acquaintances knew, acquaintances they no doubt *both* knew.

He sighed a long, woeful sound knowing he had no choice. All he could hope was the effort it took to resist her didn't eventually destroy him.

Chapter Five

A lone dark figure, nearly indistinguishable among the shadowy, swaying greenery that hugged the brick house, moved with the fluid motion of a powerful athlete up the vine-covered wall toward the second-story window. It hesitated there for the time it took to gently force the frame upon squeaking hinges. With a softly muttered curse, the man's hand shot out with unerring accuracy and grasped the tottering vase that sat like an unseen sentry upon a mahogany table placed directly before the window. A moment later, the shadow vanished over the sill and into a room the color of pitch.

A confident smile lingered over tight lips as he easily, silently negotiated himself between the desk and assortment of tables and chairs that dotted the floor space, moving with purpose directly to the file that sat unprotected upon the bookshelf. In the dark it would appear the man were the possessor of magical powers. But no, the fact was, he had been here earlier and had taken careful, if undetected, notice of the room during his last visit.

The thin file of papers was brought to the desk for a thorough examination. The very lack of a guard might have credited the general as a genius. At first glance, no one would expect these carelessly exposed plans to be of such importance. He shook his head. But no. That was not the case. Many were the times when he had found important documents in similar, casual circumstances.

There were moments when one marveled at the British arrogance. Did they not believe another could read? Was their assurance in their power and might so great that it mattered little if secrets were discovered? He knew this to be the case, for being British himself, before adopting this country as his own, he lacked none of the arrogance attributed to his former countrymen.

A grimace tightened his lips. He didn't like it, but the lighting of a candle was a necessary risk. Quickly he scanned the documents, memorizing the pertinent data.

Soft, throaty laughter interrupted his mission. Instantly the room was again thrown into darkness, the file replaced upon the shelf. His heart thundered as he stepped behind heavy velvet drapes just as the door to the library opened.

"Robert, there is no one here," Jasmine said, her surprise obvious.

A low, suggestive chuckle served as an answer and then a male voice responded as the door clicked firmly shut behind them. "So I see."

"I thought you said Merry was waiting to speak with me?" came a breathless question as she was spun about and pressed against the closed door.

"Did I say that?"

"You did."

"Well, perhaps I meant she would be waiting to speak to you if she had been here."

Jasmine shot the grinning captain a stern look of disapproval, never realizing it could not be seen in the dark. "Robert, I should be most angry with you. You realize, of course, the position in which you have placed me. I thought you were my friend."

"Darling, I've never been your friend. Certainly you know I've always wanted more than that from you."

"Robert, you must refrain from addressing me with endearments and kindly release me. I am a married lady now."

Robert laughed. "Married to that peacock? Why, the idea is ludicrous, laughable, if it wasn't so damn sad."

"In your estimation, perhaps."

"What use is he to you? I'd wager the man doesn't know the first thing about pleasuring a woman."

"And I take it you do?"

"I've had no complaints."

"Till now. Release me, Robert, or I'll be forced to make your conduct known to Anthony."

"Lord, I'm shivering with fright. Damnation, the pantywaist might even go so far as to raise his brow at me and then whatever shall I do?"

"Robert!" came her low warning, followed instantly by a sharp gasp as the man was wrenched away from her. A moment later came the sound of a sharp crack, then a dull thud and she watched as his head hit against the floor.

The shadow of a man loomed menacingly before her. Jasmine swallowed in terror as her heartbeat instantly accelerated to a choking pace. If she imagined the episode with Robert to be frightening, it was as nothing compared to facing this shadowy, unknown foe. Who was he? Where, in God's name, had he come from?

Jasmine took a deep breath, but a hand reached out to cover her mouth. It clamped itself firmly over parted lips, preventing the scream that threatened. "Silence," his low whisper warned.

Her chest heaved with fright as she struggled to bring air into suddenly starved lungs. This couldn't be happening. God in heaven, this couldn't

87

be happening!

Leaning heavily against her, caring little that his weight further impeded her breathing, he pressed her hard to the door, preventing any possible movement. "The next time you enter a dark room, make sure your companion is indeed your friend or you might find yourself suffering more than an unwanted kiss."

The words were barely spoken before his mouth lowered and warm lips replaced his hand.

Jasmine gasped again, filling her lungs with the scent of clean male flesh, horse, and leather, but barely noticing these erotic mingling of scents, her mind so occupied with his outrageous actions. Her body stiffened with shock as she reflexively squeezed her hand between their bodies and pressed, palms flat, against a muscular, immovable chest.

"Stop," she moaned on a gasping breath as moments later, he released her mouth. She was dizzy, her voice noticeably weak. "You've no right to do this. You've no right."

"Perhaps," he grunted as he ground his hips against her, clearly allowing her the knowledge of his arousal. His mouth brushed against hers again. "Nevertheless, I'm taking that right."

Surprise was her only excuse. She never expected to find a man lurking in the shadows of this room. Most of all, she never expected that man to kiss her. What other reason could there be for her lack of resistance? Why else did she accept the hint of his tongue as it brushed ever so lightly over her flesh, by parting her lips?

In truth, it was the most exciting thing that had ever happened to her. A fantasy come true, in fact. Jasmine wondered if all women had not imagined themselves in the arms of an unknown lover, a stolen moment of bliss, a few harmless kisses shared.

Amazingly, she felt no fear. Perhaps the knowledge of others nearby gave her a false sense of security, but she wasn't thinking of others now, wasn't thinking of *anything*. Her shock and fear had passed quickly into a hazy rapture that left her enjoying the taste of his mouth, the texture of his tongue.

She never realized how her body softened against him. She never knew how her sweet sigh of pleasure sounded a clear invitation for further samplings.

Again and again and again his tongue dipped into the sweetness of her mouth, absorbing the flavor, relishing in her taste, delighting in her scent, until she knew nothing but this oddly pleasant ache of longing. And if she knew not for what she craved, she found no moment to think on it, for her bodice was lowered to accommodate his searching caresses, and her freed, lush breasts became the object of aching hunger.

Jasmine groaned as the heat of his mouth seared virgin flesh. Her back stiffened and a hissing breath between clamped teeth filled the silence of the room. Her hands moved to his face, her intent to hold him closer, but his strong hands took hers and held them firmly behind her back. Vaguely she realized she should have felt fear then, but she only shivered with renewed excitement.

She whimpered in helpless need as he suckled, the drawing motion of his mouth creating an unbelievable ache deep in her belly. Jasmine pressed closer, her breathing gasping and strained, as she unconsciously searched for a means to relieve the discomfort.

His hand slid beneath the voluminous folds of her gown and knowledgeable fingers moved over silk stockings to slide beneath frilly drawers. It took him a moment before he realized he was touching naked flesh, the texture between stockings and silken skin was so akin. He smiled as her softness almost caused him a moment's pause, but his hesitation went unnoticed, for she was lost in an engulfing passion while he was totally engrossed in this enticing prize, a prize he had for too long hungered.

Her eyes were dazed as she watched him straighten and he smiled, knowing how consumed she was with her own passion. Had they been elsewhere, he would have seen to a release of their mutual needs, but here he chanced much with possible discovery. Still, it hurt no one if he showed her a glimpse of the pleasure that lay ahead for them.

Had his lips not been there, her cry of delight would surely have passed through the walls. She had surely not expected the shock of pleasure his fingers brought as they moved to the juncture of her thighs.

The ache that had been no more than a gnawing discomfort grew then into a tight band of promising . . . what? Pleasure? Pain? Jasmine groaned, unable to distinguish between the two, wanting them both. She might have thought then of her acquiescence had not his mouth taken hers again to sip and sample, to tease and taunt, to drive her wild with a longing she could not name or understand.

Her knees gave way as the final aching waves of ecstasy rolled over her desperately straining body, leaving her in the end weak and totally drained of energy. He held her securely against him lest she crumble to the floor. Long moments of harsh breathing passed before she began to understand what had happened.

Jasmine gasped and watched with nothing less than shock as he took his mouth from hers, smiled, and then deliberately licked his still damp fingers while giving a murmur of delight. "Delicious."

She groaned again as the word filled her mind. She lowered her eyes and shivered in silence, engulfed in a sense of growing shame unlike anything she'd ever imagined. How could she have responded to his kiss? What had ever possessed her to allow him such liberties with her body? What had come over her that she had clung to him, silently begging him to ease the sweet suffering the touch of his mouth and tongue had brought to life within her belly. And then groaning out her joy, his mouth the only obstacle that prevented anyone from hearing, when his skillful fingers had at last brought about their reward.

Gently he adjusted her bodice. "Go now, he's coming around" came the husky, breathless whisper, spoken just before he disappeared into the shadows from whence he had come.

Jasmine found not the will to obey his whispered order: all she could do was lean heavily against the door, her heart thudding, her breathing irregular. It took a long moment before she realized he was gone or noticed that Robert lay still at her feet, his moans of discomfort growing more pronounced as each moment went by.

And when realization set in, Jasmine cried out a choked sound of mortification muffled behind a tight fist as she stumbled on shaking legs from the room. How could she have succumbed to a man she did not know? How could she bear the shame of it? Never daring to look back, she hurried to the room set aside for the ladies, so she might repair the damage done to her hair and wipe her tears away.

She never knew who he was. Lord in heaven, it was so dark, she didn't even know what he looked like. When she had raised her hands, she'd realized he wore a mask over his eyes, but before she was allowed to follow the contours of his face, he had pulled her hands away and later, so mindlessly afire, she had forgotten to try again.

Jasmine's lips curled with an unhappy grimace as she glanced across the room and watched as her husband waved a delicately laced handkerchief, the sounds of his high-pitched, almost whining, effeminate laughter bringing a flush of embarrassment to her cheeks. She cringed and bit at her lip as the squeaking sound grated against her nerve endings and rang out with mortifying clarity over the low, murmuring voices of the party.

God in heaven, how was it she had never before noticed his laughter? She corrected herself. She *had* noticed it, of course, but it just seemed louder and shriller every time they attended one of these long, boring affairs.

Vaguely she wondered why he didn't laugh like that when alone in her company? And were her ears playing tricks or had he suddenly developed a hint of a lisp?

Jasmine shivered as she glanced his way again. And that stance! Lord but he was full of himself tonight, with his lacy handkerchiefs and ruffled shirts. If she hated but one thing, it was the popinjay. Never had she given one of his kind a second glance and now, as Essie would say, "May the saints preserve us," she had married one.

With the slightest shake of her head, Jasmine thought on her present situation and nearly laughed aloud at the irony of it. She had sworn to never marry a man such as her father. She had even gone so far as to choose this one out of a stable to ensure her free choice in the matter, and yet, in the end, Anthony had proved himself very much like her father. In truth, had he done the choosing himself, her father couldn't have done better in finding her a husband who would match him in his perverse ways.

At first she had believed the strain between Anthony and her was somehow her fault. Perhaps there was something in her that did not appeal, but the constant attention she received from the gentlemen of her acquaintance laid to rest that fallacy. Not that she wanted to appeal to him, of course. It was just . . . Too confused, Jasmine never finished the thought.

She sighed wearily. Soon enough it had grown sadly obvious that Anthony was not like other men. The oddest thing was that no matter how he might posture and pose, the resulting demeanor was not quite like that of the overly refined gentleman. His features were large, not delicate enough to be considered aristocratic but handsome and manly in the truest sense of the word, and served to make him appear all the more ridiculous when bedecked as now in his powdered wig and the beauty patch stenciled on his chin. None of this matched the man, for he was wiry but muscular in shoulders, arms and thighs, not in the least soft and feminine.

And think on it she did, only to gain nothing for her efforts. Granted, she did not know the particulars of married life, but she did know a husband and wife were expected to share a certain amount of intimacy, an intimacy that was surely lacking in their relationship. No matter that he might at times wander about their rooms in nonchalant nakedness, but for that one morning after they were married, he never forced his attentions on her.

Jasmine couldn't understand why this should cause her so many hours of unhappy thought. Hadn't she heard stories enough of the horrors of the marriage bed? Shouldn't she then feel a measure of relief that this man did not press her to do his bidding?

Indeed, she might have been satisfied with a marriage that was not a marriage at all had he not seen fit to enlighten her with the smallest of samplings, thereby letting her know exactly what she was missing. For weeks now she had thought of nearly nothing but kissing and now that she had discovered how it should be done, she realized how very much she liked it.

Her face grew crimson as she clearly remembered the happenings of just an hour past. Odd, but the man's kisses had felt exactly as had Anthony's. Jasmine shrugged, imagining in her innocence that all men kissed thusly. Determinedly, she pushed all thought of this shameful night from her mind.

Anthony hadn't kissed her since the morning after they were married, with the exception of a brotherly peck on her cheek, and that only when another might be about. No, he never touched her and, strangely, considering his feminine ways, she suddenly wished he would.

Jasmine watched as he posed and preened before two brilliantly dressed officers. She frowned with annoyance that he should so act the fool. Nearly always drunk, he lost badly, or so she heard, in games of chance. To her growing anger and misery, she imagined him ridiculed as the fool, merely kept about as resident laughingstock.

Lord in heaven, how could she have been so mistaken? How had he so radically changed? But had he really changed, or had she never truly known the man?

Jasmine shook her head. How could she have married a man whose sole interest was the cut of his clothes? And most bewildering of all, why should that fact cause her this constant nagging sorrow?

Anthony felt a moment's surprise at the anger that filled his being and forced a mental shrug as Jasmine's throaty laughter turned every male eye in the room toward her and the handsome captain of the king's dragoons at her side. Surely the lovely sight of her was enough to tempt a saint, but to hear the sultry sound of that voice was almost unbearable.

The captain lowered his head and whispered again near her ear, eliciting yet another achingly sweet sound. Anthony wondered how much longer he'd be forced to keep up this guise. How many more nights was he to lie in hopeless agony at her side, lest she discover the truthful lusty nature of the man she'd married? Dare he show himself true and jeopardize the role he had most carefully created and managed to play so well?

Nay, it was enough he had once forgotten his intent. He could never again allow her a glimpse of his true self, for he knew where her loyalties lay. She was a staunch supporter of the king and would, he imagined, surely grow suspicious of a man of such changeable character.

Anthony chose just that moment to again glance her way and felt his belly tighten with an almost painful ache. Despite her laughter, he could clearly read the sadness in her eyes and was certain he knew the reason for her bewilderment. After their first night together, she must have expected a continuation of what was so tenderly sampled. Indeed, his actions at the time had promised as much. How confused she must feel, he realized, at being a virgin still, nearly two months after her marriage!

Anthony knew well enough the torture that filled his future and prayed he had the strength to continue on in this vein.

He gave a silent curse as Jasmine's carefully guarded smile slipped and a glimpse of her desperate unhappiness made itself known. But in an instant it was gone, replaced again by the hard glitter in her eyes.

Damn the woman, he silently raged. Damn her for her beauty, for her smile, for the laughter that floated over a sea of male voices, leaving only stunned sensual silence in its wake. And damn her most of all for the pain that gripped his belly when he couldn't reach out and touch her.

Why in damnation should she so occupy his thoughts? What was she, after all, but a woman? Aye, a woman—no more, no less. A woman, he'd wager, indistinguishable from a hundred others in the dark. What had someone once said? Standing on their heads they were all the same. Aye, 'twas a fact, he swore, and then sighed with disgust, a fact he somehow couldn't force himself to believe.

Suddenly, from somewhere in the far recesses of his mind, a seed of a thought came to root and germinated into a plan of action. A moment or so later a smile of anticipation touched his lips. It was possible. Yes, judging by her passionate nature, it was more than possible.

Anthony forced aside the confident laugh that threatened and swore before much longer he'd have her in his bed. And if he was careful, she'd never even know she'd been there.

"Would you have me court you, Elizabeth? As if we were naught but youngsters still?"

Elizabeth spun around and watched, her cheeks flushing pink like a girl, her heart thudding with surprise as he rose from the library chair. "I thought the room was empty."

Richard nodded. "Answer the question, if you would."

Elizabeth's brow furrowed with annoyance. How much longer was she to bear this man's company? Did he not realize she wanted both him and her husband gone? How much longer could she keep her composure? He had to leave and it had to be soon. He was waiting for her answer, and even now she wondered if she had the courage to stand by her purpose or would she crumble beneath his magnetism. She cleared her throat twice before she trusted the sound and steadiness of her voice. "If memory serves, you have yet to do so. In truth, I was merely a convenient receptacle for a passion that could not be released upon a sickly wife."

Richard stiffened and paled at her taunting words. "Damnation! Do you honestly believe that to be the case?"

All the old pain came rushing back, blinding her to the suffering of the man before her. All she could see, all she could think was the agony he had brought upon her when he left. She didn't think to soften her words. For two months now they had rattled on in her brain and he had finally given her the opportunity to release the torment. Her smile was hard, denying the aching softness that lingered so dangerously close to the surface. "What would you have me believe? That you loved me beyond all reason?. That you forsook your vows on my account? That you protected me from the monster I was forced to marry, from the hatred I was later forced to endure?

"Nay, Richard, you are correct in one thing. We are no longer children. I, for one, do not believe in the fairy tale of love everlasting."

Richard was clearly shaken. "Are you saying there is no future for us?"

Her smile was bittersweet. "No future. No past."

He shook his head. "I'll not believe it. You cannot make me believe it, no matter the words of hate you spout."

Elizabeth's smile was heavy with sadness. "Hate? Nay, Richard, never hate. Reality, instead."

"Will you say you never loved me?"

"I will, for I never loved you. Love was an emotion given freely by the girl I once was."

"And you and the young girl are not the same?"

"Not likely. And thank God for that."

"I think you are wrong, Elizabeth. I think you are very wrong indeed."

Elizabeth shrugged and turned her back, her eyes unseeingly scanning the books upon the shelf. "Think then what you must, sir."

"Elizabeth, please, listen to me."

She appeared to have not heard him, but continued to search out a particular book.

"Damn it! I said, listen!" he snapped as he took her arm and forced her to turn to him.

"Nay, I'll not," she returned as she wrenched herself free of his hold.

"You will. I've come halfway around the world to find you. I'll not let you go again."

Elizabeth snorted a most unladylike laugh. "Halfway around the world and twenty years too late."

"What would you have had me do? Should I have abandoned her? Elizabeth, be reasonable. She couldn't be held accountable for the sickness that crept into her mind. Should I have taken you to live with me? Should I have brought such disgrace upon you? And then later upon our daughter?"

"I never asked you to abandon her. I never wanted that."

"What then? What else could I have done?"

"You could have loved me enough! You could have allowed me the choice! You could have taken us both. Taken us away. No one need ever have known. But no, not Richard Townsend, the man of superior morals and judgment to match. No, you saw fit to make your own decisions regarding our life, our love.

"I would have given anything for you. My fortune, my family, my honor meant nothing. I only wanted you."

"Elizabeth, you're speaking like a child. I had a duty."

"Damn your duty to hell!"

Richard almost burst out laughing, for it was not in Elizabeth's character to spout indelicacies. His eyes widened with surprise.

Elizabeth bit her lip, instantly remorseful. She hadn't meant to speak so harshly or crudely. An instant later she tossed her head with defiance. He deserved no better. "Does my unladylike utterance offend you, sir? I certainly hope so!" She turned to leave, but his hand on her arm brought her again to face him.

A glimmer of humor danced in his eyes. "It does not offend me. Actually, I find your anger quite refreshing."

Elizabeth sighed. "Richard, this accomplishes nothing. It is too late for us to begin again. When are you leaving?"

Richard's smile was tender. It was all he could do not to take her in his arms and kiss her till both of them were weak and breathless with need. "Not this time, Elizabeth. To be twice the fool would indeed be unforgivable. I'll not be leaving alone."

Her smile was cool. "Shall I have Jenson send over to the *Gazette* to place an advertisement for a traveling companion?"

"Your wit will not suffice here, Elizabeth. You know what I want. I shall not be leaving without it."

"You might find yourself here for some time to come, sir."

"As long as I'm with you, it matters little where I am."

Elizabeth stormed from the room, never pausing for an instant until she gained the sanctuary of her bedroom. She slammed the door and leaned weakly against it as she silently ranted at this most unfair twist of fate. No! It was too late. She was a woman grown and in complete control. Never would she again allow him the power to inflict pain. The girl who had loved him was long gone. She had managed well enough all these years. She wasn't about to give in to this weakness and bring the pain again.

Never!

Elizabeth, back stiff, shoulders straight, moved to her dressing table and began to pull the pins from her hair. Slowly, with soothing strokes, she ran her brush through the golden waves until the calmness she so

99

desperately sought came at last upon her.

She didn't blame Richard. He had done what he could to protect her. It had taken her a long time to realize that. Foolish though it might have been, he had done what he believed to be right. He never knew she was to have his child. He never knew the pain.

Although she might not blame him, he still didn't need to know that. No, it was best for all concerned if he believed her without sympathy for his cause. It was best if he believed her merely cold to his presence.

The truth of it was, it was torture simply being in the same room with him. And as far as she could see, it was not to end anytime in the near future. Elizabeth sighed. What she needed was a respite. She needed to get away for a time. She needed to gather her strength against his allure, against the need to touch him, against the need to belong to him again.

Chapter Six

"Hell and damnation! Are you sure?"

"Keep your voice down, man. The place is crawling with lobsterbacks."

Caleb Brewster grinned with confidence. "Aye, I know well enough, but methinks them more than a little short-sighted. Why, not a half hour back, I was close enough to tell you what one of them ate for dinner, what with the gravy stains on his pretty white shirt and red coat." He laughed softly and, with no little arrogance, remarked, "The bloke never knew how close he was to his final reward."

Anthony breathed a sigh of relief, knowing the man's hatred for anything British and his lusty appreciation of a good fight. "It's a good thing you kept your instincts for violence under control. It would have done little good to create a ruckus tonight. This information has to be passed on to Washington as soon as possible."

Caleb shrugged.

"Do you have it straight?"

"I understand fully. He'll know about it inside of two hours. Go back to your pretty friends and let me continue with my work."

Anthony turned to leave. "Wait! Jesus, you almost made me forget." Caleb thrust a package in Anthony's hands. "You're supposed to take this and drop it on the road at a place where it's sure to be found by the Tories."

"What?"

"You heard right. The general wants Cornwallis to think he's readying a counterattack on Manhattan."

"Why in blazes . . . ?"

Caleb grinned as he looked down from his enormous height. "You know the general. He figures those pretty fightin' boys ain't doin' much but drinking and whoring anyway. He thinks it's about time they started actin' like real soldiers. After all, why shouldn't they be worryin' a bit about one thing while the general is busy with another."

Anthony grinned, visualizing the British fortifying their defenses around Manhattan, while General Washington slipped unnoticed right by the city. God but the man was an unbelievably brilliant strategist. Silently he thanked God Washington was on the side of the rebel forces, for no matter the doubts of some, he knew that against this mighty lion, the effort would otherwise be lost.

The noisy sounds of a patrol nearby quickly sent both men about their business, Caleb to his longboat and on to Connecticut and Anthony farther into the woodland to retrieve his horse. He dared not use the roads while he held such damning evidence upon his person, for there were times aplenty when a man could not tell friend from foe. Slowly, and as silently as he could manage, he moved in and out of the swampy, wooded land of Brooklyn Heights, thinking where he could best drop this package.

Anthony smiled as an idea took hold. He knew someone who would know just what to do with this information. All he needed was a bit of luck to see his plan to rights.

*   *   *

102

Jagged bolts of lightning streaked through the black night, bringing eerie white flashes of light to the dim bedchamber while thunder crashed and boomed with jarring inconsistency. She rubbed her arms as if warding off a chill. But it wasn't cold she felt, rather a premonition of sorts. Something was going to happen. She knew it as surely as she would take her next breath.

If she closed her eyes she could imagine the sounds of a heavy barrage of cannon off one of the frigates now peacefully at anchor in New York Harbor. During the battle of Long Island, the cannon seemed never to stop and the thunder tonight was so similar to be indistinguishable.

Jasmine sighed and walked to the French doors. Everything felt so close tonight. The air, hot and heavy with moisture, left her almost breathless. She fidgeted nervously, unable to shake this oddest of feelings.

Determinedly she pushed aside the sensation. Of course nothing was about to happen. It was the storm, that was all. The storm and this endless conflict that made her a bit jittery.

Lord but she wished these rebels would use their God-given good sense. Why in the world had they created such a ruckus? Why couldn't they be satisfied under the good King George?

Granted, she wasn't overly thrilled to pay the taxes levied by Parliament, nor could she name one loyal servant to the Crown who was. But, Lord, if one took to arms over every dissatisfaction not a moment of peace would ever reign upon this planet, for there was always someone to object to one rule or another.

Again she sighed. She wanted nothing more than to see this conflict end. For a time she had enjoyed the British occupation. She smiled in remembrance. Not so long ago she had believed the British, their officers in particular, to be the most handsome of all men.

How often had the sight of their dashing red uniforms brought a flutter of excitement to a young girl's heart?

But all that had changed since her marriage. Slowly she had begun to see the English in a less favorable light. As often as not they made Anthony the brunt of a joke. They took advantage of his obvious need to belong by borrowing huge sums of money, which she had no doubt would never be returned. They knew him unable to hold his liquor, so they plied him with drink and snickered as he lost in games of chance. Chance! She snorted a rude sound. What chance had her poor husband against these arrogant rogues?

Her husband! Jasmine's brow furrowed in confusion. What was there about the man that brought about this defensive emotion? In truth, disgust should have been her primary reaction when thoughts of him came to mind, but Jasmine couldn't summon that particular emotion. Nay, it wasn't digust she felt, but rather a protective rage on his behalf. And yet it wasn't protectiveness alone. No matter how she might try, she couldn't understand or prevent the tingling awareness she always experienced when in his company.

He should have been everything a woman would want in a man. He was handsome, kind, and pleasant, ever considerate of her needs—except for one particular need! Jasmine shook her head denying the glaring truth. No, she did not want her husband. It was the coming storm that had brought on this odd sense of unease, this sense of longing.

Jasmine breathed a sigh of relief as she opened the door and allowed a gust of damp fresh air to enter the room. The breeze extinguished the candle behind her, but it mattered not. She was just as well pleased to stand here in the dark and think her darker thoughts.

The church bells chimed the hour of two and she

sighed again. She didn't put much hope in Anthony's return tonight. He often spent the night at the club, either too drunk or too tired to bother with the short trip home. Vaguely she wondered why that should bother her. Having no answer, a puzzled frown marred her smooth brow and she shrugged a slender shoulder in confusion.

Jasmine moved out to the terrace and leaned against the wall of the house, hungry for more of the agreeably scented air as it blew in from the sea and flattened her gown against her. She grinned. If nothing else, it might clear away her melancholy thoughts, for these feelings she was coming to know more fiercely each day for a man who barely looked her way were clearly ridiculous. Her husband obviously, no matter her first mistaken impression, wanted little to do with his wife.

Jasmine's thoughts returned again to the man he had been before and immediately after their marriage. She almost laughed as she remembered her desperate plans to keep him from her bed. Never would she have imagined her worries had no foundation. What in God's name had brought about this change? But had he truly changed? Perhaps he had always been thus and she had simply not recognized it.

Jasmine shook her head, her bewildered thoughts causing her brow to furrow and a sadness to show in the drooping of her lips.

He had just slipped over the railing and ducked behind the cover of a small potted tree as the doors suddenly opened and she stepped outside. His heart thudded, but it wasn't fear that suddenly gripped his innards in a breathless hold. Nay, it was a desire the likes of which he wondered if he'd survive. Blood pounded in his veins, echoing loudly in his ears, the sound blotting out the whistling gusts of wind as it rushed over the quiet city. He gasped as a streak of lightning illuminated the terrace, making it clear her white, filmy gown left nearly nothing to the imagination.

He never thought to remain hidden, for her siren call encompassed all his senses and he was standing before her, never even knowing he had moved.

Jasmine raised her eyes from the terrace floor and gasped as another flash of lightning exposed him to her view. Pure numbing terror filled her being. She wanted to scream, in fact had opened her mouth to do so, but no sound would pass the tightness of her throat. She could neither draw air in or out. Her back stiffened against the wall, her hands palm flat against the bricks as her eyes darted to the left and right, instinctively seeking a means of escape.

He moved closer and her eyes widened as fear threatened to become wild hysteria. His hand shot out and clamped firmly over her opened mouth. "Don't be afraid. I won't hurt you."

The dizziness from lack of air was easing as she breathed huge gulps into her lungs at last. It was he, the man from General Cornwallis's library! Jasmine trembled, but her fear was slipping away, replaced by a growing anger.

"Are you all right?"

She nodded.

"You won't scream if I release your mouth?"

She shook her head. No, she wouldn't scream, for she wasn't the least bit afraid of this man. She was simply furious that he should dare show himself again.

"I'm sorry I frightened you."

"Frightened me!?" she asked in outrage. "Sir, I can only pray to one day return the favor. No doubt you'd then think twice before you invade the privacy of a lady's home."

He chuckled. "But I haven't invaded your home, have I?" referring to the fact that they were outside on her terrace.

106

"Perhaps I'm in error here. Perhaps you are simply enjoying an evening constitutional." She laughed bitterly and taunted, "On the second floor."

He grinned at her sarcasm, his voice low and husky sending unwanted chills down her spine. "I'm enjoying you, particularly when the lightning allows such delicious glimpses of your attire."

Jasmine felt not the slightest flicker of embarrassment, for the man was a cad and deserved not a moment of her thought. Her lips tightened with fury. "Poor man to have never seen a lady disheveled."

He laughed again and took a small step closer. "Oh, I've seen one or two in my time, but none to compare to the likes of you."

Jasmine ordered the sudden flutter in her chest and the unreasonable pounding of her heart to cease. "If you think to convince me of your honorable intentions with a few gently spoken words, you'd best try again."

His low laughter sent another bout of those hateful thrills down her spine. She didn't want to feel this. Jasmine stiffened further, forcing aside the despised sensation. Good God, wasn't what he'd forced upon her when last they met enough? Did she want again to suffer in the agonizing throes of shame and guilt? Why was she even standing here? Why didn't she call for help? Why didn't she make a dash for the safety of her rooms?

"Indeed, I've failed at our last meeting and badly if you believe my intentions honorable."

"Sir, politeness forbids my telling you how greatly I despise you and your actions."

"Does it?" He chuckled. "And yet you've managed to make yourself clear enough." There was a moment's hesitation before he continued. "And still you stand here. One might believe your declaration had you run at the first sight. But did you? No, you faced me down and dare me still to do my worst."

Jasmine was amazed to realize she felt no fear. Why, she couldn't begin to fathom. All she knew was this man would not bring her harm. "I dare you nothing! I simply refuse to be frightened by the Shadow, a rogue too cowardly to show his face. Leave my house this instant."

His hands against the wall held each side of her head and trapped her in place, while a taunting smile lingered at his lips. "Ah, so you know who I am. You intrigue this rogue, madam. How is it you find the courage to speak to me thus? Most women would have succumbed to the vapors by now."

"All of the Colonies know of you, for your reputation travels far and wide. I am not most women, sir. I do not succumb to that ailment."

"But you will succumb to me, won't you?"

"Will I?" she asked, her jaw lifting a notch, her glare daring him.

He let the taunt pass, realizing rightly her growing anger. But it wasn't anger he longed to see, no matter how lovely she grew with flashing eyes and flushed cheeks. No, it wasn't anger he wanted from this woman.

"Why are you out here alone? Where is your— What was his name . . . Anthony?"

"My husband is inside asleep." Jasmine prayed he wouldn't hear the trembling in her voice at the lie. "I've only to call out and he will come to my rescue."

He nodded his head. "Ah, but do you need rescuing? Have I done something you might consider a threat?"

"You? Indeed I would be overly suspicious to believe so," she remarked, her voice replete with sarcasm. "Just because a man has taken it upon himself to climb two floors to my balcony. Just because it's two o'clock in the morning. Just because he masks his face like a common criminal, far be it for me to suspect a threat." She gasped, taking in a long

108

deep breath and then silently cursed as the scent of him filled her senses and brought back memories of a night she'd tried so desperately hard to forget. "No doubt I'm slightly unbalanced, but I do not fear you."

"Would you object overmuch if I kissed you?"

"Good God!" she sputtered, her outrage never more in evidence. "Of course I would object. A lady doesn't kiss a stranger." *What kind of a man is this,* she wondered? *After the intimacies shared, the liberties taken, he still asked for a kiss as if he were naught but a beau.*

"Especially a married lady. Is that it?"

She nodded.

"But you kissed me once."

"You caught me by surprise," she explained, her voice growing decidedly breathless at the remembrance.

There was a long moment of silence before he asked, "Could it be you love your husband and wish to remain faithful?"

"Of course I love him. I married him, did I not?"

"And a married lady in love with her husband would never kiss another. Am I right?"

"Now that we've settled that monumental question, will you kindly take your ridiculously masked self and leave these premises?"

The man chuckled his disbelief. "Ah, madam, you are a lady like no other. Perhaps I should never have asked."

"Indeed not!" she concurred.

"Perhaps I should have simply performed the act and then suffered the consequences, or perhaps delighted in them. Do you agree?"

Jasmine gasped as he leaned his body closer. She could feel him against her, his entire length, every inch, legs, thighs, stomach, and chest as hard and solid as the stone at her back.

109

"Do you?"

"No," she gasped as she forced her hands between their bodies. "No!" she insisted as his mouth brushed warm against her cheek. "No," she whimpered as heat, sweet blazing liquid heat rushed unwittingly through her veins and caused her heart to thunder an erratic beat. She gasped as the sensation came suddenly upon her and it took every ounce of her strength not to turn her face into his kiss.

She tried to push him away, but the man was an immovable object. She'd call out. Silently she promised, if he didn't stop, she'd call out . . . only she never did.

This wasn't happening, of course. No doubt she had conjured up the whole of it. She was asleep. She was asleep and dreaming and one had no control over dreams . . . did they?

It couldn't be that she felt this sudden unbearable weakness. It was ridiculous. It was outrageous. Simply out of the question. Oh, God, it couldn't be happening again!

Jasmine almost breathed a sigh of relief, so nearly had she convinced herself it was all imagination. But deep down she knew it wasn't. It was real, far too real to be denied.

But if she couldn't deny its reality, at least she could deny her reaction to the things he was doing to her. Firmly she insisted they brought about not the least effect on her senses. She didn't feel a thing. She refused to feel a thing. Oh, God, please.

Her lips were tingling, not from his expert kisses, but because he had yet to touch his mouth to hers. Gently his lips caressed her temple, her cheeks, her jaw, her ear, deliberately ignoring the temptation of her mouth.

"I'll call for help," she warned, her voice shaking and breathless.

"You won't," he remarked, all confidence.

"I will," she insisted, and if her voice held a slightly dreamy quality, she didn't seem to notice.

But he did.

Jasmine shuddered uncontrollably as his warm breath bathed her face in deliciously scented heat while his lips continued their taunting, teasing, until she was powerless but to groan out her need and turn her lips toward his.

His kiss was gentle, exploring, almost tentative. His tongue moved sweetly over her lips, a low growl telling her clearly his enjoyment. Inside her lip, he teased with the gentlest strokings of sensitive flesh. It was beyond her ability to resist this tender assault. With a soft cry Jasmine tilted her head and further parted her lips to afford him greater access.

He felt her soften against him while her arms slid up his body to clutch at his neck, dragging him closer but allowing not their lips to part.

Her knees gave way when he acceded to her wants and deepened the kiss. His tongue, thick and hot, sensuously rough and smooth, brought wild, dizzying sensations and Jasmine knew all was lost in this flaming contact of mouths. A soft whimpering sound of pleasure bubbled from her throat and escaped her mouth to be greedily absorbed by his. She forgot the shame she would no doubt later suffer. It no longer mattered. Nothing mattered but that she be allowed more of his taste, his touch. She couldn't have said what had come over her. She didn't understand anything but this knowledge that she'd surely die if his lips were to part from hers.

His hands were at her breasts. There was no help for it. She had not the power but to urge him on to further delicious discoveries. She wanted to tear her gown away so she might feel the roughness of his calloused palms. Feel it all. Feel the heat. Feel . . .

She was drowning in sensation. Were it not for his body pressed tightly to her, she would have crumbled

111

to the floor and yet she had no knowledge of this weakness. All she knew was his hands were beneath her gown touching her everywhere, caressing full breasts, running over her hips and stomach, lingering at the juncture of her thighs, bringing a crazed hunger that went beyond desire into searing flame, unmatched by anything before experienced.

It took a long moment for the words to register, for the raw hunger in his voice only added to her pleasure. He gasped between breathless kisses, "Inside. I don't want to take you here."

Jasmine knew had he carried her to her bed, she never would have noticed. Nay, the act would have been completed before her senses had returned, but his words were as a cold dousing in her face. Instantly she realized what she was about to do and with that realization came the horror of her actions.

Good God, what could she have been thinking, to take a lover to a room shared by herself and her husband?! She couldn't. God help her, no matter the pain of denial, she couldn't.

Jasmine sat upon her bed, her arms hugging her knees to her chest and listened to her husband's footsteps as they slowly mounted the stairs. Her door opened a crack, as if he were hesitating, and then further still, until he stood framed in the blackness of the hall behind him. Jasmine swallowed a sigh of relief. He was not deep in his cups. Lord but she needed to talk to him. She couldn't bear the strain any longer. The guilt, the shame. She had to do something. She couldn't go on like this.

For hours she had tormented herself by reliving her immoral behavior. Finally, unable to bear the guilt or shame a moment longer, she had laid the blame for her wild actions at Anthony's feet. Instinctively she knew had he treated her truly as a wife, she'd never have allowed the other his advances. Jasmine sighed wearily. It had to end, this marriage that was no marriage. She had to make him want her, lest she succumb to these sinful tendencies.

"Was your evening pleasant?"

Anthony smiled, his eyes moving over her with an appreciation he could only pray she didn't notice. He didn't have to act his usual feminine role, at least not to its fullest extent, when alone in her company; still, he couldn't allow his true self to be known. God but she was lovely. In his eyes she grew more lovely every day and every day he only wanted her more. "Indeed."

"I'd have thought you to be asleep for hours."

"I wanted to talk to you."

Anthony tilted his head toward her, waiting for her to go on, his heart pounding furiously, for he was unable to control the direction his gaze had taken. He could see her clearly beneath the diaphanous gown and the sight brought an unconscious curse to his lips and a mind-boggling ache to his belly. Lord, why wasn't she like other wives? Why wasn't she dressed to her neck in flannel, hiding beneath the heaviest quilt?

But Anthony knew it wouldn't have mattered. He'd want her no matter how she was dressed. God, how was he to find the strength to resist this vision?

"I've found something I think might be of great importance."

Again no response as he waited for her to continue.

Jasmine handed him the packet.

Anthony's expression clearly bespoke his astonishment as he scanned the papers inside. "Where did you find this?"

"Outside," she said, her cheeks flaming with guilt as she purposely allowed him to believe what he would, for, in truth, she had found it at her feet after her would-be lover had left.

"Outside?" He gave her a long look of disbelief. "Where?"

Jasmine lowered her head, unable to meet his eyes as she purposely avoided his direct question. "Someone must have dropped it. What do you make of it?"

Anthony shrugged, hiding well the fact that he had held this very packet earlier. "I can't be sure, but it appears to be orders from that rebel Washington."

Jasmine sighed wearily. "So it seems, but what is to be done with it?"

"No doubt it should be sent over to Cornwallis in the morning. It might be very important."

Jasmine nodded as she took the papers and placed them again on her nightstand. "Anthony," she said hesitantly, her heart pounding at what she was about to say, "do you suppose we could talk a bit?"

"What about?" he queried, his body stiffening with dread when he heard her softly murmured, "Us."

"What do you mean 'us'?"

"Well, I've been wondering lately." She shrugged, her fingers nervously tracing unseen patterns on the sheet. "You act so strangely. Is anything wrong?"

Anthony laughed warily. His voice was breathless and low as he answered, "Do I? I wonder how so?"

Jasmine bit her lip and shrugged, unable to raise her gaze from her knees. How was she to say it? How could she tell him the man she had known at the stable, the man she had married, was gone, leaving behind only the slightest shadow of whom she had believed him to be. And yet that was enough to have caused her to forget her plans. No longer did she look forward to her father's departure so they might part, for she oddly had begun to want this man and this marriage. How did a wife go about telling her husband she wanted him to take her to bed?

Jasmine nearly groaned aloud the torment that wracked both body and mind. There was no help for it. If she wanted things to change between them it was clear she had to be the initiator. Her face flamed, her throat tightened, but she forced her embarrassment aside and rushed on lest she lose this moment. "Well, for one thing there was a time when you touched me quite a bit and kissed me when you could. You haven't done that since . . . since . . ." Her throat seemed to close up. It was impossible. She couldn't go on.

"Oh, *that*," he remarked with all the nonchalance he could manage, his guts twisting the whole time with the agony of wanting her. He turned his back lest the need to touch her prove too great and she recognize the desire he could no longer disguise. "I was under the impression you didn't care for that part of marriage."

Jasmine's cheeks burned. Would she ever know a greater degree of mortification? "Oh, it's not that. It's not as if I want . . . you know . . . It's just . . ."

Anthony almost groaned aloud his pain. That she should nearly come right out and ask him to make love to her was almost more than he could bear. God, he breathed a sigh. If only he could. If only he could love her as he wanted. But if he threw caution aside and did as they both wanted, wouldn't she then grow suspicious? Wouldn't he have given her even greater cause to wonder who her husband really was?

Anthony forced aside the temptation. Trembling, he remarked as he began to undress, "Well, if you're not particularly interested, and I'm not, either, there should be no problem."

Jasmine sighed as she pulled the sheet over her flimsy gown, her cheeks flaming, her eyes misted with suppressed tears. "I guess not."

Chapter Seven

It was early. The sun had barely broken over the horizon, but Elizabeth had been ready for the last hour. The house was quiet. All within, but for herself and Jenson, slept.

Nervously she paced her bedroom floor, awaiting his knock. She'd been forced to wait till dawn. It would have been impossible to leave sooner, for to travel the streets under the cover of darkness would have been pure folly indeed.

She was terribly anxious to get away, but not so much that she would chance the danger that the streets of the city held for an unprotected woman at night. Patrolled by the English, there was nevertheless an occasional mishap, for ruffians were not unknown in this part of Manhattan.

Her bags were packed and she had written a note to Jasmine explaining her absence. Idly she wondered how long she'd be away, then she shrugged. How long would it take before Richard realized he had no place in her life and no hope for a future together?

She flung her cloak over her shoulders and slipped the strings of her reticule over her wrist at the discreet knock. Moments later, her baggage secured to the back of the carriage, she settled herself comfortably inside. A lap rug was placed snugly over her knees to guard against the damp morning air. The door shut and Jenson signaled the driver to be off.

Elizabeth gave a deep sigh of relief from having made good her escape. Had she just stepped from prison, she couldn't have felt a greater sense of freedom. Purposely she ignored the tiny ache that had formed in her chest. It meant nothing, she vowed. She was sorry only that she wouldn't be seeing her daughter for a time. She'd miss no one else.

She grinned at her deception. All were still abed and would be for hours yet. By the time he awoke . . . She shook her head with the silent correction. By the time *they* awoke, she'd be walking the sandy dunes outside the cottage.

Anxiously she looked forward to the peace and tranquility of her summer home. She'd be completely alone, for, by her own choice, she kept no servants there.

Elizabeth laughed as she spied her meticulously manicured hands and nails, knowing her smooth palms would soon be rough and red from the chores she intended to take on. It didn't matter. What she needed was to work herself into exhaustion so she might sleep. She couldn't face yet another night tossing in her bed, aching . . . Stop!

What does it matter now? He'll be gone before you return. Why not admit to the longing?

Elizabeth shook her head, refusing even the weakness of a thought. She would accomplish nothing if she were to pine away for the man. She might as well return to the city right now if that were the case. No, she wouldn't think of him, nor of the love they once shared. And if he was of a mind to insist the love between them remained, then that was his problem and something he'd have to overcome.

Elizabeth awakened from a slight doze to see the early-morning sun now high above the carriage. A frown marred her smooth brow as she peered out of the carriage window. They had been traveling for hours and yet not a glimmer of blue ocean showed itself beyond the thin woodland that bordered the road. They should have been there long ago. Unless she was mistaken, they had already traveled a good four hours and it took only a bit more than two to reach the cottage.

Elizabeth stared at the unfamiliar landscape, having not a clue as to where they were . . . Yes, she did, she realized suddenly, recognizing the Post Road which ran east to west on the northern part of the island. They were miles out of the way!

What was the matter with the driver of the carriage that he should grow so confused? He knew the way as well as she. Hadn't they only returned from a long weekend some two months back?

"Thompson!" she called out as she banged her hand against the carriage wall. "Thompson, you're going the wrong way."

The carriage came to an abrupt stop and she heard heavy feet pound to the ground. An instant later her door was flung open.

Elizabeth felt all the air leave her lungs at once. She leaned forward, fighting the instinct that demanded her to run. Her eyes widened with shock and no doubt her face paled as well. And yet she could do nothing but gasp her astonishment at the sight that greeted her.

"I'm afraid I've little knowledge of this area, Elizabeth. Perhaps you might direct me."

For endless moments she simply stared at him. Her cheeks flushed pink and her heart thundered in her breast. She wanted to order him to turn back, but the words wouldn't come. In truth, she could find no words at all so great was her surprise.

Finally gaining some control over the wild rush of excitement that filled her, she leaned back in her seat and sighed, knowing he would have his way. In the end it mattered little if they spent some time alone. There were no eyes here. There were no standards to maintain. And she was suddenly determined to show him there wasn't a chance of her succumbing so easily again. "Turn right at the next intersection. If we're lucky, we might find a road there leading south."

Richard hadn't realized till she spoke that he was holding his breath awaiting her response to his presence. "Yes, ma'am," he said gently, suddenly filled with joy that she hadn't ordered them back to the city. Idly he wondered if he would have obeyed, and then shrugged as he slammed the door and once again gained his seat, thankful he hadn't been forced into making that decision.

Elizabeth had read the determination in his silver eyes. No doubt she would have had a time of it if she had insisted they go back. Thankfully neither would be put to the test. Elizabeth never realized the soft glow that had come over her, nor the smile that curved her lips as the carriage lurched forward.

"Why in damnation are you doing that?" he growled as he took in the sight of her red, roughened hands. They had been here a week. A week of polite conversations that never hinted of the passions that rumbled so closely to the surface; a week of sleeping alone, tossing in bed until the sun broke over the horizon, his body aching for her, knowing she was just down the hall. How much more was he to stand? How much longer was she to keep him at arm's length?

"What?" Elizabeth asked as she looked up from her kneeling position.

"Why are you scrubbing the floor? Why haven't you hired servants?"

Elizabeth felt a moment's annoyance. What right

119

had he to tell her what to do? "Richard, I keep no servants here. I usually bring them from home."

Suddenly all his frustrations seemed to surface and he nearly bellowed, "Well, you should have done so then."

"I would have, had I wanted company," she shot back meaningfully as she wiped her hands on her apron and stormed out the door.

Richard sighed as he watched her move with a brisk pace down the endless stretch of white sand. Had she always this temper? Had twenty years washed away all her faults from his mind, leaving only a mystical, unrealistic beauty to remember? Richard grinned. He couldn't remember a time when heated words had passed between them. Suddenly he realized how good it was that he could provoke her into anger. Her cool, polite demeanor had instantly dropped away, leaving a woman with blazing eyes to answer him taunt for taunt. His eyes narrowed as he imagined what else he could provoke her to do.

"Is the meat to your liking, Richard?"

"Indeed," he remarked, desperately trying to control the almost overpowering urge to choke. He coughed into his napkin.

"I suppose you're going to tell me I should have brought along my cook as well as a maid," she snapped as she pushed the food around her plate.

Richard made a great play of enjoying his forkful of dry, stringy beef.

"You need not pretend your enjoyment. I know the roast is at best unpalatable."

Richard shook his head. "Not at all. Try some of this gravy."

Elizabeth ignored the offered gravy and almost sneered, "Last night the chicken undercooked, now the roast over. It boggles the mind why a man would

120

endure these discomforts when a short drive back to the city could fill his stomach to overflowing."

Richard grinned. He had riled her sure enough. It seemed he only had to enter a room to rile her. He wondered if there wasn't more to her quick temper than his appreciation or lack thereof of her culinary accomplishments.

"That, if I'm not mistaken, was the eighth time today you hinted I might return to the city."

Elizabeth leaned slightly forward. "Richard, I hint at nothing. Listen, and I'll tell you clear. If you're not satisfied with the fare thus far served, leave."

Richard played with the wine in his glass, swirling it up the sides as he watched her. His lips curved into a grin so mysterious Elizabeth couldn't help but shiver at the promise in his eyes.

"I begin to think it's not my lack of compliments that rankle, Elizabeth, but rather the lack of insistence on my part for us to bed."

"I knew it! I knew you would eventually bring that up!" Elizabeth jumped to her feet, never noticing her chair had toppled as she stood. "You promised you would not, and yet at the first opportunity . . ."

"First opportunity?!" he interrupted. "Woman, are you daft? We've been here over a week and every damn night, I listen to you pace. You don't sleep. You don't eat. I'll wager you're not half as afraid I will as I won't touch you."

Elizabeth's laughter was shrill, her nerves strung to the limit. She hadn't slept more than a few hours since they arrived. She couldn't take much more of this strain. "You are ridiculous."

"Am I? What keeps you awake then? Surely you work hard enough for two. You should drop into bed exhausted. Why do I hear you still when the rooster down aways begins to crow?"

"Perhaps you hear only what you wish. You'd like to think I'm pining away, awaiting a lover's touch."

121

"Not a lover, Elizabeth. *My* touch."

Elizabeth's lips tightened as she glared. "I'm going to bed."

"It will do no good, you know." He spoke to her back as he watched her move away. "Neither of us is leaving here until this is settled."

"Then we'll stay here forever!" she cried as she rushed up the narrow steps to her room.

Richard was nearly at the end of his rope. Another week had gone by and he began to reason she was either the world's most stubborn female or he was the biggest of fools. Perhaps he had seen only what he wished. Perhaps she spoke the truth and felt nothing for him.

"God," he groaned softly as he took yet another sip of the ruby claret. How was he to go on loving her as he did?

Lightning flashed, and thunder rocked the tiny cottage with its force. The wind howled against the windows, causing them to shudder beneath the blast, whipping waves into heavy white foam to crash against the smooth white sand, only to drag each sudsy crest back yet again into its black, endless depths.

A fire brought a cozy atmosphere to the small room as the world went wild outside the cottage. Suddenly the door nearly crashed open, almost tearing from its hinges as it smashed into the wall.

Richard jumped to his feet astounded to find Elizabeth standing in the doorway. She was soaked to the skin, clearly struggling against the weight of her clothes. Water ran in rivulets from her hair, over her face. Terror for her gripped his heart, for he thought she was upstairs asleep. "Jesus! What were you thinking to go out in this?"

"I . . . I was up early." Her jaw ached as she fought

to keep her teeth from chattering. "I thought I'd take a walk."

Richard cursed. "You fool. Haven't you sense enough to stay indoors when it rains?"

"It wasn't raining when I left."

Richard grabbed a coverlet from the settee. "Take those things off and warm yourself before the fire lest you come down with a fever."

Elizabeth pushed aside the offered blanket. "For God's sake, it's only water. Besides, I'm not cold."

"Damnation you're not. You can hardly stand for the shaking."

Elizabeth knew he spoke the truth, but stubbornly refused to agree. "I'll change upstairs." She moved to pass him.

"There's no fire in your room. Change here," he returned. And when she simply glared, he smiled so knowingly that she couldn't contain her shiver. Fear or excitement she knew not which, but suddenly she found it an effort to simply breathe. "If you won't do it, I will" came an almost evilly whispered promise.

Her eyes widened with disbelief. "Would you take me against my will?"

Richard laughed. "I wasn't thinking along those lines, but since you've brought the subject up . . ." He let the sentence die as they both allowed their imaginations to finish the thought.

Elizabeth was shaken by his audacity. "How dare you?"

"Do not speak, just remove your clothes."

"Never!"

She never knew anyone could move as fast as he. Suddenly his hands had knocked her saturated wrap to the floor and began to undo the dozen or so tiny buttons of her bodice.

Elizabeth pushed his hands away, but the effort proved futile, for they simply returned to their task. "Stop! Damn you, I said stop!"

123

Richard ignored her struggles. Her bodice was open to the waist and he was attempting to force the material over her shoulders when she suddenly slapped him with a jarring force.

All movement came to an abrupt stop, and for an endless moment, they stared at each other. Elizabeth bit at her lip, contrite. A red mark shone clearly upon his cheek. Unthinkingly she reached her hand to soothe the injury, while a soft sound, not unlike purring passed her lips.

His arm slipped around her waist and pulled her small body against his. "Pretend no more, Elizabeth. I've waited long enough," he murmured as his head lowered to take her mouth in a kiss that easily matched the fury that raged outside.

Elizabeth's cry was one of hopeless longing. She couldn't fight him any longer. Eager fingers helped him finish undressing her. She was naked in his arms, unashamed as she watched the wonder in his eyes.

"Elizabeth, my love," he crooned as he lowered her before the fire, to the rug-covered floor.

Jasmine sat in her hip bath and gave a disheartened sigh. Slowly she spread a thin film of scented soap over her shoulders and chest. She dreaded the evening ahead. Another party and another and still another after that. She shook her head sadly. What had they to celebrate, after all? The British held still to Manhattan, while Washington was mere miles up the Hudson. She shivered at the thought. It seemed to her he lay in wait like a wolf licking his chops while an unsuspecting lamb napped lazily in the field.

Seventeen eighty-one and still the conflict raged on. Would it never end? Would things never return to normal? Most likely not, if the French had anything to say of the matter. Curse them for their interference.

By now the rebels would surely have given up their cause were it not for their help. Jasmine sighed softly. Lord but she was sick of it. Why didn't Clinton do something? Why was Mr. Washington all but ignored? And, confound it, why did the English believe the answer to every problem was yet another party. And tonight would be the worst of all, for they were expected yet again at the Arnolds'.

How often had Jasmine forced back the words of disgust when Benedict Arnold's name came up? Most everything about both Arnolds disgusted her. Heroes though the couple might be to some, she couldn't have held them, and the general in particular, in more disregard.

Granted there were those who snickered behind their back, remembering how the one-time major general had betrayed his cause. It was common knowledge that he had bargained for a tidy sum to be paid upon the surrender of West Point, as well as a specific number in pounds sterling for every American soldier captured. And yet that was as nothing compared to the disgust she felt when remembering him to be the cause of the loss of John André. Was it only last fall? Jasmine shook her head in sorrow.

Adjutant to Sir Henry Clinton, John André was no doubt the best friend she'd ever had. Had she searched, she could not have found a man more worthy of the title "gentleman," for, although he was known to visit more than one lady's bedchamber, he had never once taken advantage of a young girl in the mad throes of her first love. And because of that, Jasmine would always hold him a special place in her heart.

He was not the spy they supposed, but merely a messenger. He did not deserve to hang because of Arnold's stupidity. What had ever possessed the man to send André, with papers that could only ensure the man's death, overland rather than by way of the

125

Hudson, aboard the H.M.S. *Vulture*?

A wry smile touched her lips. Amazingly, the beast had not taken to horseback himself upon hearing of Washington's imminent arrival at West Point. Nay, he had left his wife and children to face the rebels alone, scurrying like some water rat down the shore of the Hudson and entering safely the city of Manhattan on the English frigate.

Peggy Shippen Arnold was surely one of the most beautiful of all New York's polite society. She gave the most brilliant parties, and indeed, an invitation to her home was long sought by all. What Jasmine couldn't fathom was how the woman maintained her arrogance. Surely, she could boast of nothing in regard to her husband and in truth she might have held her head in shame at being so easily discarded when his safety was threatened. And yet the woman was obnoxiously sure of herself, so much so Jasmine wondered if she had the strength to tolerate another night in her company.

She thought ahead to tonight's gathering. Anthony would be there, of course. Her lips curved downward with disappointment. He would go straight from the club, no doubt, for he rarely accompanied her to and from social gatherings. Jasmine could only imagine tonight would be no different from a dozen others.

Afterward, he would again go off to his club and play cards well into the night. She wouldn't object, not even if her heart ached at the slight.

Jasmine suddenly gasped as the door to her room was flung open and Anthony stopped in the doorway. Lost in thought, she hadn't heard his step. His gaze upon her naked flesh in the tub brought a warmth to her cheeks. Her hands moved instinctively to cover herself, but she instantly thought better of the notion.

Brazenly she sat before him, praying he'd say something. Please God let him say something! Her

126

whole body ached to be in his arms again.

Finally a "Good evening, my dear" came from him in a dispassionate tone and Jasmine knew a crushing disappointment as her shoulders slumped and a soft sigh came to her lips. "Good evening, Anthony. I didn't expect to see you till the party."

Anthony turned from her and began to rummage through his drawers. "I was running low on snuff. Thought I'd stop by and replenish my supply."

Jasmine sighed and gave a weary shake of her head. Lord but she despised the habit. If he had to use tobacco, why couldn't he have taken up a pipe, an occasional cheroot, anything but snuff? Would someone please tell her why she loved this man? There was little enough but the physical to appeal, and yet her feelings seemed to grow each day.

She was reaching behind her, intent on soaping her back when his voice interrupted her thoughts. "Would you like me to do that for you?"

Jasmine's eyes widened with surprise. But for the one morning after their wedding, he hadn't touched her in four months. She couldn't believe she was hearing him right, but when he came suddenly to the tub and knelt at her side, he repeated, "Would you?"

Jasmine could only nod her head. No words would pass through a throat gone suddenly dry.

Anthony cursed his thoughtless words and actions. He hadn't meant to say it. He hadn't meant to come to her. What could he have been thinking? Did he imagine himself of such strength as to be able to resist this creature once he touched her?

The soapy cloth was in his hands before rational thought returned. How was he supposed to avoid touching her when she sat naked and glossy wet before him? He couldn't remember a time when he hadn't wanted her and had resigned himself to the fact that there would never come a time when this aching would end.

His voice was husky, sending chills down her spine when he whispered, "You are so pretty, Jasmine." Silently he cursed the idiotic remark. To say she was pretty was liking the Atlantic to a puddle. The cloth slipped from shaking fingers and his hands smoothed over her soapy skin, bringing them both to a state of near delirium.

Anthony gave a silent curse. He must have been out of his mind to touch her. How was he going to find the strength to stop?

"Am I?" she whispered, her breath coming in huge gasps as she noticed his gaze fastened to her naked breasts.

"These are pretty as well," he remarked, his breathing growing more strained with each moment. Without thinking, he reached a soapy palm out to caress the beckoning softness.

Her eager sigh of delight nearly finished him as the sound mingled erotically with the silkiness of her flesh and the sweet, clean scent of her bath crystals. Her head fell back against the rim of the tub. Her eyes half closed with passion while a strangled, "Oh, Anthony" whispered past soft lips.

He felt himself drowning in her, knowing only he had to have more of this delight or risk his very sanity. Anthony suddenly stiffened. What in blazes was he doing? If he didn't stop now, he'd never find the strength.

His lips tightened with determination as he leaned back and dropped his hand into the water. Quickly, he swished the soap away and stood. "You'd best hurry, dear, or we'll be late."

Jasmine's eyes widened with disbelief. She couldn't fathom it. Again he ignored her explicit invitation. Anger seethed through her suddenly tense body. Enough! Good God, she'd had enough!

Purposely she rose from the tub, never bothering to

turn her back or reach for a bath sheet. Slowly she walked to her bed and slipped her robe over her nakedness. "I'm afraid I won't be going tonight. You will extend my apologies, won't you? I feel the beginnings of a headache."

Anthony swallowed, unable for a moment to speak, the luscious sight of her body bringing a pain he wasn't sure he was able to bear.

He had to clear his throat twice before the words would come. "I hope it isn't anything serious, dear. Is there something I can do?"

Jasmine turned to face him and gave a long, cool smile. "Not a thing."

Moments later Anthony left not at all sure he liked the look in her eyes. What the hell was going on in that beautiful head. He didn't even want to think what she might be planning.

Jasmine slid naked beneath the cool, crisp sheet, a wry smile twisting her lips. No need for modesty on her part, for she could, as actions had proved, walk around the room naked and not stir her husband. No, there was no cause for her to worry over immodesty. He was rarely there, in any case, and she much preferred the freedom of sleeping in the nude.

She hadn't lied. She did have a headache. The thought of seeing the old crowd again brought no pleasure, and Anthony's final—and she would make sure it was the final—rejection had been enough to bring on a full-fledged throbbing headache.

She was dozing off when the same question came again to haunt. Why had he tricked her into marrying him? He had no need for her money. She held no great position in society. He wanted her neither in bed nor on his arm. Why then? Jasmine sighed as she rolled to her side and snuggled into the soft feather mattress. No more. She didn't care why. She only knew it was finished.

The gay sounds of laughter and music drifted from the large house in pleasant waves over the darkened lawn and penetrated into the surrounding, thick foliage which concealed an even darker shadow. Dark eyes scanned the area watching for any sign of movement. They gleamed out of the shadows, alive with excitement, eager to be about this mission.

Two guards, with brilliant coats of red and highly polished buttons, stood like beacons of light in the murky darkness. Each was positioned at opposite corners of the house. He smiled, for he imagined they supposed themselves hidden in the dimness. He imagined, too, another set would be found at the front corners of the house.

From the long windows that faced the balcony, he could see the graceful swirlings of the many who danced. Two couples stood in the shadows of the terrace, one in a light embrace, the other obviously taking a breather from the oppressive heat of the ballroom.

The Shadow cursed, knowing he should have waited till later, till the revelers had gone and the master and his guest had retired for the night. A smile touched his handsome mouth. Yes, he should have waited for later, but he had plans for later, plans that could no longer be delayed.

Under the best conditions, it wouldn't be a simple matter to enter this house. And yet enter he would, for he had to know when and on which ship the counterfeit money would arrive, paper money that would destroy an already tottering Colonial government. He knew to expect its arrival soon. What he didn't know was exactly where and when.

As silently as possible, he followed the line of

foliage along the side of the house, praying the sounds inside would hide any crunching of stone beneath his boot. Midway between the front and back stood a door, no doubt a servants' entrance.

The Shadow was no more than a dark blur of motion indistinguishable in the night as it moved between trees and shrubs toward the house. At last he hugged the wall, breathing easier as he inched his way to the door, knowing himself unnoticed against this blurred background as he slid silently into the house.

Directly before the door stood steps that no doubt led to the servants' sleeping quarters. To his right was a hall, which most likely ended at the kitchens. The Shadow took the steps quickly. He hesitated at the first landing, crouched in the darkness listening for any sound. A moment later he began a systematic search of each bedchamber, until he came at last to the one he sought.

It was the best of the rooms; spacious, it held the largest bed and had its own private balcony. No doubt the general had taken this room for himself. Quickly he moved to the desk and lit a candle. His eyes widened with surprise, for here in plain view was just what he sought.

A moment later the information was committed to memory and he was sliding over the balcony, eager to be gone. He landed hard on the ground below and unwittingly uttered a soft sound, but it was enough to alert the guard at the front of the building.

More so than ever, it was imperative he not be caught. If it were known he had already visited the general's chambers, the time and date of the ship's arrival would no doubt be changed.

He flattened himself against the ground, praying the guard would never notice this darker shadow amid the shrubbery. The young soldier walked right by, never knowing death lay only two feet to his right.

Jasmine moaned, lost again in yet another stirring dream. Lord but it felt so warm, so wonderful. She hadn't imagined it could be this good. Yes, she had, but it had been so long since she'd dared. So terribly long.

It took her some time before she realized she wasn't asleep. She wasn't dreaming again. Jasmine gasped as the shocking knowledge came to assault.

She gasped again as hands moved down her body, hands that nearly seared her flesh with their heat. Feebly, almost automatically, she attempted to rebuff the daring caresses, for Jasmine, no matter her lust-filled longings for her husband, was an innocent. It was hardly a common occurrence to awaken in the loving arms of a man, and her first instinct was to deny them both this pleasure.

But he wasn't to be denied. Not tonight. Not ever again. And she secretly gloried in his insistence, for she wanted more. She wanted all he had to give. Her body trembled beneath his touch and they both knew she was starved for him.

She gasped as he took her mouth. His tongue, hot, thick, hungry, as hungry as her own plunged deep inside and Jasmine was helpless but to moan her acceptance. "Yes," she whimpered as she clutched his naked shoulders, pulling him closer, glorying in the feel of warm, hard flesh and the exquisite sensation of weight pressing her deep into the mattress. "Yes," she whispered again as her hips rose to meet the delicious thrill of warm, wandering hands.

"Anthony, oh, God, Anthony," she murmured as she reached for him. But her effort was instantly stilled as her hands were held securely above her head. Still, she felt no fear, for this man, this wonderful, confusing man could give only gentleness. "I want to touch you."

"Nay, tonight is for you," he whispered just before his mouth came to slash over hers again in a kiss that promised an end to this aching need at last.

Jasmine knew a moment of shattering disappointment at the whispery sound of his voice, for she realized it wasn't Anthony loving her. She shook her head almost sadly, her heart twisting with pain for what could never be. Her heart hardened with determination as she pushed the emotion aside. She didn't care. She refused to care. She needed to be held, to be cherished, to know at last the intimate workings between a man and a woman. And that need overrode any instinctive resistance. She'd worry later the repercussions of this hour. For now it was enough to want this masked man of mystery.

Chapter Eight

"I've waited forever. I want to savor this night."

Jasmine barely heard the words so lost was she in the sweet magic of his touch. It boggled the mind, lifted the spirit until she thought of nothing but this exquisite sensation. How had she gone so long never knowing the wonder?

Her body squirmed eagerly beneath his touch and he chuckled knowing she was as lost in her need as he.

Her groan was low, deep, almost delirious as he kissed her again, his tongue teasing the senses, exploring her sweetness, absorbing her essence while imitating the act that was to follow.

His body stiffened as she answered his gentle thrusts with tentative strokes of her own, but when she instinctively sucked at his tongue, it was nearly his undoing.

She was floating in a haze of ecstasy, drowning in his taste, breathing in his clean scent. She felt her whole being disappearing willingly, more than eager to become a part of him. There was nothing that wasn't his to do with as he wished, nothing that remained undiscovered by gentle, searching caresses.

"Oh, God," he moaned as he tore his mouth from a kiss that threatened to break his control and pressed his face hungrily into the sweetly scented flesh of her throat, her shoulder, her chest.

Jasmine moaned as his mouth lowered to the softness of her breasts. She arched her back, desperate for this sampling. His mouth and teeth brought an ache not unlike a slight cramp to blossom to life somewhere in the pit of her belly. His tongue was hot, almost burning as it soothed the tiny injury left by his hungry assault. And finally his lips gently plucking at her hardened nipples intensified her longing to mind-boggling proportions.

He released her hands only to capture them again holding them at her sides, fingers entwined as his body slid down the length of her. Inch by heart-stopping inch, lips, tongue, and teeth worked a magic that bordered on torture until she was no more than a mindless creature searching for release from this exquisite agony. She was panting, gasping, unable to remain still as his mouth came dangerously close to the heart of her passions, moaning, mindless with a need that knew of no possible means of satisfaction.

"No!" she gasped, her body stiffening with shock as his lips brushed a light kiss over soft, inviting curls.

He laughed at her belated attempt at maidenly shyness, eager to instill this new knowledge, knowing he'd never again have or want a more willing and delicious partner. He trembled, fighting for control as his face buried itself in the softness of her belly. Never had he known a hunger to match this. He hadn't been able to think of anything but this for months.

He growled with deep satisfaction as his mouth settled upon her at last and moaned as she cried out a helpless choking sound, unable to fight the need to lift her hips to his kiss.

Jasmine had often imagined the marital act and

knew a bit more about it than did most ladies of her station, thanks to an inquisitive mind and her mother's accurate if blushing answers. And yet she wasn't prepared for something of this magnitude—never could have been prepared for it.

From somewhere far off, between heavy, gusting breaths, she heard sounds, primitive, almost animalistic sounds, but never attributed the mindless broken words and groans of delight to herself. The discomfort in her belly grew. The ache expanded into a hard band that approached pain. She might have wondered what was happening had she the sense to wonder at all. But her mind knew nothing but feeling, and hunger for more. "Please," she muttered desperately. "Please," she said again, never knowing she'd spoken the words nor for what she asked.

His answering growl was muffled against her hot, moist flesh as she opened for the wonder of this the sweetest of intimacies.

"Ohh," she groaned, unable to reach for that elusive something that would bring blessed relief. "I can't," she gasped. "Please, I can't," she implored.

But she could. Suddenly it was within her grasp, suddenly the ache had spread into a twisting hard band over her belly, squeezing, tight, tighter, promising relief with every movement of his tongue.

Her body stiffened as the first spasm came to rock her into near madness. She grunted, her hips rising from the bed as she greedily accepted the contraction and another took its place and then cried out as still another shook her to the center of her being. Her body trembled helplessly, caught in the aftershocks of blinding passion released.

Dazed from the inner explosions, she never noticed him move. His mouth was hot and wet, tasting of her, coaxing to life again a need she had imagined satisfied.

Slowly he eased his body between her relaxed

thighs. Mouths clung, breaths mingled as his body slowly entered the tempting tightness that forever beckoned.

She jerked with only the slightest discomfort as he pushed himself past the thin fiber, proof of her innocence. He filled her to overflowing, deep, deep into a heat that threatened to rob him of his mind.

Tight! Oh, God, she was so tight. His eyes squeezed shut in agony as he forced his body to remain still, giving her body the time it needed to accept him.

His mouth, never satisfied, began another assault on her senses. He never knew how he managed, but he waited until her hunger rose again, nearly matching his before he began to move.

She couldn't breathe. It didn't matter. Nothing mattered but this moment, this ecstasy. The weight of him pressed her deep into the mattress. Gently guided, she learned quickly to meet his thrusts. His movements grew harder, almost vicious, as his hunger threatened loss of control. She welcomed the pain as his fingers tightened on hers, for even pain added to the moment.

His tongue imitated his body's movements and Jasmine thought she might die of the pleasure. Slick with sweat their bodies moved together, apart and together again.

She felt the bubble of sound begin deep in her throat. She couldn't stop the mounting ache that grew ever stronger inside.

"Help me," she gasped as the pain intensified to a blinding mindless force.

"Put your legs around me," he gasped, his voice low and strained. "Let it come, don't fight it," he soothed.

He covered her panting lips with his, stealing the last of her breath as her head flung back with an almost keening wail.

"Oh, darling," he groaned, feeling the spasms tighten around him, drawing him deeper into a world where she alone existed. With a shudder that shook him to the core, he gave in to the need at last, but she never heard his agonized cry, "Jasmine, Jasmine, my love."

Jasmine groaned with discomfort as she came slowly from sleep, and the ache between her legs made itself known to her conscious state. She snuggled deeper into her pillow, willing the discomfort away as a smile touched her lips. Three times he had brought her to ecstasy. Three times she thought she might die of the pleasure. She sighed with delight at the memory.

"Are you feeling better, my dear?"

"Much better," she said as she blinked her eyes open to a sunny day and stretched comfortably, unmindful of her nakedness as the sheet slipped to her waist.

Jasmine stiffened. Good God, Anthony was in her bed. She must have fallen asleep and never knew her husband had returned. An almost hysterial giggle threatened as she imagined her husband and lover to pass each other outside her door. Surely Anthony would wish him a good night, for she doubted anything but a snag in his hose would upset him greatly.

"Jasmine!" he gasped.

"What is it?" she asked, suddenly wary, wondering what could have caused him to raise his voice.

"Must you go to bed like that?"

Jasmine shot him a nasty look, her mouth turning grim at his astonished expression. "What difference does it make? Surely there is no one here to see."

Anthony made a short sound that might have been disgust in his throat.

"Does it offend your sensibilities, Anthony?" she

138

asked, her anger plainly obvious. It was his fault. It was all his fault. Why should she hide in shame her shameful act? Suddenly she scrambled to her knees, her head thrown back in defiance, her hands at her waist as she dared him to object to this deliberate flaunting.

Anthony soundly cursed his stupidity, knowing too late he never should have let her know he'd taken notice. Never did he see her that he didn't want her. Even now, especially now, with her hair a mass of deliciously messy curls, her skin golden pink and warm from sleep, he could feel the proof of his desire spring instantly to throbbing life.

Determinedly he pushed aside his need, forcing the picture of midnight curls cascading over golden, naked flesh from his mind. "Of course not, my dear. I was merely surprised is all."

Angrily, Jasmine muttered something beneath her breath.

"What was that, dear?"

Leaning against the top of the bed, she drew the sheet up over her breast. "Anthony," she breathed on a long weary sigh, "I think it's time for us to talk."

He smiled pleasantly as he moved from the bed and began to dress.

"I believe I've inadvertently chosen a husband more like my father than I would have imagined."

Anthony's brow furrowed in feigned confusion as he glanced her way.

"Do you deny your preference for men over women?" she snapped.

Anthony laughed. "Jasmine, I think both of the sexes excel, each in their own way."

"That does not answer my question. I'm not surprised. You have a talent for dodging the issue."

"What issue is that?"

"Anthony, I want an annulment."

A vein ticked in the side of his throat. "I'm afraid

that's not possible. We've both admitted to the intimate side of marriage. Have you forgotten?"

Jasmine knew he spoke the truth. No matter the absence of a relationship, all believed they had one. To deny it at this late date would only bring tongues to wag. "Very well, a total termination of the marriage, then."

"Why?"

"Why? How can you ask such a question? Have you once acted the husband?"

"I thought I was a very good husband, actually."

"Actually, you don't come near to being good."

"In truth? What then would you have me do?"

Do?! she wanted to scream. *Act like a man, for one thing! Worry less of your clothes and their fit! Look at me! Look at me the way you once did.* But Jasmine said none of her thoughts. Instead she remarked softly, almost dully, "I've taken a lover."

Jasmine was astonished at the red flush that came to his cheeks. His mouth thinned. If she wasn't sure of the impossibility, she would have imagined him angry. His next words relieved her of the notion. "How very sophisticated of you," he laughed, that same high-pitched shrill sound she'd grown to hate. "I didn't think that to be part of your makeup, my dear."

"Nor I," she breathed on a weary sigh.

"Of course, the idea of termination is out of the question. You would never live down the disgrace."

"I grow to care less each day what society thinks. I am most unhappy, Anthony."

"Perhaps this chap is not the right one for you then. We all must learn to take our happiness when we can, my dear."

Anthony's smile was almost fatherly as his lips bestowed a light peck to her forehead. And if his voice was tight, strained with control, Jasmine, lost in her own misery, never noticed. "This will pass, my dear.

140

All in due time. I ask only for discretion."

Jasmine watched with wide-eyed amazement as he finished his dressing and left the room. Never would she have thought to see the day when her husband granted her permission to carry on a liaison. She should have felt relieved, but she could only manage despair.

Jasmine sat upon Hercules and watched as Benedict Arnold and her husband went charging over the small grassy mounds of Central Park while she and Mrs. Arnold trotted their horses behind. "I hope you are quite recovered from your malady."

"Quite," Jasmine replied, her smile tight, revealing none of the disgust she felt as her gaze settled upon the two men as they spun their horses around and trotted back.

"I do so hate being indisposed," Mrs. Arnold remarked. "You have my sympathies, dear."

Jasmine wanted to laugh, for she'd never suffered, as did some, of female problems. She supposed it was most unrefined of her, but she never fainted, nor was she ever sick. And yet she wasn't around this woman five minutes before a raging headache came upon her. Actually, it had begun when Anthony informed her an outing with the Arnolds was planned for this morning. "Shall we ride," she asked, unwilling to be drawn into the intimate chitchat Mrs. Arnold seemed disposed toward.

Jasmine was off, racing down a wide path before any of her three companions realized her actions. She heard her name called, but only increased her pace, most anxious to be gone from their company, happy for the chance at a moment's peace. Leaning low in her saddle, she reveled in the power of horseflesh beneath her and laughed aloud as Hercules's mane whipped up and snapped in her face.

Suddenly from out of a side path came a rider. Jasmine breathed a sigh of relief as he pulled his horse up short. She was beyond him in a flash.

Moments later strong arms reached around her and lifted her easily from her seat. Jasmine turned astonished eyes toward the man holding her as he trotted his horse to a stop and quickly dismounted.

Once he had settled her on her feet, he asked, "Are you all right?"

"Are you insane?" she returned as she adjusted her hat and repinned it in place.

"Excuse me?" he asked, his eyes widening with appreciation as they took in her beauty and form while a smile began to twitch at his thin lips.

"I believe you heard me, sir. Whatever possessed you to behave so outrageously?"

"Are you telling me you weren't in need of assistance?"

"Indeed I was not."

A long moment of surprise followed. Suddenly he laughed a deep, somehow familiar sound. "Allow me to extend my apologies, Madame Montgomery."

Jasmine studied his face for a moment. How was it that he seemed so familiar? She was positive she didn't know this man. How was it he knew her name? "Have we been introduced?"

"I'm afraid I haven't as yet had the pleasure."

"And yet you know my name."

"We have mutual acquaintances who told me your name. I saw you once. Actually, we bumped into each other once in Lawson's Sweet Shop."

Jasmine's eyes brightened and she laughed as she remembered the day when all her licorice drops had flown into the air to bounce at her feet. It had been her fault really. She had been talking to Deborah and hadn't been watching where she was going. Suddenly she had slammed into something so hard she had first imagined it to be a wall. Only the quickness of his arms had saved her from joining her spilled candies on the floor.

"I should thank you again, sir, for saving me some measure of embarrassment."

"You need not, for I'd do as much for a lady only half so beautiful. I confess it gave me a chance to hold you in my arms. A pleasure I could only dream."

Jasmine caught her breath and blushed hotly. He was terribly bold and deserved a good setting down. And yet the twinkle of amusement in his eyes brought a slight fluttering to her chest and dared her to do more than accept his words of praise.

The sounds of horse's hooves pounded the earth behind them. Suddenly her husband's worried voice rang out. "Good God, Jasmine. Must you ride like that? I thought for sure . . ." His words came to a sudden end as he apparently recognized the man standing at Jasmine's side. He was off his horse moving toward them, his hand extended toward the man who had yet to take his eyes from her. "Joseph? Joseph Gaspar? Good God, is it really you?"

Jasmine stood close enough to both men to realize their amazement at this chance meeting had somehow never reached their eyes. Suddenly a wild thought came to life as she watched them embrace. Could it be? Were they lovers? Was this man the reason why Anthony would not come to her? She shook her head at the ridiculous notion. She might have believed it of Anthony, but not of Joseph Gaspar. Not by the way he looked at a woman.

Surely this meeting was as it first appeared. Her imagination was playing tricks, for she could fathom no reason for such an act. As the two men embraced, her eyes met Joseph's again. Jasmine felt an unexplained trembling, her brow furrowing as she wondered why this man should instill the sudden, wild beating of her heart.

Somehow she knew it wasn't the man himself who

so intrigued. Nay, it was the way he looked at her. He reminded her of someone. But who?

He moved silently along the wharf. The distant sounds of laughter echoed over the silent city. Ahead was the *Mercy*, her black hull rising above the water's edge and blocking from sight the silver light that shone upon New York Harbor.

He grinned. A merchant ship. He would have imagined the shipment sent under the guard of the Royal Navy, but no, the English either thought this a ruse no one would suspect or believed their might in such an extreme that no one would dare to interfere with its delivery.

White teeth flashed in the dark. It mattered not their reasonings. Royal Navy or merchant, the counterfeit bills would never have a chance to be circulated.

"Were you waiting for me?"

Jasmine gave a small start of surprise and then smiled as she watched his dark, shadowy form move to join her at the balcony railing. Strong arms circled her waist and Jasmine sighed as he pulled her to lean back against him.

"Your arrogance never ceases to amaze me. As you can see, I've been watching the harbor."

He chuckled near her ear. "If you enjoy watching a fire, perhaps we could start one of our own."

Jasmine tried desperately to ignore his deliberate sexual taunt. She wasn't in his company ten seconds that she didn't want to hold him, have him hold her. "You wouldn't know which ship burned, would you?" she asked, trying to ignore her need of him.

"I believe it's the *Mercy*. Why?"

Jasmine shrugged. "Do you know what happened?"

"I'm afraid I couldn't say," he breathed near her ear, and Jasmine knew no hope of resisting.

She nodded. "I knew you would come."

"Did you?" came the low, laughing whisper that never failed to set her nerve endings into an uproar. "I wonder why?"

"You know my husband, do you not?"

She felt his shrug. "You might say we have a passing acquaintance. Why?"

"You know the nights he visits his club. Am I right?"

"Perhaps."

Jasmine laughed a low, sultry sound. "What would you do if he suddenly walked into this room?"

"What would you have me do? Shall I accept the challenge he would no doubt offer?"

"Would you?" she asked, and then slid out of his arms. On silent feet he followed her to her bedroom. She had no need to look, she knew he was standing behind her. Slowly she turned to face him, the dim light of a dying fire behind her outlining her body beneath a diaphanous gown. This was wrong, so very wrong, and yet she couldn't stop the need he brought to life. He didn't have to touch her, he didn't have to speak. Just being in the same room was enough to change her into the wanton she'd become.

His voice was rough, low, sending chills of excitement up her spine. "For you there is little I wouldn't do."

Jasmine reached for the tie that held her gown at her shoulder. A moment later she was exposed to his view, the filmy material puddled softly at her feet. "Will you tell me who you are?"

His voice trembled slightly at the vision standing so proudly before him. "I will, but not yet. Sometimes it's best not to know all."

"The Shadow," she said softly, her voice gentle with an emotion she couldn't name.

She watched as his mouth split into an engaging grin that tugged at her heart and seemed oddly familiar. "As a loyal subject to the Crown, you should have long ago turned me in."

"I expect I should have."

"You haven't a dragoon of His Majesty's forces hiding in the closet perhaps, awaiting a most inopportune moment to interrupt?"

Jasmine laughed and moved toward him. For two months he had come to her rooms. For two months she'd known nothing but near diabolical pleasure. And yet she found she needed more. She wanted to know this mysterious lover. She wanted to understand why he so willingly chanced his life for a cause that went against everything she believed in. "Are you the villain others would have me believe?"

"Do you believe it?"

"Nay." She shook her head, her long black hair swaying gently about naked, lushly rounded hips.

"What is it you believe?"

"That there are times when politics run a weak second place."

His heart was thundering in his chest, almost obliterating the sound of her voice. His fingers worked the string at his throat and his cloak fell to the floor. His voice was hoarse with need. "To what?"

"To this," she murmured as she closed the distance between them, opened the buttons of his black shirt and slid her hands inside.

"It matters not then our beliefs?"

"I'm afraid not. Ever so foolish of me, don't you think?"

He reached out, his palms gently guiding her naked breasts to rub erotically against the thick

146

golden hairs of his chest. A choking sensation gripped his throat and he was barely able to manage, "If so, then I'm equally the fool."

"Why don't you take them into the house?"

Startled, Jasmine spun around at the sound of his voice. "What?"

"For weeks you've been sneaking out here to play with them, why not bring the kittens inside?"

Jasmine frowned. "Anthony, I do not sneak. If I wanted them inside, I would have done so."

Anthony shrugged. "I can't see what harm it can bring."

"No harm at all, I imagine. I simply prefer them to remain here."

"I wouldn't mind if you kept them in our room."

"Thank you but I think not."

Anthony gave what appeared to be a careless shrug, while his blue eyes carefully searched her face for the reason behind her odd behavior. Fancy had, since the first night, found her spot at the bottom of their bed. But since she had her litter—four kittens that Jasmine professed not to care about and yet at every opportunity was in the barn playing with—the cat had not been allowed in the house.

Surely a box in the corner of their room would cause no problem. Anthony couldn't understand her professed lack of interest.

The conversation around the dinner table was always strained, tonight it was even worse. Jasmine's face was white and a flicker of fear shone in her eyes as she answered her father's question. "The cats are in the barn. I know well enough your dislike of animals."

"Explain to me, why then am I suffering?" Jami-

147

son Huntington, as if to prove his point, sneezed loudly into his handkerchief.

Anthony said nothing, knowing the cat and her kittens were upstairs. He'd meant them as a surprise for Jasmine, never realizing her father would have such a reaction to cat hairs.

Jasmine, having no knowledge of her husband's hand in this, shrugged. "Perhaps another malady affects you."

"A long sea voyage might be just the thing to clear up what ails," Anthony politely volunteered, his mask of innocence almost but not quite hiding the true desire behind his words. It was obvious to all that both men had disliked each other on sight. Anthony cared little of Jamison Huntington's preferences in the bedroom, but he did care of the man's treatment of his daughter, treatment that, as far as Anthony could determine, was completely undeserved.

Elizabeth, eyes flashing with an inner beauty that was almost breathtaking, barely controlled her urge to laugh while Jamison snarled a "Perhaps."

"You might take Anthony's advice into consideration, Jamison. Surely you must suffer a degree of boredom. I doubt the pleasures so easily obtained in London are readily available here."

"Are you asking me to leave?"

Elizabeth sighed. She very much wanted him gone, but dared not say the words lest he remain, if only to spite her. Legally the man was her husband and had every right to occupy her home. "You may of course stay as long as you wish."

"How very accommodating," he remarked snidely.

"That tone is unnecessary," Richard announced, his silver eyes turning to pewter with a clear threat as they glared across the table.

Jamison laughed. "Is it? Have you then made yourself so at home in my wife's bed that you are now

148

giving orders in this house?"

Jasmine gasped with shock as she came to her mother's defense. She jumped to her feet and leaned forward, never noticing the wine splashing red over the white tablecloth. "How dare you?! How dare you so casually defame my mother?"

Jamison surveyed his daughter with clear distaste and snickered evilly. "Tell her, Elizabeth. Tell your daughter about the nocturnal visits. Why, a person can hardly get a wink of sleep with the doors opening and closing at all hours."

"Mother," Jasmine turned to a white-faced Elizabeth, "you don't have to listen to . . ." Her voice faltered as she took in Elizabeth's guilty expression and suddenly knew the truth of what she'd believed were slanderous words.

Jamison laughed at the horror clearly written on his wife's face. "You never were one for subterfuge, Elizabeth." He gave a shrug as he began again to eat.

"Unlike my husband, of course."

"Of course," Jamison answered almost happily.

"I'll never believe it! Not my mother! She doesn't do things like that."

Anthony smiled as he strolled beside his wife through the gardens at the back of the mansion. The cool rays of silver moonlight illuminated Jasmine's flashing eyes as she dared him to disagree.

"Your mother is a very lovely woman, Jasmine. Would you sentence her to live her remaining years alone? Deny her the pleasure and comfort that is but a normal way of life?" Anthony bit his lip and prayed Jasmine in her present state would never notice the words he spoke nor dare him to practice what he preached.

"I'm telling you she's not like that. She doesn't need . . ."

149

"A man?" He laughed. "Are you sure? She knew the touch of a man once. Are you so positive she found the chore so great she would spurn a would-be lover? Especially a man like Richard?"

Jasmine nodded, if a bit unwillingly. "I can see why she might find him attractive, but . . ."

"Have you seen the way he looks at her?"

"How?"

"Like a man in love."

"But . . . but they barely know each other."

"How long did you know your . . ."

"That's different," she interrupted quickly, a blush creeping up her throat.

"Is it? I wonder why?"

"Because she's my mother!"

Jasmine turned, ready to stomp toward the house. "One more word. Have you ever noticed his eyes?"

Jasmine blinked her confusion. "His eyes?" She shook her head.

Anthony nodded. "Look at him. Really look at him."

"What are you hinting at?"

"What are the odds, do you suppose, of meeting two people in one lifetime with the exact same eyes?"

Jasmine's spine stiffened further. Her eyes rounded with fear. "Are you telling me he's my . . ."

"I'm telling you nothing. Just look at him."

Jasmine scowled. Her anger was never more apparent in her swift stride and the tense hold of her shoulders as she left him in the dark.

Anthony's words echoed again and again in her mind. "The exact same eyes . . . exact same eyes. The odds, what were the odds?" Jasmine was gasping for breath as she raced up the stairs, running as fast as her feet could carry her. Running from the truth? God in heaven, was it true? Was Richard her father? She wouldn't believe it. She'd never believe it. No! He couldn't be. Please God, no! But no matter her silent,

150

desperate cry, she knew the truth of the matter.

Richard had not come to marry her. From the first he had eyes only for her mother. There was no doubt in her mind that he loved her. And if Jasmine read her mother's shy glances correctly, the feeling was returned. Until this minute, she'd been too involved with her own problems to take real notice.

Jasmine felt the bubbling threat of hysterical laughter. It had all been for naught. My God, she had brought it all upon herself. She had foolishly married a man she didn't know in order to escape her own father! Jasmine allowed a low, silky, mocking laugh. In all these colonies, was there a fool greater than she?

It was an hour later that Anthony entered their bedroom to find a now calm Jasmine sprawled upon the floor laughing as the kitten crawled over her.

"I see you took my advice."

Jasmine blinked her surprise. "I didn't. I found them here when I came in."

Anthony grinned. "Did you? I wonder who could have brought them from the barn?"

Jasmine smiled, her heart fluttering in her chest as she took in his warm expression. "Thank you, Anthony." And indeed she had much to thank him for. He knew before she the stigma of her birth and yet it mattered not at all. He accepted her for who she was, not as the bastard some would claim.

He shrugged away her gratitude. "It was nothing."

Jasmine held a kitten in the palm of her hand and rubbed its silky fur against her cheek. "I should bring them back. My father," she shot him a knowing look and then smiled softly, "cannot abide animals. He never allowed . . ." She couldn't finish as haunting memories of terror came to haunt. Terrors never lessened even now that she'd grown to adulthood.

Anthony never realized her fear as he plopped down upon the bed. "Too bad. If he doesn't like it he

151

can always leave."

Jasmine watched him as he stretched out and cupped his head in his hands. For a long, silent moment, through eyes half closed, he watched her. She raised her gaze to his and perhaps for the first time in her life, she felt truly safe. No matter his powdered wigs and beauty patches. No matter his frilly handkerchiefs and high-pitched laughter. Somehow she knew she had nothing to fear, not with this man at her side.

A longing so great it nearly left her breathless came suddenly over her. God but she wanted him. What would he do, she wondered, if she stood and took off her clothes. Suppose she was bold enough to make all the moves. Would he reject her again? Or would he accept her love and give his in return?

Jasmine almost gasped her surprise as she realized the depth of her love for him. Desperately she sought to deny the emotion. It couldn't be. She couldn't love one man and yet lust for another. But Jasmine knew the truth of her thoughts. And the truth brought about nothing but shame and disgust.

What had she done to her life? She had married one man to avoid another. Then, like a fool, she'd fallen in love with her husband, a husband who could not love her in return. Jasmine had no doubt Anthony felt a certain fondness for her . . . but *love?* Nay, she knew for a fact that, unlike her, Anthony felt none of the passion that bubbled in her veins for his mate.

Chapter Nine

"Noooo!" came the bloodcurdling scream of pure anguish. Anthony, his before-dinner drink flung carelessly to the carpet, was on his feet and running before the sound came to an end. He was halfway up the stairs when it sounded again. "Noooo!"

Anthony smashed the door into the wall as he rushed into the bedroom. His eyes widened with surprise, for at first he could see nothing amiss. Not, that is, until he came abreast of Jasmine and saw the direction of her horrified gaze.

Tears ran unchecked over her cheeks as her gaze held to the pitiful sight on the floor. The mother cat and four baby kittens were lying lifeless at her feet. From the odd positioning of their heads, Anthony realized their necks had been snapped.

"Jesus," he muttered at the gruesome sight and automatically took Jasmine into the comforting circle of his arms, pressing her face gently to his chest.

"I told you. I told you," she whimpered as her arms reached around his shoulders and clung to him.

"What, Jasmine? What did you tell me," he asked as he attempted to soothe her with gentle caresses up and down her back.

"I told you to leave them in the barn. I told you,

and now he did it again."

Anthony stiffened, his face turned white with shock. "He? Your father? Your father did this?"

Jasmine nodded, her face pressed into his shoulder. Tears flowed freely, soaking his shirt, and sobs broke from her throat as she spoke. "When I was a child, he killed my dog. He killed him and made me watch, because it was raining and I brought him inside."

Anthony trembled with horror at her story. How could a father have done that to his child? But *was* she his child? Could it be Huntington knew she was not and that was why he hated her so? Anthony breathed a long sigh and held her tightly to him. "Come downstairs, darling. I'll have Jenson see to this."

Jasmine was wiping at her tears, her husband's arm around her waist, as she moved into the library. Suddenly she came to an abrupt stop. Hatred glittered in her eyes as she spied her father comfortably seated before the small fire.

His malicious grin couldn't have shown better his satisfaction. "Crying again, Jasmine? You always were a sniveling brat. I can remember still how as a child you would forever cry over one thing or another. A most annoying child," he finished with clear distaste.

Anthony's lips tightened as he fought a battle of control. Lord, but he wanted to smash the man's face in and if the bastard said another word, he might do just that.

"You monster! Why did you have to kill them?"

Unconcerned of her suffering, Jamison smiled pleasantly as he examined a perfectly manicured fingernail. "I told you to keep them out of the house. We've been through this before. Indeed, one would have assumed you to have learned your lesson the first time. But then, you always were a willful child."

Anthony's low rumbling murmur of rage grew to

an all-out bellow of fury at the man's coldness. Suddenly he was standing before his father-in-law, his hands on the man's coat, as he yanked him from the chair. No sooner did Jamison come clumsily to his feet than Anthony knocked him to the floor with a mighty punch.

Blood gushed from what was likely a broken nose and ran over his mouth to cover the front of his crisp shirt, but Anthony took no notice of the damage inflicted. Again he picked him up and again he knocked him down. Once more he repeated the act and might have continued the dull, thudding punishment had Richard not suddenly arrived to pull Anthony off the bloodied, dazed man.

His legs widespread, he stood over the injured, moaning man. Anthony found himself breathing heavily, less from exertion than anger. His voice was deep, heavy with menace as he warned, "If you hurt her, if you touch her or anything she loves again, I'll kill you." And when no response came forth, Anthony reached down, grabbed him again and shook him savagely. "Do you hear me?"

Jasmine watched her father hang limply in her husband's less-than-gentle hold. His eyes wide, she thought if it was possible to die from terror, this man was about to meet his just reward. Sadly she felt not the slightest flicker of pity. She cared neither if he lived or died. She cared only for Anthony, for her father was not without powerful influence.

"Darling," she soothed as she slid her hand around Anthony's arm, unconsciously pressing the back of his arm to her breast. "I don't want you to get in trouble. He's . . ."

"I don't give a damn who he is," he remarked almost without thought, glancing at his wife and then turning a murderous gaze upon the man at his feet. "I want you out of this house tonight."

"You've no right."

"I'm taking that right," he whispered so evilly that Jasmine felt a shiver race up her spine. Where had she heard that before? Why did the words and tone sound so eerily familiar?

"I have nowhere to go."

"Get yourself a room until the next ship leaves for England."

"With what? I have no money," he snarled. "I can't buy a ticket. You took the only chance I had . . ."

"To sell your daughter?"

Silence.

Anthony breathed a long, calming sigh as he turned from the sight with disgust. "I will absorb the cost of the room. You'll get your money and then some on the day you sail."

"I'm afraid you got more than you bargained for when you married me." Jasmine's voice was soft, her gaze filled with love and gratitude that he had defied her father and come to her defense. Her emotions were little more than a mass of confusion. She hadn't noticed at the time that his feminine ways had completely disappeared during the confrontation. How was it this man had suddenly lost his whining, high-pitched voice and growled out his hatred in the deepest masculine tone? Jasmine wished she could understand him, but if his actions brought about a degree of confusion, she felt none in regard to her feelings. She loved him as she could never love another. And if he refused to take her to his bed, she'd accept that as part of him.

Anthony smiled, his eyes warm with regard, his body aching as always with the need to hold her near. "Do you think so?"

Jasmine shrugged. "My family," she remarked,

almost apologetically, her hands held out palms up.

Anthony grinned. "No doubt you'd whip them all into shape if you could."

Her smile was the merest flicker of movement at the corner of her lips. "I think I'd best start with myself."

"Do you? I've not found cause to complain."

"Anthony, the very least you can expect from your wife is for her to be faithful."

A pulse pounded noticeably in his temple and yet his voice remained almost disinterested. "Does this mean you've broken it off with the other fellow?"

Jasmine nodded. "I have, as of right now." She shot him a puzzled look, for oddly enough the sound of his sigh didn't seem at all happy.

He laughed and Jasmine almost moaned aloud her despair, for the sound did terrible things to her insides. "So you love your husband, do you? Is that why you don't share his bed?"

"I share his bed," she insisted as she paced before the small fire in her room.

"And he doesn't touch you?" he remarked, his voice rising slightly, filled with amazement.

"What makes you think he doesn't . . ."

The tall, masked form moved suddenly before her. He laughed again. "Have you forgotten, I was the first? You cannot deny you were a virgin. A virgin after months of sharing his bed?" He laughed, the sound cruel and vicious to her ears. "I know well enough what I speak. He does not touch you."

Jasmine's lips thinned. She truly didn't like this man, no matter the sensual glory he offered her. "There's more to a marriage than . . . than . . ."

"Sex," he supplied, his mouth twisting into a delicious smile. "The word you're searching for

157

is sex."

"All right!" she snapped. "There's more to a marriage than sex."

He grunted in disbelief. "Suppose you tell me what else is half so delightful."

"There's companionship. There's trust. There's friendship."

He grabbed her hand and pulled it to his groin. Suggestively he moved against her palm. "A woman, like a man, has many needs."

Jasmine wrenched her hand free and snarled her disgust. "That's all you have to offer."

"What more do you want?"

"I want my husband."

Jesus, no. He couldn't let her go. Not yet. It might be months before he could . . . Damn, but he wasn't handling this at all well. He should have appealed to her sympathies instead of arousing her anger. Still, all wasn't lost. How far was anger from passion?

"Will you give this up? Will you be satisfied with a bit of hand-holding when you can have this?" He leaned down to capture her lips with his and gave a low chuckle of victory when he heard the soft sigh of her surrender.

His laughter brought her to her senses. She didn't want this. She didn't love this man, she loved the one man who couldn't love her in return. "No!" she gasped, furious with him and his insistence and with herself for giving in so easily to this temptation. He laughed again, but the sound came to an abrupt end as her hand smarted his cheek. Jasmine gasped at her reflexive action and took a step back with astonishment as the loud crack seemed to vibrate again and again in the silence of the room.

His mouth thinned in anger as he took a menacing step toward her. Jasmine meant to move again, but his hand was suddenly buried in the thickness of her hair, pulling so hard that tears misted her eyes. She

158

had no choice but to raise her face toward his.

"Aye," he said, his voice low and insistent. "You will be mine until I say nay."

"I will not," she gasped through the pain as he tugged harder, bringing her mouth nearer to his. "You cannot force me."

Again he laughed, his warm breath fanning her face. "Can I not? Shall I show you then the power I have over your body?"

Jasmine gasped, her eyes showing her fear. They both knew it would take little to force her to acquiescence and, once in his arms, she had no will. Lord but she hated herself for this weakness. "I love him. You'll have nothing but a body," she warned. "I can give you no more."

He forced aside the ridiculous sensation of pain her words inflicted. He didn't care, he swore. He wanted her and it didn't matter her feelings. It mattered only that she came to him and would always come to him. "Now and every time I want you, you will be available to me."

And when she didn't, couldn't, respond, his mouth took hers in a searing kiss that left her gasping for breath. Still, she didn't respond.

His hand reached beneath her skirt, sliding under her frilly drawers and into the flaming heat he knew he'd find there. There was no gentleness in his touch. He meant to show her his complete mastery over her body and he did just that. Long fingers penetrated her body with an almost vicious thrust. He smiled as he felt her legs give way and heard the soft, unwitting exclamation.

"Won't you?" he insisted as his fingers brought about an almost instant climax.

Jasmine gasped as the shuddering convulsions claimed her. There was no help for it. She had not the power to resist. "I will," she choked out on a broken sob. "Oh, God, I will."

He grunted with satisfaction as he took her in his arms and brought her to the bed. "Then a body will have to suffice."

Jasmine sat alone in her darkened bedchamber. Her eyes held sightlessly to the flickering red-gold flames of a dying fire as her mind raced on desperately seeking a solution to the problem that seemed suddenly to have taken control of her life. A soft sigh of remorse slipped unnoticed past her lips as again and again she relived this night of sin spent in a stranger's arms.

How was she to get out of this? It was obvious the man wanted her. It was obvious, too, that he would listen to no claims on her part that these meetings had to end.

How had it come to this? What kind of a woman was she to love two men? Jasmine shook her head sadly as she allowed the knowledge full rein. That she did love both Anthony and this masked man was a truth she could no longer deny, but what did that make her? Certainly not the moral lady she had once believed herself to be. Jasmine gave a low, pain-filled laugh. Nay, certainly not a lady, moral or otherwise. For morality was now a thing of the past. Honor meant less than nothing. Even her beliefs of God and country had been pushed to the sidelines so she might indulge in this most grievous of sins.

From the first she'd known him, if only by reputation. Were she the loyal servant of the Crown she had once supposed, she would have turned him in. She would have plotted to see the end of the Shadow, for none among the rebels was more hated and feared, with the possible exception of Mr. Washington himself. But had she done it? Nay, she was besotted with his tender whispers, his gentle searching hands, so besotted, in fact, she refused to think on the matter. And now, now it was too late.

Jasmine fingered the small note that had dropped from his cape pocket. A frown marred her smooth brow. Indeed, the man was careless, for often as not she found evidence such as this after a heated encounter.

Jasmine stiffened as the almost debilitating thought came to hold. *How* often? Nearly every time? "My God," she groaned aloud. And like the dutiful subject of the king she'd thought herself to be, she'd turned that information over to someone in authority. Information that, she'd wager on her soul, was false.

Why had he done it? Jasmine laughed at her own naïveté. Not to discredit her surely, for she held no position of authority. A hard smile twisted her lips. What better way to mislead the enemy than through a lover?

For months he'd been feeding her these tempting morsels of information, information that held just enough truth, or possible truth—enough reasonable doubt in any case to be believed.

"God," she groaned again. Certainly he believed her to be the greatest of fools.

Jasmine's laugh was chilling to her own ears as she came to her feet and threw the note into the dying fire. It might have taken her some time, but she was finished playing the fool.

"You dance beautifully," Jasmine remarked as she moved with graceful ease at her partner's side and granted him a most alluring smile.

"I do believe you are flirting with me, Madame Montgomery. I beg you to desist and take pity on this poor man."

Jasmine's laughter floated deliciously over the merry sounds of yet one more party as she dipped toward her partner. Had she been another, Joseph Gaspar would have been greatly tempted to sample the taste of that beautiful mouth, for the looks she bestowed from beneath thick black lashes were tantalizing to say the least. The fan she held, high and open upon her chest, did little toward hiding the delicious display of more than ample curves swelling above the low neckline of her gown.

"Poor man, indeed," she laughed with supposed gaiety. "You cannot deceive this lady, Mr. Gaspar, for I've grown wise to the ploys of a young man."

"And what ploy would that be?"

Jasmine's smile never reached her eyes. "What better way to ensnare yet another victim of the heart than for a man to profess a weakness he does not possess?"

"And you know for a fact men possess no such weakness?"

"None that I'm aware of."

"And their declarations of love? Are they all false, then?"

Her smile was touched with sadness. "I've found that such declarations often have some other reality in fact."

"Surely you speak not from experience."

Jasmine laughed, her eyes glowing suddenly as hard as diamonds. "Am I not? Why would you believe me exempt from a suffering that has afflicted so many?"

He shrugged. "Anthony strikes me as a man who would not bring suffering to one he loves."

"You are right there, I think," she answered truthfully. And then finished in silence, The only problem is, he doesn't love me.

"Do you doubt it, Mr. Gaspar?"

Joseph smiled at this lovely woman and watched

as she blotted the perspiration from her cheeks and throat with a lace-edged handkerchief. They were standing on the terrace, taking a much-needed breath of air, the sounds of the party muffled behind closed French doors. "I think we have a way to go before all is finished."

"And the outcome?"

"Inevitable, don't you agree?"

"I do, now that France has entered into it. In the end the rebels will be victorious, God help them."

Joseph smiled. "Does that surprise you? Surely you can understand their reasonings."

"I'm afraid I cannot, for I feel an affinity with England that no distance can sever."

"Do you believe the rebels then, as some, to be ungrateful wretches?"

"I prefer to believe them misguided, I think. Led by a small, select group of fanatics."

"Have you given any thought as to where you will go once the hostilities cease? Will you be returning to England?"

"I think not," Jasmine shook her head. "There is nothing for me there."

"You cannot remain here. I doubt the rebels will take kindly to those who did not see justice in their cause. Canada, perhaps?"

Jasmine nodded. "Perhaps.

"And will you continue on in your chosen endeavors?"

Joseph's smile caused Jasmine's heart to thud with surprise, her eyes widening with recognition. She knew that smile. From the first she'd known he reminded her of someone. Suddenly she realized why he seemed so familiar. It was the Shadow! For a second she wondered if Joseph and the Shadow were not one, but instantly knew the impossibility of that notion. Joseph was the captain of a merchant ship and sailed to and from the West Indies, while the

Shadow was constantly about, growing more and more notorious. "In truth, to a sea captain it matters little the victor, for there will always be a need to trade."

"Do you have relatives here, Mr. Gaspar?"

Joseph's eyes widened with surprise at the sudden turn in conversation. "Why would you ask?"

Jasmine shrugged. "You remind me of someone."

"Do I?" He laughed. "I'm afraid I remind most people of someone. I have that kind of face, I suppose."

Much to Joseph's relief, Jasmine had no chance to speak further on the subject, for Deborah chose that moment to step outside for a breath of air.

"Lord but it's hot in there," she remarked as she made good use of her fan.

Jasmine smiled as she noticed Joseph's obvious reaction to the small blond woman. She almost giggled as she realized the poor man looked nearly thunderstruck. "Have you met my friend, Mr. Gaspar?"

And at the silent negative shake of his head, Jasmine introduced the two. A moment later, feeling very much the third wheel, she made her excuses and left them to some privacy. Jasmine smiled as she moved away, knowing neither realized she was gone.

It was as if rockets had exploded in Deborah's head. Her body stiffened. She felt as breathless as if she'd taken a blow to her stomach. Joseph Gaspar! Deborah fought desperately against the blackness that edged its way around her consciousness. She wouldn't faint. Not now! My God, she couldn't believe she'd run across him by accident after all those years of searching. José Gaspirilla, the notorious murdering pirate of the Caribbean. How she hated that name. Deborah marveled at the man's audacity. Joseph Gaspar. José Gaspirilla. Did he think his enemies fools not to relate the two names?

Deborah fought to keep her expression pleasant. She forced her lips to move, praying words of sense came from them, for she couldn't quite believe she faced her father's murderer. She smiled sweetly, never knowing what he said, determined not to allow the hatred she felt in her heart to show. No. She had plans for this murdering beast. Plans that would end, she prayed, with his limp body swinging from a rope.

Sadly Jasmine held little hope, but she knew she must try one more time. Somehow she must bring her husband to her.

Unable to resist the Shadow and the passion he could so easily bring about, she knew a self-disgust unlike anything before imagined. Tonight, she swore, tonight would see the end of this suffering. One way or another, she would be finished with him.

It was late. The house had been quiet for hours. Jasmine sat in her bath, readying herself for the flagrant display she had planned. She stiffened as she heard his footsteps. For a second she almost panicked, but forced the emotion aside. Nay, she would not scramble into bed and pretend sleep. She would see the end of her plan, no matter how her pride might suffer.

Jasmine was just stepping out of the tub when the door to her room opened. A slight smile curved her lips as she heard Anthony's soft exclamation of surprise. "Still awake?" he asked needlessly, and then cursed the undeniable trembling of his voice.

Jasmine closed her eyes on a silent prayer. She turned to see his gaze move over her nakedness. That he wanted her was something he could not deny, for the heat of his eyes scorched her skin, hotter than flame.

"Tired?" she asked gently as she listened to his long, steadying sigh.

"A bit."

"Here, let me help you," she said as she moved toward him.

"You'll take a chill. Perhaps you'd better dry off first and cover yourself."

"In a minute," she said as her fingers aided him in discarding his coat.

"Jasmine, I can do this myself." He almost choked as the warm, clean scent of her invaded his brain. He swallowed hard wondering how in tarnation he was to stand this? How much more could he take before he lost all control and took what she so obviously offered.

"Let me help you. I can see that you're tired."

Oh, God, Anthony groaned in silent agony as she opened his shirt and ran her fingers over his heated flesh. He jerked as her cool, wet breasts came in contact with skin that threatened to burst into flame.

"Thank you, my dear," he managed stiffly, forcing aside the need to throw her to the bed and take her without another moment's hesitation. The time wasn't far off—if he lived through this night, that is—that he was going to use every bit of the knowledge he possessed to drive her insane with the same need that threatened his very soul to madness.

"Anthony," Jasmine murmured as she snuggled closer to him, her mouth brushing feather-light kisses along the side of his throat.

Dear God, no one should have to go through this kind of torture. How was he to survive the pain. He trembled, his arms hanging nearly useless at his sides. He couldn't find the strength to push her away.

"Yes?" he asked, praying for the strength he must find if he was to live through this temptation.

"Would you love me, Anthony? Just this once?"

Anthony took a deep, calming breath and then

silently cursed as he again took her scent to fill his mind, to further weaken his resolve. He was drowning in her. God in heaven, why had he taken this torture upon himself? "I would, dear, but I'm a bit tired tonight." He almost cried with relief as he felt her stiffen against him. "Can we make it for another time, do you think? Tomorrow night, perhaps?"

"Tonight, Anthony." Her voice hardened a bit. "I'm afraid it must be tonight," she said, forcing aside the beginnings of anger. Jasmine never knew where she found the courage, but she forced her trembling hand down the length of him, past his waist, and cupped his rigidness in her palm. She almost smiled her relief. He wanted her. She could see it in his eyes. She could feel it in his body. Why was he fighting against the need they both shared?

"I'm afraid I must insist, my dear," he managed at last, and with trembling fingers at her waist, stood her away from him. A wave of dizziness overcame him and he wondered if he'd survive this moment. Sweat glistened his skin, his heart thundered with distress, his breathing grew near nonexistent. His mind might be of one course, but his eyes refused to obey the commands so far issued.

God but she was beautiful, so perfect, almost mystical. His heart was breaking as pain tore through him. If he lived to be a hundred, he'd never tire of looking at her, of touching her, of claiming her as his own. The sight of her alone was driving him out of his mind, but he didn't care. He couldn't take his eyes from her sweet breasts, her slender waist and lushly rounded hips. He could no longer remember why it had been so important not to touch her.

"Jasmine," he choked, knowing the game was over. He couldn't hope to win out against this.

But Jasmine had gone as far as she dared. She had

167

offered him everything there was, only to have it thrown back in her face. She couldn't bear another minute of this shame. Jasmine shook her head and turned away. Her eyes lowered to the floor. "Never mind," she said dully, the pain in her chest so sharp it took every ounce of her strength not to crumble beneath its force. "It's late. I understand."

His hand reached out, but it was too late. Before he could take another breath, before he had a chance to show her how much he wanted her, her nightdress was thrown over her head and she was beneath the sheet, her back to him.

Jasmine sighed as she neatly folded the last petticoat upon the stack of clothes already packed. She was taking only day dresses and the necessary under things, for she expected that she'd have no need of fancy clothes in the country. Even with that, the trunk was filled to overflowing. Jasmine shook her head with dismay. She'd have to leave behind more than she had thought. She shrugged a slender shoulder. It mattered not if she wore rags. The country cottage was miles from the next neighbor and she'd be entertaining no visitors.

Somehow she'd known this day would eventually come. She was leaving, leaving the Shadow and the sin she couldn't resist, and Anthony and this sham of a marriage forever. She was done with it. Done with the pain, the confusion, the hurt. That she had lasted this long was a miraculous feat. But no more. The punishment she'd taken to her pride was not to be borne.

Idly she wondered if he would even take notice of her absence. Not for a time at least, she reasoned, her lips curving in a sad semblance of a smile. Jasmine lifted her chin and forced aside the tears that threatened. She wouldn't cry. What was there to cry about? Her husband didn't want her. Surely there was no crime in that. She had only herself to blame for being so foolish as to have fallen in love with him.

Jasmine gave a low, painful laugh. Ignored by the man she loved, enslaved by passion to another, she couldn't despise herself more. She shook her head with disgust. Anthony couldn't help his feelings any more than could she. There was nothing to be gained by staying. And before she lost what little remained of her mind, she was leaving.

Jasmine reached into the back of her closet for her heaviest cloak. She knew from experience that the nights would be cool, and unless she wanted to spend every evening inside, she'd best prepare for the winds that would sweep in off the waters.

The back of the closet was darker than usual. Jasmine smiled as she realized that Anthony's clothes, of which there were many, brought the closet to overflowing and prevented any light from reaching the back. Jasmine felt along the wall. Her cloak was fur-lined and easily recognizable once she touched it.

Odd, she hadn't remembered the closet to be quite so shallow. Her hand hit against the ragged edge of a board and she gasped as a heavy splinter slid beneath her fingernail. Jasmine wasn't prone to tantrums, but this pain came at a time when she was truly at her lowest ebb. In truth, for some time she had been balanced on the edge of wild hysteria, but suddenly the injustice of her life seemed too much for her to bear. With a vicious curse that was as foreign to her nature as violence, she kicked the offending wall. As her foot connected with the slat, the bottom moved sharply in, causing the top of the wood to come crashing down on her head with stunning force. Jasmine gasped as pain sliced into her foot and up her leg. A soft moan at her own stupidity slipped past her lips as she leaned against the wall, dazed from the blow taken to her head. For a moment she couldn't imagine what had happened. Why should a solid wall suddenly come loose. Her amazement couldn't have been greater as she watched the offending slat fall to the floor, exposing a shallow space behind a wall that should have been solid.

Chapter Ten

Jasmine threw the delicate figurine across the room with little hope of satisfaction. She watched as it burst upon impact into a thousand tiny pieces of porcelain and then grimaced with disgust, for the action brought no relief. At the moment, rage and shame battled for prominence and she could not say which emotion was the greater. That she had been played the fool was obvious indeed. Her lips twisted into a sneer. Too bad he hadn't known that was the one insult Jasmine could never tolerate.

Her lips tightened as she allowed mortifying memories to return. Her hands balled into fists and struck uselessly at her thighs. She shivered in shame, her pride in tattered ruin, as she paced her darkened room.

She hadn't, of course, hesitated to report him to the authorities. Jasmine shook off a niggling twinge of regret and denied her actions might have been a bit hasty.

Surely he would hang for this, but Jasmine refused to care. At the moment she could only pray the execution to be a public affair, for she couldn't imagine greater sport than to see his lifeless body swing at the end of a rope. Her eyes hardened and a bitter if slightly strangled laugh escaped her lips.

Silently she swore it didn't matter the consequences. Nothing mattered but that she extract her revenge. In truth, whatever the punishment bestowed upon the beast could never be enough to satisfy the months of torment he'd put her through.

No doubt the perpetrator of this most monstrous deed had laughed mightily at her naïveté. But, God, were it her last action on earth, she'd laugh last.

The twinge of regret was determinedly pushed aside and berated as a sign of weakness. She wouldn't be sorry. She'd be thrilled to see justice done to the beast. She lived for the moment as she had for nothing else in her entire life.

He fingers twisted the black silk scrap of material and she cursed again his duplicity as she restrained the urge to rip this damning piece of evidence to shreds.

A hard smile touched her lips as she examined the timepiece at her bodice. It was growing late. If he was coming, it would be soon. Jasmine almost laughed aloud knowing the anger he'd feel once he realized his game was up and she was the one responsible for his capture.

She flattened herself against the wall near the balcony doors. Other than the soft glow of a small fire, the room was almost completely dark. Silently she took the sword she'd previously leaned there into her hands and waited in breathless anticipation for him to enter the room.

Suddenly he was there facing the bed, his back to her. Jasmine's heart gave a jolting leap of surprise. It was amazing how he could move with such silence. One moment the room was empty and the next he was there, as if a ghostly apparition appearing from out of the darkness.

Her heart thudded so loud she thought it impossible for him not to hear. Silently she breathed a long, steadying sigh, praying for a measure of calmness, of control. She longed to rail at him, to fling his treachery in his face, to attack him physically, but she would not, for to show that loss of control would give him the edge and she dared not allow him any advantage if she wished to best this beast.

The point of a sword jabbed with threatening menace into the small of his back. He stiffened and gave a silent curse, wondering who had lain in wait for him.

"I'd advise you, sir" came a softly spoken whisper, "not to move a muscle, lest I take the pleasure upon myself that the Crown awaits."

"Who are you?" he asked, not recognizing the husky sound.

A soft laugh. "No doubt I should be asking that of you."

He breathed a sigh of remorse, for at the sound of her laugh he knew. He'd have known that laugh anywhere. "Should you? But you know who I am, Jasmine."

"I thought I did."

"I've never denied being the Shadow. Why should you suddenly hold a blade to my back?"

Jasmine threw the mask she'd been holding for the last two hours over his shoulder. It floated to the floor. "I found this in the closet."

"I see," he whispered, knowing the rage she must surely have felt at finding the hidden compartment and the clothes within.

There was an almost imperceptible movement. A hunching of his shoulders, a straightening of his spine, and she knew he was ready to pounce upon her. "I wouldn't," she warned as the blade pressed more firmly to his back.

He chuckled softly. "Will you hold me here indefinitely?"

"Only until the militia arrive."

"You've sent for them, then?"

173

"I have."

He shrugged and moved away from the blade. "You don't mind if I relax while we wait, do you? I tend to get a bit stiff standing with a blade at my back."

By the time he finished his nonchalant remarks, he was sitting on the bed leaving her with no choice but to allow him his way or run him through.

"Indeed you are brave, Anthony," she remarked from the safety of a room's separation. "Even a blade at your back brings not a moment's pause. Have you no fear of death?"

Anthony laughed. "Not at your hand, wife."

"Your first mistake then, for I have every intention of seeing justice done."

"Am I supposed to be frightened? Do you imagine you could keep me here if I wanted to leave?"

"The point is moot. I expect the militia to arrive at any moment. The house will be surrounded. You will not be leaving here. Not under your own power, in any case."

Anthony nodded, then leaned back on one arm and smiled. "You are angry."

"I cannot imagine it put in milder terms."

"Would you kill your own husband, Jasmine? Shall I make a run for it and put you to the test?"

Jasmine's lips curved into a cold semblance of a smile as she fingered the blade still held in her hand. "Indeed, the idea brings much pleasure to mind. Why not give it a try?"

Anthony chuckled as he came to his feet. He did not move toward the safety of the dark balcony, but rather walked slowly back to stand directly before the pointed sword. "A kiss then, my sweet," he said, so softly she thought she might have misunderstood. "One final kiss before we say goodbye."

He leaned forward and gently lowered her arm to her side. His arms took her tightly to him and his

174

mouth brushed gently across hers. "A word of advice for future reference. Don't ever hesitate. If there's something you want to do, do it."

Jasmine's palm smarted from the blow she delivered to his cheek. "Like that?"

White teeth flashed with something akin to admiration as strong arms tightened his hold.

If Jasmine had been slightly less enraged, she might have noticed the glitter in his eyes. As it was, her mind being more than a little preoccupied with fury, she was unprepared for the sudden movement.

"Exactly," he muttered as his mouth swooped down and took hers in a kiss, the power of which seemed to threaten the very depths of her soul. Jasmine, as always, was helpless at the onslaught. Her knees weakened as she leaned helplessly against him for support. The sword clattered unnoticed to the floor.

Had she a moment to think on it, Jasmine would have been amazed at her reaction, for never had she felt such wild abandon. But his mastery was such that all thoughts of revenge flew from her mind. She couldn't think of anything but the taste of his mouth, the scent of his warm breath, and the heat of his hands.

She pressed close and murmured a soft sound of delight as his hands roamed freely over her lush curves. She wanted him. Perhaps it was the extreme emotion she had suffered these last hours that only seemed to make her want him more.

"They come," he muttered hoarsely against her mouth as the sounds of running footsteps clattered up the stairs.

But Jasmine was lost in the throes of a passion gone wild. She never heard the sounds, nor his words. His hand pressed to her neck. An instant later Jasmine slumped unconscious into his arms.

The door to her room burst open. Six British

soldiers hurried into Jasmine's bedchamber accompanied by a sleepy-eyed, befuddled Jenson.

Orders were issued and a quick search initiated.

"You will explain, Captain, this outrageous invasion of privacy" came Elizabeth's angry voice.

"I'm afraid I must search your house, madam" came the stiff retort.

"Am I to know why?" Elizabeth asked as she gathered her dressing gown more firmly around lush, obviously naked curves.

The captain didn't miss the movement and stared for a long moment at her beautifully disheveled appearance, cursing the instant stirring at his loins. The fact was that this woman was a lady and what had suddenly come to mind was out of the question. That she had been either in the midst or just finishing a good toss was obvious from her swollen and reddened lips and the darkly sultry eyes that had not quite lost their sheen of passion. "We've," he cleared his throat and cursed again the helpless reaction his body was having to her. "We've received information that the Shadow would be here."

"Here?" Elizabeth asked, a touch of obvious ridiculing humor in her voice.

"What is it, darling?" came the deeper sound of a man as he recognized the hunger in the officer's gaze and slid his arm around Elizabeth's waist in a definite and most possessive manner.

Elizabeth hadn't noticed the sudden gleam in the young captain's eye. Neither had she realized Richard's unspoken claim on her person. Her eyes widened in amazement at what she'd just heard. "Surely there's been an error."

"I'm afraid not" came the stiff answer as one of the soldiers handed the captain the discarded sword and silk mask. "As you can see, he's been here."

"Might you know the whereabouts of your daughter, ma'am?"

"Jasmine?" Elizabeth looked blankly around the room for a long moment before realizing it was past two in the morning and Jasmine was not in bed. "Oh, my God!" she cried out as she slumped against Richard. "Has he taken her?"

The captain shrugged. "I'll have the men search the grounds."

"Oh, hurry! Please do hurry!" she gasped. Her skin paled to her lips, her eyes grew huge as fear came to tingle every nerve ending, and her heart threatened to break through the wall of her chest with its pounding.

"Go dress, Elizabeth," Richard whispered. "I'm afraid our guests will be here for some time."

"I'll have to search all the rooms, Mrs. Huntington."

Elizabeth nodded, not paying all too much attention to his words as her mind tried to absorb the enormity of this development.

The soldiers, at a nod from their captain, filed out and began their search. "I can see you are upset, but you might take consolation from the fact that you weren't the only one duped."

"Excuse me?" Elizabeth asked blankly.

"Your son-in-law."

"Anthony? What about him?"

Captain Hall frowned. "I thought you understood. It is he for whom we search."

Elizabeth blinked. "Why? Why would you be searching for Anthony? Has he been taken as well?"

"Madame, I'm afraid he is the one doing the taking. Anthony Montgomery is, in fact, the Shadow."

After a long moment of stunned silence, Elizabeth giggled in relief. Lord but she'd taken such a fright. Now she knew there had been some terrible mistake. "The notion is absurd, Captain. If you knew my son-in-law . . ."

Captain Hall interrupted, his face reddening, for he did indeed know Anthony Montgomery and the knowledge that he, too, had fallen for the man's expert act did not sit at all well with him. "Is this your daughter's hand?"

Elizabeth looked with surprise at the note thrust in her direction. The smile that hovered about her lips soon turned into a grimace of horror as her eyes scanned the clear writing. She had no doubt her daughter had written it. But why? Why would Jasmine accuse her own husband of so dastardly a crime as treason? Didn't she realize the man would surely hang if the charges proved true?

"I cannot believe it."

"Would your daughter rouse the militia in the dead of night on a whim? Have you ever known her to be a liar?"

"No." Elizabeth bristled at the insult. "Of course not. It's just that this is impossible to believe."

"Nevertheless, it is doubtless true," Captain Hall remarked as he took the note from Elizabeth's trembling fingers and returned it to the inside pocket of his coat, all the while cursing the fact that the Shadow had been within his grasp and he had never even suspected. Damn, he might have been a major today had he been less believing of the popinjay.

It was almost dawn before the search was given up and the soldiers left them in peace. Elizabeth sighed knowing there was not a corner of her home left undisturbed. Soon she would rouse the servants yet again and direct the resettling of her home.

Richard and Elizabeth were in bed, but Elizabeth was clearly too upset to sleep. Richard leaned against the headboard, holding Elizabeth's shapely back to his chest as his arm circled her slender, naked form and caressed the tempting curves.

178

The room was warm and no cover had been drawn up since they had discarded their clothes for the second time that night.

Richard knew Elizabeth was deeply worried, but he tried to relieve her mind of its fear. "You know, of course, that I'll never get enough of holding you like this. You absolutely have the most beautiful breasts, soft, lush, heavy. There are moments when I'm sorely pressed not to reach out and touch them, no matter the scandal it would cause."

Elizabeth turned and glanced up into silver eyes. "You mean in public?"

"In public, in private. Everywhere. Anywhere. I love you beyond reason."

Elizabeth sighed as she snuggled closer, her cheek caressing his hard chest. "Richard, you don't mind, do you, if we do nothing more than rest for a time? I am worried about Jasmine."

"I know you are, dear, but you need not. Remember she is with Anthony. Surely you know he will bring her to no harm."

Elizabeth nodded. "I know, but . . ."

"No buts, Elizabeth. Anthony is a man of great strength. His honor is above reproach, no matter his views differ with ours. I've known this from the first."

"Richard, I'm afraid his views do not differ with mine."

Richard chuckled as he snuggled his face in the warmth of her neck. "Are you telling me you support the rebel cause?"

"I'm afraid I do."

He sighed with delight as his palms cupped the heavy softness of her breast and his thumbs almost absentmindedly caressed the rosy tips into tight buds. "Do you realize how very much I love you?"

Elizabeth's eyes widened with surprise, not at his declaration of love but at what she took to be agreement with her political stance. "You, too?"

Richard chuckled and shook his head in the negative. "Darling, I sympathize with your plight, but I'm afraid I'm a staunch supporter of the king. Still," his eyes lit up as he teased, "there's always the possibility you might convince me of the error of my ways."

"Is there?" Elizabeth turned shining eyes on the man she'd loved for all these years. Her hand moved over his chest and down his stomach. "One wonders how I might go about such a chore?"

Richard groaned as he snuggled his face into the curve of her neck. "I'm open to suggestions."

Elizabeth giggled like a young girl. "Shame on you, Richard. Where is your resolve? Your fortitude?"

"I'm afraid I have none where you are concerned," he groaned, his voice low and husky as he captured her teasing hand and held it against him.

"You mean to say I can mold you to my liking?"

Richard breathed a long sigh. "If Jasmine is as stubborn as her mother, Anthony's sure to suffer a bit at first."

Elizabeth smiled as she lifted her gaze to his again. "Only a bit?"

Richard grinned. "Lord but I feel sorry for the men of this family. They don't stand a chance in hell against their women."

Elizabeth took his one hand and ran its palm over her rounded belly to the juncture of her thighs. She sighed with delight as his fingers eagerly sought out her warmth. "I wouldn't feel too sorry, darling."

Anthony's back felt as if it was breaking in two. It had been hours before the house had settled again into silence, and still he waited. Jasmine had regained consciousness just as the voices in her room were beginning to fade. He felt her take a huge breath into the darkness, no doubt ready to scream. Again he had pressed his fingers to her neck and she had crumbled once more into oblivion.

When he felt her stir again, he whispered near her ear, his hand holding tightly to her mouth, "Make not a sound unless you'd prefer to sleep again."

Jasmine broke out in a clammy sweat, her heart pounding with a mindless terror. Desperately she tried to control the urge to scream. Her voice shook. "Where are we?"

"In the closet."

She barely heard his answer as panic seeped into her every pore and terror filled her mind. She was having trouble breathing. "Why?"

"The militia were here."

There came a long moment when only the sound of her gasping breath was heard. Finally she asked, "*Were?* Have they gone then?"

Anthony chuckled, attributing the breathless sound of her voice to despair. "I'm afraid they have, darling."

Jasmine tried to pull away from his embrace, for she was crushed almost breathless against him. She needed air. She needed room. She had to get out of here. Darkness invaded her senses, bringing with it a terror, the strength of which she hadn't known since a child.

"No!" she groaned as if in pain. "I have to get out."

"Not yet."

Jasmine began to fight a desperate battle. She couldn't breathe. She had to get out. She couldn't stand the confines of small places. It had always been thus ever since, as a child, her father had punished her by forcing her into a black closet. Only this time it was worse than she could ever remember. "I have to. I have to," she repeated, her voice growing in volume. Suddenly, like one driven over the edge of reason, she was scratching and kicking with unbelievable strength.

"What's the matter with you?"

"Let me out!"

Anthony cursed as he again felt for the pulse at her throat. Damn but he didn't want to do this. How often could this hold be administered without resulting in permanent damage?

Anthony muttered a sharp curse as the hooks that held his spare clothing dug deep into his back, for the space allotted was not meant to hide people, especially not struggling people.

An instant later she again slumped against him.

Anthony sighed as he listened at the bedroom door. The house remained silent. Apparently the militia had gone. He crossed quickly to the balcony and whispered a foul curse. Below the balcony stood a guard and Anthony had no doubt another was stationed at the front door and probably still another at the back.

His gaze moved to the still figure upon the bed. Damn, she had nearly torn the skin from his body in an effort to free herself. Never would he have imagined her to suffer such fear of small spaces. How in the world had she come to know this terror? What had happened to her?

Anthony forced aside the silent questions. There was no time to think on it now, nor to question her as to the cause. He sighed with disgust. He had little choice in the matter. Because of the guards, he would be leaving her behind, at least for the time being. But not for long, he swore.

Anthony glanced at the sky. In less than an hour it would be dawn. He smiled as he moved to the balcony, silently vowing to return, for she would be with him no matter her objections. He almost laughed aloud as he moved over the rooftop and jumped to the next building. For that she would object, he had no doubt. A light of anxious anticipation burned in his eyes. He couldn't wait to see the anger flare to life in her eyes, for anger was merely a heartbeat from desire.

Jasmine came suddenly and sharply awake with a short gasp, for she imagined herself still enclosed in the coffinlike confines of the secret closet. Her eyes were wide with fear and her heart pounded as if she'd run nearly a mile.

She tried to get up, but slumped back upon the bed, her legs and arms trembling still as she fought to regain control. Wildly her gaze searched out the room. She sighed with relief to find herself alone. It took some time, but after a few moments her breathing grew even and the weakness of her limbs began to ease.

As Jasmine's terror began to fade, so did her lips tighten with fury. Tonight he'd given her still another reason to hate him. Suddenly her mouth curved with self-mockery and she laughed, the sound foreign to her ears, for it was more an ache of remorse than a sound of merriment. How in God's name had she ever imagined herself in love with him? The man she thought she loved did not exist. Why hadn't she realized this obvious fact before? Why had she allowed an occasional tender word and the magnificence of his form to convince her otherwise?

Surely there were others as handsome, thousands of men who possessed an equal width of shoulders, the slimness of his hips, skin that glistened bronze in firelight, eyes that were as blue. She shook her head and nearly cried out in despair. God, he couldn't be the only one to so entice.

Jasmine's eyes hardened with resolve as she came

slowly to her feet. But he did not entice, she silently insisted. Surely she had only imagined the emotion. Of course, she reasoned as the smallest of smiles touched her lips, it was the oddity of their relationship that had instilled these erroneous thoughts. Nothing more.

The man was a traitor to the Crown. And she as a loyal English subject had done her duty. The disgust she felt at being taken in by his act was as nothing compared with her hatred for this man. She swore before God she'd find a way to bring him to justice, and she knew in her heart that she'd never rest until she found her means of revenge.

"You can't imagine the relief I felt to see you walking into this room. I thought he had taken you with him and worried half the night away only to find you were in your room all along."

Jasmine smiled at her mother from across the breakfast table. "No doubt it was the arrival of the militia that interrupted his plan." Jasmine's cheeks grew pink as she remembered exactly what the soldiers had interrupted. She shuddered. "He held me in the back of the closet until all was clear."

"Well, thank God you didn't call out or Anthony would now be in dire straits."

"Mother, I didn't call out because he pressed my neck a number of times and caused me to lose consciousness. Had I the chance I would certainly have done so."

"And turned your husband in?" Elizabeth asked, clearly aghast at the notion and ignoring the fact that it was Jasmine's note that had brought the militia in the first place.

"Elizabeth!" came a note of warning from Richard.

Elizabeth shot him a look. "Don't try to stop me, Richard. It's time Jasmine knew how I stand on this matter."

Jasmine's brow furrowed with confusion. "What matter?"

"Almost from the first I've been sympathetic to the rebel cause. And in truth, I've supported it financially."

Jasmine gave a low laugh of disbelief. "Mother, you jest."

"I'm afraid I do not, Jasmine. Without our aid, the patriots stand little chance."

Jasmine's eyes widened with shock. "How could you?"

"How could I not? Their cause is just. England has no right to take and give nothing in return. Why, they've reduced us to little more than indebted servants, taking until there is no more to give. We have no voice and yet we must pay their taxes."

"But . . ."

Elizabeth ignored the interruption. "Aside from the fact that your husband held political beliefs opposite from yours, would a dutiful wife have done as you?"

Jasmine stared at the woman across from her, unable to believe her ears. Her words of protest were feeble at best, for she knew in her heart, the truth of the matter. She had reported him out of rage, not for any sense of loyalty to the Crown. Her voice was low and held almost a childish sulk as she responded, "I did what I thought was right."

"Knowing Anthony, if caught, would surely hang for treason? Jasmine, you realize of course that the English government considers this as merely a rebellion. Your good King George will not recognize this action as war?"

Jasmine's confusion couldn't have been greater. She had never expected her mother to give her a setting down for remaining loyal to the Crown. "I didn't think . . ."

"I can see as much. One hopes that in the future you might try thinking before you act. It matters not if you agree with your husband's beliefs. Your duty as his wife is to stand by him."

"Why? You didn't stand by yours."

Elizabeth gasped at Jasmine's daring. "You are correct in that. But I left my husband. No matter how despicable, I didn't turn him over to the authorities."

She gave a slight sound of self-disgust, knowing she had miserably failed her daughter. Jasmine had no notion of the tenets of loyalty involved in the relationship between husband and wife. In truth Elizabeth couldn't fault her on that, for one could only learn from example. "Unlike Jamison Huntington, I doubt your Anthony gave you a moment's suffering."

Elizabeth snorted as she clearly read the truth in her daughter's eyes. She shook her head wearily and breathed a long sigh. Jasmine loved her husband and yet she had turned him in. "I believe it past the time for you to grow up." And with that last statement, Elizabeth rose from her seat and silently left the room.

Chapter Eleven

"I'm afraid we're all suspect."

"Why?"

"They assume he did not work alone." Joseph shrugged. "More than likely they're right."

"You cannot mean everyone. No one was closer to him than I. And yet, I . . ."

"I'm afraid I do."

"But I swore allegiance to the Crown. Does that not count for something?"

"Many have sworn. Most believed it prudent at the time to allow the English to believe what they would."

"But I meant it!"

"Nevertheless you had best watch your every action for a time."

Jasmine sighed and nodded unhappily. They both knew her possible disloyalty was not at the root of the problem, for no one had proven themselves more loyal to the Crown than she, but she knew, as did he, the whispers behind fluttering fans and false smiles. She had heard the praise but louder than words was the condemnation clearly read in the faces of those who were once her friends.

"Her own husband!"

"Imagine a wife like that!"

"How could she have done it?"

How had this come to be? Hadn't she done what was right? Why then did they turn from her?

They didn't know, of course. Not even her best friends knew, for she'd never tell another living soul the terrible thing he'd done.

She knew now why she had done it. It wasn't so much his betrayal of the Crown as his betrayal of her.

She had believed herself in love with a man who couldn't love her in return. In desperation she had sought solace in another's arms, only to find out her lover was her husband. Wracked with guilt, she believed she had loved one and lusted for the other when they were one and the same. God, what a fool she'd been. Her mother had been wrong. She had suffered greatly at Anthony's hand and it seemed her suffering was not due to end in the near future. The long empty nights that brought torture to abound in both body and mind weren't enough. How often had she lain awake till dawn, aching for his touch, trembling with the traitorous pain of arousal he had awakened in her body?

For more than two months she had stayed close to the house, venturing out seldom for an occasional afternoon tea, a ride in the park, or a visit to the dress shop. Devoid of spirit, she often felt lethargic, at times even physically ill, especially in the mornings. The ailment had grown in strength as each day had gone by until she found it an effort to simply get out of bed. Jasmine felt no little disgust at this newfound weakness of character.

Lord but she didn't want to miss him like this. How had he come to mean so much? How had she ever allowed him to affect her like this? All she wanted was to banish his memory from her mind, to pretend he had never existed. It had taken months, but she knew it was time to pull herself from the edge of despair.

And now that she had finally roused herself from her lethargy, she had come up against a new obstacle. She had done what she knew was right—indeed, what was expected of her, no matter how her conscience might plague—but through no fault of her own, she was suddenly shunned by much of New York's polite society. How terribly unfair!

During the conversation between Joseph and Jasmine, Deborah had moved from the chair facing her friend and was now standing before one of the library windows. Idly she examined a nail and spoke as if to no one in particular, but in truth she responded to Joseph's last words of warning. "I doubt the need, if one has nothing to hide." Deborah gave a long, elaborate sigh. "I imagine the life of a coward most trying, wouldn't you agree? Never knowing on which side of the fence to hide must be quite unnerving."

Joseph reddened, his lips tightening with anger, while Jasmine gasped at the out and out insult.

"Meaning?" His voice was low with a clear threat. Jasmine hadn't a doubt that were Deborah a man, Joseph would have called her out to the spot.

"Meaning?" she repeated, imagining her look of confusion belied the hatred that had instantly blazed to life. "Good heavens, Captain Gaspar, you don't mean to say I meant anything by that statement? Surely you've hinted often enough that women, children, and dogs have much the same mental capabilities. A pat on the head usually satisfies."

Joseph ground his teeth at her barely veiled disgust, his eyes narrowed with fury. Unable to let her comment go, he insisted again, "You are calling me coward, Miss Windstock?"

Deborah laughed softly. "Whatever made you think that? You don't have a guilty conscience, do you?"

Damn! What was there about her that set his teeth on edge the moment she entered a room? Why did he allow her to rile him to a point of near madness?

Jasmine's eyes moved back and forth between her only two real friends left in the city. She had held such hope at first. They had seemed so attracted to each other. What had happened to bring them to this? Why did they find it necessary to fight? Could they not spend a moment in each other's company without going for the kill?

It was obvious Joseph believed Deborah merely a flighty piece of fluff, having no interests other than the right parties, friends, and clothes while she, speaking clearly her mind no matter the consequences, accused him more than once of being a stodgy bore and, to Jasmine's embarrassment, a stupid one at that.

Jasmine sighed. Lord but these two made a stunning couple. Deborah with her petite blond beauty and Joseph so very tall and handsome. She shook her head sadly. She had so hoped they would . . . Jasmine shrugged. It mattered not what she had hoped. Now she only prayed they could find the control needed to refrain from physically attacking each other.

"I'm sure Deborah didn't mean . . ."

"The hell she didn't!" he growled.

Deborah laughed airily, unconcerned by his obvious rage, as she retrieved her wrap and reticule. "I'll see you at the dress shop, dear. I have an appointment I really should see to." To Joseph she said nothing as she turned her back, rudely ignoring him as if he simply did not exist, and walked out of the room. A moment later the front door slammed announcing her exit.

190

Joseph's lips tightened with suppressed fury. "The little witch! If she was a man . . ." He let the sentence hang as he imagined all manner of delicious things he might do to relieve himself of her company forever. Damn Anthony! Where the hell was he and how much longer would he be forced to watch over this wife of his?

It had been more than two months since he left. And the time spent since squiring his sister-in-law about town was surely about to do him in. God, how he hated this life. How many more millineries and dress shops was he to visit before his brother took up his own responsibilities?

Although not nearly as rough as some, Joseph was a seaman at heart. Fancy clothes and manners were not his forte. No, he much preferred the straight talk of real men, the peaceful existence aboard his ship, and the majesty of the sea to an afternoon tea spent in the company of giggling, simpering, dim-witted women. Most of all he disliked the fluttering females who seemed to hang on to his every word as they batted eyelashes and stared with empty-headed adoration. Were those practiced little stances, and he had no doubt they were practiced, meant to entice? Joseph shook his head. God, but he could barely stand them. Certainly he couldn't talk to them, for they knew next to nothing but for the arrangement of their hair and the newest fashion smuggled in from France.

Too bad they couldn't be more like Jasmine. He didn't mind her company in the least, for she was articulate and bright. Indeed, his sister-in-law, although she didn't as yet know she was his sister-in-law, was a fine woman, if a bit impulsive and thick-headed. All in all, Anthony could be proud to call her his wife. But the rest? Joseph shuddered his disgust.

Still, women did have their place. And that little witch, who had just insulted him and left without so

191

much as a by your leave, would do nicely spread upon her back. Nicely, that is, if he could gag her mouth, for he disliked nothing on earth more than a woman who refused to realize her place.

"Shall we go, Joseph?"

Joseph looked up with surprise to find Jasmine waiting for him. He was to escort her to the dress shop, for she had her final fitting for the dress she would wear to the party tonight, a party she seemed more than anxious to attend, since the invitations to her were so rare in coming these days. He dreaded the afternoon chore as it was, but the thought that he would no doubt run into the nasty Miss Windstock was nearly enough to cause him to beg off.

Joseph was obviously bored. More than anything he longed to return to the sea. Standing here in the dress shop, he allowed his mind to return to the delight of running his ship as he leaned against a table and absentmindedly fingered a flimsy piece of lace. It took little thought to imagine the smell and dampness of salty air as he walked his decks. God, how he longed for the peace and serenity, knowing the soothing balm it brought always to his soul.

Joseph hadn't at first realized the direction of his gaze, for his mind was otherwise occupied. It was with some shock that the sight before him finally penetrated his thoughts and caused his body to stiffen. Through clamped teeth Joseph inhaled a soft, hissing breath. Of all people, it was Deborah who had just entered the tiny cubicle and forgotten to draw the curtain completely back in place. There she stood behind the partially drawn curtain awaiting the help of a salesperson in her dressing. An unbelievably tiny waist, a waist he had no doubt he could easily span with his hands, was corseted. She wore no shift. Her breasts were clearly visible to his

192

gaze and, due to the tight bindings just below, jutted temptingly high and lush, ready to fill a man's hand. Because she was facing the long mirror, Joseph was blessed, or cursed, depending on one's point of view, with the vision of loveliness, both front and back.

In his thirty-three years, Joseph had seen most everything and the female form had long ago ceased to bring a measure of surprise. But this woman, half naked, her hair disheveled as if she'd just come warm from her bed, the long golden waves draping over creamy shoulders and down her back, took his breath away.

He should have averted his gaze. It was the gentlemanly thing to do and he knew it, but he suddenly found himself incapable of movement. No part of him, no matter how he silently berated his actions, would move—most especially his eyes.

Deborah's blue eyes suddenly rose to meet Joseph's through the mirror. He gasped as the tiniest flicker of a smile touched her pink lips. A wave of dizziness swelled over him. She knew he was watching. Their eyes held. There was no way she couldn't know. She knew it and yet did nothing to hide her nakedness.

Sweat beaded along his upper lip. Blood rushed to his loins and pounded in his ears. He could feel himself growing thick, throbbing for release of a desire so powerful and sudden it nearly knocked him to the floor. It was all he could do to remain in place. Every nerve called out to his brain, imploring, demanding him to go to her, to order the saleswoman out and take this woman right here, without a word spoken between them.

A blue dress was slipped over her head, hiding the deliciousness he knew to lurk beneath and Joseph could only breathe a long sigh of relief, knowing the worst of his torture had passed.

"Are you all right?"

Joseph turned at the sound. It took him a moment

193

to realize he no longer stood alone, so dazed was he at the sight he'd just witnessed. He smiled at last and remarked, "It is I who should be asking that of you, considering your weakness of late."

Jasmine shrugged away his concern, knowing it the workings of her own mind that had brought about this odd, unshakable lethargy. "I told you, whatever it was that plagued has gone. I feel perfectly fine." She moved a bit closer, her eyes narrowing with concern. "You seem a bit flushed." Her hand reached out to touch his forehead. "Are you warm?"

An understatement to be sure, for he was beyond the point of warmth. A raging heat burned within, a heat that, he instinctively knew, would burn on, never to be extinguished until he possessed that one particular woman. "I'm fine. It's a bit warm in here." He smiled at her concerned expression. "Are you ready?"

Jasmine smiled and nodded. "I promised Deborah we'd drop her at her place." And at his pained look, she asked, "You don't mind, do you?"

"Not at all." If his reaction to the news of spending time in the lady's company was a bit stiff, Joseph allowed Jasmine to believe it was because of their earlier harsh words.

"Joseph," she sighed, "I really wish you two could try to get along."

Joseph took her hand and smiled down at the sweet pleading in her eyes. "I can see it's important to you Jasmine. I promise I'll do my best."

The ride home was a delightful surprise. Gone were the usual nasty comments and cutting gibes. Jasmine never noticed the tension between the two; they merely seemed a bit subdued and she hoped her plea, if not for friendship then at least tolerance, was finally being acted upon.

Jasmine, her eyes wide with astonishment as she caught one tender exchange of timid smiles, was

194

suddenly filled with burgeoning hope for their future. She merely smiled her understanding when Joseph suggested, in a strangely strangled voice, that she be dropped off first, even though it was definitely not on the way as he professed, hoping her two favorite people might put to good use these few moments of privacy.

Jasmine alighted from the carriage with a carefree smile and a promise to see them both later at the Chandlers' party.

Deborah smiled almost wickedly as the carriage lurched forward again. "Do you think we can manage the ride to my house without tearing at each other?" she asked Joseph.

He watched her for a long moment, a grin teasing the corner of his mouth. "I imagine there is more than one reason for a man and woman to tear at each other."

Deborah nodded knowingly. "Indeed, but a man and woman would first feel some measure of attraction, if that were the case."

"And, of course, *we* are not besieged with such emotion."

"Of course not," she agreed sweetly. And almost laughed aloud with pleasure. It was working. Good God, she couldn't believe how easily she had taken him in. First, she had brought about interest with anger and now lust. She didn't care if it meant she'd soon share his bed. She'd do anything to see this animal brought to justice.

She'd sent word for help, but it would be some time before they arrived. And she had to keep him here.

She wouldn't trust this man to the law. Deborah almost laughed at the idea. What had the law done when she most needed help? Nothing! Nothing but stand by while he murdered her father and pirated her family's ship. No, she'd take matters into her own hands this time. Soon the world would see the last of

195

the infamous pirate Captain José Gaspirilla.

"You wouldn't be teasing me, would you, Miss Windstock?"

"Certainly not," she returned primly, but the ghost of a taunting smile in her blue eyes belied her words.

Joseph gave what he hoped was a devastating smile. "Jasmine would be pleased if we could refrain from our usual bickering. If I use some effort, do you suppose we might grant her wish?"

Deborah laughed and Joseph squirmed uncomfortably at the soft, lilting sound. "I suppose I could try to contain myself."

Joseph extended his hand. "Agreed?"

Deborah didn't think but to do likewise.

He smiled with satisfaction as he held her hand and listened to the soft gasp as sensation raced up both their arms. "Agreed," she murmured shakily, surprised by the odd shiver that raced through her. It didn't matter, of course. It didn't matter what he made her feel. It only mattered that she keep him occupied until help came. She'd crawl on her belly through hell to make sure this beast got what he deserved.

Suddenly she was pulled across the space that separated their seats and flung upon his lap. Her eyes widened with surprise, her back stiffened with outrage. "What do you think . . ."

Joseph caught her chin with his hand and forced her to face him. "I think we should seal our agreement with a kiss."

"I think not, Captain," she said breathlessly, not liking at all the effect his nearness was having on her. "You take much upon yourself."

"Perhaps, but I'm going to kiss you nevertheless."

"And if I don't want you to?" she asked, silently cursing her thundering heart and the tingling sensations that were racing up her spine.

"Don't you?"

"Captain Gaspar," she said quite primly, no matter her present position, "I'm not in the habit of kissing mere acquaintances."

"I'm afraid after what happened in the dress shop, I don't believe you."

"What happened?"

"You knew I was watching you, damn it! You wanted me to watch. You enjoyed it."

"Did you?"

"Did I what?"

"Enjoy it?"

"Oh, God," Joseph groaned as he slashed his mouth across hers in a kiss that bordered on violent. He was drowning in her scent, her taste as he plunged his tongue deep into her warmth. He wanted her here and now. He couldn't wait a moment longer.

"I want to see them again," he gasped breathlessly as he pulled his mouth free of hers and then, unable to resist the temptation, kissed her again, this time with infinitely more gentleness as his fingers undid the buttons of her bodice.

His hand reached inside and a soft groan slid from his mouth to hers as his hand filled with the rich pleasure of her. His mind reeled at her reaction to his touch as she squirmed wantonly upon his lap, her rounded bottom brushing enticingly against his arousal.

Deborah's mind grew dazed. Vaguely she knew she should put up more resistance, but the touch of his mouth caused a weakness that was new to her senses, a weakness she couldn't resist. Did he know the gentle stroking of his tongue on the sensitive flesh inside her lips caused a fluttering in her stomach and was about to drive her out of her mind? Of course he did. Idly she wondered how many others had been so blessed as to know this man's kiss?

God but she didn't want to lose control in his arms,

She didn't want her body to soften to warm liquid beneath the touch of his hands. No, she needed every ounce of willpower lest her plan fall to ruin.

She tried to laugh, to keep the moment light, but the chuckle sounded more a desperate groan as his lips, tongue, and teeth slid down her throat. "Surely you know the female form, Captain Gaspar."

Joseph couldn't think. This had never happened to him before. All he knew was her touch, her kiss, her taste. All he wanted was more of her. It took him a long moment before he realized she had spoken. "Call me Joseph. I want to see you again. Open your dress for me. Pull it down."

"We are almost at my house."

"I don't care."

"Captain Gaspar. The carriage has stopped."

Joseph groaned in frustration and flung his head back against the high leather seat, taking huge gulps of air, fighting for the strength it took not to tear her clothes from her body. Damnation, when was the last time a woman had affected him like this? Never, he realized. Never had he known this almost insane desire. He was gasping for breath, unable to believe this tiny, nasty woman was the one to have brought about such loss of control.

With shaking fingers, Deborah refastened her bodice, straightened her hat, and adjusted her skirts.

"You don't mind if I don't see you to your door, Miss Windstock."

Deborah's blue eyes widened with surprise and a devious smile touched the corners of her mouth. "I was going to invite you in for tea." She gave a nonchalant shrug. "Perhaps at a future date then?"

Dumbfounded, Joseph stared for a long moment into her eyes. She looked at once the innocent young miss and the temptress. He'd never met anyone like her before and didn't quite know what to think. What exactly was she offering him?

"Tea?" he asked, his voice low and thick, not yet able to control his rampant emotions. His heart was pounding as he prayed he was reading correctly her silent invitation.

Deborah felt her skin grow pink. She knew what he was asking. What she didn't know was how to answer him, for she had in mind an afternoon of seduction. But she was new at this game and didn't quite know how to go about arranging it. "I have spirits if you prefer, Captain."

Oh, Lord, Joseph groaned the silent prayer. Was he correct in his interpretation of her or was he only imagining the promise in her eyes?

He paid the driver and followed her to her door. She knocked. Again and then again. No sound came from within. "Oh, dear, I forgot I let the servants go for the afternoon."

Joseph couldn't control his low groan and felt his legs begin to shake. She was driving him out of his mind and the cooler she grew the hotter he became. He cursed as he leaned against the wall of the house for support and watched her reach into her reticule for her key.

"Did you say something, Captain?"

"No," he barely choked out.

Deborah gave him a long, searching look. "Perhaps we should make this for another time. It really is most unseemly for me to entertain a male guest without . . ."

"Open the door."

Deborah bit back her smile and shrugged as she stepped inside. She said nothing as he followed her in and purposely locked the door behind them.

Her hat joined her wrap on the peg in the hall and she smiled as she faced him. "What shall it be, Captain, tea or . . ."

"You," he interrupted.

Deborah managed a weak, if nervous, smile.

Determinedly she ignored his obvious statement and her voice was more than a bit breathless when she finally said, "Tea it is then," glancing toward the sitting-room door. "If you'll make yourself comfortable, I'll be right back."

"Forget the tea." He took her hand and began to move toward the wide stairway that led to the second floor and the bedrooms.

Deborah offered no resistance as she meekly allowed him to pull her along. Her heart thundered with pure fright, but she forced the emotion aside. This was what she wanted, wasn't it? She'd wanted to entice him, to make him crazed for her. Surely she'd be a fool to back out at this late date.

"Which room is yours?"

She nodded, unable to force the words past her throat, toward the door at the end of the hall.

The door was barely shut behind them when she was flung up against it, his body pressing tightly against her. His hips held her in place as if he was afraid she'd bolt at the last minute, while his fingers began to work on the fastenings of his clothes. A smile touched the corners of his hungry mouth as he murmured, "Now we can both get comfortable."

She forced a gentle smile, and if her lips quivered just a bit, he didn't seem to notice, for her small hands reached to the buttons of his shirt and joined him in the disposal of his clothes. It took but a few minutes and yet it felt like a lifetime had passed before he managed to rid her of the hundreds—at least it felt like hundreds—of underthings. By the time she stood there as naked as he, he was gasping for breath, ready to burst with the need of holding her in his arms, of tasting those sweet lips again, of burying himself deep, so deep in her body he might never be able to come back. Joseph had never felt a desire to equal this. Blood pounded in his ears, his groin, his throat. She was in his arms and then suddenly upon the bed, his body holding her securely beneath him.

Joseph fought for control, which was minimal at best. His hands moved down the length of her, roughly seeking, plundering in his need.

Had he been a bit more rational, he might have noticed her slight stiffening, but Joseph was too far submerged in this insanity. He felt the warm wetness of her and assumed she was ready to accept him, but Deborah was not nearly as far along in passion as her partner. She couldn't help the cry that escaped her lips at his sudden forceful entrance.

Joseph came to his senses then, realizing what he had done and knowing it was too late to do anything more than enjoy this beautiful woman. He breathed a long, almost woeful sigh and stilled his movements. Gasping for breath, he forced aside the need to take her now and instead began a slow torturous exploration of her body and mouth, an exploration that would lead the two of them to mindless ecstatic discoveries.

Jesus Christ, she had been a virgin! Joseph's arms trembled still with the aftershocks of a pleasure that had never before been equaled. His breathing as yet labored and unsteady, he tried to understand what had happened. He looked down into eyes still dazed from passion and wondered in confusion at her behavior. Why had she made him believe her act nothing more than a coy tease, meant only to excite him beyond endurance. And that he had been excited, was in truth still excited, he couldn't deny. Damn her to hell for her trickery. Why had she done it?

His body stiffened with rage as an idea suddenly occurred. Did she by any wild stretch of the imagination believe he would now feel obliged to marry her? Of course she did. Damn her and all her conniving breed to hell. Well, this one had a surprise

201

coming, a surprise he could hardly wait to deliver.

Joseph couldn't keep his fury from spilling out. His lips were tight with the need to thrash her. "I suppose you expect me to apologize."

Deborah shrugged, and then stretched as best she could while lying still beneath his long body. She knew he would be angry and she almost laughed at how predictably he had fallen beneath her purposely spun web of seduction. Being a novice, she hadn't supposed it would be quite this easy. Why, the man had been so desperate he'd nearly dragged her up the stairs and into her room. Her clothes almost ripped from her body, he had given her no chance to object as he took her with a desperation she could only have dreamed possible. Even now, after what could only be described as an hour of sheer bliss, when his body should have been sated, she could feel again his arousal.

He glared down at her satisfied expression, for no matter her feelings toward the man, he could and did bring her body to a point where she wondered of her sanity. The fierceness of his gaze almost caused her to laugh, for she wasn't the least bit frightened and, most of all, she wasn't finished with him yet. "If it makes you feel better," she finally answered.

"It won't."

"Then kindly don't bother to do so."

Dark-blue eyes searched her face for a long moment, finding none of the remorse he might have expected. "How in hell can you be so calm about it? I took your . . . your . . ."

"I believe the word you're searching for is virginity, Captain," she offered at his obvious hesitation.

"Do not speak, please. I'm trying to tell you I'm sorry."

Deborah blinked and allowed a measure of

surprise. "Are you? Well that makes one of us, I suppose."

Joseph's eyes widened with amazement. "Are you telling me you have no regrets?"

"It was with me long enough, don't you think?"

"What do you talk about?"

"I'm simply trying to tell you I appreciate the favor."

"Favor? What favor?"

Deborah sighed with elaborate patience. "I wouldn't want anyone to know I was a virgin, not at twenty-four."

"What is the matter with being a virgin?"

"It does tend to get in the way, don't you think?"

Joseph was dumbfounded. He had expected tears, perhaps anger, for he had certainly given her no chance to refuse his advances. But what did she do? Lord almighty, she thanked him. Finally he managed to ask, his eyes narrowing almost in a threat, "In the way of what?"

Deborah smiled. "Captain Gaspar, you are a man of the world." She gave a slight shrug. "That's why I chose you to be my first. Now I can enjoy myself without . . ."

Joseph pushed himself up on his arms. He couldn't believe his ears. Surely she wasn't . . . "Enjoy yourself? Chose me? What are you saying, that you're now free to whore for whomever you please?"

Deborah growled out in instant anger as she shoved him off and yanked her hair from beneath his arm. "Nothing! I'm saying absolutely nothing. Lord but I despise men like you." She stood unconcerned of her nakedness, hands planted firmly on her hips. She glared her hatred. "I take it it's all right for you to indulge in an afternoon of pleasure, but not me. Well, for your information, Captain, you'd have had a time of it trying to do this alone."

"So?"

"So, how does that make me less than you?"

"It doesn't," he returned uncomfortably as he realized the truth of her words.

"Really?" she sniffed with disbelief, while tossing her golden curls behind her shoulders. "Is that why you're so ready to accuse me of being a whore?"

Joseph's lips tightened with fury. "I can't remember a woman who has caused me to lose my temper half as often as you."

"Leave then. I believe I'm finished with you for the time being."

"Sonofabitch!" Joseph lunged to his feet. For one terrifying moment Deborah wondered if she hadn't gone too far. She'd never seen a man so furious, nor one so close to losing all control. "I'm leaving, all right." He grabbed at his pants, shoving his legs inside with such force, Deborah wondered how the material didn't rip to shreds. "Actually, I can't wait to get the blazes out of here. But first you're going to tell me what is going on in that mind of yours."

"Mind!? You mean to say you admit to my having one?"

"Jeeesus!" He groaned with frustration. "I repeat. What is it you're planning?"

Deborah gave him a low, husky laugh as she moved toward her silk robe that lay over the bed's bottom rail. She slipped it over her nakedness and tied it tightly at her waist. "Planning, Captain Gaspar? Indeed, I have no plans at the present. I've accomplished all I've set out to do."

Joseph felt he had been used by Deborah and the notion did not sit well. Is this how the women felt, he wondered? Did they feel used after an hour or so of pleasure when he so carelessly left their beds? "I suppose you think you're now quite experienced."

Deborah laughed again as she began to push her

brush through her waist-length hair. "Not likely. One afternoon spent in a lover's arms, even a lover as accomplished as you, hardly qualifies me as such." She shrugged and gave a secret smile. "No, I think I'll need further tutoring, don't you agree?"

"Not from me, madam. I don't like being used."

"No, you'd rather do the using, I assume?" She shrugged again when she received nothing but a snarl for an answer. "No matter. There are many who would gladly offer their services."

Joseph glared at her for a long moment. If he didn't get out of here right now, he was going to kill her with his bare hands. His rage was so great he couldn't speak, and he wished to blazes he could understand why. Why should he care in whose bed she lay? It was nothing to him if another came to know that luscious body. *She* was nothing to him, nothing but a godalmighty irritant to his body and soul. Jesus, but he felt sorry for the next poor bastard to fall under her spell. Thank God he had realized the truth about her before it was too late.

Dressed in merely seconds, he nearly knocked her door from its hinges as he slammed out of the room.

He almost ground his teeth to dust as he heard her soft, peeling laughter. His fists ached to punch something, anything, as he stomped down the stairs and stormed out of the house.

"Ah, Captain," Deborah commented happily to the empty room, "you mustn't take on so. I've only just begun to make you suffer."

Joseph scowled darkly as he watched her from the sidelines of the dance floor. He couldn't count the men she'd danced with tonight. What he didn't understand was why he was ready to kill every bastard who put his hands on her. Why should he care if she danced with every man here? What did he care that she shamelessly batted those long dark lashes at every male in the room? What did he care if she snuggled scandalously close to more than one of her partners?

She was most obviously searching among those in attendance for her next unsuspecting conquest. Well, he hoped she enjoyed herself, because he cared not one whit what she did.

Suddenly she laughed at something that was whispered in her ear. Joseph's heart pounded in his throat cutting off his breath as he watched her and her current partner walk toward the wide doors that led to the dark terrace.

He was not aware he had moved. He never felt the people he shoved aside. He never heard their exclamations of surprise or offered a word of apology.

He was outside, his eyes searching the dimness of the terrace for a sign of her. He could see nothing. He could hear nothing above the raging of blood pounding in his ears.

Suddenly a soft laugh, her laugh, came from the darkened corner. He never thought of the consequences as he moved toward the sound and his hands reached out, flinging away the man blocking her into the corner.

Deborah's brows rose a fraction as she watched him struggle for control. Calmly she awaited his next move. His hands tightened into fists at his side, for the temptation to thrash her within an inch of her life was almost more than he could bear.

"Now see here" came a disgruntled voice at Joseph's side.

Joseph never heard him. His full concentration was on the woman who so bravely faced his rage.

"It's all right, Henry. Captain Gaspar and I have something to discuss," Deborah explained softly. "We'll talk later."

The man gave Joseph a killing look and then shrugged at the pleading in Deborah's eyes. Without another word, he turned and walked back to the festivities.

"Do you think so?"

"What?"

"Do you think I'll allow you to *talk* to him later?" His exaggeration on the word plainly told her he knew she had more interesting things than talking in mind.

Deborah's laughter was as close to ridicule as she dared, considering the thin thread of control he seemed to be holding. *"Allow?"* A delicate shrug of a shoulder told him clearly her indifference. "Your caveman antics will not suffice in polite society Captain."

Joseph laughed a sound depicting not a trace of humor. "Where will they suffice then?"

"Perhaps aboard your ship." Suddenly she grinned and moved up against his stiff form, her hands sliding over his chest, entwining at his neck like a silken web he suddenly knew he had no hope of ever escaping. Her body pressed close against him as she murmured throatily, "Perhaps in bed."

Joseph gasped with surprise at her outrageous comment. He had expected her to cower in fear. He'd wanted to shake her till her teeth rattled, till she begged him for forgiveness for the suffering he'd endured every time a man took her into his arms and out to the dance floor, but the words wouldn't come as desire suddenly flooded his mind.

He stood stiffly before her, unable to utter a sound, for she teased as if already a practiced courtesan and yet she held just enough innocence to make a man wild. "Shall we try it and see?"

Joseph let go a string of vile curses as he snapped out of his trancelike state, grabbed her hand, and yanked her out of the corner. Without another word, he led her down the stone steps toward the garden, deep into the night shadows. His first thought had been to bring her to his ship, but he instantly discarded the notion. He needed her now, this very minute. Idly he wondered if he could wait even the few moments it would take to get her to a more secluded area. His ship would suffice for a later time. Right now, nothing on earth was going to stop him from taking her and he didn't give a good goddamn of the danger to her reputation should someone come across them.

"What are you doing? Where are you dragging me?" Deborah asked breathlessly as she struggled to keep up with his long strides.

Suddenly, beneath the darkness of a thickly branched tree, he came to an abrupt stop, turned, and took her in his arms.

"If you think . . ."

"Shut up!" he growled as his hands reached for her hair and, pins flying every which way, buried his fingers in its lush, silky length. She was fighting him, but he gave her resistance barely a moment's notice as he forced her mouth toward his. "I'll bring you to bed later. Right now I'm going to show you how a caveman takes a woman."

Chapter Twelve

He was gasping for breath, finding the thought of releasing her quite beyond his ability to bear. He held her pressed against the trunk of a tree, his hands cupping the length of silky thighs, securing them firmly about his hips.

Joseph took a deep, steadying breath. Nothing in his life had ever come close to the madness he suffered every time he came near her. Again and again he fought for control, but the emotion seemed to forever slip from his fingers the moment she opened her mouth.

He breathed a sigh and leaned his forehead against hers, waiting for his heart to calm and the strength to return to his limbs.

"Hardly up to your usual expertise, Captain," she remarked coolly. Clearly her tone meant to imply her boredom.

Joseph dropped his hold on her legs and watched her struggle to gain her footing, her hands reaching out to clutch at the front of his shirt. Bitch! She could hardly breathe. She certainly couldn't stand, and yet she was bound and determined to appear unaffected by what had passed between them.

Joseph glared, adjusted his clothing, and watched her futile attempt to bring her hair into some semblance of order. He knew he should turn his back and walk away. No, damn it, he should run, for he didn't trust himself to stay in her company more than a few minutes at a time lest he thrash her within an inch of her life or give in to her overpowering allure and make love to her again.

Curse her to hell, he wasn't about to run from this. No, he wasn't going to give her the opportunity to laugh again at his frustration. With some effort Joseph controlled the urge he felt to fling her over his shoulder and show her just who in tarnation she was playing with. This tiny woman had thrown his calm, orderly life into an uproar. All too quickly she was becoming a thorn in his side and he'd be damned if he'd suffer this affliction alone. She was going to admit to the ecstasy that raged out of control between them.

"Tell me that wasn't good and you're a god-damned liar."

Deborah laughed. "If it means that much to you, Captain, you were wonderful."

Joseph cursed. He knew well enough the truth of the matter. It was his mouth that had absorbed her low cries of pleasure, his arms that had felt the shuddering response of her body. He knew she'd found more than a little satisfaction in this spontaneous coupling. She had said the right words, but her tone had belied their meaning.

"You might try growing up, Miss Windstock. It's not necessary for us to like each other to admit that our encounter has been an unforgettable experience."

Deborah's lip curled into a sneer of hatred. Her laughter was no more than a hiss. "Not like you? Lord, but that's an understatement of mammoth proportions. I don't dislike you, Captain. I despise you and all of your kind."

Joseph nearly took a step back, so amazed was he at her venomous statement. What had he done to inspire such hatred? Why, he hardly knew her and she certainly had no knowledge of him. How could she hate so fiercely?

He forced the dozen or so questions from his mind, giving in to the impulse to strike back. "Perhaps, but you melt fast enough once in my arms," he returned arrogantly.

Deborah was tempted to slap his face, but instantly realized any show of violence on her part might very well backfire. She stiffened her spine and lifted her chin a notch. Her eyes glared her rage. "Are you calling me a whore again?"

"I never called you a whore, Miss Windstock. I was merely stating a fact. We make good bed partners. Why can't you admit to it?"

Deborah laughed. "Is your male ego so fragile, Captain, that you cannot leave a simple coupling without a bravo or two?"

"Indeed, Miss Windstock, if you believe what has transpired between us to be a simple coupling, you are in need of some further experience."

"Exactly my thoughts on the matter, sir."

"And you thought tonight to further your education?"

"I did." The lie came so easily she couldn't help feeling a moment's surprise.

Joseph, angered nearly beyond endurance, noticed nothing amiss. "And you expect me to stand by and watch?"

Her brow rose, her expression pure disgust. "Are you a voyeur as well as an unconscionable bore?"

"What?" he asked. What was she ranting on about now?

"You said I expected you to watch."

Joseph couldn't help the grin that curved his lips. He was angry enough to cause her physical harm and yet she made him laugh. "I didn't mean . . ." He interrupted himself with helpless laughter. Without a thought he took her stiff form in his arms and cuddled her close against him. She felt his mouth near her ear, his breath sending unwanted chills down her spine as he whispered, "It's probably just as well I'll be leaving in the morning. If I spent much more time with you, I'd soon be a babbling idiot."

"You're leaving?" she asked, her voice tight and filled with a desperation he took for excitement.

"You don't have to sound so damn happy about it," he said, his anger instantly returning. Lord but this woman had his emotions seesawing out of control. One minute he was laughing, the next enraged. Why did it bother him that she should be so pleased to see him go? What did he care what she thought or felt? He'd gotten what he wanted, hadn't he?

Why then was he haunted with the thought that she'd soon be in another's arms? Why did the idea cause a burning ache in the pit of his belly? And why had he thought of nothing else all afternoon? Damn but she was driving him out of his mind.

"Let's go," he ordered as he placed his arm around her waist and guided her to the side of the house where the long line of carriages and drivers were waiting for the guests to depart.

"Where? Where do you think you're taking me now?"

"I'm going to show you my ship."

Deborah stiffened. "I'm afraid not, Captain. I've no interest in seeing your ship."

"Why?" He suddenly stopped and turned her to face him, truly puzzled. They both knew he had no interest in showing her his ship. He wanted to take her somewhere private and she knew it. Suddenly an idea dawned. Joseph grinned. "What do you think I'll do? Kidnap you?" He hadn't imagined how intriguing the thought until he'd actually said the words, but he knew, the moment they were said, exactly what he was going to do.

Joseph wasn't the kind of man who allowed a woman a moment's thought once an enjoyable encounter had reached its conclusion. In truth, although his body might feel a measure of satisfaction, he very often couldn't recollect what that particular partner looked like. Indeed it was unusual for him to want more, but, amazingly such was the case now. He almost breathed aloud a sigh of relief, for he realized at last why she had caused him this unusual degree of anguish. He hadn't gotten enough of her. It was simple. What he needed and needed desperately to end this dilemma was more. And in order to get more he'd have to take her with him. After he was done with her, after she was out of his system, it wouldn't matter in the least to whom she turned.

"I wouldn't put anything past you."

Joseph grinned. "Lord but I can't imagine how you should have gotten such a low opinion of me." Wisely he refrained from adding that in this instance, her opinion was most deserved.

"Is something wrong?" Jasmine asked as she clutched her cape around her shoulders against the morning's cool dampness. Her heart had been pounding with trepidation by the time she boarded the ship to find Joseph awaiting her arrival on deck and she struggled still to gain an even breath.

The sun was just breaking over the horizon, causing the calm blue waters of New York Harbor to glow a soft pink. Behind them the streets of the city were coming awake. Peddlers began shouting their wares. Sailors stumbled a precarious path along the dock searching for their ship and whatever constituted their bed. Some came alone, others were accompanied by bedraggled ladies of the night.

Almost all were in a drunken stupor.

"I hope you don't mind that I sent my man for you. The ship's hold is full and I must leave for the West Indies on the tide." Directly after I make a quick stop along the Carolina coast, he silently added. "And I didn't want to miss saying goodbye."

Jasmine's eyes went wide with surprise even as relief threatened to buckle her knees. Was that all? Had the whole house been awakened before dawn and she nearly dragged from her bed by a sailor who would take nothing but her acquiescence for an answer just because Joseph wanted to say goodbye?

Jasmine bit back the temper that flared suddenly to surface and forced a brightness she was far from feeling to her smile. Something was not right here. Seaman Majors had come pounding at her door, allowing her barely enough time to dress, stating Jasmine's presence was needed with all haste, giving her the very definite impression that Joseph was in some sort of trouble.

Surely Joseph knew of his intended departure last night. Why hadn't they said their goodbyes then? And why did he find the need to say them in person? Even a friend as close as he could have penned a short note. After all, it wasn't as if she'd never see him again.

Jasmine's eyes narrowed with suspicion. Something was wrong and yet she couldn't imagine the reason behind his odd behavior. "Not at all," she replied at last. "Now that I'm here, have you the time to show me your ship?"

"Certainly." Joseph smiled and breathed a long sigh of relief. He hadn't dared to hope it would be this easy. Joseph had no doubt he would soon see the last of her cordiality. For a moment he was greatly saddened, for he wanted nothing more than to be held in his sister-in-law's esteem. Gallantly he offered her his arm.

"What's in there?"

"That's my cabin. I'm afraid it's a bit of a mess or I'd show it to you."

Joseph almost laughed at the understatement. The room was a shambles. Obviously there was nothing left to break, or perhaps she'd simply grown exhausted, for not a sound had come from the room for the last hour or so. No doubt she'd be beating down the door if she knew Jasmine now stood on the opposite side.

Joseph was anxious to be on his way. Although he had the running of his ship to see to and had little time to spare, for this woman he'd make the effort. He didn't want to scare her, but she'd have to know what was about to happen and the sooner he got it over with the better.

"Jasmine, there is something I have to tell you."

Now it comes, Jasmine silently remarked. She had been waiting for the explanation to his odd behavior. She glanced up and waited for him to continue.

"What I have to say may come as something of a shock."

Jasmine tilted her head to one side and waited.

"Your husband and I are brothers."

Jasmine gave a short laugh, her eyes widened with something close to merriment. "For a moment I thought you said . . ."

"I did," he interrupted.

"But that's impossible. You have different names."

"Half brothers to be more accurate." He saw the confusion in her eyes. "I'm afraid I haven't the time to explain right now. Suffice it to say Anthony has sent for you."

Jasmine's mouth fell open with shock. Her eyes filled with incredulity and almost swallowed her face, so huge did they grow. Her skin lost all color and she forgot to breathe.

He thought she might faint. She definitely swayed.

Joseph cursed and reached out to her lest she fall at his feet. "Are you all right?"

"No." She breathed a shaky reply and moaned an agonizing sound as the truth of his statement hit her. Lord, what was the matter with her? Had she some terrible need to constantly be hurt? Would she go on the rest of her life acting the fool? Again she'd been taken in. Once more she'd been used. Was there no one she could trust? "I thought you were my friend."

"I *am* your friend," he returned, forcing aside the guilt he felt at his deceit. He was guiding her toward a cabin, his arm supporting her at her waist. Lord but this was far worse than he could have imagined. If she had put up a fight, if she'd shown a measure of anger, he might have felt justified in his actions. As it was, her pitiful expression nearly broke his heart. For a moment he almost relented. He almost called to his first mate the order to see her to shore when he heard her sudden growl and the whispered promise, "I'm going to kill him for this."

Joseph grinned. This woman had spirit. Caught as she was, she hadn't wasted her effort on escape. No gentle plea had come from her lips. Obviously her mind was already on greater plans. No doubt she was already imagining the ways she'd bring suffering down upon her husband's head. For a second he felt a surge of pity for his brother. An instant later he was smiling, knowing both of them to be equally willful, he a touch too arrogant, she a bit spoiled. Lord, he almost wished he had the time to see the outcome of this drama. Wickedly, as in the way of many a younger sibling, he hoped his brother was brought down a peg or two, and if anyone could do that, it was his lovely wife.

Before she came to her senses, Jasmine was seated upon a bunk in a cabin. She was alone. The door was closed and locked. From the first, she instinctively knew no amount of pleading would suffice. It was obvious, even in her dazed state, he was not happy to be about this chore. And yet any effort on her part to beg help would have been a waste.

Jasmine sighed wearily. Joseph had played his part so well she never imagined them to be brothers. She cursed her stupidity, realizing all too late why Joseph had always seemed so familiar.

He didn't look like Anthony but for his size and the color of his eyes. It was his stance and mannerisms that were much alike. Jasmine sighed wearily. Why hadn't she remembered his smile? A smile that was so like the Shadow's. It might have saved her much of the suffering.

Idly she wondered if Joseph held to the same convictions as his brother. Was he, too, in fact, a rebel? Jasmine shrugged. It mattered not. What mattered was the anger she felt at being duped again. Lord but the men of this family had a thing or two to learn regarding honesty. And she for one couldn't wait to teach at least one of them a lesson he'd not soon forget.

Joseph guided his ship into the secluded harbor along the deserted stretch of the Carolina coast, searching the shore for a sign of Anthony's presence. Below his position at the wheel stood Jasmine and Deborah locked in an embrace.

Jasmine didn't know whether to laugh or cry as she embraced her friend. "Have you been here all along? Silly question. Of course you have," she corrected, knowing they had not put to shore since they left New York almost a week ago. "Why?" she asked. "Why are you here?"

Deborah was obviously stunned to find her friend also aboard ship. Had she, too, been kidnapped? Was the captain taking his pleasure with Jasmine while he waited for her to calm down? For three days she had thrown a continuous tantrum. No one had dared come to the door of the cabin, with the exception of a silent, burly seaman who had quickly shoved a tray of food inside three times a day. She had seen no one and spoken to no one. Till now she hadn't realized how desperate she was for human companionship. "It seems our captain takes what he will, no matter who might object."

"He kidnapped you?" Jasmine asked, aghast at the thought, but she knew the truth of it the moment the words were spoken. No one but the captain would have dared. No one but the captain held the power of life or death over those aboard his ship. "Why?"

Deborah shrugged, knowing very well why, but was loath to speak of such intimacies.

"Has he asked for a ransom?"

Deborah could only shake her head.

"Has he said when he'd let you go?"

Again came a negative reply.

The two women were freed from their cabins for the first time since boarding. Neither was quite able to believe they were not completely alone in this bizarre happening. Together they moved to the wooden crate Jasmine had just vacated. "Lord, this is a mess, isn't it?"

Moments later both knew the plight of the other, a fact that went far toward lifting both their spirits and made them feel not so very alone.

Jasmine could only imagine the fright Deborah must have suffered and her heart went out to her friend. But after a moment's conversation, she realized her concern misplaced. This was no ordinary kidnapping. There was something between the captain and his very lovely captive. A very definite light of anticipation shone in Deborah's eyes every time his name was mentioned. Jasmine relaxed in her worry, knowing instinctively that Joseph, no matter his high-handed actions, might very well come out the loser in this contest of wills.

The women turned at the sudden sound of the heavy anchor splashing into the water. Jasmine felt her heart flutter with something like excitement, for she hadn't a doubt that her meeting with Anthony was close at hand. How would he act? How would she?

Indeed she hadn't long to wait before she'd find out. A boat was lowered into the water and, after their quick, teary goodbye, Jasmine was helped over the side of the ship.

Silently Deborah waved to her friend from the deck. For just an instant Jasmine read her friend's expression. Suddenly her brow quirked with laughter, and she almost felt sorry for her newfound brother-in-law, knowing he would most assuredly get his just deserts.

Joseph's whistle was answered by a familiar deep chuckle, a chuckle that brought a shiver down Jasmine's spine. For a moment she tried to understand her reaction to the sound. Was it revulsion? Fear? Jasmine couldn't be sure. All she knew was her heart was pounding and her breathing grew strangely inadequate, causing her to suffer a sense of dizziness. A moment later Anthony stepped from the dark foliage that lined the shore.

"You make too much noise. Hush, for the redcoats regularly patrol this area!"

"What would redcoats want with a bird?"

"What bird?"

"The one I was imitating."

Anthony gave a strangled laugh. "You'd best be practicing if that godawful sound was meant to be a bird."

The two men were laughing as they embraced, each slapping the other on the back, while Jasmine's gaze narrowed with rage. She denied the hunger for the sight of him that squeezed at her chest. She hated him as she never hated before.

Silently she watched their embrace. In truth, she never knew which Anthony to expect. Certainly not the arrogant stablehand she had first known, but that was whom he most resembled now. Jasmine's heart fluttered in her chest. He was tanned to a deep bronze, while his hair had grown longer and was now liberally laced with blond streaks. He seemed taller, brawnier than since she'd last seen him. His teeth flashed white when he smiled. Tiny laugh lines crinkled at the corners of his clear blue eyes.

Her husband had never looked more handsome to her, Jasmine thought as she listened to the conversation between the two brothers.

"What in hell took you so long?" Anthony asked.

"I might ask the same of you. Jesus, I was about done in from New York's society. I'll take a good battle any day over one of those polite afternoon teas."

Anthony grinned imagining his impatient brother being forced into polite conversation and shrugged a shoulder. "I was with Sullivan up north routing out the tribes."

Joseph grinned, knowing the uselessness of that particular mission, since all five nations, with John Burke as their leader, were now safely in Canada and the Indians, in league with the British, had wreaked havoc upon the farmers in western New York and Pennsylvania.

"I imagine you heard of the mess that turned out to be." He sighed wearily and rubbed a hand over his face. His voice was filled with disgust. "All we accomplished was to destroy their towns." His voice was heavy with sarcasm. "No doubt that will make them even more fond of us."

"I see you brought *her*," Anthony remarked almost

220

offhandedly as he glanced, apparently for the first time, toward his silently fuming wife. Jasmine was not used to being ignored and that seemed to be exactly what this oaf was doing.

Were it anyone else but his brother Joseph would have imagined Anthony had just noticed her presence, but Joseph knew his brother was keenly aware of her and that his behavior toward his wife was clearly with purpose.

Anthony had watched her from the moment she had scrambled over the side of the ship, his heart pounding with excitement as she approached the shore. God but she was beautiful. He'd almost forgotten just how lovely. Her black hair, freed from her straw bonnet had lost its pins and flowed gently behind her in the breeze. Her eyes glittered a devastating silver in her silent anger. He couldn't wait to hold her again and had a time of it concentrating on the conversation with his brother, so desperately did he long to turn to her and devour her loveliness with eyes, hands, and mouth.

He was finding it a test of will to simply refrain from touching her. He could feel the need rushing through his body.

The two men quickly embraced, knowing the danger to his ship should they prolong this meeting. They each wished the other safety till their next meeting.

Joseph grinned at Anthony's matter-of-fact order to his wife. "Let's go," he commanded, turning his back and heading toward the safety of the forest.

Jasmine was beside herself with rage. Over the last week she had often wondered on his welcome, but she never expected him to ignore her. No, even her wild imaginings hadn't come close to this.

Her eyes spit fire and rebellion. If he thought he could simply wave a finger or issue an order and have her obey, the man was in for the shock of his life.

221

Jasmine stood her ground.

Anthony realized immediately, of course, that Jasmine had ignored his easily spoken order. He had agonized long and hard over how he should greet his wife, considering the dramatic circumstances at their parting, and even as he watched her walk up the sandy shore, he had yet to find the right method. Obviously, the one he had chosen had been less than effective, for she was ignoring him and it was clear that no amount of orders was going to do a damn bit of good. Anthony sighed, wondering how to bring about her acquiescence with as little fuss as possible but he could think of nothing. He hadn't a doubt of her anger, but it wasn't anger he wanted from this woman, and he didn't have an inkling as to how to go about bringing a smile to those lovely lips. Finally he simply reached for her hand and none too gently pulled her along.

"Where do you think you're taking me?"

Anthony grinned down into eyes gone pewter with rage. Her bonnet had fallen to her back, held there by silk pink ribbons at her throat. Ribbons that matched perfectly her low-cut dress, and tendrils of midnight curls were stirred by a gentle breeze against her angrily flushed cheeks.

Lord but she was a lovely creature. Countless were the nights he had lain upon his pallet swearing her beauty with only his imagination. But he knew that wasn't true. She was, if possible, even more beautiful than he'd remembered. A never-ending ache grew to alarming strength in the pit of his belly. God, he could hardly wait for tonight and the chance to get her into his bed.

And for Jasmine, it was all suddenly too much for her to bear—his deceit, his disappearance, the despondency she'd known these last months. Without thinking, her hand suddenly flung out and contacted with a sharp slap to his cheek. Unfortunately that action brought not the slightest relief to her, but rather it merely opened the floodgates of violence and, to her astonishment, she found herself striking him again and yet again.

Anthony had a time of wrestling her hands to her sides. Jasmine muttered a curse of pure frustration to find her arms bound tightly behind her by his one hand. Wordlessly she glared at his satisfied expression. "Happy to see me, I take it?" He grinned at her ferocious growl. His eyes twinkled with delight and then closed momentarily with pleasure as he yanked her closer. "In a bit of a temper, are we?" he teased unmercifully, holding her tightly to him, his hips moving suggestively against her. "But I have the remedy for what ails," he whispered as his mouth lowered to lips parted with incredulity.

Just before his mouth touched to hers, she turned her head away. His lips brushed her cheek. She could feel the laughter in his chest. "If you think it will be that easy . . ."

"Sweetheart, nothing's been easy since the first day I saw you in the barn.

"But there's one thing I know . . ."

"Good grief, you mean you know something?" she interrupted snidely. "Which one thing is it?"

Anthony chuckled at her sarcasm. "I know you're a sucker for my kisses."

"Bastard!" And she would have hit him again had not her hands been held secure.

He laughed. "And you like what comes after as well."

"Do I," she asked, her mouth tightening and her eyes glaring her rage. With all the control she could muster, Jasmine smiled, "I wonder what damage it might cause to that overinflated ego of yours if I told you I only behaved as I did for the information you so willingly supplied? I hated every minute of it."

Anthony laughed again. "That might have been

223

the excuse you used to appease your guilty conscience, but it isn't true, is it?"

"It most definitely is."

"Is it?" he asked as he yanked her tighter to his chest, bringing every part of her body into contact with his, his eyes widening with supposed innocence. "You mean you hated it when I touched you here?"

Jasmine gasped as his palm covered her breast, his finger flicking back and forth over the tip.

He smiled and silently applauded her determination when she whispered in only a slightly breathless tone, "I did."

"Then you must have despised this," he said as he dragged her toward the privacy of the woods and lifted her skirt to cup her sex.

"Anthony," she warned, trying desperately to break free of his hold. Her voice broke as sensation flooded her body. "Stop it this minute!"

"You haven't answered me." He was grinning as he moved his hand over her warmth. He could feel the dampness, the heat, and almost gave in to the urge that had allowed not a night without torture since he'd last seen her. She could deny her feelings till it snowed in hell, but her body wasn't lying.

Jasmine closed her eyes, determined to hold out against this deliberate taunting of her senses, but when his fingers purposely grazed the sensitive spot of her passion, she trembled and gasped. His mouth was ready for that reaction and her deep breath only took into her lungs his manly scent and brought almost instantly to her mind the most delicious lethargy. Against her will she felt her body begin to relax against his.

A soft murmur broke from her throat as his tongue dipped deep into her warmth and rediscovered her taste, her scent, her texture.

"Oh, God, I've missed you, too," he groaned as his mouth tore itself from hers to hungrily run over her

224

arched throat, her jaw, and again take her mouth with an intensity equal to nothing either had ever known.

Jasmine moaned, unable to fight the daze of passion he could so easily instill. His hand moved to her waist and slid beneath her frilly drawers. Instinctively she pressed her hips up and forward, hungry for the feel of his hand against her. She wanted to cry out her despair, for she knew she needed this more than food, drink, even air. His touch, his kiss were the necessary ingredients to sustain life.

What did he mean missed her, too? came a whispery voice from the far recesses of her mind. Desperately she struggled to free herself of this fog of desire. Silently she swore the lie. She didn't miss him. She'd never missed him. In her whole life she had never been happier than when he had gone. And she certainly would have told him just that if only he would free her mouth from his wonderfully drugging kiss.

Jasmine found herself suddenly free of his hold as well as his kiss, his hands held her at her waist as he leaned his forehead against hers and whispered, "Someone is coming."

"Oh, so the missus finally arrived, Captain?" came a voice tinged with mirth.

"We were just saying hello, Boggs. I'll be back shortly."

"Of course, sir," the man returned.

Jasmine gave a low, anguished moan. Her cheeks flamed. She was positive he had seen Anthony's hand up her skirt. Lord, how was she to ever face the man again?

"Don't worry of it, sweetheart. Boggs has been married for years. He knows the way of things between a man and his wife."

"Oh, God," she muttered as he, with his arm at her

waist, guided her to the rebel encampment.

Jasmine railed at his daring. How dare he? How dare he treat her like this? How could he calmly take her in his arms and kiss her, very nearly make love to her, as if nothing were amiss? As if they hadn't parted enemies. As if he'd never deceived. As if he'd never sorely abused her trust.

Jasmine's eyes widened with surprise at what could only laughingly be called an encampment. There were perhaps some dozen or so battered two-man tents set in a half-circle around three fires. Jasmine screwed up her nose as she noticed the men who apparently occupied these tiny enclosures. They were gathered about in small groups talking in easy camaraderie while they saw to the care of their weapons. Jasmine's mouth gaped open, for they were easily the dirtiest, most ragtag group of misfits she had ever seen. Bearded faces held tired eyes that smiled with unabashed appreciation as they glanced her way. Hair that had escaped its ties hung dirty and unkempt around their faces. Their clothes were ripped and filthy, so much so in some cases that Jasmine could only breathe a silent prayer of thanks that she stood no closer.

To one side stood a group of five young women, dirtier, if possible, than the men. Bedraggled and uncombed, they stirred huge pots over open fires.

"Take that look off your face," Anthony ordered. "I won't have you looking down on these men. In a week, perhaps less, you'll look very much like the rest."

Jasmine laughed, a short sound of false bravado. "No doubt I would, were I to stay."

"And you don't think that to be the case?"

"Not likely." Jasmine eyed the women with particular distaste, wondering which of them had given comfort to her husband at night. Oddly enough, the thought brought a measure of discomfort to her chest. Determinedly she pushed aside the picture of Anthony in the arms of another woman. What did she care, after all? To be sure, she didn't want him and it mattered not how many women warmed his bed, as long as she wasn't one of them. "I have no intention of becoming a camp follower."

"Intentions aside, that is what you are."

"It will hardly be worth the effort, Anthony," she warned, "for I shall run at every opportunity."

"Where?"

She shrugged. "It matters not."

"You have no experience, Jasmine. You'd never survive the woods without assistance. And even if the impossible happened and you did survive, do you think it likely one of your own will come to the rescue?" He shook his head. "Think again, wife, for they will surely abuse you, having gone so long without."

She shrugged again, having every intention of escaping him, no matter the fear he tried to instill. She didn't believe him in any case. No English soldier would mistreat a lady, on that she would wager her life.

Anthony breathed a long sigh at the determined tilting of her jaw and the defiance that shone in her eyes. "I see my warnings matter not in the least." There was a long moment before he spoke again. "That leaves me with a bit of a problem. How would you handle this, were our positions exchanged?"

Jasmine smiled. "I'd bring myself to the first town we came across and hire the necessary means to see me home."

Anthony chuckled. "A coach perhaps?"

Jasmine shrugged. "Perhaps."

"Sweetheart, we are days from a settlement.

227

Perhaps a month from one with such a convenience."

Jasmine gasped. "I don't believe you."

It was Anthony's turn to shrug. His voice was indifferent as he spoke. "You will, of course, believe what you must. In the meantime, I expect you to hold down your share of the work. You will see to my meals and take care of my tent and clothes."

Jasmine laughed. "Get one of your women to do it, for I shall not lift a finger."

Anthony took her by the arm and directed her toward his tent. With a shove, she was inside. "I have no woman here but for you. And if you will not work, you will not eat."

"Fine," she snapped as she spun around to face him. Her hands were on her hips as she silently dared him to do his worst.

Anthony ignored her sneer. "You might start with my clothes. This pile needs washing," he said as he bent to the ground to retrieve the clothing in question and shoved it in her direction.

And a moment later it was thrown every which way, a few pieces landing over the small table he used as a desk, others littering the floor and bed. Anthony answered her defiant gesture with only the slightest of nods. "After you're done, you eat."

Chapter Thirteen

Jasmine could not remember a time when she was so consumed with fury. Openmouthed with amazement she had watched him stalk from the tent. She knew he had to have heard the crash of the table as it hit the floor, but he ignored the sound and the subsequent curses that trailed after him.

The blinding fury had finally run its course, but not before the tent was in a shambles. Not even his trunk, nor the papers, clothes, boots, and shaving apparel inside had escaped her fury.

Jasmine sank wearily to her knees. There was no place to sit, for she had upened his cot and smashed the small stool repeatedly upon the ground until one of the legs had finally broken off. She eyed the cot with some longing, but pushed aside the need to lie down. She wouldn't give him the satisfaction of being in his bed—for any reason.

Lord, had there ever been a man so easy to hate?

Jasmine sighed with despair and shuddered at the trick fate had played. Tears of self-pity misted her eyes. How was she to survive this? She hated him with every ounce of her strength. Never would she submit to his arrogance. Never would she act his servant. She didn't care if she starved to death, for death was preferable to his offhanded use of her. She was a lady, not a servant, and it would serve him well to remember that!

Jasmine glanced around at the chaos she had caused the small tent and shrugged. Let him have one of his women clean it up, for she'd die before she'd lift a finger.

It grew dark, but Jasmine remained firmly in place. She'd not stir. She'd not move a muscle. We'll see, she mused in cold silent fury, just who would win out.

She was asleep by the time he returned. Anthony shook his head and sighed as he lifted his lantern over his head and surveyed the inside of his tent. Lord but the woman had a temper. Vaguely he wondered if he was equal to the strength of it. Which one of them would be the first to give in?

Anthony straightened his cot and covered it once again with blankets. For just a second he was tempted to let her remain where she lay but instantly thought better of the notion. No, whether she liked it or not, this woman was his wife and, as such, would share his bed. Besides, he wouldn't chance the chill she might take lying the night on a dirt floor.

Anthony stripped down to his bare skin, pulled back the blankets, and retrieved his wife. Jasmine, exhausted from weeks of mental anguish and more than half asleep, offered no objection as he removed her clothes and installed her within the comfortable, if narrow confines of the cot. He sighed with pleasure as he cuddled her close to him. Lord but it had been so long. His body ached to take her, but he held back, knowing how tired she no doubt was. No, when he took her he wanted all her senses about her. He wanted to feel again her passionate responses. He wanted to make love, not simply relieve this almost debilitating need.

Jasmine had no recollection of his removing her clothes. Even after she awoke the next morning to find him searching through the mess at his feet for a fresh shirt, she had yet to realize her nakedness. She blinked in confusion, unable at first to comprehend what she was seeing. Finally she remembered where she was and sat up, never realizing the blanket had fallen to her waist to reveal lush, womanly curves.

Anthony noticed the movement and straightened as much as he could. The roof of the tent obviously preventing him from reaching his full height, he stood, hands on hips, and grinned down at her. His body tightened at the sight of warmly flushed, naked skin. "I hope you're satisfied. Now I can't find a clean shirt."

"A shame," she returned, her voice dripping sarcasm as she pulled the blanket up to conceal her nakedness. She hadn't missed the direction of his gaze.

"Indeed," he concurred. "It's going to take you hours to straighten this mess."

Jasmine laughed as she lay down again. "It probably would if I were to clean it. But since I've no intention . . ." She let her voice falter and shrugged.

"You'd best have every intention, Jasmine. I imagine you're getting a bit hungry by now."

"Not in the least," she lied, for she was ravenous after missing yesterday's midday and evening meals.

"We'll see," he remarked as he found a shirt, slid it on, and began to work the ties at the neck closed. Whether it was clean or not, Jasmine couldn't say, nor did she care. Turning her back to him, she pretended to fall back asleep.

Suddenly the blanket was torn from her. Jasmine gave a short shriek of surprise just before finding herself flipped to her back and Anthony lying full length upon her.

Anthony grinned at her surprise. "You might think to win this point, wife, but you will not. Your hunger will grow each day while your strength lessens. Have you a prayer of escaping me in a weakened state? Will you not need all your wits and strength to carry out the plan I know to be uppermost in your mind?''

Jasmine flushed guiltily. Did he know her so well, or was he merely guessing at her thoughts? It mattered little, she supposed, for even though he had reasoned correctly her state of mind, he'd never know when or how she'd pull off this scheme. In truth, no clear plan had as yet come to mind.

If she had the power to reason coolly, she'd have realized he was right. But she couldn't reason right now. Right now she was filled to overflowing with seething anger. And if she suffered due to her own stubbornness, so be it.

Anthony sighed as he watched the workings of her mind play out in her expressive eyes and the further tightening of her lips. She wouldn't be giving in, not yet. Idly he wondered how long he'd be forced to wait.

His lips brushed against hers and Jasmine gasped, not expecting the sudden touch of them, for her mind had been on plans of escape and revenge. He pulled back and smiled ever so slightly, and again his head dipped and his mouth brushed hers.

He didn't kiss her exactly, but Jasmine's heart thundered nevertheless. The touch of his lips was like a jolt of tingling sensation speeding throughout her body. Lord but his lips were soft. Her mind swam. Pliable and sweet, they moved back and forth, shaping, reshaping, teasing with only the merest of touch.

Jasmine felt the moan come to her throat, but managed in time to force back the sound. No, he might be practiced in this art of sensuality, a master, to be sure, but she was determined his kiss would bring about no reaction.

It was easy enough to swear to her stubborn

thoughts, but Jasmine soon had a time of it remembering exactly what those thoughts were. She felt the tingling to her toes, and her lips parted, forgetting completely her sworn lack of response, suddenly eager for a continuation of this bliss. The tip of his tongue ran over the pliable surface of her mouth and then the softer more sensitive area just inside her lips. Her breathing grew erratic. God but this felt delicious. She wanted more. Much much more. Unconsciously her hips arched into his and she allowed the groan at last. Her arms circled his neck and she pulled his mouth more firmly to hers.

Suddenly it was she who was kissing, she who demanded. She cried in delight as his hands slid down the length of her, shuddered and groaned when he sought out her warmth, strained against his moving fingers. And at last it was she who whimpered as his fingers brought her to mindless ecstasy.

"I'll be back before the midday meal" came his ragged whisper. Jasmine purred like a kitten and curved into his body, never hearing his words. "See that your work is finished by then." She blinked with astonishment as he moved away. Suddenly he was gone.

Jasmine came to her feet, her lips curved in a sneer. Without thinking, she did the first thing that came to mind—kicked at the clothes that littered the floor, remembering too late this particular pile covered the overturned table! She almost howled as blinding pain shot straight up her leg to momentarily wash away every other thought in her mind. She gasped and took deep, steadying breaths, forcing aside the need to cry out.

Damn him! Damn him! Lord, how she hated the beast. "I'll give him finished work," she muttered, and then vowed, "And I'll finish him along with it."

Jasmine had every intention of escaping this madman she had so foolishly married, but not before she did the swine in. Lord but he was going to pay for his callous abuse. She'd make him worry. She'd make him curse the day he'd thought to bring her here.

Jasmine's body tensed, but she refused to look in his direction as he entered and gave a long-suffering sigh upon spying the condition of the tent to be no better than when he had left. No doubt the noonday sun was at its zenith, for the heat that filled the tent was suffocating. Perspiration caused her hair to stick uncomfortably to her neck and dampened her gown. Still, she sat silent and determined among the strewn articles of clothing that covered the floor.

She knew he was watching her. She could almost feel his gaze upon her, but forced aside the shiver that threatened. She wouldn't show him a moment's weakness. If he thought he'd win simply because she suffered a bit of discomfort, well, the beast could think again.

What in hell was he to do? Anthony suddenly felt both the woman and the situation beyond his control. Why had he believed his wife would give in to his demands? Hadn't he long ago realized her stubbornness? Hadn't he known she was no woman to cower before a stronger foe?

How in hell had he got himself into such a hopeless situation? Even if she eventually gave in to his demands, how could he claim victory? Anyone would grow manageable if starved into it. And if she grew ill? He almost groaned at the terror of the thought.

Anthony gave another long sigh, knowing no matter the pain suffered, he'd not back down from her anger, for to do so would only convince her of his weakness. More important than power in this stance, she had to know she was his wife and, despite her wishes to the contrary, always would be.

234

She sat in profile, her eyes straight ahead. Midnight curls fell loose about her shoulders and down her back to her hips. The silence stretched on as Anthony strove for control against his body's almost instant reaction to hers. Just one look could bring back with vivid clarity the softness of that now rigid body, the scent, the taste. His lips tightened as he forced aside the aching need for her.

"Hungry?" he finally asked, thankful that she kept her gaze upon the wall of the tent, for he had yet to gain complete control and she needed not this added weapon to use against him.

"Not very."

"Thirsty?"

Jasmine lifted a slender shoulder in an unconcerned shrug.

"Jasmine, no matter your denials, I know you must hunger and thirst. There is no need for you to suffer like this. You need only . . ."

"Rid myself of a certain man?" she asked, the jeering in her voice not to be denied.

"The trouble with you, my sweet, is you are too accustomed to having your own spoiled way."

Jasmine came to her feet, her hands and fists at her hips as she snarled her contempt. "The only trouble with me, *my sweet,* is *you!*"

Three days. How much longer was she to suffer before the beast let her out? Granted, she had been brought food and drink, but she was kept a prisoner in this tent. She couldn't take much more of this solitude. What was she going to do? The action she had chosen was getting her exactly nowhere, for Anthony had proven himself at least as stubborn as she.

They hadn't spoken since her first day here. When he came to the tent, he studiously ignored her as she had him. It was only at night that he spoke. When she was deep in sleep, he would join her in bed. Then she heard his whispers, felt his gentle caresses. He did not try to make love to her although he had every opportunity, for she would have offered no objection while half asleep. Idly she wondered if this action only led to further confusion on her part. She couldn't decide if she was angry, or happy that he had not pressed his advantage.

Jasmine shook her head as she tried to free herself of these unwanted thoughts. She had to do something. She had to get out of the tent. Jasmine laughed as the plan of sweet revenge took hold. Her eyes glittered as she took in the disarray. Oh, she'd straighten up this mess all right. And the minute she was finished, she'd gleefully burn the whole damn thing to the ground.

Jasmine waited for the sound of his footsteps and smiled when she heard the soft shuffle of his boots scrape upon the ground just outside. The flap of the tent opened, and he entered.

"Very nice," he said as a smile played at the corners of his mouth. His eyes warmed with appreciation and clung to hers. Anthony breathed a great sigh of relief to find her smiling. She had every right to be furious. And he had felt no little measure of guilt at his abuse. She was his wife and had every reason to expect him to treat her with due respect. The problem was, he didn't know how to treat her.

He had never sought to completely control this woman. He loved her spirit, her fire. He'd come ready to make a truce, to offer her anything just so she might smile again—anything but her freedom! Now he thought better of the notion. If she had forgiven him his ghastly treatment, he wouldn't be foolish enough to remind her.

"Would you like to go for a walk before supper?" he asked gently, so gently, in fact, that Jasmine felt a moment's remorse for what she was about to do.

"I've just one more thing to do," she answered, brightly turning her back to him, determined to fight against this weakness he so easily brought to surface in her. Quickly she opened the glass that shielded the candle's flame and slid a folded piece of paper inside. A moment later she flung the now burning paper to a small mound of crumbled papers, clothes, and melted tallow that she had earlier prepared.

There was a soft puff of sound as the mound caught fire. Jasmine grinned with relish. In a second the whole side of the tent would be in flames. She turned to face her flabbergasted husband and smiled sweetly. "I'm ready now."

Anthony cursed, lunged forward, and shoved her out of the tent. Jasmine wanted to laugh at the rage he was sure to feel, rage that might even grow to equal hers. Only she didn't laugh because she suddenly realized she was outside the tent alone.

Anthony was still inside!

"Nooo!" she screamed as she sped back inside, heedless of the danger. Without thinking, she took a quick breath and began to choke, for the tent was already filled with black smoke. She couldn't see him through the density of it and couldn't hear him as the roar of flames grew to cover any sound.

"Anthony!" she screamed. "Anthony," she cried amid harsh, choking sobs as she searched, blinded by tears and smoke, for his tall form.

Hard arms circled her waist and dragged her back, pulling her from the almost instant inferno. Jasmine fought against it, but was powerless against this mightier strength. "No! He's inside! Get him out!"

"I'm here" came the shaken reply.

But Jasmine was wild with fear for him and never heard Anthony's words. She didn't even know it was he who held her.

She was sobbing in earnest now as she beat against

237

a solid chest. "Get him out. Please get him out."

"I'm here, sweetheart," he said again, this time caressing her back with hands that had yet to begin to hurt. He never felt the pain. All he could hear were her cries. His heart soared with pleasure at her desperate pleading, for he knew she felt more for him than she had thus far admitted, perhaps even to herself.

Jasmine was sobbing into his chest as his softly spoken words penetrated her consciousness at last. She gasped and looked up to a tender smile.

Suddenly she pushed herself out of his reach and glared. Forgotten was her fear for his safety. How dare he smile his disgustingly smug all too male smile? How dare he laugh at her suffering? "How did you get out?"

"The same way you did." He nodded toward the tent that was now totally engulfed with flames. His mouth tightened with annoyance. "A neat trick. First you clean it, then you burn it. Why?"

"You told me to clean it."

Anthony shook his head and forced aside the smile that threatened. She had done it to spite him, of course, not to cause him loss of possessions. There was nothing inside that could not easily be replaced. He had grabbed at his maps and was making his way to the tent's opening when he had nearly stumbled over her. His mouth tightened as he realized he could esaily have missed her in the smoke. By rights he should beat her for her defiance. Because of her rash actions either of them could now be dead, or at the very least seriously injured.

Anthony breathed a long, calming sigh and reminded himself they were safe. He couldn't stop the rush of relief that filled him and was incapable of mustering the anger he needed to cower this woman into place.

"You all right, Captain?" asked one of his men as they came to a running stop at his side.

"Fine, Cooper. You think you might come up with some ointment. I'm afraid my hands . . ."

He left the sentence unfinished as Jasmine gasped and then spied his blackened palms. "Your hands! My God, Anthony! Look at your hands."

Another tent was found, from where Jasmine couldn't imagine. A cot, blankets, and spare clothes were gathered for the captain's use. Jasmine sat at his side as he dozed upon a cot. Wracked with guilt she lowered her eyes in silent contrition. Why had she done it? Oh, Lord, but she was sorry to have brought this man such pain. In her anger she'd wanted nothing more than to see him suffer, but now, in the aftermath of fury, she was aghast at what she'd done.

The worst of it, of course, was his treatment of her. His kindness only led to her further self-abuse. Why hadn't he railed at her idiocy? Why hadn't he ordered some suitable punishment?

Jasmine breathed an audible sigh. It was time, past time to put aside her willful ways and listen to the advice her mother had given. It was time to grow up. This man, whoever or whatever he might be, was her husband. It was time to reconcile herself to the fact, lest disaster result.

It mattered not his actions, nor her sworn hatred of the man. She was his wife and no amount of childish trantrums would change that fact.

Jasmine was besieged with the glaring truth that she had wanted him, had longed for his touch, had suffered the agonies of hell while secretly praying he'd come for her. And when he had brought her to his side, what had she done? She had acted the fool. She couldn't explain or understand her actions. All she knew was she'd never forgive herself if she'd crippled him for life.

Damn him! Why had he shoved her out only to run

back? Were maps not replaceable? Why had he not thought of his safety? Jasmine shivered as she realized how close each of them had come to death today.

"Are you cold?"

Guilty eyes rose to his tender gaze. "No. Are you feeling better?"

"I'm afraid not. My hands hurt like the devil."

Jasmine nodded. "Mr. Boggs left this for you when you awoke."

Anthony glanced at the pewter tankard, suspecting correctly its laudanum-laced contents, and shook his head. "I cannot remain in a drugged state. There are things that must be done."

Jasmine nodded as she lifted his head from the pillow and pressed the cool lip of the tankard to his mouth. "All in due time. You won't be much help to the men in your present state."

Anthony choked down the bitter brew. "Where are my men?"

"Gone on patrol. They'll be back shortly."

Anthony nodded as the strong dose quickly began to ease his throbbing fingers. "Awaken me when they return."

His hands were stiff, but the injury was not likely to leave any lasting damage, barring a scar or two. The swelling had lessened as had the throbbing. Already he was able to flex his fingers without a groan of pain escaping.

Anthony's eyes widened with a touch of surprise as Jasmine entered the tent. She'd had every opportunity to make good her escape during this last week and yet she had rarely left his side.

Countless were the times he had awakened to find her at his side, sometimes offering him liquids, sometimes draping cooling rags over his feverish

240

forehead. Always there, always eager to bring comfort. Idly he wondered if she was of a mind to ease one particular form of discomfort that had suddenly come to plague. He repositioned himself in an effort to hide the damning evidence.

Jasmine smiled as their eyes met. "No moaning this morning?" She nodded as she spoke, her voice gaining in cheer with every word. She put aside the tray she held and placed a cool hand on his forehead. She smiled again, for his fever had broken last night and had not returned.

"What have you got there?" he asked, his gaze moving to the tray resting upon a small chair at the side of the bed. "No more laudanum."

She smiled. "No more. I've brought you a feast fit for a king." And at his puzzled frown she went on. "A pot of tea, a slab of ham, and fresh bread with a huge glob of butter."

"Butter?" he asked in amazement.

Jasmine raised suspicious eyes as she went on to explain. "It appears the Widow Frame, whose farm you recently visited, found out about your injury. She seemed a mite upset, more so since your wife has joined you and you will not be seeing her again."

Anthony grinned. "Who told her I won't?"

Jasmine shrugged, her cheeks gaining in color as she remembered her cool confrontation with the lovely woman. "Will you?"

"Nothing happened, Jasmine," he said gently.

She studied his steady gaze for a long moment before she dared to breathe a sigh of relief. "Through no fault of the lady, I take it?"

Anthony shrugged, unwilling to lay blame at the pretty widow's feet. It was not in him to judge. He well knew and sympathized with the lady's loneliness. Idly he wondered if he would have taken her up on her discreet offer had he not been anticipating Jasmine's arrival. Would his wife's beautiful face have come between them to mar a stolen moment of pleasure? Anthony gave a mental shrug, happy now he had not put the temptation to test. "I stopped there but once to buy supplies. I was not alone."

Jasmine grinned as she placed a napkin beneath his chin. Her heart filled with unexplained joy. She hadn't expected him to declare his innocence, for she knew the ways of men and realized her husband might dally with a comely woman, which she knew the widow to be, when given the chance, especially in times of war. The idea did not sit well, still she believed a woman would be a fool indeed to expect faithfulness from a man. "Once, hmm? You do leave lasting impressions, sir."

"Once," he repeated, for some reason feeling it imperative she believe him.

And she did.

He ate hungrily, but since he hadn't had solid food in a week, he was unable to eat more than half of what she'd prepared. "You'll wither away with such a paltry amount."

Anthony smiled. "No doubt my appetite will increase in time."

"More tea?"

He shook his head.

"Can I get you anything else?"

"I've a need to use the chamber pot."

Jasmine turned beet red and then silently cursed her squeamishness. What had she expected? Of course he'd feel such a need. She had helped him when in the throes of fever. Why was this moment so different? Determinedly she put aside her embarrassment. "You'll need help."

Anthony looked at his bandaged hands and gave the slightest of shrugs, unable to hide his grin. "Get me to my feet."

Jasmine did as he asked, trying desperately to ignore the fact that he was stark naked. His arm rested along her shoulders as they managed the few steps to the corner of the tent.

Her face flamed as they reached their destination. She was terrified he was going to ask more of her, so terrified, in fact, that she never noticed she spoke aloud her fear. "Don't ask me to hold it."

Anthony's eyes widened at her pained expression. He chuckled. "The idea is deserving of some merit, but I doubt I'll be able to do what needs to be done if you offer further assistance."

Jasmine groaned and reddened further still as she realized he had answered what she had imagined to be only a thought. It seemed to take forever, but he was finally finished with his chore and wobbling back to his bed.

"It's that damn drug you've been feeding me," he groaned as he collapsed upon the cot. "I haven't the strength of a kitten."

"You needed the laudanum. You'll regain your strength soon enough," she said as she covered him again.

"I want a bath. I smell like a dead skunk. Have one of the men bring in a barrel."

"The men aren't here. I'll get it."

"No, it's too heavy for you. Get me a bowl of water and I'll . . ." Anthony cursed in frustration as he remembered and glanced down at his hands.

Jasmine left his side only to return moments later with a bowl of warm water, a bar of yellow soap, and pieces of toweling.

Anthony gave a silent groan when he saw her reenter the tent, for he hadn't a doubt as to the suffering that awaited him.

243

Chapter Fourteen

For the next three days, Jasmine continued on in blissful ignorance to her husband's suffering. She bore his ill humor with gentle patience, filled as she was with a goodly measure of guilt, and attributed his grumpy state to the pain he was no doubt experiencing. In that case, she was quite correct, for Anthony was indeed consumed with pain, but of an entirely different nature than she supposed.

Her days began at dawn when the low sounds of early morning camp brought her from Anthony's side. Snubbed from the first by the slovenly camp followers, she was grateful today to find they, all five, slept late. After last night she wasn't eager to see their grinning faces.

Jasmine, who, not that long ago, would have turned up her nose at these women, was amazed at the charity she had not before suspected she possessed. Where once she would have judged them, she realized now what they did was clearly their own business. Even the obvious fact that they weren't at all particular about whose bed they shared, on any given night, did not rankle. What *did*, however, was their blatant interest in her husband.

Jasmine found her temper severely stretched to the limit to find all five of them crowded into her tent early last night—and even worse, was her husband's obvious appreciation of their company.

He was smiling at something one of them said, his blue eyes twinkling in a darkly tanned face when she entered. Two women were seated on the cot, one on each side, the other three hovering close by, and Jasmine had felt an unreasonable urge toward violence at the sight. The urge did not lessen in any measurable degree as the night slowly progressed.

It took some doing, but she finally managed to clear the tent of what was, for her at least, unwanted company by professing the lateness of the hour. After one withering glance, Jasmine refused to look again at her husband's grinning face. She should have known he would be grinning. Damn the man! She wouldn't have been surprised to find him sprouting feathers and prancing around this tent like a damned peacock, so proud was he of his conquests.

At her prolonged silence, Anthony asked, "Is something wrong?"

Jasmine's eyes narrowed at the humor he only barely managed to suppress. The last thing this beast needed was more reason to gloat. She turned her back to him and began to undress. "Not a thing."

In her rage Jasmine forgot her husband lay but a few feet from her as she readied herself for bed. She had done as much every night for more than a week, only she had done it in the dark, and usually while Anthony slept.

Anthony nearly strangled on his breath as he watched her carelessly discard her clothing. His voice was tight with the throbbing need that suddenly filled his being at the sight of her naked back. Lord but he ached to see her turn and walk to him, her arms open with invitation. "Are you sure? You seem a mite upset."

"Do I? Perhaps that's because I'm trying not to do you bodily harm."

245

"Me?" he asked, his lips twitching as he feigned surprise. "What did I do?"

"Not a thing," she grunted as she grabbed a shirt and slid it over her nakedness.

But Anthony wasn't of a mind to allow silent anger. He wanted a reaction from his wife, and he'd be damned if he'd let the matter rest. "You were very quiet tonight. Did you find the evening enjoyable?"

Jasmine glared at his oh so smug grin. "Not as enjoyable as you, surely."

"Oh," he asked in all innocence, "did I give that impression?"

"Indeed, sir, you did."

"I was merely being polite."

Jasmine ground her teeth, forcing aside the urge to physically wipe the grin from his lips. Regardless of the fact that his wife was present, Anthony had flirted with every woman in attendance and he now dared to label his reprehensible actions as "merely being polite"? "Is that what you call that type of behavior? In that case, I can hardly wait to be as polite to a few of your men."

"Jasmine . . ." he began, his tone holding a note of clear warning.

"Is that why you keep them here? So you might practice the art of social niceties? Is that what you did before I came?"

"I don't keep them here. Washington doesn't forbid it. The women follow their men. How can I stop them?"

"I know well enough the practice. And I haven't asked you to stop them. You can do anything you please. Only the next time I find them in attendance, I'll not stand by like a fool and watch. I'll look for another who . . ."

"Jasmine, were I you, I wouldn't even think it."

"Wouldn't you? Unless I'm greatly mistaken, you were thinking exactly that tonight."

246

As he leaped to his feet, Anthony cursed both his foolish actions and her threat of retaliation. This had not gone the way he'd expected. Granted, he'd wanted her to feel a measure of jealousy. In truth, he'd prayed she'd feel it, for only then might he shake her from this damn cool control. Only then might he know the depths of her feelings. What he didn't want or expect was her rage and the easily issued threats that didn't bear thinking on.

"Come over here," he ordered.

Jasmine gave a sneering laugh. "Not likely. I'm not one of your doxies."

"Goddamnit! They are not mine," he insisted in a low whisper as he began to stalk her.

"Someone should tell them then, for they believe it to be so."

"I told you to come over here."

Jasmine snorted something like a laugh and warned in an unsteady voice, "Keep away from me, Anthony." Damn the man! Why did the sight of him standing there naked bring on this sudden thudding of her heart? Why did his blatant masculinity cause her only to relish the fact that she was a woman? She should have been disgusted, shocked at his careless stance. Any virtuous woman would be. But not her. Oh, no. She couldn't stop her gaze from greedily taking in his form. God but he was beautiful, tall and lean, chest wide, waist and hips narrow, he was everything she could physically want in a man.

Still, she wouldn't give in to this need. Not after tonight. Not consumed as she was with rage.

Anthony grinned as he watched her move closer to the door. He gave no indication of noticing his naked state as he stood before her. "Will you run from the tent dressed as you are?" he dared.

Jasmine looked down, her eyes widening as she realized she wore only a shirt. While it covered the necessities, it could hardly be considered proper

247

attire in which to leave the privacy of their tent.

Anthony wasted not the moment her attention was diverted but instantly closed the distance between them. His body was pressed the length of hers, his arms holding her securely against him before she had a chance to glance up.

Jasmine stiffened with surprise to find herself locked in his embrace. Silently she swore she detested the man. The last thing on earth she wanted was to be this close. "Let me go!"

Anthony chuckled at her struggles to free herself and only pressed her closer. "Be still. You're going to hurt yourself."

Jasmine glared into blue eyes warm with laughter. She opened her mouth, her intent to hurl every insult she could imagine upon his head, when his bandaged hand clutched her hair and pulled roughly at the loose, heavy mane. Jasmine stiffened further and hissed an indrawn breath at the discomfort. He ignored the sound and pulled harder, forcing her face to lift.

Blue eyes darkened to a midnight hue. A slight flush crept over lean, tanned cheeks. His nostrils flared as he fought to even his breathing. Anthony grimaced from the pain in his hand, but pushed aside the sensation as his mouth lowered purposely to hers.

He had meant to take her mouth with gentle persuasion, to savor the feel of her, the scent and taste, but the moment they touched he forgot his intentions. Mind-boggling need washed throughout his body, bringing it alive as never before and blotting out his usual care to coax her into submission. In truth, he no longer wanted submission on her part but equal aggression.

The gentle brushing of soft lips instantly became a hungry assault, a sizzling onslaught of heat Jasmine was helpless but to answer. She could feel the fever. She was melting against it as surely as if engulfed in

248

fire. Her whole being became liquid. Her legs threatened to give way. She steeled herself to keep from falling and moaned as she pressed her lower body tighter to his. His tongue slid between her teeth to explore, to rediscover her warmth, her texture, her taste.

Her hands trapped between their bodies moved to his waist, her hands boldly, hungrily they explored his naked flanks. For days she had administered to his needs. She had bathed him, fed him, but never once had she given in to the desire to linger in her touch as she'd most desperately wanted.

Jasmine heard his low groan as her fingers squeezed his bottom and slid down his thighs, only to return again to the muscled buttocks.

Anthony eased his hold and moaned against her lips, "Open the shirt."

Jasmine never thought but to obey. She had wanted this for so long—for the months after he had gone, for the days since she'd come to his camp. It mattered not the times they had previously come together, for Jasmine had not known she was making love to her own husband. She felt this moment to be new, to be the first, and in a way it was, for this was the first time they had come together as husband and wife.

His mouth was devastating to her senses, his head angled for greater access. Eagerly he sipped at the sweet nectar, greedily he took all she gave into his mouth. Time and again she forced herself to remember his request, for her fingers strayed constantly to his chest, his waist, the deliciousness of his hard, throbbing sex. Impatient, she tore at the buttons, never hearing the material rip as she strained to close the distance between them. She wanted to feel him warm and hard against her. She'd die if she didn't.

The material fell to the floor at last, and Jasmine

breathed a sigh of sheer delight as she moved eagerly into his warm embrace. She trembled as her body brushed against his. The rough hairs of his chest became an aphrodisiac to her senses and brought a moan of pleasure from deep within her throat. Her nipples hardened as she purposely rubbed against him. She breathed his scent and the world spun away. There was no thought but to experience this ecstasy, to relish this sweet torture, to hunger for more of the promise of his body.

They were lying upon the cot, she sprawled comfortably upon him, their mouths never breaking contact. For a dizzy instant Jasmine wondered how they had managed the distance, for she had no recollection of moving, but moments later she lost the thought as he, his arms under her shoulders, slid her body up the length of his.

He couldn't use his hands, but he silently implored she use her body in their stead and Jasmine felt no need to refuse this erotic delight. On her hands and knees she hovered above him. Eyes closed against the beauty of sensation, she slid herself over the length of him, barely touching, her breasts, belly, and thighs teasing his burning flesh from knees to shoulders.

She heard his choking breath, felt his trembling, and smiled as she realized the power she held over him. "You smell so good," she murmured, never knowing she'd spoken.

"Do I?" he asked, his voice tight as he sought to control the need to take her now.

"Mmm," she murmured her answer. Her tongue flicked out to increase his torment. "I've wanted to do this for so long."

"Oh, God," he groaned, his body stiffening, his loins pulsing rock hard with an ache only she could ease. Dangerously close to his limit, he nevertheless found it beyond his power to resist a further sampling of this exquisite pleasure. Her mouth left no portion of him untouched. He thought he'd surely go mad if she didn't soon bring this ecstasy to a close when she suddenly took him deep into the wet heat of her mouth.

Anthony cried out, his body tensed, his hips arched eagerly as he lay panting helplessly beneath her. "Jasmine," he choked. "Too much, stop."

But Jasmine was of a mind to further her power over this man. His wild reaction to her touch set off the deepest thrill of satisfaction to echo throughout her body. She couldn't believe her lusty enjoyment of him. Where touch had once been all she desired, it was now not enough.

Jasmine moaned her delight and then cried out her disappointment as he dragged her up his body. "No more," he choked in breathless wonder. "God, I can't take any more," he murmured as he positioned her legs on either side of his hips.

He was so hard he was near ready to burst. If she didn't take him into her body soon, it would be too late.

Mindless with equal need, Jasmine instinctively followed his lead. She raised herself on her knees and came down hard, taking his throbbing sex deep into the moist heat of her body. Their mutual cries of delight went unnoticed as the pounding of blood blotted out all sound.

Her head flung back, long, silky, ebony hair teased his thighs. Her mind went blank for feeling, and the sensation alone was almost more than she could bear. He pulled her forward and captured the tip of her swaying breast between his teeth.

They cried out in unison as he suckled and bit down. Jasmine went wild. Her nails bit into his shoulders, her hips moved frantically as he viciously brought their fevered bodies to an ecstasy neither could have imagined.

With a deep groan Jasmine crumbled upon him.

She gasped for breath, knowing the impossibility of ever moving again. Never had she felt anything to match this. Never had she imagined anything like this. Their previous encounters had been laden with guilt, a guilt that had apparently robbed her of experiencing her passion to the limit.

His chest was slick with sweat and Jasmine sighed with delight as she breathed her full and nuzzled her face into the moist, hair-covered flesh. "You smell so good," she breathed as she waited for the pounding in her chest to ease.

"Umm," he growled. "So you've said."

Jasmine's head snapped up, her eyes wide with surprise. "Did I?" she asked, not remembering. "What else did I say?"

"Only that."

Jasmine laughed with relief, for a moment terrified she might have said something more. Only she couldn't define exactly what might have so frightened her. "You taste even better," she sighed as she flicked her tongue out and took his male scent into her mouth.

"I want to touch you."

"You are touching me."

"With my hands."

Jasmine raised her silver gaze to his and bit at her lip with obvious contrition. "I'm sorry, Anthony. It was a childish thing to have done. I never thought you'd be hurt."

Anthony shrugged. "The bandages will be off in a day or so."

Jasmine sighed and relaxed against him again, her fingers idly drawing patterns in the hairs of his chest.

"Why didn't you run?"

Jasmine reacted with obvious confusion to the question. Her body stiffened and her eyes widened with shock. What had she been thinking? No greater opportunity was liable to come her way and yet she had not taken advantage of the moment. Why?

They both knew he had been incapable of stopping her should she have chosen to leave. The truth was she had forgotten. What she couldn't understand was why? To cover her own confusion she finally shrugged and laughed a low, tantalizing sound that, like her touch, sent sizzling jolts of sensation up his spine. She leaned upon her elbows and brushed the black cloud of hair from her eyes. "That wouldn't have been very sporting on my part. Wouldn't you agree?"

Anthony grinned. "Is it a game we're playing, then?"

Jasmine smiled and returned her attention to his chest. God but the man was beautiful. Tanned to a bronze tone, his chest heavily furred with golden brown hair beckoned her touch, a silent call she could not resist. "Of sorts," she murmured as she touched her mouth to him again.

Anthony swallowed his groan. He had to keep his senses about him. He had to know of her plans. "Does that mean I can expect you to run the moment I'm well again?"

In truth Jasmine couldn't say. She didn't know what she wanted. Not anymore. From the moment she had noticed his burned hands she had but one thought and that was Anthony. She tried to imagine herself gone from him. The mere thought brought a crushing loneliness and a measure of pain she wasn't at all happy to acknowledge. What had happened to her spirit? Where had her determination gone? Jasmine gave the slightest shake of her head, forcing aside the unanswerable questions. "Certainly not dressed like this," she returned with a low, delicious chuckle.

Anthony pushed aside the thrill he felt at the sound of her laughter. God but he'd give her anything if she'd simply tell him she would stay. It wouldn't do for her to know the weakness she caused, the desperation he felt to keep her near. He forced a firmness he didn't feel into his voice. "You didn't answer me."

"Didn't I?" she sighed happily.

"Jasmine, don't force me to keep you here. If I have to, I'll bind you naked to the cot every time I have to leave camp."

Jasmine's head came instantly from his chest. "You'll what?" she asked, unable to believe what he was saying after the glorious moments they'd just shared.

"You heard me."

"Damn you, Anthony," she grunted as she tried to get up, only to find his arms around her again forcing her to lie stiffly upon him.

"I want your word."

"I'll give you words enough to sizzle your ears if you don't let me go."

"I want your promise."

"I promise to see you in hell before I give in to such threats."

Anthony grunted. No doubt he was on his way, especially with a wife who wouldn't grant him a moment's peace of mind. It took some effort, but he finally managed to reverse their positions.

Jasmine struggled to free herself, but knew instantly the impossibility of the notion. She was trapped beneath him. Even though he wasn't as yet completely recovered, she was no match against his strength. She bucked against his weight and nearly cried out her frustration. There was no way she could throw him off.

Despite the pain in his hands, he gripped her arms and held them over her head. The position prevented her head from moving. Helplessly she watched as his mouth came closer. "If you think this makes a difference, you're wrong. You cannot keep me a prisoner here."

Jasmine was amazed at her own words. Did she truly want to be gone? Did she? Lord, what was the matter with her? Why couldn't she understand her own wants, her own desires?

"You'll stay all right," he grunted just before his mouth took hers. "I'll make sure of it."

Jasmine could only moan her denial, for his lips prevented her words. She groaned as she felt the helpless wave of desire flood her senses yet again. She didn't want this. God, she didn't. Please, she didn't. She wanted to cry, for she knew the lie. She wanted this and more. She wanted everything he could give her.

"I hate you," she gasped as he tore his mouth from hers at last.

Anthony chuckled at her rage. "You won't in a minute."

His arrogance was more than she could bear. She bucked her hips again in an effort to dislodge his hold. "Get off!"

His tongue licked her nipple and he smiled as he listened to her gasp of surprise. "You don't hate that, do you?"

"Bastard," she groaned as she helplessly arched her back offering herself to his mouth.

Only Anthony had more in mind than titillation. He was going to make her wild with need. Before he was through, she'd beg him to take her, beg him to let her stay.

He smiled at her sweet offering but purposely ignored the tempting morsel. No, it wouldn't be that easy. His mouth moved instead to the long, delicious column of her throat and lingered at the sweet hollow of her shoulder.

From there, burning lips drew a moist path between her breasts. He breathed in the luscious scent of her and sighed with pleasure as his mouth nipped

255

at the fullness of her soft flesh. Slowly he circled her breast, watching with satisfaction as she slipped ever further under his spell. Her eyes fluttered closed and she moved restlessly beneath him, her back arched, silently begging him to take her into his mouth.

She was wild for him, desperate to feel the heat of his mouth, almost crying in frustration as he teased her flesh unmercifully. Jasmine cried out with pleasure and pain as he finally took her deep into the flaming heat of his mouth. Engorged nipples grew harder and sensation raced up and down her body as he bit down, almost too hard.

It was more than she could stand. Tears of ecstasy misted her eyes and a hard, painfully delicious ache came to life in the pit of her belly as his mouth suckled.

"Anthony," she breathed. "Oh, God, Anthony," she murmured as her hands freed of his hold came to his head and mindlessly pressed him closer.

She was aching, almost sore, and yet she wanted more. Anthony ignored the tugging of his hair as she tried to keep him in place. He had more to offer. Despite her moaning protest, his mouth slid lower.

Her ribs, her waist, her belly—nothing was left untouched by the heat of his mouth. Her muscles quivered as his mouth lingered at her thighs. She cried out as he nuzzled the backs of her knees and then gasped as his mouth slid up the inside of her thighs.

It was worse than she could have imagined. It was torture. It was hell. It was heaven. Blinding lights flashed behind her closed lids and she gave up her struggles, allowing him to carry her where he would.

He breathed her moist, musky scent and fought against the trembling that suddenly took him in its fold. God but she was lovely. Long, soft, lushly curved, delicately boned, he couldn't have imagined a greater delight than holding her in his arms.

The experience was new. It might have been the

first time for him, so great was his reaction to her scent, her feel. Anthony felt a flicker of remorse, for his reasons were not to bring her pleasure but to establish his undeniable hold over her. Purposely he set aside the guilt, knowing he'd do anything to keep her with him. Steeling himself against her powerful allure, he buried his face in her moistness.

Jasmine knew this was a purposeful seduction meant only to gain his point. She knew he wasn't so deeply involved as she, and yet she couldn't force aside her response. He worked his magic well and she was powerless to combat the need he so easily brought to life.

He was kissing her, biting her, sucking at her moist, sensitive flesh. She thought she might die. She wasn't prepared for this. Not this much. She recognized the ache and felt it grow to profound proportions. It spread in whispery waves of heat over her abdomen and threatened to tear her asunder. He had to stop. He had to release her from this torment.

Broken sobs mingled with mindless, urgent words to fill the small tent. Her head tossed back and forth as her hips rose helplessly to his greedy mouth.

She ached. Her groans became heavy with pain. She was lost somewhere between heaven and hell and she didn't care. Nothing mattered but that she find the pleasure that stood just beyond her reach.

And then suddenly, amazingly, blessedly it was there. She cried out. Her head came from the pillow, her body stiffened as she welcomed the pain and shuddered in reaction to the first onslaught of blinding ecstasy. And then again. And again.

He didn't stop until the last aftershock had slipped away. He slid up the length of her and cuddled her against him, knowing she hadn't yet realized he'd moved. Her felt her relax, heard her soft, deep, shaking breath, felt her warm sigh of utter satisfaction against his neck and smiled.

His legs slid easily between pliant thighs and Jasmine murmured with surprise to feel him enter her again. "Anthony," she groaned almost drunkenly. "I can't."

Anthony smiled as he watched the softness in her eyes fade away, replaced by a flicker of light as he moved deep within her. He saw the slight flush darken over her cheeks. He listened to the pattern change in her breathing. "Can't you? Are you sure?"

"Anthony," she whispered, giving up her feeble murmurs of protest.

"Ah, Jasmine," he sighed, his eyes closing with pleasure as he buried his face in her neck. "I feel like I've been waiting forever to hear you, to feel you. I wonder if I'll ever get enough."

Jasmine wondered much the same thing as hours later she awoke once more mindlessly responding to this need.

Jasmine felt her cheeks burn as his low voice behind her murmured gently, "Have you recovered from last night?"

How long had she been standing there dreaming of their time spent together? Her cheeks burned as she realized he knew exactly what she'd been thinking. She felt very much the fool.

Shoulders stiff, she turned to face him with a cool smile. "I thought you were still asleep. Are you hungry?"

"Not as much for food as for you," he answered silkily and smiled as he watched her blush.

Doing her best to ignore his teasing remarks, she ordered, "Sit then, I'll get your breakfast."

He was saddling his horse, having taken most of his bandages off earlier this morning. His fingers were tender. Half the skin had blistered while the rest was sore enough to cause him to wince.

"Your hands are sure to fester. You should have waited a few more days."

"You can take care of them when I return. You will be here, won't you?"

Jasmine shrugged. She didn't want to give a simple yes or no. He had to be made to understand his actions last night were reprehensible. Even though she might have enjoyed his lovemaking, they both knew it wasn't done for enjoyment but rather to assert his control. If she was going to stay, it had to be her decision. Half turning from him she remarked, "Anthony, you can't force me to do your bidding with . . . with . . ."

"Sex?" he offered, his smile one of pure male enjoyment. Purposely he ignored the slight discomfort her words brought. He refused to feel guilty. She was his wife and he'd use any means available to keep her with him. "Perhaps not, but I can give it a good try."

Jasmine's lifted eyes filled with inner turmoil. What did she want? Oh, God, was she ever to know the truth of her feelings? There was a time she thought she loved this man. She knew now the man she loved did not exist. What should she think now? He had so many sides to him. Was she supposed to suddenly switch her feelings to this new Anthony?

Did he honestly expect her to swear her loyalty to a man she barely knew, to a cause she couldn't in all good conscience take as her own? What was it he truly wanted from her? She knew he felt no depth of emotions. It was his nature to exhibit tenderness. If he appeared lusty in bed, it was probably due to the fact that they had been separated for some time. He didn't love her, of course. Jasmine felt a moment of shock. Did she want him to? Finally she shook her head and breathed a long, sad sigh. She had no answers but one. "It won't work. If anything, these deliberate, emotionless actions only increase my need to be gone."

Anthony's lips tightened at her rejection. Damn her to hell. What was he going to do? Would he be forced to tie her to the bed as he'd promised? His smile was grim, his voice stiff as he answered her at last. "I'm sorry you said that. Sorry, too, that I put you through last night for no apparent reason."

Jasmine's head spun as he whirled her around. A moment later she was inside the tent, watching with no little amazement as he stripped the clothes from her back. She came to her senses as he struggled with the ties of her petticoat. Her hands pushed at him. "What are you doing?"

"I'm making sure you'll be here when I return."

"Stop it!" She shoved at his chest, cursing as he easily ignored her efforts.

His eyes flashed with anger as he pulled her stockings from her. With one he tied her hands behind her back, with the other her feet. She was dressed only in her shift and drawers as he flung her upon the cot and covered her.

"Anthony, you can't keep me here. The heat," she said. "I'll suffocate."

"I'll be back before the full heat of the day begins," he promised, for they both knew how intolerable the inside of a tent could grow in the middle of the day.

"I'll scream," she warned.

He shrugged, unconcerned. "And give the women quite a show, I imagine. But none of them will dare to release you lest I order them banished from camp."

Anthony stood over her for a full minute watching her useless struggling. "Will you give me your word?"

Jasmine's answer was a hate-filled glare and a silent gritting of her teeth.

Chapter Fifteen

Anthony dismounted his horse and made immediately for his tent. His lips grew grim and his chest squeezed uncomfortably tight at the sight of her. He cursed against the helplessness that suddenly filled him. Not once had she left his mind all morning. Thankfully they had not encountered a British patrol, for he knew he would have been near useless leading his men against their foe in his present state of worry.

He moved closer to the cot, steeling himself against the angry words that were sure to blister his ears. Her eyes were closed, her lips parted slightly, deliciously so, in sleep. A heavy film of perspiration coated her skin, for the tent was almost unbearably hot. Tendrils of midnight curls clung damply to her cheeks and neck, while her honey-tinted skin held an unhealthy flush.

Anthony cursed first his earlier actions that had brought her to this condition and the pain that sliced through his chest at seeing her helplessly bound and obviously suffering from this stifling heat. He had been gone longer than he'd expected and the full heat of the day was now beating down upon the tent.

This wouldn't do, of course. He couldn't allow either of them to go on like this. He'd be forever useless when about his future missions, thinking of her and her suffering, while she would only grow to hate him more each day. He shook his head knowing he had but one choice. No doubt Jasmine would find little to celebrate when she learned of his decision.

In the corner there was a small table upon which a pitcher and bowl stood. Anthony dipped a small piece of toweling into the tepid water and moved it over her face and neck, bathing at her heated flesh.

Jasmine's eyes fluttered open. A smile touched the corners of her mouth. And her eyes, softened and blurred with sleep, seemed to hold a moment's tenderness. Anthony gave a silent curse as she came more fully to her senses and felt the tenderness evaporating as if it had never existed. His chest tightened in vague discomfort. What wouldn't he give to always see that softness when she looked his way? Anything, he vowed. Anything but her freedom.

He reached behind her and untied her wrists and feet, forcing back his own grimace at her soft moan of pain. He wouldn't do this again, for though it was her hands and ankles showing the evidence of his brutality, it was he who truly suffered at the sight.

"I won't be tying you again," he muttered, forcing aside the pain that constricted his breathing as he took her hands and rubbed them gently between his.

"Are you letting me go?" she asked, her gaze meeting his, searching for the meaning behind his statement.

Anthony almost offered her her freedom, but the fear that she might, in truth, jump at the chance to leave him was more than he could bear. No, he might not ever again tie her to ensure her company, but he couldn't let her go. He loved her. There was little doubt in his mind as to the truth of it now. He had wondered at his feelings for some time. He'd missed her horribly when he had been forced to leave her behind in New York and found boundless joy upon

262

seeing her again, but, until seeing her moments ago, he had not completely realized the depth of his feelings.

Anthony gave a silent sigh. He loved her, but should she discover that fact, would it not only add to the arsenal of weapons she already used against him? Would she not then know her power over him? Would she use it kindly? He couldn't be sure and he wasn't about to put it to the test.

No, it was best that she believe he merely wanted her at his side. She didn't have to know the reasons why.

"What would you do if I offered you your freedom?" he asked her and for a long moment Jasmine said nothing, simply staring into his eyes trying to understand his reasoning. A wide range of emotions assailed. Was he offering her freedom? Did he trust her to stay at his side without his insistence, without force? Or was it that he simply didn't care if she stayed or not? Jasmine forced aside the lump of fear that had suddenly formed in her throat. "Are you offering it?"

Anthony sighed with almost crushing defeat at the sight of what he believed to be hope flare to life in her eyes. What had he expected her to say? Had he truly hoped to hear her declaration of undying love? He shook his head, silently berating himself for a fool. "I'm afraid not. I won't be tying you again, but neither will you be going home soon."

"Where then? Where am I going?" Jasmine couldn't deny the relief that flooded her stiff body.

"Nowhere. You're staying with me," he said with not a trace of tenderness.

She tightened her lips with dismay. It was one thing to know he wanted her but quite another to be forced to remain at his side like some prisoner. "Anthony . . ."

"It matters not if you fight me, Jasmine," he

interrupted. "I want you here and here you will stay. In the future, I'll be taking you with me wherever I go."

"On patrol?" she asked, her amazement obvious.

"Exactly."

"And I'm to stand silently by and watch you slaughter English soldiers?"

"Is that what you believe I do?"

"Don't you?"

Anthony sighed, striving for patience. "Jasmine, in the first place, I don't slaughter anyone. My purpose here, for now, is to secure supplies for Washington. Supplies stolen, I might add, by your English comrades. In the second place, we are fighting a war for freedom . . ."

"You are mistaken there," she interrupted. "The king's forces are merely putting down a rebellion."

"Damn it, woman!" he snapped, his patience stretched to the limit. "I know your thinking on this matter. You might say what you will, but the fact remains that it is a war we fight.

"Can't you imagine what it will be like to be free, to live without tyranny? Can't you understand that freedom is the most basic of every man's needs?"

Jasmine laughed. "And this from a man who has just untied my hands?"

Anthony had the grace to flush at the obvious truth of her words. He settled her in his arms and watched her with almost overwhelming tenderness. "You may not agree with my methods, but you'll one day see the truth of my words." He ignored the slight shake of her head. "In the meantime, if you accompany me on my missions, you can see for yourself that I slaughter no one."

Jasmine swatted at the pesky mosquitoes while crouched behind the cover of thick foliage. Mindful

264

of her surroundings, she carefully made no slapping sound that might alert the small patrol of painted Indian braves not ten feet away. Annoyed that the tiny insects seemed determined to sample a tasty morsel at the base of her throat she swung again, the slightly more vehement movement taking her off balance. She struggled to regain her foothold, but the leaves beneath her feet were slippery after the morning rain. Her mouth twisted into a grimace of disgust as she lost her balance and with a soft whooshing sound plopped on her backside into a small cavity filled with rotted leaves. The stench was instant and gagging. Jasmine disallowed the thought that more than leaves occupied the slight depression.

From this position Jasmine glared at Anthony's silent laughter. She opened her mouth to rail at his lack of sensitivity, tempted to wipe away the muck and clean her hands on his shirt, when his eyes lost their mirth and he grew suddenly alert. In the next instant she was flat on her back, his body stretched out over hers, his hand held firmly to her mouth.

She stiffened, her eyes wide with alarm, for she heard the footsteps then, so soft she might have thought them a rustle of leaves in the wind. Her brow creased with puzzlement as another sound came to her ears. Was someone pouring water?

One look at Anthony's grin and she knew the origin of the sound. One of the braves had stopped perilously close by and was using the forest as his personal chamber pot. Jasmine found herself still capable of blushing beet red.

Certainly she should by now have become used to such happenings after nearly a month spent in the company of Anthony's men, men who never knew or simply ignored social niceties and often forgot her presence. To their credit, they had at first shown a measure of embarrassment when committing their blunders against good manners, while mumbling red-faced apologies. Soon they had rarely bothered with such niceties, for they had grown used to her company and apparently considered her as one of the men.

The sound dribbled at last to a stop and the whispery footsteps were again heard over the pounding of her heart. A moment later Anthony released her and came to his feet.

Dismayed, Jasmine realized the whole of her back was now coated with the vilest matter. Her voice was no more than a whisper when she asked. "Did you have to push me into it?"

Anthony grinned. "You were about to yell at me. I could see it in your eyes."

Jasmine shivered with disgust. She wore nothing beneath the shirt and only her drawers under the borrowed brown skirt, realizing from the first how much easier to ride astride and move about in these woods without the encumbrance of petticoats. Now the moistness had seeped through her clothes. She could feel the material clinging to her back. "I have to get this off. It's disgusting." She shivered again.

Anthony nodded. "You can have my shirt."

He was opening the ties at his throat and pulling the shirt over his shoulders before Jasmine thought to ask, "What will you wear?"

"My vest is enough."

Jasmine realized the truth of his words, for his leather vest covered all but his arms and a thin line of his chest. But she hadn't time to think upon the intriguing sight of his chest peeking through the open vest. All she could think was to rid herself of this stench. Unconcerned with her nakedness, she had flung aside her hat and quickly pulled the foul-stenched material over her head. She was using the soiled shirt to wipe away the all-too-thick coating of leaves on her bottom when she came to a jerking stop at the sudden intake of Anthony's breath. She glanced up. The gleam of hunger in her husband's eyes could not be denied. Only now did she realize she was standing there naked to the waist and Anthony was taking every advantage of the sight.

Jasmine's heart skipped a beat and then thundered wildly in her ears. His eyes grew nearly black, the blue all but disappearing as hunger shone clearly in their depths. He wanted her. Jasmine's mouth went dry, for she couldn't deny the answering need that had leaped to life in her breast.

Her hair had fallen down her back when she pulled off her hat and was now in wild disarray about her shoulders. Her skin glowed honey-gold in the dim light of the forest while the shadowy movement of leaves danced over flawless flesh.

He felt his mouth go dry, and a thickness began to throb to life in his groin. It had been weeks since he'd last touched her or seen her thus, for each night the light was put out before she undressed. An unspoken truce had formed between them, a peace Anthony instinctively knew would be destroyed if he asserted his husbandly rights. Wisely he realized they had to grow to know each other. She had to come to love him, for he'd never be satisfied with anything less.

And so night after night they had come to share the same cot but little else. How long, he wondered as a desperate yearning filled his soul? How long before she came willing into his arms?

Anthony mumbled a curse and quickly handed over his shirt at the sound of rustling leaves. Her fingers moved clumsily, but she managed at last to smooth his shirt into the waistband of her skirt just before three of his men came upon them.

"What kind of a name is that?"

Anthony shot her a glance across the campfire, the sound of her voice interrupting his plans for the next

267

morning. "The kind to instill terror in many a brave man."

"Dragging Canoe?" Jasmine snorted her disbelief, her lips twitching in thinly veiled humor as she refilled her cup with the hickory blended coffee. She took a sip of the hot, bitter brew and grimaced her disgust, wondering vaguely why she was trying to acquire a taste for this horrid mixture. "It sounds ridiculous to me."

"I'd wager you'd rethink your opinion should you and he come face to face."

Jasmine shrugged. "I hardly think I'd ask his name if that were the case."

The men chuckled at the obvious truth of that statement. "Aye, missus," said Boggs. "You'd disappear faster than bird piss in rain. And I'd be hot on your trail."

"As I was saying . . ." Anthony interrupted his men's knowing laughter. "There are five wagons, heavy with supplies and moving slow. Each one has a driver and guard. Two more on horseback hold the point. Beyond that there should be no problem, assuming Dragging Canoe," he shot Jasmine a stern disapproving look, "and his bunch are not in the area."

Jasmine swallowed another burning mouthful of coffee, her eyes filled with doubt, her heart pounding with sudden fear. The Indians were indeed in the area this morning. What made Anthony think they'd be gone tomorrow?

"Boggs is our best shot. He'll pick off the two riding point, while the rest of us will split up coming in from both sides. Hopefully it will be over in seconds."

"May I have a word with you in private?" Jasmine asked, coming quickly to her feet.

Anthony nodded and joined her moments later in their tent.

"I won't be a party to murder," she stated once he entered.

"What murder?" Anthony asked, obviously unable to understand her meaning.

"It's murder to ambush those men."

Anthony sighed, his voice tinged with disgust. "Jasmine, do you think they'd hand over the supplies if I were to ask politely?"

"I imagine they'd do just that if it were shown they had no choice in the matter."

"Meaning?"

"Surround them. Order them to lay down their arms."

Anthony smirked with disbelief. "Just like that?"

She nodded. "Just like that."

Anthony breathed a long sigh. "The idea is worthy of merit, Jasmine. Had I more men I might do as you suggest. As it stands, I'd endanger my men if I agree to your plan."

"You endanger them regardless."

A light of humor danced in his eyes. The woman was nothing short of amazing. Was she now about to tell him how to conduct his business. "Do I? How so?"

"The Indians and English have but one common cause. And that is to rid this area of every so-called patriot. Am I right?"

Anthony refrained from remarking on her sarcasm, anxious to hear what she had to say. "You are."

"We know for a fact that the Indians are in the area, perhaps close enough to hear the shots you plan to fire and come rushing to the assistance of their friends."

Anthony shrugged, knowing the truth of her statement. He knew the danger of taking the supplies but it didn't matter. The rebels marched barefoot with stomachs growling from hunger. They needed these supplies desperately. He had no choice but to do as he must.

"If you suddenly came from the brush . . . If your men took them unsuspectingly."

Anthony watched her for a long moment while imagining the possibility of her plan. She was right about the sound alerting the Indians. He'd been prepared to take that risk. Suddenly he realized it just might be a risk he needn't take. Finally he gave a long sigh, his eyes filled with tenderness as his gaze moved over her worried features. He nodded. "It just might work."

They could hear the squeaking of the wheels long before the wagons came into view. Silently they hid among the heavy undergrowth along the side of the dirt road, some on horseback, some on foot. Jasmine felt a shiver of fear race up her spine as a thin film of perspiration broke out and chilled her entire body. What if she was wrong? What if this encounter turned into disaster? What if these men were shot? What if they were killed? It would be her fault.

She might not agree with their beliefs, but she no more wanted to see them dead than she did her countrymen.

Jasmine gave a silent tormented groan. What if Anthony were hurt? Would she be able to live with herself knowing he had given in to her plea and suffered because of it?

Jasmine didn't have long to think on the matter, for the line of wagons was suddenly upon them. She pushed herself back from the road, further into the underbrush, suddenly sick with apprehension.

"Your attention, gentlemen." Anthony spoke as he moved out of hiding to face the two men who led the small column.

There was a shout, dozens of curses filled the air, but to Jasmine's relief no shots were fired as the rebels quickly stationed themselves one on each side of every wagon, guns drawn and pointing with deadly menace at the drivers, not three feet away.

"Your weapons, if you will," he asked politely and Jasmine almost cried with relief when, after a long moment of stunned silence, she heard the heavy dull thud of metal hitting the ground. She hadn't realized until that moment she'd been holding her breath.

"Now, if you would be so kind, gentlemen. Line up over here."

"Cooper, would you accompany the men to the center of the road and assist Billings with the rope?"

Jasmine listened to the enthusiastic curses as the men were unhappily tied together. Still, the sounds made were less filled with hate than surprise, for she imagined each had at first believed this day to be their last spent on earth.

The wagons were hidden beneath the cover of thick foliage. Hidden so well, in fact, that one might walk into them before seeing them. It was late. Some of the men had already turned in for the night, while a few sat at the campfire discussing the day's events.

Jasmine covered her mouth with her hand as she yawned and then came stiffly to her feet. They had ridden miles today. Every muscle ached, particularly those in her bottom. She was literally covered with dust, dust that had adhered to her skin, hair, and clothes as the heat of the day grew in strength. Idly she wondered if she'd ever be really clean again. How much farther would they travel before coming upon Morgan and his men?

"Would you like to clean up before bed?" Anthony asked, suddenly beside her, his head bent, his mouth close to her ear, his eyes shining with an emotion she could not read. "It's dark enough to ensure privacy if you want to bathe at the river."

271

Jasmine sighed, a flicker of a smile showing in her tired eyes as she imagined the feel of the river's cool water upon her. Each night she had washed as well as she could in the privacy of her tent, but she hadn't taken a bath in more than a month and the temptation to be really clean again was more than she could refuse, no matter she'd have to bathe outside. She grinned at the thought. "I'll get the soap."

Moments later they were at the gently flowing river's edge. The night was indeed dark and Jasmine had no fear of being seen should anyone suddenly take it into their heads to do the same. Not that any of Anthony's men were likely to harbor such a notion, for she had never met a more slovenly bunch.

Quickly she shrugged out of her clothes and boots, thankful that she had thought to wash her pink dress days ago, for it had taken almost that long to dry in this damp heat. She had been forced to wear the same things every day for almost a week and, with disgust and relief, she dropped the offensive-smelling articles to the ground.

Due to the pitch of the night, she was comfortable in her nakedness. She gave Anthony a puzzled look to see his shadowy form settle itself upon a fallen tree. "Aren't you coming in?"

Anthony could see little more than the vague outline of her, but knew well enough she stood before him naked. It took two tries before the words would clear his constricted throat. Finally he nodded, although she couldn't see the movement. "I'll keep watch while you bathe. You can do the same for me."

Jasmine smiled. "Do you think your men have the same interests as we?"

"It's not my men I watch for," he said, fingering the rifle he held.

"Indians?" Jasmine asked as a shiver of fear raced up her spine.

"Perhaps," he shrugged, "or redcoats. It's best if we don't let down our guard."

Jasmine couldn't ever remember feeling quite so comfortable. Her hair was clean, as was her body. Still damp, she had hurried into her clothes. She was lacing up her boots when Anthony came out of the water. They did not speak as he dressed, but when they began the short walk back to camp, Jasmine couldn't hold back her gratitude another minute. "Anthony, I want to thank you for today. You managed to do as you had to without the loss of even one man. For that, I'm grateful."

Anthony beamed with pride as he saw the esteem in his wife's eyes in the soft candlelight inside the tent. "I wish every encounter could be as bloodless, for your tender words of gratitude are not wasted."

"Can't it be?"

Anthony laughed. "Jasmine, what kind of a war is it if no one gets killed?"

"An extremely civilized one, I'd imagine."

He laughed again. "No doubt." His smile disappeared. "I only hope those left alive today remember the mercy bestowed upon them and in turn, offer the same to my countrymen."

"Why would they not?"

"Jasmine, the Brits are not known to show mercy toward the rebels. Indeed, many are slaughtered with the least suspicion."

"I don't believe it."

"Perhaps not, but the fact holds truth in any case."

"They are not barbarians," she defended.

"All men are barbarians when at war. They are no worse or better than us."

"I won't believe it," she stubbornly insisted.

"Believe this then, for it is naught but fact. Tarleton, welcomed at the home of a certain Mr. Richardson in South Carolina, sat at the man's table and partook of his hospitality. After the evening

273

meal was done, Tarleton then calmly ordered his men to drive all the cattle, hogs, and chickens they could find into the barn. He then set the building ablaze.

"Afterward he compounded his dastardly deed by torching the main house. The women of the family escaped, of course, but with little more than the clothes on their backs. They now live in what could only be referred to as a hovel. And all because Richardson was suspected, and falsely, I might add, to be a supporter of our cause."

Jasmine opened her mouth to object, for one couldn't assassinate the reputation of every English soldier for the uncivilized actions of one.

Anthony interrupted her before she began. "Of course I harbor the hope that the patriots might have been slightly more merciful."

"Of course," she returned, her disgust for his way of thinking more than obvious.

"Still, they have their own dastardly deeds for which they must answer." Anthony smiled at her surprised expression. She had never expected him to defame those of his own viewpoint. "Of those, there are no doubt many. As happens in times of war, no one side can be held without a moment's dishonor."

Chapter Sixteen

Jasmine bent her knees, unconsciously squirming her backside against him in the small confines of the narrow cot. It was impossible for the two of them not to touch, for the bed was hardly wide enough for one. On his side, his knees were bent behind hers, her head rested upon his outstretched arm.

She knew he was awake, for his breathing had yet to regulate into the even, deep sounds of sleep. She could feel the warmth of his breath against the side of her face and wondered why she couldn't sleep?

Anthony felt her stiffen as his arm snaked out beneath her shirt to circle her waist and pull her more tightly against him. "Relax," he breathed.

"It's hot. I can't sleep," she answered. Even leaving the flap of the tent partially open had brought no relief from the heat, for not a breath of air stirred inside or out.

The long shirt she wore to bed each night had slid up with her restless movements. Her backside was now pressed up against his front, without the barrier of cloth that usually separated them. She knew she should pull the shirt back into place, but it was so unbearably hot, she was loath to make even that small adjustment. Had she the nerve she'd have come to bed naked. The thought had indeed crossed her mind, but knowing how Anthony would have interpreted that gesture, she'd immediately thought better of it.

She should have insisted they make up a pallet and sleep outside. Had she less fear of all things creepy and crawly, she would have done so, for she imagined even the hard ground to be preferable to this breathless heat.

"Lie still. Sleep will come."

She squirmed against him again, trying in vain to find comfort. She could feel the hardness of his arousal pressed against her soft, rounded buttocks and wondered if it were merely the same phenomenon that often afflicted him upon awakening each morning. No doubt it was, for if he'd wanted to take her as his wife, he'd had more than ample opportunity. Every night for the past month they had lain thus and he had not, but for that one time, asserted his husbandly rights.

Jasmine couldn't help but wonder why. Why had he gone to the trouble of bringing her here, of keeping her here, if not for the private moments a husband and wife shared? She couldn't fathom his reasoning. Certainly that was what men wanted, wasn't it? Not that she wanted it as well. She didn't, of course. But she wouldn't deny him if he made some kind of advance toward her. It was, after all, her wifely duty, wasn't it?

Jasmine smiled with some amazement at her thoughts. When had she begun to think of herself as a wife? When Anthony had begun to treat her thus, she silently answered. He did, in fact, treat her better than a wife. She knew there were few who respected their wives enough to ask her opinion. There were fewer still who would treat her as an equal. And through it all he managed to hold her in his gentle care.

Without thinking of the consequences, Jasmine turned over. Her leg slid between his thighs, her arm flung with casual nonchalance over his waist. God, the heat was unbearable! She might not have minded the heat, at least not quite so much, if she could have managed to relax. But this position was even worse than the other. Now the hairs of his chest tickled her nose and she could smell the musky heat coming from his skin. What was the matter with her tonight? What was it that caused this unease?

Her body pressed against his, having no alternative to do otherwise. She sighed a sound that was far from happy.

"What is it?" Anthony asked as his big hand smoothed her damp hair back from her face and neck.

"I'm hot, is all."

"It's been hotter, Jasmine. Does something else cause this restlessness?"

She wanted to ask him why he had brought her here, if not to make love to her. But she pushed aside the words that nearly formed, afraid if she brought up the subject, Anthony might believe she still harbored thoughts of leaving. "No," she finally breathed a sigh. "I was just wondering how much longer before this is finished."

Jasmine's hand came between them to rub her nose, for the hairs of his chest continued to tickle. The back of her hand lingered on his warm flesh long after she should have pulled it away. She finally did so but with great reluctance. Her arm did not return to his waist, but rather to her own hip.

Anthony's heart pounded in his chest. He wondered just how much longer he was to suffer this agony before she'd finally come to him, a willing participant in their lovemaking. He moved her hand back to his chest. "Keep it there," he remarked. "I like it when you touch me."

"You don't mind?" she asked.

Anthony grinned in the dark. "I only mind when you don't."

"Then why . . . ?" The words came of their own accord. She hadn't known she was going to ask until she heard the sound. Instantly her throat closed and she very nearly choked on the effort it took to bite back the words. She couldn't ask him. Not right out.

"Why what?"

"Nothing," she sighed. "Nothing important."

"Tell me," he whispered, shifting his head so that his mouth came close to her ear. His breath caused chills to run down the length of her spine. "Tell me your thoughts. I meant to give us time to get to know each other, but how can I know you if you won't share them?"

Jasmine moved her head back, trying to see his expression in the dark. But the open flap allowed only a minimum of light to enter and she could see little more than his shadowy form and the slightest glitter of his eyes. Could that be it? Is that why he hadn't taken advantge of opportunities such as these? Is that why he hadn't touched her in more than a month? Her face flamed, but she forced aside her embarrassment. She had to know. "Is that why you haven't made love to me? Because you want us to get to know each other better?"

Anthony breathed a shaky sigh, filled with almost desperate need to hear her say the words. "Oh, God," he choked. "Are you telling me you want to make love?"

Jasmine shrugged. "I don't know." And after a second's hesitation, she added, "That's a lie." Silently she blessed the darkness, for it hid flaming cheeks. "I'm embarrased to tell you. Ladies are not supposed to want that sort of thing."

"So I've heard." Anthony grinned into her hair as he pulled her gently back against him. "Do you believe everything you hear?"

"Isn't it true?"

"I think a lady isn't all that different from anyone

278

else. Some like it, others do not."

"How . . . ? Never mind. I don't want to know."

"Jasmine," he breathed, forcing aside his need to crush her against him and take her without another word spoken. Dare he hope it was jealousy he heard in that softly spoken question? Oh, God, he hoped so. "I've not lived the life of a monk, till I met you, that is. You cannot expect . . ."

"I don't," she interrupted. Jasmine stiffened and lifted herself to her elbow. "What do you mean till you met me?"

Anthony shrugged and breathed a long sigh. "I've come to realize celibacy is not a particularly pleasant experience. It does not clear the mind or increase energy as some might suppose, but rather allows a constant, unsatisfying ache that interferes with even the most mundane everyday happenings."

"Celibate? Are you telling me there has been no one else since you met me?" she asked, clearly amazed.

"Did you expect there to be?"

Jasmine shrugged. "Well, I'd thought you being a man and all . . ." she let the sentence falter.

"And men don't remain faithful to their wives. Is that it?"

"I don't know, do they?"

"They do when they know to take another would do little toward easing their needs. When there's only one woman who entices. Only one who can satisfy."

"Are you suggesting only I can do that?" she murmured as she lay down again. Without thinking, she gave in to the need to taste the warmth of his chest.

"Oh, God," he groaned as he felt her lips and tongue against him.

Jasmine moaned a soft sound of enjoyment. "I never thought a man would smell this good."

"No? What did you think men smelled like?"

279

She shrugged. "I don't think I ever thought about it."

"And a good thing, too," he grinned as he turned her to her back and lay partially upon her, his bent elbows supporting most of his weight, his hips cradling deliciously against her softness. "I can't have my wife sniffing at every man she meets."

Jasmine giggled at the absurd picture his words brought to mind. "In fact, that was one of the first things I noticed about you."

"You noticed I smelled?" She heard rather than saw his grin.

"I noticed you smelled good. I couldn't understand it. You worked in a barn but smelled so clean."

"That was because I didn't work there."

"Why did you let me think you did?"

Anthony grinned down at her, remembering the first time he'd seen her in the dim light of the stable. "Shall I tell you the truth of it?"

"You had some girl in the back and didn't want me to know."

"How the hell did you come up with that?"

Jasmine gave a soft laugh. "I was teasing. Tell me why."

"I'll have to set the scene a bit."

Jasmine nodded.

"I had just come back from a meeting pertaining to my work."

Jasmine interrupted with a most unladylike snort. "Spying, you mean."

"Actually a trip to relay a message, if you must know."

Jasmine nodded, a satisfied gleam in her eyes.

"There I was, soaked to the skin and freezing. So I took off my coat and shirt."

"Of course. Doesn't everyone take off their clothes when they're cold?"

"I told you they were wet. And who is the one

telling this story?"

"All right," she laughed. "Go on, I won't interrupt again."

"There I was, taking care of my horse—the damn stable boy being nowhere in sight—when I heard the sounds, the delicious sounds, I might add," he leered down at her, "of a woman's laughter. Needless to say, I was intrigued."

"Because I laughed?" she asked in disbelief.

"I thought you weren't going to interrupt me again?"

"Sorry," she choked, biting at her lips to contain her mirth.

"Anyway, where was I?"

"You heard me laugh."

"Right, but I didn't know it was you at the time."

"Did you think it perhaps my horse?"

He glared at her.

"I'll shut up."

Anthony grinned and began again. "I heard this delicious laughter and then some shocking conversation about a certain lady's disreputable escapades."

"What escapades?"

"You're doing it again."

"My lips are sealed."

"Needless to say I had to see for myself this woman who would dare dance three times with a married man. The same woman who, I'm not happy to report, left the church picnic with Tommy and, worst of all, thought a decent man to be a boring prospect."

"Good God. How did you remember . . . ? Sorry," she said in a small voice, cutting herself off at what she imagined to be his most fierce look.

"And when I saw her, she proved to be so beautiful, I just knew I had to have her."

"Did you now? But suppose this lady wasn't agreeable? What would you have done?"

"I had no specific plans in mind at first except to get to know her a bit. Actually things didn't seem to be working out at all. I was on the verge of making a clean breast of it while praying she wouldn't hate me forever, when she asked me to marry her."

"But she didn't mean to marry in truth."

Anthony ignored that remark. "As you can imagine, I was at first dumbfounded. But the idea soon grew to hold some merit in my eyes."

"Why?"

"Why?" he repeated, clearly surprised by the question. "Because, by that time I was starting to fall in love with her, of course."

"Of course," Jasmine gasped on a ragged breath. "Did you?" she forced herself to ask.

"Did I what?"

"You said you were starting to fall in love. Did you do it? Did you fall in love?"

Jasmine saw his teeth flash in the tent's nearly black interior. "Shall I tell you?"

Jasmine shrugged as if unconcerned and ignored the pounding of her heart as she examined a fingernail, an impossible task considering she could hardly see her finger, much less the nail. "Only if you want to live beyond this moment."

Anthony laughed. "Oh, in that case, I expect I'd better."

After a moment's silence, she said, "Well?"

Anthony grinned. "You don't think I'd be a fool to tell her, do you?"

Jasmine's arms slid over his chest and shoulders, not stopping until they linked at the back of his neck. With little urging she managed to bring his mouth closer to hers. "I think you could never be a fool."

His lips touched lightly against hers, briefly brushing over the sensitive softness, moving away only to return again to tease, to entice, to drive her slowly beyond reason. She grew softer, sweeter, more pliant beneath him. Her lips ached to feel the heat of his, to feel the pleasure only he could bring.

"Anthony," she murmured, her impatience evident, her breathing erratic, her pulse pounding with an urgency that was quickly growing out of control.

"Mmm?" he asked in return, already dizzy with the deliciousness of touching her, breathing her, tasting her.

"It's terribly unkind of you to tease."

Anthony chuckled, his mouth pressed into the damp warmth of her neck. "Do you want me to kiss you?"

"I do," she breathed, and then moaned softly as his mouth nuzzled the sensitive hollow of her throat.

"Tell me then," he breathed shakily. "Tell me how."

"Like this," she demonstrated as she dug her fingers into his hair and pulled his lips back to hers.

"No," he returned, needing to hear the words. "Tell me. Tell me what I should do."

"Put your mouth on mine."

"And then?"

Her breathing increased to a gasping sound. "And then open your lips."

He nodded. "And then?"

Her voice was little more than a strangled cry. "Anthony, please." She took his head between her hands and brought his mouth to hers. Hungrily she kissed him, using lips, teeth, and tongue.

"Ah," he gasped as he tore his mouth from hers at last. His body shook with the effort it took to control the need her kisses brought about. "I see what you mean. You want me to use my tongue."

"Anthony," she moaned, frustrated that he felt this need to talk.

"Shall I tell you what I want?"

"Oh, God," she gasped helplessly, caught under his spell as he whispered near her ear. Her body

283

trembled as his words brought erotic pictures flashing through her mind.

His fingers opened the buttons of her shirt. "I want to touch you, kiss you everywhere. Do you want that?"

Jasmine swallowed. Her heart pounded. She was panting, unable to take in enough air to relieve her starved lungs of their ache. "Yes. Oh, yes!"

"Shall I start here?" he asked as his one finger trailed a sizzling path between her breasts and then grazed his nail against the rosy tips as it moved suddenly to the left and right.

Her back arched reflexively. Her body hummed, every nerve alive and throbbing. "I can't stand this."

"Yes, you can. We both can. And it will be better for our efforts."

"Oh, God," she moaned, knowing the torture that was sure to come. "It can't be better than the last time."

Anthony chuckled at her unthinking compliment. "Shall I tell you where I want to touch you?"

"No," she breathed heavily. "Don't say any more. I can't stand for you to say any more."

He ignored her pleading, he needed to see her wild with longing. Wild with wanting him. He whispered again near her ear and Jasmine shivered uncontrollably at the thoughts his words brought to mind.

"Where first?"

Jasmine was beside herself with longing. Burning, she imagined any minute to burst into flames. "Don't ask me, I can't tell you," she whispered. And in truth she couldn't, for although he hadn't as yet touched her, he might as well have, for she knew no difference so clearly did she imagine the exquisite pleasure that awaited her.

"Here, I think," he murmured as he slid down the length of her and cupped her backside, lifting her, bringing her closer, more comfortably to the angle on his mouth.

Jasmine's body jerked at contact and she bit her hand, lest she cry out and alert the entire camp as to the happenings in this one tent. She was creamy wet and warm, but his mouth was flame, burning hot against her flesh. He hadn't shaved since early that morning and his sharp whiskers grazed. His tongue laved her, his teeth nibbled, his breath seared.

Jasmine felt the twisting in her belly tighten to a pressure-filled, mindless ache. "Too fast," she choked out in a breathless whisper. He had enticed her with words to the point where the merest touch was already bringing her pleasure to an end.

Anthony moaned as he felt her strain anxiously against him, her yearning desperate in the broken, mindless sounds she uttered. His mouth opened wider, hungered beyond reason, eating at her as if once starved and now allowed to feast.

Her head twisted wildly upon the pillow; she was half crazed with a need only he could satisfy. He growled his satisfaction as she bit back a cry and stiffened beneath his mouth. The tiny nub grew pebble hard as he continued his unrelenting, almost ruthless massage. He felt the shudder, listened to the helpless guttural groan. His mouth felt the spasms sharply distinguishable against his tongue. He felt the trembling widen and relax the entrance to her body.

Anthony breathed a soft sound of delight as he absorbed her taste. "Ah, Jasmine, do you know how delicious you are?" he asked against her slippery moistness.

Jasmine breathed a soft sigh as her body relaxed at last. She expected him to move then, to cover her body again with the pleasure of his weight. But he didn't move. As he continued on, his tongue apparently no closer to finding what it sought than when he'd first begun, she murmured almost drunkenly, "Anthony, enough."

Anthony's chuckle was muffled against her. "You said it yourself. It was too fast."

She was so sensitive she didn't think she could stand another second of the pleasure that had started as an ache, grown to blissful ecstasy, and was now beginning as an ache all over again.

"I can't. Anthony, stop." Feebly she struggled to free herself.

He laughed again, his nose, mouth, and chin buried against her sweetness. "More. I want to feel you lose control again."

"Oh, God," she moaned, helpless against his need, a need that served to bring hers suddenly, wildly alive again.

She couldn't stop the cry this time. She wanted to scream. She knew she wouldn't be able to do anything less, for the ache was agonizingly strong and her release promised to match it in strength. Desperately she pulled the pillow from under her head and pressed it over her face as her body responded as it would of its own accord.

She felt the blessed comfort ease a lethargy into the marrow of her bones. She barely had the strength to breathe. Her body was slick with sweat. She wondered if her heart would ever beat normally again. "I hope you're satisfied," she mumbled from beneath the pillow.

"Not quite," he grinned as he lay full length upon her. "Are you trying to hide from me?" he asked as he realized the pillow was over her face.

"Would it do any good?"

"Can't say as it would."

"If you ever do that to me again . . ." she warned.

Anthony laughed. "You'll love every minute of it," he returned knowingly.

Jasmine chuckled and threw off the pillow. "In that case, I'll just have to find a means of retaliation."

"Later," he groaned as the enticing picture she hinted at nearly caused him to lose what was left of his thinly held control. "There is something I have to do first."

"Is there? I wonder what that could be?" she asked as he knelt between her open thighs, his hands again under her hips, lifting her, ready to guide himself deep inside.

"Think," he grinned at her pretense.

"Check your weapon?" She almost but not quite bit back the giggle. It was the first thing that came to mind, for it was something he did constantly. And she'd said it before she realized the double entendre.

"Jesus," he groaned, knowing instantly the way of her thoughts. He was going to burst if she started talking like that.

"Is it primed and loaded?" she dared, straining for an innocent note.

"Oh, God." He smothered a moan, doubled over, his face pressed against her belly.

"Cocked?" she asked brazenly, biting at her lip to prevent the laughter that threatened to bubble forth.

The tent filled with the sound of his gasping words, "I'm going to get you for this."

Jasmine chose to ignore his words and asked deliberately. "Will you let me rub it sometimes?"

She felt him stiffen and ran her hands down his chest, over his belly. "I watch when you oil it. The way you run your fingers over it . . ."

"Shut up."

But Jasmine only grew bolder knowing the effect she was having on him. "Will you teach me how to aim it?" She stroked him and guided him closer to her heat. "Fire it?"

"Jesus, I can't," he grunted, the last of his control gone as he plunged almost viciously, deep, deep into her softness.

Jasmine hissed a startled breath between clamped

teeth, for the beauty of this moment was more than she could bear. She moaned softly her disappointment as he pulled back, so far as to nearly separate them, but then groaned a foreign sound of nearly diabolical pleasure as he again immersed himself into the depths of her body.

Anthony felt the pleasure coming. It was too soon, but he was beyond the power to control it. His broken whisper of apology was lost on Jasmine as her muscles squeezed against him. He felt her shudder and knew a moment's surprise, for he hadn't expected her to be ready. A moment later he collapsed upon her, following her into a gasping moment of golden bliss.

Long moments ticked by before he finally managed the strength to pull his face from her throat and speak. His voice was filled with humor. "I never realized you felt this strong an affinity with my weapon."

Jasmine giggled and even in the dark felt her cheeks start to burn at her daring. She hid her face in his shoulder. "Odd, isn't it? I think I've only just come to realize how much it means to me."

"Exactly what does it mean?"

"Well, it's a very necessary piece of equipment. Wouldn't you agree?"

"I would."

"No soldier should be without one."

"Forget about soldiers. We're talking about my . . . ah . . . rifle."

Jasmine burst into laughter at his hesitation. "And now you no doubt wish for me to bestow all kind of honor upon it simply because you've learned to use it well?"

Anthony hugged her close to him and laughed as he rolled over to his back pulling her atop him. "I never knew my wife to be quite so wicked."

"Have I shocked you?"

She could feel him shake his head. "Surprised, perhaps, but a most delightful surprise."

Anthony sighed into the top of her head as his hand moved down her naked back to cup a softly curved hip. "God, this feels so good."

Jasmine grinned. "Don't get too comfortable. You're hogging the whole bed."

"You can sleep here," he announced as if it were indeed the solution to all their problems.

"I could, if I didn't have these two bumps squeezing into my chest."

"What, these?" he asked as he ran his hands over the plumped-out sides of her breasts.

Jasmine laughed and swatted at his hands. She leaned back, supporting herself above him with her arms and brushed the heavy black cloud of hair from her eyes. "This isn't going to work at all. At this rate the sun will be up before either of us gets any sleep."

It almost was.

Chapter Seventeen

It was barely dawn, but Jasmine didn't roll out of bed as usual. She was *flung* out, landing almost on her face. She murmured a short exclamation of surprise and blinked, trying to awaken her sleepy senses and not a little amazed to find herself sprawled upon the tent's dirt floor. She rubbed at the aching shoulder which had been unlucky enough to have taken the brunt of her fall. Her mind was groggy, since she had had no more than an hour or so of sleep. She turned puzzled eyes to Anthony who stood opposite the bed, muttering vile curses as he dressed with all haste.

"Hurry," he said, never realizing his shove to awaken her had knocked her upon the ground.

"Hurry and what?"

Hearing her voice come at him from boot level, he turned and glared at her. "What in hell are you doing down there? Get up! Get dressed. They're here."

Jasmine came to her feet and slid her chemise over her head. "Who's here?" she asked no one, for by the time the garment had slid over her hips, she was alone.

Jasmine followed his lead. Her fingers shook as she finished dressing hurriedly, not unaware of the ruckus outside, the shouts and running footsteps.

Her heart pounded with trepidation. What in the world had happened? Who was here? Could the Indians have trailed them and come to steal the supplies for yet a third time? No, she thought not, for Indians would have come in silence, never giving their sleeping enemies a chance to prepare a defense.

Giving up on finding pins, she secured her hair in a ribbon at the back of her head and stumbled from the tent. The activity in the small camp was almost dizzying to watch. Men ran in every direction, the hungry gleam of approaching battle glowing in their eyes, while the camp followers did much the same, except when they ran it was to search for a safe hiding place. Orders were barked out and instantly obeyed.

The wagons were rolled from the cover of undergrowth, their axles and wheels creaking under the imposed weight. In record speed each was hitched to the horses and headed away from camp.

Jasmine couldn't see beyond the thick cover of trees, but she knew Anthony would have ordered the supplies dispersed in the opposite direction of danger. Slowly, fearfully she turned to see what that danger might be.

Her heart nearly stopped at the sight that greeted her eyes. Did one among them truly believe they could win out against odds such as these? Hundreds, perhaps a thousand men stood in row upon row of brilliant white and red as they all but covered the sloping hill facing the tiny camp.

Jasmine forced aside the sudden gurgle of hysteria that threatened to grow into a full-fledged scream of terror. There would be a battle today. She had no doubt that Anthony would turn at some point and make his stand. That his stand would be a useless endeavor would matter not. That he would surely die, or at the very least be captured and then hung, since there was still a price on his head, would not enter his mind.

She was frozen into place, terrified at the thought of losing him. She barely noticed the strong arms slide around her waist and beneath her knees. She was held against a hard chest as Cooper took her up in a run, heading for the moving wagons. Without a word spoken she was deposited upon one of them, a gun pressed into her hand. "The capt'n says take this and use it if you must."

Unlike most young ladies, Jasmine was not ignorant in the use of firearms. In truth, she was an expert marksman with a gun as well as a bow and arrow. Many were the hours spent—usually at the shore, and sometimes in the wooded regions north of the city—in enjoyable competition with Deborah as the two ladies made excellent use of their targets. But her ability to shoot and hit a target did not extend to killing a human being. She could never use the weapon against a man. She shivered with horror as she eyed the heavy, long-barreled gun.

Did Anthony truly think her capable of killing someone? Especially one of her own? Never. She grunted a sound of disgust and almost flung the weapon from her. But before she had the chance, the smallest of doubts perked her thoughts. Could it be that a time might come when she'd find the need for the gun? If Anthony took his stand and was overrun—a forgone conclusion as far as she was concerned—would the English treat her as the enemy? Surely they would. No doubt her explanations would go unheard. Unheard, at least, until it was much too late, for no matter her declarations to the opposite, Jasmine hadn't a doubt as to her misuse if captured.

Her heart pounded with a fear she was sure could never be equaled as she slid the gun into her skirt pocket.

* * *

292

Jasmine sat in the company of a dozen or more camp followers, sheltered from English fire for the time being by distance and the row of supply wagons. Behind them ran the Broad River, effectively cutting off any means of retreat. All knew this battle at Cowpens would be won or lost today. This time the rebels would not—indeed could not—run.

Perhaps a hundred yards beyond the wagons, Lieutenant Colonel Washington's cavalry pawed nervously upon the ground. Before him stood General Morgan's line of Continentals and before him Colonel Pickens's North Carolina, South Carolina and Georgia volunteers faced, almost two to one, Lieutenant Colonel Tarleton and his crack militia.

Jasmine almost giggled aloud at the absurd turn her life had taken. A year ago it would have been impossible for her to imagine that she would one day be witness to a battle of this or any proportions. This morning she had realized upon spying the patriots just over the rise from their camp that it wasn't Anthony whom Tarleton wanted, but Morgan. Their tiny group of rebels just happened to have gotten caught between these two deadly forces.

The relief she had felt upon spying General Morgan and his men had been almost palatable. They weren't going to die, after all. Now, hours later, she wondered if she hadn't drawn her conclusions too soon.

The drums beat down upon her, the sound surely as suffocating as the noonday sun. Hour upon hour, they directed wave after wave of men to the front line. Would they never stop? Was Anthony one of them? Was he lying maimed or dead upon the blood-soaked earth? How many more would die before she heard again the delightful sound of silence, broken only by the stirring of a gentle breeze over this once-peaceful meadow.

Helpless despite her shivering disgust, her lungs

strained for every breath. And with every breath came the acrid burning of gunpowder and the gaggingly sweet scent of blood as a gentle breeze drifted huge clouds of the odious stench of war over her head.

Curses and screams of agony, sounds she'd never forget, echoed over the once peaceful valley. The foes met almost at dead center—an appropriate bit of wording, she mused, for nearly everything at the center was dead.

Jasmine left the rest of the women cowering, shivering with fear, behind the wagons. In truth, she was no braver than the rest. She simply could not bear the waiting. She had to know how the battle progressed, if Anthony still lived. She believed not knowing was worse than anything she might see.

She was wrong.

Nothing could have prepared her for the carnage that lay before her. Her eyes widened with shock, for she knew the manner in which a battle was fought, but what was spoken of in drawing rooms and seen firsthand were too decidedly different matters. The English had brought to the front two pieces of field artillery. Systematically and repeatedly they fired upon lines of men whose only protection against exploding steel was a rifle.

Jasmine gagged and her hand came to her mouth in a reflexive action as she watched another volley of shots dismember a man who had foolishly stood in the line of fire. Another quivered uncontrollably upon the ground seconds after his left arm was blown twenty feet into the air.

Jasmine greedily accepted the self-protecting cloak of numbness that descended upon her. She didn't think, she didn't feel, knowing there would be a later time for her to bemoan this horrible maiming and loss of life. All she could do was watch the English line advance. Colonel Pickens's men retreated. The English advanced farther. Again the patriots withdrew. Fifty paces they stopped and regrouped. An order was called out. Suddenly the patriots charged with bayonets. The English fled, leaving their field pieces to the rebels' possession.

It was then that Washington's cavalry moved. They circled behind Tarleton and successfully surrounded his entire militia. Jasmine blinked her astonishment. But for a straggling shot fired from the brush that lined the hillside, the battle was done and the rebels had proven themselves the victor against this mightier force.

From her position Jasmine watched as Tarleton and a few scattering infantry hurriedly mounted wagons and made good their escape, leaving behind much needed baggage for rebel use.

Later she would realize that there were over four hundred dead or wounded, not an inordinate sum considering these men fought from straight lines that offered no protection against the answering fire of their enemies. But to Jasmine four hundred looked to be four thousand. She'd never before seen death firsthand and death of this magnitude was incomprehensible.

Jasmine whimpered and shivered with horror as she stepped over still another body. Heat was a horror here in this valley of death. Flies buzzed sickeningly, lapping up the spillage of blood. Bodies began to bloat. Jasmine swallowed her disgust, forcing aside the threatening nausea, keenly aware of the sickening stench growing stronger every minute. She almost fell when her foot slipped in a puddle of blood that lay upon a discarded leather pouch. Her back was aching, but she kept turning the dead over. It didn't matter anymore that most of them wore red. What mattered was she couldn't find him anywhere.

Tears blurred her vision. She wiped at her eyes

with the backs of her hands, never realizing her hands were covered with blood. The result was ghastly. Covered with the dust and gunpowder, smeared with blood, she was almost unrecognizable.

"What are you doing?"

Jasmine glanced up at the sound of his voice, only to hear his sharp curse. Instantly she was pressed tightly against him. His voice was barely recognizable as he forced aside his panic. "What happened? Where were you hit?" His fingers moved gently but purposefully through her hair, searching for the wound as he spoke.

It took a moment for her to realize he was actually standing there amid the grisly carnage, alive and well, holding her in his arms. Jasmine choked back her cry of joy and collapsed with relief against him.

But Anthony took her cry to be one of pain. "My God," she heard him mutter. His face grew sickly gray, his lips only a thin white line of anxiety. "Jasmine, please." His body trembled with stark terror. "Show me where it hurts."

Jasmine had to think about his words for a moment, for she couldn't remember being hit, and right now nothing hurt. He must be referring to when he had pushed her out of the bed this morning, she silently mused. She shrugged. "My shoulder. It's nothing. Where were you?"

Anthony held her from him, glanced to her shoulder and then back to her face. His brow furrowed with confusion. If she was hit in her shoulder, shouldn't she be bleeding there? Why then was it her face that was covered with blood?

"Are you all right?" she asked, her voice breaking on a sob as she blinked tears that ran a white path over her blood-smeared cheeks. "I couldn't find you anywhere."

"I'm fine," he assured her. "Morgan sent a few of us after Tarleton. That's why you couldn't find me.

"Show me where it hurts."

Jasmine shrugged again and replied honestly, "It doesn't really hurt."

"Where?" he insisted, his voice holding a note of desperation. God, was she delirious? Is that why she was talking nonsense?

"I told you, my shoulder. I bumped it when I fell out of bed this morning."

"But it's not blee—" He never finished the sentence. His body stiffened with outrage. Only later would he know it was merely his fear for her that had brought about this anger. At the moment, however, he knew only anger, anger that she should have subjected him to what he believed was needless suffering. He thundered louder even than the cannon this morning, she thought.

"What?"

Jasmine jumped at the sound and looked up with nothing less than amazement.

"Your shoulder? You're whining over a sore shoulder?" Suddenly he grabbed that same shoulder and began to drag her from the field of death. "Sonofabitch. Everywhere you look men are dead and you're . . ."

Jasmine twisted free of his hold. Feet widespread, hands upon her hips, she glared, daring to face his anger. "Whining? Who's whining? Why did you ask if you didn't want to know?"

Anthony took a deep breath, fighting for a degree of sanity in this madness. But he was hard put to win out against the rage that assailed. He'd thought her seriously injured, only to find her playing on his sympathy. "Would you mind telling me what you expected to gain by pretending to be hurt?"

Jasmine only stared at him bewildered. "Pretending?" What in God's name was the beast talking about?

"Your face." His gaze moved carefully over her.

"Your hands. Why have you covered them with blood?"

Jasmine looked quickly at her hands and her eyes widened with surprise to see their condition. Still, her anger was not in the least diminished by this phenomenon. She again glared at him as her lips twisted into a sneer. "I have no idea and I wouldn't tell you if I did."

She spun on her heel and headed toward the river. *Bastard! And to think I was worried.* Well, worried was putting it a bit mildly, she reconsidered. *I was terrified.* Terrified for his safety? She made a disparaging and most unladylike sound.

"Jasmine! Come back here."

Jasmine came to a sudden stop. She spun again to face him, ready to bombard him with just a sampling of the anger that raged within. From the corner of her eye, she saw the boy move. At first she thought it her imagination. An English soldier was moving closer. Her eyes widened with surprise as she watched him raise his rifle to his shoulder and take aim.

Jasmine gasped. She tried to call out a warning, but in her fear for Anthony only gibberish came forth. She thought to lunge and push him aside, but he stood too far from her. She knew with a certainty that by the time she reached him it would be too late. She remembered the gun he'd given her earlier. Without thinking of the consequences, she reached into her pocket and pulled it free. In an instant, and without so much as taking careful aim, she fired. Less than a second later another shot was heard, but the shot had gone wide. The young soldier never knew he had reflexively pulled the trigger. He was already dead.

Anthony stood there, his mouth open with shock, wondering why he felt no pain, wondering why he wasn't dead. He had watched her draw the gun and, with seemingly little care, aim it. She couldn't have

298

missed. No more than ten feet separated them.

Why had she done it, he wondered? Why had she killed him? He waited for the pain to spread throughout his chest and, when it did not, he dared to look down. Slowly his gaze moved over his chest and belly. Nothing. Good God, she had missed! He felt his knees weaken with a wave of relief. Cold sweat chilled him to the core. A moment later unspeakable rage took the place of relief. He moved toward her stunned form and grabbed the gun from her limp hold with a vicious twist.

In the flood of emotion that shook him, Anthony never noticed the blank look in her eyes. Neither did he realize the lack of resistance in her body as his fingers snaked into her hair, grabbing a fistful of the silky black cloud and lifting her from the ground as he yanked her face within inches of his. "Bitch!" he pulled harder, almost out of control. "I should kill you for that." His eyes filled with disgust as he uttered a vile curse and flung her from him, leaving her to lie among the dead.

Jasmine never made a sound as she landed with a dull thud upon the ground. The side of her head hit against the steel barrel of a forgotten rifle and her own blood slid over her cheek to merge with the red stains on her face. Only vaguely did she realize his hatred, his rough treatment, for her mind could not shake the horror of what she had done. Her eyes were level now with the soldier she had killed. She silently watched the blood dribble from the grotesque wound in his neck. She watched until no more came and then she simply got up and walked away.

Anthony never saw her leave. He never glanced her way again as he supervised the unloading of the wagons. It wasn't until dark, when all were sitting around their campfires, that Anthony began to wonder where she might be. All afternoon he had refused to think about what she had done. After the wagons were unloaded he found work among those who were injured. He wouldn't think. He didn't dare.

Twice Boggs had tried to talk to him, for Boggs had been standing near enough to know the truth of it. And twice Anthony's murderous look had brought his words to a stumbling end. The bitch needed no one to come to her defense. Jesus, if anyone needed defending it was him. There was no telling when next she might try to cut him down. Anthony shivered with dread. How could he live with a wife who might murder? How could he have ever loved a woman such as she?

Odd but he hadn't believed till he saw it with his own eyes that she had it in her to kill. Even this morning he'd held little hope that she would use the gun as he'd suggested. A wry twist of his lips formed a grotesque smile in the flickering light of the campfires. Last night—a small sound of pain came from deep within his throat—last night he had nearly reached heaven in her arms and today he'd been as close to hell as he'd ever hoped to get.

"I'm going to say what I got to say. If you bash my face in, I'll just say it when you're finished."

Anthony shot his longtime friend a look of disgust. He sighed, closed his eyes, and leaned his head back upon the rough bark of the tree. "I hadn't realized you were so far under her spell to become her champion."

Boggs ignored the taunt. "Capt'n, your little girl's out there alone in the woods. Has been all afternoon."

Anthony laughed, not believing him for an instant. Jasmine wouldn't be fool enough to walk deep into the woods. She knew the dangers of straying too far. No doubt she was just out of sight waiting for him to come and search for her. Well, she had a long wait coming. "Don't you feel a small measure of compassion for the poor creatures who

300

live there when you imagine what she might do to them?"

Again Boggs ignored his words. "She left right after you flung her around like she was nuthin' but a rag doll."

Anthony glared at the man, daring him to say he wasn't correct in his treatment of her. "I suppose you're going to tell me a man should take it for granted that his wife will try to kill him. How often has Mrs. Boggs tried to do you in?"

"If you ain't the stupidest . . . How'd you ever get to be Capt'n? I thought officers were supposed to be smart."

"I used to think I was," he replied wearily.

"Yeah, so did I."

"It took a bit, but I finally figured out you thought she was tryin' to kill you, right?"

Anthony allowed a small smile of ridicule. "And you're going to tell me she missed on purpose."

Boggs laughed. "She didn't miss nuthin'. And a damn good shot it was, too."

Anthony stiffened. "What do you mean she didn't miss? The fact that I'm standing here is proof that she did."

Boggs sneered his disgust. "The redcoat she was aimin' at. Killed him clean in one shot." Boggs shrugged, "'Cause he was already down, but it was her shot that finished him off."

"Are you trying to tell me she killed an English soldier?" Anthony blinked in sheer amazement.

"I ain't *tryin'* to tell you nuthin'. I'm tellin' you straight out."

"Why? Why would she do it?"

"'Cause the Brit had you in his sights, is why."

"Jesus!" Anthony was so shaken by this news he rocked unsteadily on his feet. Having no knowledge of Jasmine's marksmanship, he didn't for a minute believe she had actually hit what she'd aimed at. He

301

knew she was trying to kill him, he knew by the anger he saw in her eyes. That she had killed another man was purely accidental.

Boggs nodded knowingly, believing he had convinced his captain of the truth. "Yep, he might be the one you'd be facin' right about now if it weren't for your lady. But I doubt it. I suspect more'n likely it'd be Lucifer welcomin' you with open arms."

Anthony gave no response to the gibe. With a curse he pushed himself from the tree knowing he had put off their confrontation long enough. It was time to find her and force her to face up to what she had done. Would she deny her cold-blooded attempt at murder? Would she expect him to believe his eyes had lied? His mouth turned grim. For her sake she'd best hold her tongue on that score, for he doubted he'd be able to withhold his fury, should she try.

Jasmine stopped to rest against a tree. She knew they would find her soon. This was not the first time she had wandered too far. She smiled, for she imagined at any minute to hear her mother's voice calling out directing her back to safety. Not that she wasn't safe, mind you. How could she be anything but, here on the immense acreage that bordered her family's home.

Jasmine raised her face to the branches overhead. She laughed with childlike pleasure as she watched a bird flit noisily from branch to branch, apparently not at all happy that she had invaded his domain. "Shall I remind you, Mr. Bird, that this is my property and it is you who should beg admittance?"

Jasmine was oblivious to the hunger that had raged through her for the last three days. Her lips were cracked, her throat parched, but she never gave the discomforting thirst a moment's thought, so deeply had she reverted back to the time of her childhood when she knew no terrors, she witnessed no death, she suffered no pain, no hatred. Her father's abuse had yet to come and all she knew was her mother's love and the safety of her home.

Jasmine's eyes widened with surprise as she came upon a clearing. "Are you a poacher?"

Curses spilled from two pairs of lips as Jebodiah Smith threw himself away from his partner, Hopeful, sitting before the fire. The two men rolled wildly upon the ground. They stopped as suddenly as they'd begun and were now deep in the shadows, facing toward the sound of her voice, rifles ready, fingers held at the trigger. Jebodiah breathed a long sigh of relief and willed his thundering heart to quiet as he watched Jasmine walk fearlessly into the light of his campfire.

"Jesus, lady! You just about scared the bejesus out of me."

"Mother says only nasty people use those words," she admonished with childlike innocence.

Jebodiah's joints creaked with age and too many nights spent unprotected among the elements. He came to his feet. They stood staring at each other for a long moment before either of them moved. She followed him back to the fire and sat uninvited beside him and Hopeful. It took a few moments but she finally managed to adjust her skirt.

Jebodiah shrugged at their uninvited guest and sent his longtime companion a puzzled look, for the elaborate movements were odd considering the plainness of her costume. One would think she had yards of lace to see to with all the flutter. Her eyes grew huge as the light from the fire allowed her to take in Jebodiah's long, white, shaggy beard. "Are you one of them?"

"Where'd you come from, girl?"

Jasmine nodded behind her shoulder. "Over there."

"What are you doing here by your lonesome?"

"I'm on a picnic. I think I got lost." Her voice lowered conspiratorially. "Mr. Kensington's our neighbor. He shoots poachers. Are you a poacher?"

Jebodiah's eyes narrowed. "How old are you, lassie?"

"Eight. How old are you?"

Jeb's white brows rose with surprise. He didn't look at Hopeful imagining the black man's eyes would be wide with dawning fear at her answer. Eight? Did she take him for some kind of fool? He could see with his own eyes she was a woman growed. Jebodiah bit back the sneer he was about to make at the look of wide-open innocence in her eyes. He felt a sudden chill race down his back. Was something wrong with her? Was she some witless fool? If she was, how the hell did she get this far from a settlement?

"It's impolite to ignore a question," Jasmine stated primly.

"What question was that?"

"How old are you?"

"Fifty-nine."

Jasmine's eyes widened as might any child's when hearing something that amazed. "Fifty-nine?" she repeated. "I never knew anyone that old. My mother's twenty-six, but she's very pretty," she said as if it were all right to be twenty-six as long as you were pretty.

Jebodiah gave her a long, searching look, having not a doubt that the girl spoke the truth. No one who looked like her could have come from an ugly woman. Why, if he was twenty years younger . . . Jebodiah forced aside the thought with a silent curse of self-disgust. No use thinking about what could never be. Someone must be looking for the girl. He wondered where she'd come from.

In the flickering light of the campfire, Jasmine

304

took in the color of the man across from her for the first time. Her eyes rounded and she gasped with surprise, "You're black!"

Hopeful shrugged. He'd never heard his color so obviously remarked upon. "You're white," he replied.

Jasmine giggled. "Of course I'm white. I take a bath every night. Doesn't your mother make you wash?"

"And you figure I'm this color 'cause I don't wash?"

"Aren't you?"

"Ain't you never seen a black man, girl?"

Jasmine shook her head in astonishment.

"Well, you have now," he remarked as he bit into a piece of hardtack.

"Mother says it's impolite to eat in front of anyone."

"Your mother sure has a thing about being polite, doesn't she?"

"It's very important, you know," she explained with complete seriousness to the two men, her voice slightly sing song. "We must always be polite. It hurts people's feelings if we're not."

Hopeful shot her a look of disgust, while mumbling a curse.

Jebodiah shrugged. "You wanna eat?"

"If I may," Jasmine responded with a sweet smile. "I am a bit hungry, but I'm more thirsty."

"What is this?" she asked as Jebodiah handed over a portion of his meal after she had emptied his canteen of water in seconds.

"Hardtack."

"It's not very good, is it?"

Jebodiah shrugged again, his eyes never leaving her face. "It serves its purpose."

"Don't you have a wife or a housekeeper who will cook for you?"

"Nope."

"You mean you're all alone?"

Jebodiah's wizened eyes narrowed at her question. What the hell was she up to? What was she doing out here wandering through these woods alone. Suddenly a thought occurred. Maybe she wasn't alone. Maybe whoever she was with was out there waiting for a signal that all was clear before he came in. Jebodiah came suddenly to his feet. If there was someone out there, he'd sure as hell find out.

"Where are you going?"

"I'll be right back." And to his partner he said, "Don't let her wander off."

Jebodiah returned with the knowledge that she was indeed alone. If anyone was out there, he'd have found tracks beside hers. There wasn't anyone alive who could track better than him, and that included an Indian. For a long time he watched her as she struggled to get the hardtack down.

"You gotta chew it better than that. What'dya wanna do, choke?"

Jasmine obediently followed his instructions, almost drowning herself when he told her to take a little water with the meat.

He had to slap her on the back to stop her choking. Damn, she'd scared him shitless again.

"What's your name?" he asked after they'd both calmed down a bit.

Jasmine smiled as she spoke. "Jasmine Huntington. I'll be Lady Huntington when I grow up."

"You will, eh? How come you ain't a lady now?"

"Oh, I am, but Mother says the title's not to be used until I'm older."

"Where you from?"

"I told you, here."

"Where's here?"

Jasmine laughed. "Don't you know where you are? Have you gotten yourself lost?"

306

Jebodiah shrugged and shot Hopeful a look. "Guess maybe I have."

"We're in England. Do you know that?"

Hopeful cursed. Jebodiah nodded, figuring it couldn't hurt to play along with her for a while. "What part?"

"Huntington," she announced proudly. "The same as my name."

"You mean these parts were named after you?"

"Oh, no. My ancestors named this village."

It was an hour or so later, and Jebodiah cursed himself for being a damned fool as he watched her sound asleep snuggled deep inside his own warm blankets. Hopeful hadn't cared if the girl froze. He had taken his own blankets and settled himself by the fire for the night. Why the hell did Jebodiah feel he had to give up what was rightfully his? Why should he care if she was cold? It should be her sleeping, or trying to, under the loose fur pelts that insisted on falling to his side very time his chest moved to breathe.

It was a long night, and he breathed a sigh of relief as the sky began to lighten. Jebodiah's joints creaked as he came into a sitting position. It would be an hour or more before the sun began to creep its light over the horizon, but he figured he'd had as much sleep as he was likely to get.

Before long a pot of coffee was brewing upon the fire while he warmed up some leftover beans and Indian meal in bacon fat.

"Help yourself to some coffee," he said when he saw her stretch and sit up.

"I'm not old enough to drink coffee. Besides, I much prefer hot chocolate."

Hopeful grumbled his disgust at that.

"Well, I ain't got no hot chocolate. It's coffee or nuthin'."

Jebodiah cursed as he saw tears fill her eyes. He had

307

no call to go yellin' at the girl. Shit! It was obvious she wasn't in her right mind. Now he had hurt her feelings and she was going to cry. If it was one thing he couldn't stand it was watching a woman cry. If he wasn't so stupid, he wouldn't have forgotten her story. Well, he silently excused himself, looking at her it wasn't easy to remember that she was supposed to be eight.

What bothered him now and had bothered him most of the night was what was he going to do with her? He couldn't leave her here although he was sorely tempted. It would be easier to travel if he didn't have Hopeful scowling at him every minute. But she'd die for sure, and that was just one more thing Jeb didn't want to answer for. He'd have to take her to a settlement. He shrugged. Maybe he'd take her to Charleston. It would only take a week or so of riding. He could sell his pelts while he was there. It shouldn't be too much trouble, he reasoned.

If they hadn't come across the baby, it probably wouldn't have been.

Chapter Eighteen

Jebodiah cursed as they came upon the wagon. "Goddamned stupid pilgrims," he grunted as he spotted the charred wooden remains. What kind of fools would travel these parts alone? Jesus! You would have thought they'd know better. His shrug of nonconcern belied the disgust and impotent rage that twisted his features. Well, they sure as hell did now.

The ground was littered with objects torn from the wagon. A chest of drawers was tipped upon its side and leaned at a drunken angle against a child's wooden cradle. Its drawers were pulled out, lying empty now upon the tall grass. Mattresses, torn pieces of clothing, a child's toy, and ripped blankets littered the area around the still smoldering wagon. In the center of the debris lay a dead man, his back grotesquely supporting the gaily feathered end of an arrow.

Ominously, there was no sign of the woman, even though torn petticoats, drawers, and a crushed bonnet lay discarded upon the ground in a silent proclamation that there had been one. She was gone. Jeb hadn't a doubt the Indians had taken her. He knew, too, she was better off dead.

"Why did you stop?"

Jeb turned to Jasmine, who sat high upon his pack mule directly behind him, her eyes bright with childish inquisitiveness. "Are we there?"

There was no way he was going to tell her what lay across their path. There was no way he was going to let her see it neither. No tellin' how she might react if she'd seen somethin' like this. He eyed a silent Hopeful at his side. "This is the wrong way. We got to turn around."

Jasmine nodded, having no doubt he spoke the truth. He was taking her back to her mother. Instinctively she knew that any man who'd go to that kind of trouble could be trusted completely.

Then they heard it. Jeb refused to believe the sound for what it was. Hopeful pretended he hadn't heard it at all. "What was that?" Jasmine asked, her head tilted as she listened for it again.

"Nuthin', probably a bird."

"I never heard a bird that sounded like that."

Jeb tried to turn them on the narrow path. Desperately he pulled on the reins of his horse, while one hand tugged at his stubborn mule. "It was a bird, I tell ya," he insisted, his voice growing in strength, for he knew in his heart it was not. What in hell did he look like, some goddamned parent to lost children? It was one thing to help out this simple-minded woman, but there was no way he was going to cart a baby all the way to Charleston. Even if he managed by some miracle to avoid the Indians, he hadn't an iota of an idea how to go about taking care of it, and he wasn't stupid enough to try.

It was bound to die, in any case. No tellin' how long it had been out here. At least since last night, he reasoned. It was better off gettin' it over with.

"It's a baby!" Jasmine cried, her eyes wide in obvious astonishment as she heard the sound again.

"It's a bird," he continued to insist. "What the hell would a baby be doing out here?"

"Maybe Gypsies left it." She scrambled down from her perch high above the tied fur pelts. "Mother told me they sometimes camp on our property."

Jebodiah cursed. "Didn't your mother tell you to keep away from them?"

"Of course she did." Jasmine stopped and turned to face his scowl. "They sometimes steal children," she added with a hint of fear in her huge silver eyes. Suddenly she smiled, and Jeb's heart twisted with a longing he dared not name at the beautiful sight. "But they must have forgot this one." Jasmine was running toward the sound, unmindful of Jeb's sharp curses.

Jasmine's eyes saw the destruction, but something had happened to her mind when she shot the soldier. It was as if a safety valve had closed off somewhere, preventing her from absorbing further horror. The same thing refused to allow this scene of destruction to penetrate her mind. She searched for the sound, mindlessly stepping over the fallen man. A moment later she smiled as she moved a piece of underbrush just beyond the campsite. A minute or so later she was cheerfully walking back toward a cursing Jebodiah and a silent Hopeful. "I told you it was a baby. Look." She proudly held the infant up for the men's inspection.

Hopeful cursed. "I ain't goin' anywhere with that. You think I'm lookin' to get myself dead?"

Jeb spit and scowled his disgust. Just what he needed. First a half-crazed woman and now a baby. What in hell was he supposed to do? He glared at his longtime friend. "You wanna stop bitchin'? Ain't I got enough to handle?"

"I think she's hungry."

"How'd you know it's a she?"

. But Jasmine either never heard his question or chose to ignore it as she cooed at the child. "Isn't she pretty? I'm going to ask my mother if I can keep her."

"Christ!" Jeb grumbled sourly as he ran his gnarled fingers through his long white hair.

"What are you going to feed it?"

Jasmine smiled. "I'll ask Mrs. Kensley when we get home. She's our cook. She has six children. She knows everything."

Jebodiah closed his eyes, lifting his face toward the heavens, silently wondering why God had seen fit to cause his life such a ruckus. He didn't ask for much. All he'd ever wanted was to live the last of his days in peace. He'd had a family once, but the Lord had seen fit to take them. Was the Lord now expectin' Jeb to take these two misfits under his wing as a substitute? Well, the Almighty could just think that one through a bit more clearly. He had no intention of being saddled with a family. Not at this point in his life.

What in hell was he going to do? Now it would take him twice as long to reach Charleston than he'd originally planned. He'd have to stop and hunt regularly. And it would be a good idea if he could find a cow along the way. Jebodiah chuckled in ridicule at his own thoughts. He was gettin' as daft as this woman. Sure, he reasoned in silent sarcasm, all he had to do was wish for one and a cow was sure to appear.

"I think she wants milk," Jasmine remarked as the baby began to squirm in her arms. "And she's wet all over."

Jebodiah sighed wearily. "Ain't that just what I wanted to hear." He dismounted and angrily began to throw his pelts to the ground. "Sit there till I get back."

Jebodiah stormed off in search of something, anything he might find that the baby might use. A few minutes later he fought his way back through the thick foliage. If there was a cow, the Indians had taken it. He grimaced with disgust. How in hell was he supposed to keep this little thing alive with-

312

out milk?

His arms filled, he dumped the blankets, a few tiny dresses, a soft bonnet, and material he supposed was used for changing a baby when it was soiled at Jasmine's feet.

Jasmine cried out with glee. What fun! She didn't need dolls anymore. Now she could play with her very own baby. And the very first thing she was going to do was change her.

Two days later they found the cabin.

"I don't give one damn what you do. I ain't leavin' her. I left my wife and son and found the Indians had had a good time with them while I was gone."

"She ain't your wife. The Indians won't bother her. They's scared of her kind."

"Is that what's plaguin' you? Are you a scared of her?"

Hopeful shot him an angry look. He weren't no nigger to shiver in fear at every sound in the night and he weren't scared o' that half-crazed lady neither. He just didn't want to be bothered with this whole mess. It wasn't his problem what happened to her. He just didn't like most folks. Especially white ones. "The baby is sick. It's sure to die."

"I know that."

Hopeful shrugged. "It don't matter none if it dies here or on the way to Charleston."

"You wanna go? Go. Take your share o' the pelts. I'll catch up."

Hopeful cursed, but he didn't go.

One day grew into the next as they waited for the baby to grow in strength or die. In the meantime Jeb and Hopeful repaired the damage long years of abandonment had done to the cabin. They sewed their pelts together, creating warm comfortable bedding. They repaired holes in the cabin's roof.

They hunted. They cooked. And when Jasmine grew exhausted, they took turns rocking a baby that seemed never able to rest.

Hopeful even managed to fashion a broom of pine needles and Jasmine, when she wasn't attending to the child, swept the place clean.

Two weeks had gone by and the baby seemed no better than the day they'd found her. There was no milk, and being miles from a settlement, no possible way of finding any. Jasmine fed the child, dipping a clean corner of her torn petticoat in warm sugar water or broth, allowing the baby to suck it dry. But nothing she did made a difference. It was a rare moment that the baby quieted enough to sleep or, for that matter, managed to keep the liquid down.

Both men knew they'd be moving on soon. And neither, although they'd deny it to their dying day, looked forward to the moment, for both Jeb and Hopeful had grown oddly content and happier than they could have imagined with their makeshift family. Amazingly, even Hopeful's grumpy attitude was sometimes known to slip, a tender smile curving his harsh lips when he cuddled the suffering baby in his arms.

In days, perhaps hours, the baby would die, no matter how they struggled to keep it alive. Both of them dreaded the moment and wondered how Jasmine would accept the inevitable.

It was late. Jeb heard the sound and was standing pressed flat against the cabin wall with rifle aimed into the darkness, long before the stranger emerged from the shadows.

"You be wantin' sometin', mister?" Jeb asked the man, his rifle pointing directly at Anthony's stomach.

Anthony heard the voice, but looked beyond the dark figure of a man. His gaze was drawn to the open door and the woman inside the cabin. He felt a wave of knee-weakening relief, but the emotion was short-lived at best, as anger came to fill him to the core of his being. He was suddenly almost beside himself with rage that she should have fared well while he had suffered the agonies of imagining her injured or dead. He wondered with no little amazement at his ability to remain so apparently in control when every nerve ending screamed for him to go to her. He closed his eyes and silently cursed his weakness, for he should put his hands to her throat and squeeze until his agony was no more, and yet all he could think, all he could want, was to take her in his arms and feel again her softness against him.

He stood bathed in the light from the doorway and nodded toward the woman he could clearly see inside. She was pacing back and forth while holding a baby against one shoulder. And right now he couldn't decide what he wanted more, to kiss her or kill her. "My wife."

Jeb's lips tightened and he felt his heart give just a little twist of regret. He'd known from the beginning he'd have to hand her over someday, but he hadn't expected it to happen so soon. For just a second he allowed the thought of pulling the trigger. If Jasmine had no husband, maybe she'd stay with him. Maybe he wouldn't be so lonely. Damn but he hadn't known he was lonely till she came. And he was just getting used to her, too.

"Maybe she don't want to be your wife no more."

"Maybe you should mind your own goddamned business."

"I figure, since I've been carin' for her for the last two weeks that maybe it is my business."

"Look, old man, I don't want to fight with you. I just want my wife back."

"Why'd you let her go?"

Anthony breathed a long sigh, straining for a control he was far from feeling. "It's a long story."

Jebodiah shrugged and relaxed his stance a bit. "I

315

got time."

"It's private."

"I ain't lettin' anyone take her till I find out what happened to her."

"What do you mean? What happened to her?"

"I mean she's not all there." Jebodiah pointed to his head with one finger. "I wanna know why."

Anthony started with dawning fear. What the hell was he talking about? Was he trying to tell him something was wrong with her? Anthony breathed a long sigh of relief as he listened to the sound of her voice singing to the child she held. "If anyone's crazy, it's you." Anthony was about to rush by Jasmine's self-appointed guard but was brought up short by the rifle pressing deep in his belly while another poked him hard at the small of his back. Sonofabitch! There were two of them. What in hell was she doing here? How had she come so far? How did she find these two and what was she doing for them that they should be so loyal? "Jasmine!" he called out.

"Jeb" came a fear-filled voice from across the small cabin as she backed to the far wall. Jasmine's eyes grew huge as she stared at the open door. She couldn't see out into the darkness, but she could hear and what she heard caused her heart to pound with fright. What she couldn't understand was why? "Is something the matter?"

"Everthin' fine. Hopeful and me, we're just talking to a friend. You can go to sleep now."

Anthony opened his mouth to call her again but felt the rifle press harder into his gut. Wisely he closed his mouth again. "Suppose you leave the little girl alone and just tell me the problem."

Jasmine had just snuggled down with the baby upon a bed of soft fur when she heard the sound of his voice.

"Jasmine . . ." Anthony tried, but he couldn't remember a time when he'd felt closer to murder. He had feared her dead, having searched the wilderness for two weeks only to find her safely ensconced in a ramshackle cabin with two diligent watch dogs. He should have known not to worry. Her kind always managed to land on her feet. Aye, her kind always would.

Jasmine looked up from the pallet of furs, her eyes wide, as Anthony came slowly into the cabin. Indeed, her eyes told the whole of it had he been willing to see. Confusion. Childish inquisitiveness. They rounded with surprise as she watched this visitor enter their little home. "Hello." She smiled sweetly as she came to a sitting position.

Anthony bit back the curses that threatened. "Hello? Is that all you can say?" he railed as he stood menacingly over her.

Jasmine gave a weak smile, never hearing the disgust in his tone. But she did hear the anger. She looked past him and smiled as Jeb and Hopeful entered the cabin. The sudden pounding of her heart lessened with their comforting presence. "Are you Jeb and Hopeful's friend?"

Anthony shot her a look of pure hatred. So she was determined to carry this hoax to the end. Did she imagine her power over him so great that he'd believe this outrageous performance?

"Why are you pretending? Am I supposed to believe you don't know who I am?"

Jasmine gave him a wide-eyed look of true confusion. "Do I?" A flicker of fear shone in eyes gone suddenly huge. "Do I know you?"

"Go easy on her. I told you . . ."

"Shut the hell up," Anthony flung at Jeb, not realizing till that moment the man had followed him inside. "She's my wife and I'll treat her any way I see fit."

Jasmine blinked her surprise, wondering who this man was and why he should speak so rudely? Her eyes clouded with a trace of fear, but she bravely protected her friend. "Mother says only nasty people use those words."

"What in hell is going on here?"

"I told you before. She's . . ."

Anthony interrupted with a curse of disbelief while silently swearing there was nothing wrong with her. She had lost a bit of weight, but she was just as lovely as ever. Couldn't they see that? Couldn't they see there was nothing wrong? "Can't you see she's faking?" A terrible thought came suddenly to mind. Anthony would realize later he'd never have allowed such a thought had he not been half crazed with worry.

"Or maybe you can," he answered his own question with a knowing sneer. "What did she promise you if you went along with her game? She whorin' for the two of you? Is that why . . . ?" Anthony never got to finish his sentence, for a mighty fist suddenly made contact with his mouth.

"You sonofabitch!" Jeb grunted as he stood over Anthony's dazed figure. "I don't give a damn if you're her husband or not. Nobody ain't goin' to talk about her like that."

But Anthony wasn't dazed for long. An instant later Jeb was flung back, his head landed with a dull thud against the wall. Slowly he slumped to the floor.

Jasmine screamed as she scrambled from beneath the covers and ran to the older man. Bravely she knelt at his side and cried. "Stop! Don't hit him! He's my friend."

Anthony never noticed the barrel of the rifle pressing suddenly into his back. All he could do was stare with amazement at his wife as she knelt at his feet. His heart tripled its beat as almost paralyzing fear crept into his body, the force of it nearly causing him to crumble at her side. Her voice and actions were those of a child. She wasn't faking. What the hell happened to her? His throat was so tight, he could hardly get the words out. "What did you do to her?"

Jeb shook the fuzziness from his head and came slowly to his feet. "I figure it was you who did the doin'."

"You shouldn't have done that," Jasmine said as she, too, came to her feet. She shook her head as if realizing his shame. "Mother says it's very wrong for one person to hit anoth—" Jasmine's voice faded as her eyes widened with dawning understanding. Suddenly her voice lowered to a whisper, her confusion unmistakable. "Anthony?"

Her heart swelled with a mixture of joy and pain. Had he ever been so handsome? Tanner than ever, his hair even more liberally streaked with gold, his skin stretched tight across his features. He'd lost weight, but the new gauntness of his face only caused him to appear more appealing. She almost raised her arms in welcome. An instant later, all memories came rushing back. Her smile froze and then faded until a frown of pain stole across her face.

"Did you think it that easy to escape me? Didn't you think I'd look for you?"

Jasmine didn't bother to tell him she had forgotten his very existence till this very minute. That she'd never thought to escape him, that she'd wandered off in shock at the horror she had done. She never remarked upon the hardship she'd suffered wandering alone in the forest for three days before she stumbled upon Hopeful and Jeb. She wanted to laugh at the absurdity. And he thought it had been easy?

But she didn't laugh, couldn't laugh as the pain came rushing up to fill her throat. She gave what she hoped was a nonchalant shrug and forced the words past the tightness that nearly robbed her of her

319

breath. Her voice was low and rough, filled with the emotion. "You found me."

Anthony had expected many things. He thought she might rant at him. Perhaps cry. Perhaps beg him for forgiveness. Plead her case. Offer some kind of an excuse. Her almost uncaring attitude left him momentarily speechless.

"Is that all you've got to say? You've found me?"

Jasmine sighed. She was tired. She didn't have the strength or the will to do battle with him right now. She felt like crying, for she remembered too clearly the life she had taken and the blood that seemed to endlessly ooze from the wound. A wave of guilt assaulted. What must his mother feel? How could she bear the news that her son had died? How could any mother live with that kind of pain? And how could she? "What do you want me to say? I'm happy to see you again?"

Anthony gave a harsh, bitter chuckle. "You might try, but I wouldn't believe it. Not after what you did."

"What you *thought* I did," she corrected.

He gave a grim, humorless smile and nodded. "I was wondering how long it would take you to deny what you did."

Jasmine stared at his contemptuous expression for a long, silent moment. She remembered clearly now his mistreatment after she'd saved his life. She realized that he hadn't known her intentions, but what hurt was he hadn't bothered to find out. Pain slashed into her heart. He never asked, even after the night they had spent in each other's arms, he had thought her capable of murder. Obviously that night hadn't meant to him what it did to her. Lord but she was tired of it all. What she wanted more than anything in the world was peace. Somehow she knew she'd never get it with this man.

She wouldn't defend herself, not at this late date. If he thought she'd tell him now, after how he treated her, he could think again. She felt her heart harden. She'd never tell him. Let him think what he would. "Go to hell."

Anthony gave a harsh laugh. "No doubt I will, madam, and meet you there."

"I'm already in hell, Mr. Montgomery. Marrying you put me there."

"Good," Anthony grunted, denying the pain that ripped into his chest. What had happened to them? How had they ended up with this kind of antagonism between them? After the night they'd spent in each other's arms, he'd thought . . . Anthony shrugged. It didn't matter anymore what he thought. "Get ready. We're leaving, now!"

"I can't leave. Amy is just getting over the fever."

"Who the hell is Amy?" he asked as his gaze wandered about the small cabin, forgetting completely the child he'd previously seen her holding.

Jasmine walked back to her pallet and pushed down the blanket that covered the small, sleeping form.

"Where did you get her?"

"She's mine."

Anthony breathed a sigh of disgust, his mouth twisted in a sneer of ridicule. "Jasmine, we both know it takes nine months before a woman can deliver a child. We've only been apart for two weeks. She is not yours."

Jasmine lifted her chin in defiance. "I never said I bore her. I said she's mine, and she is."

"Where did she come from?"

"I found her."

"Where are her people?"

"Dead." Pain flashed in her eyes as she remembered for the first time the smoldering wagon and the body she had stepped over. Lord, how had she managed to forget that fact till now?

Anthony nodded and rubbed a hand over his face.

321

He tipped his head toward the two men standing at the opposite end of the small room. "What happened to you. How did you find those two?"

"I thought they were poachers," she said before she thought.

"You what?"

Jasmine shrugged. "Nothing. I came across their camp. They were kind enough to help me."

"Exactly what kind of help did they offer? If they touched you, I'll . . ."

"It's a bit late for this sudden show of concern, don't you think?" Jasmine looked at her husband for a long moment before she sighed with untold disgust. "I'm tired. I'm going to sleep."

"I told you to get ready. We're leaving."

"And I told you I can't go. Amy isn't well enough to travel."

"Leave her here then. I've wasted two weeks searching these damn woods for you. I'm needed back at camp."

Jasmine's laugh was hard and held not a trace of humor. "I wouldn't want you to waste another minute on my account. You can leave now."

"I'm not going without you."

"And I'm not going without Amy."

"Another day or so shouldn't make that much difference," Hopeful remarked as he moved into Anthony's range of vision. His rifle hung with supposed negligence at his side, but Anthony didn't miss the man's finger lightly caressing the trigger. He watched Hopeful's cold, almost lifeless expression, knowing without a doubt the black man would use the gun in an instant if he thought Jasmine in danger. How in hell did she inspire such devotion?

Anthony smiled almost sadly. Hadn't he at one time felt much the same? Lord but it was a curse to love a woman such as she. Thank God he loved her no longer. He felt a pang of sympathy for these two

322

men to be so taken in by this deceitful creature and wondered if they'd ever come to know the truth about her.

Anthony gave a long sigh, knowing he had no option but to comply, for to fight both men would be folly indeed. For now he would wait, and while he waited he'd plan all the delicious ways he'd make her suffer. "All right. We'll wait a few days."

Anthony cursed as he walked into the cabin. He had heard the laughter from across the clearing where he was chopping wood. She never realized he had entered, for her laughter did not cease as it often did when he was nearby. On her hands and knees, her face was snuggled into the baby's belly. Anthony felt a grin threaten as he listened to the happy, gurgling sounds as she tickled the child.

"You like that, do you?"

The baby had grabbed handfuls of dark hair and was now pulling her fist into her mouth. "No, darling," Jasmine murmured softly as she disengaged the tiny fingers from her hair, "You mustn't eat that. Hair is to tickle your belly with."

Again, the sound of laughter as Jasmine allowed the heavy mass to trail over the baby. Jasmine took the baby in her arms and sat back. "Oh, Amy, you are just so adorable."

"And healthy, I take it?" Anthony asked.

Jasmine's heart lurched at the sight of him leaning comfortably against the doorjamb. Silently she cursed the sudden leap of her pulse. Why did the mere sight of him do this to her? Why couldn't she simply ignore his presence?

Thank God he had not suggested they share the same pallet. Thank God for Jeb and Hopeful's presence, since she knew what would happen if either of them let down their guard. She knew she wouldn't offer a murmur of objection if he wanted to take her in his arms. God help her, she could deny it until forever, but the truth was she hungered as never before for his touch and she hated herself for this weakness.

"There's no use waiting any longer. We'll leave in the morning."

Jasmine shrugged, for the baby did seem much improved. "Fine."

"You needn't sound so overjoyed," he bit back, his voice harsher than he would have liked, for he didn't want to imply he was bothered by her lack of enthusiasm.

"Oh, but I am overjoyed, Anthony. Can't you tell?" she remarked, never bothering to hide the sneer in her voice.

Anthony cursed. "Just see to it you're ready." A second later he was gone.

Jasmine cuddled the baby close to her breast. "To hell with him, Amy." Her voice grew soft and husky as she struggled against unshed tears. "We don't need him, do we? You and I were just fine before he came." She brushed her cheek against the baby's head and silently wondered if any of them would be "just fine" again.

Jasmine leaned her head against the rough pole that supported the porch roof and sighed. She was tired, her back and arms ached from hours of holding the baby, and yet she couldn't sleep. The moment she closed her eyes, vivid pictures of lovemaking assailed. God, how she wanted him. What was wrong with her to so crave his touch, knowing he felt nothing but disgust for her?

She should tell him the truth and be done with this ache. What mattered of pride if it only brought this unbearable suffering? It didn't matter anymore what he thought of her. She wanted her husband to hold her. She needed desperately to be held.

Jasmine started, her body stiff as she suddenly realized she was no longer alone. She smiled, imagining her wish to have brought him here. Lord, if only everything in life were that simple. If only she could simply wish and have it done.

Strong arms slid around her waist and, finding no resistance, pulled her gently to rest against him. She felt his breath against her ear as he sighed with obvious relief. "You shouldn't be out here alone."

"I couldn't sleep."

"You should have awakened me."

Jasmine smiled as she leaned comfortably against him. Why couldn't they always know this sweetness, this tenderness?

"God but I love holding you," he groaned as he buried his face in the warmth of her neck. "I didn't know if you'd ever let me hold you again."

Jasmine smiled as she leaned her head back upon his shoulder. "Didn't you?" Jasmine turned into the circle of his arms. "I can't imagine a time when I wouldn't want you to hold me."

She felt him tremble with need as his mouth leaned down to hers. Jasmine moaned as she parted her lips for the hungry assault of his tongue. The passion between them was instant and wild. His touch brought her body to life and she strained against him, wondering how had she lived these past weeks without his touch?

Her arms came to his shoulders and wound sweetly around his neck as his hands pressed against her back flattening her breasts to his chest.

"I want you. I want you," he gasped as he tore his mouth from hers only to hungrily take it again. "It doesn't matter. God, nothing matters when you're in my arms," he groaned as burning lips slid to her cheek, her jaw, her throat, and then back to her mouth again.

"What?" she asked, her mind drugged with his kisses, her body alive with the feel of his hands.

"I don't care what you did. I have to hold you, kiss you," he breathed shakily as his fingers sought out the softness of her breast.

"What did I do?" she asked breathlessly, not quite understanding his meaning.

"Jasmine, I realize now that you didn't mean it. You were angry. It just happened."

Jasmine pulled back, her arms at his shoulders preventing his lips from continuing the scorching path down her throat. Her voice was dull, her body cold, her passion gone as if it had never been. "I was angry, so I thought I would kill my own husband?"

"You didn't realize what you were doing. You won't do it again."

Jasmine laughed, the sound, low and throaty, filled with great sadness. Her heart felt bludgeoned, aching and sore at his words. How could he simply assume her capable of so dastardly a deed? What did this man feel for her? Was it passion alone? Did he believe even passion this strong could survive when there was no trust? She answered honestly, only he never knew the meaning behind her words. "You are mistaken, Anthony. I knew exactly what I was doing. And I would indeed do it again."

She waited an endless, breathless moment, willing him to ask the one question that threatened to separate them forever and then gave a sad sigh as Anthony's arms dropped to his sides.

He watched her for a long moment, forcing his hands to refrain from clutching at his chest, for the pain that came from within was not to be borne. He wondered if his heart hadn't broken in two, for he could imagine no agony worse than this. She was telling him the truth. He could read it clearly in her eyes. She had meant it! She'd wanted to kill him! How was he to live with her as his wife? God in heaven, how was he to live without her? Without another word spoken, Anthony turned on his heel and walked back into the cabin.

The soft sound of the door as it closed might have been a gong so loudly did it vibrate in the silent night. To Jasmine's mind, it marked the end of their relationship. Idly she wondered if they'd ever really had one.

Her arms ached. Her back ached. There wasn't a place on her body that didn't ache. It was probably the endless hours she spent holding the baby in the saddle, she reasoned. It couldn't be that she was ill. Of course she wasn't. She never got sick. Why, she couldn't remember the last time.

Anthony was driving them hard. If Jeb hadn't complained, she wondered if he'd have stopped even at dark. But the wizened old man's insistence that they were pushing the horses to their limit, plus the obvious fact that they would no doubt be moving in circles particularly on nights when there were no stars to guide them, had caused Anthony to acquiesce to the older man's demands.

Jasmine smiled as she remembered Anthony's surprise at finding Hopeful and Jeb ready to leave with them. No doubt he had thought to have her alone, but they had insisted they were going in the same direction, and it was safer to travel together. Anthony had had no choice but to allow their company.

Her head was pounding, and with each step the mule took, it grew worse. "Jeb," she muttered, softer than she imagined.

But Jeb had been watching her since this morning. He'd seen the glassiness in her eyes. He'd watched as she swayed upon the mule.

Instantly his mount was beside her. "What?"

Jasmine offered a weak smile. Her face was flushed and she shivered even though the heat of the day was at its greatest. "Could you hold the baby for a spell. I hate to ask, but my arms are so weak. I don't want to drop her."

Jebodiah cursed. Why hadn't he thought of this before? Why hadn't he fixed up a spot for the baby so Jasmine wouldn't have to hold her from morning till night? Even if she hadn't been ill, the strain of holding the child would have been too much.

"I think it's time for us to stop."

Jasmine glanced up at the brightly lit sky with surprise. "But it's not dark."

Jebodiah nodded, his eyes hard as he easily took the baby from her shaking arms. "We're stopping anyway."

Jeb was just about to call ahead when he heard the unmistakable sound of an arrow as it whistled through the air. From the corner of his eye he saw Jasmine give a sudden lurch. A gasp of surprise slipped from her lips, followed closely by a low groan of pain.

Chapter Nineteen

Jasmine blinked, her feverish eyes wide with astonishment as she turned to see the cause of the sudden aching discomfort in her leg. It wasn't until she actually looked that the pain registered fully and grew to excruciating proportions. Her eyes grew wide with confusion as she took in the sight and wondered with no little amazement how in the world had an arrow come to be sticking out of her calf?

Jasmine hadn't time to think the matter through, for she was suddenly knocked from the mule by an avidly cursing Jeb and flung with a bone-jarring thud to the ground. It was then she screamed, for the horror that they were being attacked finally sank in.

She was lying between the mule and Jeb's horse. For the moment, the damage to her leg was forgotten. Stark terror overrode every other thought and consideration.

Jeb, beside her again, dragged her beneath the cover of underbrush. She lay there panting, almost paralyzed with fear as arrows whistled with near silent menace through the air.

As fast as they were loaded, guns were fired blindly across the road into the cover of woods. Frustrated curses mingled with bone-chilling screams. The riderless horses and mule scurried down the dirt road, adding their own terrified sounds to the melée.

From the comparative safety of underbrush, Jasmine saw him emerge from cover, tall and dark, covered only by a loincloth, his face and chest painted with oddly drawn lines and figures. He inched toward the center of the road. Jasmine's gaze moved toward his intended destination. It wasn't until that moment that she realized Jeb had dropped the baby where they had fallen. Amy lay unprotected, in the open, between the two deadly combatants.

"No!" she cried as she watched the brown arm snake out and grab at the baby. "Stop!" she screamed as she came to her feet. She never noticed the pain slice up her leg. She wasn't thinking of her safety. In truth, she wasn't thinking at all. She only knew Amy belonged to her and no one was going to take the baby away.

The pain should have grown to excruciating agony as she put pressure on her leg. It might have robbed her of her breath, had she thought on it, but she easily ignored what had become only mild discomfort, for her mind was set with but one purpose.

Her leg was stiff, the arrow still protruding, holding her skirt at the same angle as when she sat upon the mule. She walked with a limp. An arrow whizzed by, but Jasmine either ignored or never noticed the danger. "Put her back!" she ordered the man who had dared to touch what was hers.

Silently the Indian had slithered back under the cover of underbrush. She was in the clearing now—alone, as each antagonist hid along either side of the road among the trees and thick foliage. She never gave a moment's thought that she was standing directly in the line of fire without any protection. Her hands were placed firmly on her hips as she called out, "Bring that baby back here immediately!"

All sounds of fighting instantly ceased. Anthony, Jeb, and Hopeful froze with shock. An instant later vile curse words pursed silently upon their lips. Anthony tried to scramble to his feet, his intent obvious. He was a wild man, his fear for her uncontrollable. A moment later he was wrestled to the ground and held in place, with no little effort, by his two wiser and far calmer fighting partners.

Anthony's curses died on his lips as he realized the sudden, ominous quiet. God, please, no! Nothing more could happen to her. He could never find the strength to go on.

Three pairs of eyes turned toward the road. Helpless, they watched with shock and horror. She was standing in the open unprotected, while their silent enemies watched and listened as the beautiful white woman demanded her child returned.

Above all things the Indians held courage in the highest regard. Among the small hunting party that lay facing her, hidden in the foliage, there wasn't one who believed it unusual for a woman to be brave, since many among their own were equally so. It was the fact that this brave woman was white that so astonished, for white women were notoriously known to be cowardly in the face of their enemy. They cried. They screamed out their terror. They whimpered their fear and became great sport among the men once they were captured.

Of course some might pick up a gun and help their men, but most shivered like children in mindless fear when facing their enemy.

So it was that each man held Jasmine's bravery in the highest regard and silently honored her as they might any man among them. And because of her courage they believed it only right to honor her request. They watched her with great respect as she stood her ground and called out again. "I want that baby returned, now!"

Jasmine's eyes widened as the foliage parted. She'd heard not a sound. The Indian was simply and suddenly there, the baby in his arms.

They met in the center of the road. She never noticed his look of respect as she took the baby from his extended arms. An instant later he was gone.

Jasmine limped to the opposite side of the road and an instant later she, too, had disappeared into the foliage.

The battle continued on in earnest, as if there had never been an interruption. Anthony was at her side, cursing as he reloaded his rifle. "What the hell did you think you were doing? Goddamnit! I couldn't believe it when I saw you walk out and call for the babe."

"The baby is mine. No one will take her from me."

Anthony cursed again, knowing it would be nothing short of a miracle if any of them lived beyond this day, and this fool woman was worried about the life of a baby, a baby who was sure to die in any case. It seemed she was the only one who didn't realize that fact.

"Can't you shut her up?" he grumbled, knowing every cry only alerted the bastards across the road to their position.

"She's afraid. The guns are scaring her to death."

An arrow came to land with a soft thud inches from Anthony's position. "Sonofabitch!"

"Give me a gun."

Anthony shot her a quick look, his fear for her fueling his anger, his lips thin with humor at her request. "Right. This way you can finish what the Indians leave."

Jasmine ignored his taunt. "Jeb," she called softly, "give me a gun."

A moment later a handgun was slid beneath the brush. Jasmine placed the baby under her body and retrieved the gun. Wordlessly she cradled its heaviness in her hands, knowing she would use it without the slightest qualm. For these weren't English

332

soldiers and she didn't feel the camaraderie she felt toward her own. These men were the enemy. Ruthless, bloodthirsty, and as vicious as wild dogs, they would kill any and all if they weren't stopped.

She didn't see him until it was almost too late. Somehow she felt a presence behind her. She turned and almost reflexively aimed and shot the weapon.

Anthony started at the sound, then jumped as a heavy weight fell suddenly over his body. Curses filled the sudden quiet as he rolled the lifeless form off him.

Jasmine wasn't looking his way, occupied as she was with reloading the gun.

Anthony couldn't believe his eyes. She had killed the Indian with one shot. How the hell . . . ? He never finished the thought as another loomed suddenly above them.

Anthony and Jasmine fired simultaneously. He never knew which of them had delivered the deadly shot. The Indian crumbled silently to the ground, sprawled mere inches from them.

They lay there a long time listening. Finally, the mounting silence grew too much for even the calmest soul and Jeb and Hopeful left to scout the area. They returned moments later to report they counted five dead. As near as they could tell, there were four more, gone now, as were all the horses.

Jasmine sat rocking the baby as a silent Anthony shot her alternating looks of amazement, dawning respect, and guilt. He had no doubt that his wife knew how to handle a gun, and that she was an excellent shot spoke for itself. What he wondered now was how he was going to bring up the subject of his idiocy. Would he ever convince her to forgive him, to give him another chance? What could he say that would make a difference?

Jasmine seemed to easily ignore his presence as she had since the moonlit episode some three nights back. The three gathered around her. They'd have to take the arrow from her leg. She knew that. What she didn't know was if she could bear the pain of it.

The burning that had grown wild in its intensity had lessened for now to a throbbing ache. She almost begged them to leave it be, for she knew to remove it would cause untold agony.

"Jeb . . ." Jasmine pleaded softly as she watched the man kneel before her.

Anthony bit back the threatening snarl that she should turn to this man for comfort and help rather than him. He gave a silent curse knowing there was no one to blame for their estrangement but himself. He should have known her innocence right from the beginning, but he wouldn't allow the truth. Why? What was he afraid of? Why couldn't he believe she cared enough to protect his life? Boggs had told him the truth of the matter and still he'd stubbornly refused to believe.

Hopeful retrieved the horses. Supplies were taken from the packhorse. Jasmine was made as comfortable as possible. Hopeful took the baby from her arms. "I'm afraid," she whimpered, almost beneath her breath.

"Lordalmighty, girl," Jebodiah remarked as he lifted her leg in his calloused, capable hands. "Any woman who has the guts to face down a hunting party by her lonesome can sure stand a little splinter."

Jasmine gave a weak imitation of a smile through trembling lips. "A splinter? Is that all it is?"

Jeb nodded. "That's all. Why, I never saw a punier, skinnier arrow in my life. What do you think, Hopeful?" Jeb smiled as he asked his friend's opinion.

"So I'd be a baby to cry, right?" she said. Her voice wobbled slightly with fear, her hand lifting to wipe away the sheen of tears that threatened to spill.

"Damn it, girl! You just do anythin' you feel like. I figure after what you did, you got every right." Jeb kept his attention on the wound and grunted his approval that it had penetrated only the fleshy part of her leg. To remove it would be more painful than dangerous. "If'n you want to scream, go right ahead." He smiled. "Why, I remember a time when one o' these things found its way into Hopeful's shoulder. Now you never seen a bigger baby in your life. He was agruntin' and agroanin' like you can't imagine. He thought he was a goner for sure."

Hopeful grinned as his black hand patted the baby's back. He nodded his agreement. "Never took much to pain."

Anthony knelt at her side, silently cursing his helplessness, for he'd never felt more useless in his life. He wanted to hold her in his arms. Would she spurn his attentions? Would she welcome his belated concern? Would she ever forgive his asinine accusations? Damn! What was he going to do?

Jasmine moaned as Jeb, without warning, broke off the end of the arrow. An instant later he pushed the thin piece of wood clean through her leg. Anthony took her into his arms and she cried out her agony against his shirt. She moaned again as the worst of the torment passed, her lips thinned and white with pain. Anthony's heart twisted. He wished it was he who suffered. His head grew light, a low sound escaped his throat, and he swayed weakly as he saw the blood gush from her wound.

"Don't look," Jeb ordered, noticing Anthony's movement and distinctly green coloring. A moment later he poured a liberal amount of whiskey over the injury.

Jasmine screamed a terrifying sound of pure anguish. She writhed mindlessly against him and clutched his shirt, her whole body stiffening against an agony she could never have imagined. It took forever, but the all-encompassing pain began to lessen at last. Soon it was little more than a throbbing ache again.

Jasmine slowly relaxed her hold and lay weakly gasping for breath in her husband's arms. "Thank you," she whispered as Jeb went about the task of bandaging her leg.

Jeb gave a slight shrug of his shoulder and grunted his response. When he was finished he looked at Anthony and grinned. No matter the cause of their separation, it was clearly a thing of the past, and it was clear this man surely did love his woman. Rarely had he seen one suffer so for another's pain.

"We can't make camp here. Them Injuns will be back to collect their dead."

Anthony nodded. "I know of a place not far from here."

Jasmine moaned as she lay snuggled in her husband's arms. Her brow creased with puzzlement, for it wasn't her leg that brought about discomfort. Indeed, compared to the cramping in her back, she hardly felt her leg at all.

She was burning up with fever. Anthony heard her low, garbled groan and brushed tender, anxious kisses against her forehead. His own body was stiff with dread. What was the matter with her? How had she become so suddenly and desperately ill?

No matter his need to hurry, he dared not quicken their pace, for even the least movement seemed to bring her untold pain. She moaned again, the sound muffled, her slackened lips pressed against his chest.

Anthony cursed with a mastery born of terror. She was sick, terribly sick. And apparently had been for some time. Why hadn't she told him? Did she believe he would have thought she pretended illness in order to delay their leaving? Of course she did. Goddamnit! What in hell was he going to do with this woman?

Hours of aching discomfort finally terminated

when an excruciating cramp sliced into her lower back and threatened to rend her body in two. Her back had ached since she'd awakened this morning, but nothing in her life had come close to pain such as this. Even through the debilitating daze of fever she knew something was wrong. She shouldn't be hurting like this. Not from a fever.

"What is it, darling? Is it your leg?"

Sweat beaded her face, but no matter the heat that burned within, she couldn't stop the shivers that had taken control of her body. Her lips were parted as she took short, shallow breaths. She was suddenly soaked with perspiration and looked at his concerned expression with dawning fear. "What's the matter with me?" She gasped at the intensity as another pain held her in its agonizing grip and squeezed the breath from her lungs.

"Don't be afraid. I'll take care of you," he said, reading correctly the confusion and fear in her eyes. Anthony could only pray she didn't notice the trembling in his voice, for he didn't have the slightest notion what to do.

"I have to . . ."

"What?"

"Oh, God," she grunted in a voice thick with agonizing pain. "Put me down, I have to—" she emitted a guttural, almost animalistic sound as the pressure came suddenly upon her. She couldn't think. She couldn't breathe. Her body stiffened as the need to bear down came upon her. For a second the thought came that she was about to disgrace herself. A moment later, her finger bit into his arms with a stranglehold. She clung to him with the strength of three men, and yet Anthony had to use all his power to merely keep her vibrating form from flying out of his arms.

Shaking with chills, burning with fever, she had no choice but to give in to the workings that wracked her body. A moment later she moaned as something warm and sticky slipped down her legs.

Through the murky thickness of fever, she realized at last what had happened. Too late. She'd realized too late. A strangled sob escaped her throat as tears of remorse slid down her cheeks. She welcomed the blackness as it swept the edges of her consciousness and sighed with relief as it swiftly enveloped her in its soothing cloak of forgetfulness.

Anthony was wild with fear. What in the world had happened to her? Had the fever proven too much? Had she suddenly succumbed to some sort of seizure? His heart pounded with terror, for he knew it wasn't sleep that held her relaxed in his arms.

His arms brought her firmly against his chest. His knees tightened, his heels dug into the sides of his horse. Heedless of the danger, he raced the animal through the forest. He never knew the words he muttered were a wild mixture of threats, curses, and prayer. He never stopped saying them until the farmhouse came into view.

"Sonofascumbitch!" He rolled the curse words as one, his heart beating triple time as he took a staggering step back. A breathless horror struck him suddenly immobile. He couldn't think what to do.

"She miscarried," Ann Frame remarked as she worked quickly to clean away the blood.

He never heard the explanation, his mind registering nothing but *blood!* The small bedroom swam in a red, dizzying haze. All he could see was blood. It covered her from hip to knees and had soaked into her drawers and petticoats like water. God in heaven, how could she bleed like that and live?

"Anthony, get me clean bedding," Ann ordered.

He looked at her from across his wife's prone, half-naked body. He knew she had said something, but the words wouldn't penetrate the fog of terror that gripped his body and mind.

"Anthony! In the closet," the tiny blond woman motioned over her shoulder. "Get me clean sheets!"

His hands shook as if palsied as he handed her the needed bedding. He couldn't speak as he watched her roll a torn portion into a pad and place it between Jasmine's legs. He'd never felt as helpless in his life. He wanted to help. He wanted to do something, but his hands wouldn't stop shaking.

The Widow Frame left the room and returned moments later with a nightdress, a pan of water, and toweling. She was finished in a matter of minutes and was trying to slide the nightdress over Jasmine. "Help me, Anthony. Lift her."

Again he did as he was told, but he acted as if dazed. His movements were jerky and uncoordinated, his complexion a sickly gray, his breathing harsh and erratic.

Ann groaned as she noticed his coloring. He was going to faint. Obviously he'd never seen the results of a miscarriage before. She had to get his mind off what had happened, and she had to hurry before he crumbled to the floor. "Pick her up while I change the bedding."

In an instant the bloodied sheets were whipped away and replaced by smooth, clean cotton. Ann sighed as she noticed his skin. The gray was disappearing. "You can put her down now." And when he seemed to not have heard, she said more forcefully. "Anthony, I said put her down!"

Docile, Anthony did as he was told. His shaking nearly caused him to fall into the chair at the bed's side. Dumbly he watched as Ann checked the padding. It was obvious, even to his befuddled mind, that the river of blood had eased considerably. "What was the matter with her? Why was she bleeding like that?"

"She lost the baby, Anthony."

"Baby?" He looked confused, thinking for a second she meant Amy. But Amy wasn't lost. "What baby?"

"Didn't you know she was pregnant?"

Anthony's eyes widened with shock. His low moan of anguish answered her question as no words could have. Silently she left the room.

Cool, wet cloths were pressed to flaming skin and each application brought a murmur of pain, but he was relentless in his administrations. It mattered not the discomfort she suffered. It mattered only that he bring this fever down.

He dribbled a few drops of water against her parched, cracked lips. A murmur came again as she slid her tongue, eager for more.

Anthony rarely left her side. When he slept it was for short, restless moments in a chair at her side. He dared not leave her, for he trusted not even Ann with her care. He watched her constantly, fearful to look away lest her fever grow worse or some further complication arise. All the while he listened with dread for any changes in her breathing.

It was the morning of the third day when she opened her eyes to find him changing the dressing on her leg. Jasmine must have made a sound, for his gaze moved instantly to her face. His smile was one of pure joy to see her finally awake.

"Am I very sick?"

Anthony smiled again. "You were."

"Have I been sleeping long?"

"Three days."

"Can I have some water?"

Anthony held her against him as he lifted the glass to her lips. "Not too much."

But Jasmine ignored his words and greedily

sucked at the liquid. "Easy," he said as he took the glass away.

He laid her down again. A moment later he pushed aside the covering sheet and lifted her gown to her hips. Jasmine hadn't the strength to stop him, even had she the understanding of what he was doing. With efficient, clinical movements he replaced the pad between her legs with another.

Their eyes met as he repositioned the coverings.

Her eyes widened as a sadness filled her being and ripped into her soul with an agony so severe she wondered if she'd survive the loss. She was pregnant. No, that was wrong. Silent tears filled her eyes. She had been pregnant. She'd lost the child, even before she knew the thrill of carrying her.

Odd how she seemed to know it was a her.

"Did you know?"

Jasmine gave a slow shake of her head. The tears overflowed and ran over her cheeks into her hair. "I lost the baby," she whispered pitifully.

The words sliced into his chest and he thought his heart just might break, for he'd never in his life heard words so sad. Anthony thought there could be no greater pain. He gathered her close to him and rocked her gently. "Don't, darling," he soothed as he ran his hand over her back. "It's over. We'll have other children. I promise you as many as you want." Anthony groaned against her hair as the room filled with the sound of her crying.

Jasmine cried until she slipped back to sleep. Now only an occasional hiccupping sob broke the silence of the farmhouse. Jasmine wasn't going to be pleased when she found out where he'd brought her. At the time he'd had no choice, for he knew not another for miles that could help. Right now he'd give just about anything to see a spark of anger in her eyes.

Her fever broke that night. Anthony almost cried with relief to see the sweat forming over her now cooling skin. He spent hours fussing over her. It wasn't until the sun began to rise that he drifted off into a deep sleep.

The crashing sound of falling glass brought him instantly awake. Jasmine's hand was extended toward the nightstand. She bit at her lip. "I'm sorry. I didn't want to wake you. I needed a drink."

Anthony's heart was pounding in his chest. Suddenly the endless nights of worry combined with almost no sleep proved to be too much. He lashed out unreasonably, "What the hell do you think I was sitting here for? Do you think I like sleeping in a chair?"

Under normal circumstances, he knew Jasmine would have snapped a biting answer in return. Anthony just about died with the pain that sliced into his chest as her eyes filled suddenly with tears. "Oh, damn! I'm sorry," he groaned as he sat upon the bed and cradled her in his arms. Slowly he rocked her back and forth. "Don't cry. I didn't mean it. You scared me, is all." He felt a moment of near panic. Except for when she realized she'd lost the baby, he'd never seen her cry. Even in the midst of agonizing pain, he'd not seen tears. "You want to hit me? I'll get you a stick."

"I'm not crying." She swallowed, trying to get some control over this unusual need to weep. Anthony had snapped at her before. Why did his words suddenly bring her to tears?

"You're not?" he asked as he cupped her face in his hands and gently wiped away her tears with his thumbs.

Jasmine shook her head, unable to speak. Her throat was tight, for the tender caress brought fresh, burning tears to surface.

"Shall I tell you something?"

She nodded.

"Your eyes are leaking."

342

Jasmine smiled at his teasing, then was suddenly crying and smiling at the same time as she pressed her face into his shirt. "I'm still thirsty," she managed a short time later between shuddering sniffs and, sipping at the glass of water Anthony hastened to bring her. She gazed up at him with searching eyes. "Where are we?" she asked as she looked around the strange room.

"In a farmhouse." Quickly he changed the subject, fearing to upset her again. His first mistake. "Are you hungry?"

She shook her head. "Thirsty."

Again he helped her up so she might drink.

"Is Amy all right?" she asked the moment she lay down again.

He nodded, knowing in his heart this was the right thing to do. She could wait until she was stronger to face the truth. His second mistake.

The baby had appeared to rally and gain some strength after taking milk, but the nourishment was too long in coming. Weakened beyond help from the effects of the fever, Amy had died two nights ago. "She's been taking milk. Kept most of it down." That part at least had been true.

Jasmine breathed a sigh of relief. Thank God for Amy. Perhaps the loss she suffered would be easier having her. "Can I see her?"

By a sheer act of will, Anthony managed to keep his expression pleasant. Jasmine never noticed the strain in his voice. "I don't think that would be a good idea. She might take sick again."

Jasmine nodded her agreement, never for a moment suspecting the truth. "You haven't shaved," she said, noticing for the first time his growth of whiskers.

Anthony grinned as he rubbed almost a week's worth of stubble. His personal hygiene had been the furthest thing from his mind while she lay burning with fever. If Ann hadn't forced it on him he wouldn't have eaten, and even when he had given in to her nagging, everything had seemed tasteless. His eyes were warm with tenderness as he explained. "I figured since I wouldn't be kissing you for a while the shaving could wait."

Jasmine swallowed against the ache in her throat. She knew he was trying to ease her pain by teasing. "And you were so sure you wouldn't be giving me even one kiss?"

He leaned forward and smiled as he placed his palm against her cool forehead. He'd done it a hundred times during the night but constantly found the need to reassure himself. "You know what happens when I kiss you."

Jasmine smiled. "No. What happens?"

"I don't want to embarrass you."

Jasmine's eyes widened with surprise. She grinned at the deviltry that twinkled in his eyes. "Go ahead. Embarrass me."

Anthony grinned and then shrugged trying to maintain a look of innocence. He failed miserably. "Well, you know how you go all out of control. I'm afraid you're a bit too hot-blooded for the likes of me."

"Why you . . ." Jasmine took a deep breath as she forced aside her laughter. "Just for that beastly lie, I think I'll cry again."

"Don't!" he said, his eyes widening with dread.

Jasmine laughed quite cockily. "I think I'm going to enjoy this newfound power."

Anthony's moan was real, even if it brought a smile to Jasmine's lips. Newfound? He felt totally in her thrall, so intense was her power over him.

"Jasmine, I want to tell you how sorry I am."

"About the baby?" she asked, instantly feeling the need to cry once again.

"Yes, about the baby, but also about what happened at Morgan's camp."

Jasmine blinked back tears of self-pity, silently cursing this almost overwhelming and definitely uncharacteristic need to cry. "You could have asked," she reminded in a voice suddenly dull and lifeless.

Anthony knew an instant fury, for his guilt was not to be borne. If it weren't for him, she'd never have left. She'd never have suffered the fever or the loss of their child. And he was ready to take responsibility for what had happened. Therefore, no one was more shocked than he to hear the words come tumbling from his mouth. "I said I was sorry, damn it! What more can I do? Shall I crawl?"

Jasmine gasped at his cruel tone. She never realized her overreaction as all thoughts of self-pity were instantly replaced by righteous anger. The weeks spent consorting with his men had not been entirely wasted, for if nothing else, they had increased her ability of phrasing a thought. She knew how to give as good as she got, and in language he'd clearly understand. She bared her teeth and growled, "You? Crawl? And pray tell how would you manage the feat with that stick up your ass?"

At any other time, the indelicate words might have brought a smile to Anthony's lips, but he was too consumed with his guilt to appreciate the most unladylike remark and he came instantly to his feet and cursed. Damn the woman! He'd tried to make amends and what did she do? She damn near threw his apology back in his face. Well, she could go to hell if she thought he'd apologize again.

Jasmine watched him pace the floor. Damn him. Damn him to hell, she silently ranted as the dull thudding in her head grew to mammoth proportions. She didn't need him. She didn't need his care. What she needed was peace. What she needed was for him to be gone forever. "Go away."

Anthony turned, his expression nothing short of astonishment. "Is this the thanks I get? *Go away?*" His mouth twisted with anger and he continued on before she had a chance to interrupt. His lips were tight and not a flicker of tenderness shone in his eyes. "Don't worry. I'm going all right. I'm getting out of here now."

"It can't be soon enough to suit me."

Anthony ran his fingers through his hair and watched her closed, tight expression. "I should have known this would be a waste of time." Childishly he struck out, having not the least intentions to see his threat put to use. "You might not appreciate my company, but there are others who enjoy it well enough."

"Anthony" came a soft, southern, feminine voice from the doorway.

Both sets of eyes moved with surprise at the sound to find Ann Frame standing just inside the room. "I thought you might like a cup of tea." She smiled at Jasmine. "You're better, I see. Well, that's a relief." She smiled again, growing slightly uneasy at the glaring silence that filled the room and realizing too late she had interrupted something. "I'll bring a pot for the two of you."

The door closed softly behind her. Anthony, dreading what he would see, turned to find his wife's accusing stare. "It's not what you think."

"Isn't it?" Jasmine gave a harsh, bitter laugh, feeling very much the fool as her mind raced to obvious conclusions. She had little trouble imagining what had happened while she lay ill with fever. Even from this short visit, it was clear the pretty widow was still enamored of her husband. And from the guilt on Anthony's face, Jasmine doubted he spurned her sweet advances overmuch. "Isn't she the one of whom you spoke? The one who would enjoy your company?"

346

Jasmine shrugged, trying desperately to hide the pain that ripped through her chest and crumbled her heart to tiny bits. "I imagine taking care of me no great chore, since the lovely Widow Frame hovered nearby ready to bring comfort."

"You'd do well to imitate her qualities."

Jasmine's eyes widened. Pain sliced tenfold into her chest. Had he used a knife, he couldn't have inflicted greater agony, for his words brought clearly to mind the differences between the two women. And to Jasmine's way of thinking, she came in a weak second place to the lady.

Where Jasmine was dark, tall, and slender, Ann was blond, petite, her figure nothing less than perfection. Her mannerisms and speech were gentle and sweet. She was everything Jasmine was not.

Jasmine's voice was flat and dull as she responded at last, "Meaning, of course, I have none of my own."

Anthony cursed the foolishness of his tongue. What was the matter with him? He'd never meant to say that. How could he have so callously compared Jasmine to another? Lord, there wasn't another on earth to equal this woman. Why hadn't he controlled this need to lash out? Why hadn't he realized his guilt was running away with his reason?

"Go to her, then. I'd never stop you."

Anthony shot her a long look. Did she mean it? Did she care so little? Anthony searched her face for a sign of softening. He could find none.

"You couldn't, in any case." Anthony ignored the soft gasp that sliced pain into his heart. An instant later he slammed out of the room and leaned up against the closed door. He ran his hand over his face and groaned. Jesus, he'd made a fine mess of things. What had come over him? Why hadn't he realized she'd not yet recovered from her illness and was not up to straightening out their misunderstanding? Why had he allowed his guilt to loosen his tongue and say the most ridiculous things?

Jasmine hobbled from the chamber pot to the bed and sat with a shaky sigh of relief. Her leg was sore but gave her little trouble. Every day she was able to stand upon it longer.

Her bleeding had stopped two days ago and she could feel her strength slowly returning. She hadn't seen Anthony in more than a week, not unless she counted his nightly visits to check on her when he thought her asleep.

It was Jeb who served her her meals and looked after her welfare. He never mentioned her obvious estrangement with Anthony, nor did she.

Jasmine smiled as she listened to the voices outside her door. She wished she could convince them to bring Amy to her. Lord, but they were protective of the child. Surely she posed no danger, for she'd had no sign of fever in days. She smiled again. Amy was so good. Why, she hadn't heard a whimper of sound since she'd come from her fever. A sudden thought almost took her breath away. Fear clutched at her chest as she desperately tried to quiet the pounding of her heart. Was that normal? Shouldn't she have heard the baby cry? At least once?

Jasmine staggered to her feet and, forgetting her borrowed robe, she lunged for the door. The living area was directly outside her door. She held to the wall and faced the startled glances of three men and one woman sitting at a long table, not ten feet away. Her eyes were wide with fear. "Where is she?"

All three men exchanged looks of guilt and came to their feet. Jasmine's heart sank. Something was wrong. Something was terribly wrong. Where was Amy?

"Jasmine," Anthony said in a low soothing tone. "You shouldn't be out of bed."

348

"Where is she? Where is Amy? Why haven't I heard her?"

Anthony swallowed. Jesus, he hated to be the one to tell her. He knew how she'd taken to the baby. He pushed his fingers through his hair and sighed.

"Tell me!" she demanded.

"Amy died."

Jasmine never realized the sympathy in his eyes. She never realized anything but the dull ache that had come to her breast. She heaved a long sigh. The hurt was almost more than she could bear, for it seemed to magnify her loss. Only she had known this child. She had grown to love her. "I imagine her dying brought some measure of relief. I know you had no use for her."

Anthony swallowed, dumbfounded by her accusation. "That's not true."

"Isn't it? Didn't you want me to leave her behind?" Jasmine knew she wasn't being fair, for it was impossible to believe he'd want a baby to die, but she couldn't stop the words. She had to lash out. She had to speak or die of the pain. And it was to Anthony she directed her helpless rage.

"Jasmine . . ." he began.

"No!" she almost shrieked as he moved toward her. If he put his arms around her she'd fall apart. "Don't touch me. Don't ever touch me again."

Instantly she was back in the bedroom, the door slammed in his face, huge sobs tearing at her throat urging their release. Her eyes burned as she forced back the tears. She wouldn't cry. She'd only known the baby a little more than two weeks. Certainly Amy hadn't come to mean so much to her in that short a time.

She was acting the fool. Babies died every day. Hadn't her own? People accepted their death as normal occurrences. Why then couldn't she? God, how had she come to love this baby so desperately?

Almost from the first she'd known, as had the others, that the baby would die. She'd known it to be only a matter of time. Even so, it had come as a shock, simply because she hadn't wanted to face the obvious. She'd wanted so desperately to believe there was a chance.

Jasmine lay on the bed and touched her hand to her empty stomach, imagining her own child who had once lain growing in the warm confines of her womb. A hiccupping sound came unexpectedly from her throat. Suddenly the effort proved to be too much and she gave up the struggles to keep her tears at bay. They streamed down her face accompanied by wrenching sobs.

Jasmine hid her face in the pillow, lest those beyond the room hear. Despite her efforts, they did.

Chapter Twenty

Anthony came awake at the sound. His body grew instantly stiff as he lay there listening. Someone was moving about in the dark. His heart hammered in his chest. All were asleep and no one guarded them at their most vulnerable moments. Jesus! How had he allowed his mind to grow so full of this woman that all his usual precautions of safety evaporated like the early morning mist under the heat of the sun? Why hadn't he thought to keep guard?

Anthony slid silently from the pallet and reached for his trousers. On bare feet he moved toward the door, wondering if whoever prowled outside was alone. Had another already entered? His eyes searched out the shadows of the room, his body stiff as if he awaited attack. He could find nothing amiss—no open windows, no doors left ajar. The house was silent. All slept within.

A film of sweat suddenly broke out over his body as a horrifying thought occurred. Did they in truth sleep? A moment later he breathed a great, if silent, sigh of relief. They did, for in the stillness of the night, he could hear Jeb's snores.

His rifle leaned against the wall near the door. Anthony retrieved it, and with a prayer of thanks that the hinges had recently been oiled, for they made not a sound, he stepped outside.

His eyes searched out the darkness for a hint of movement. It was then he saw her. His knees nearly wobbled as relief filled his body.

"You shouldn't be out here. It's not safe."

Ann Frame spun around, the slight squeak of sound from her startled lips telling him correctly her surprise. "I thought you were asleep."

"I was. I heard someone walking around."

Ann's smile was lost in the dark night. She gave a slight shrug and sighed heavily. "I couldn't sleep. I didn't want to awaken the others."

Anthony glanced out into the darkness. He knew the nearest neighbor had to be more than five miles away. Indians were constantly spotted nearby. The only reason she hadn't already been victimized by a hunting party was the fact that the rebels regularly camped or patrolled her property. What would happen when they left? "You shouldn't stay here alone. It's too dangerous."

She smiled again. "This has been my home since I was a child. Where would I go?"

"Family?" he offered.

She shook her head. "Dead."

Anthony sighed. "Still, you shouldn't stay here alone. One woman would have no chance against . . ."

Ann gave a short laugh. "Are you offering me your protection?"

Anthony gave her a long look and found nothing that did not appeal. Long blond hair framed a delicately pretty face. The robe, tied at her waist, displayed her lush curves. And yet Anthony felt none of the longing he'd known when first they met, a longing he knew now was derived from sheer loneliness. Despite her obvious but discreet attraction toward him, he'd somehow known then, as now, no one but his wife would satisfy. And this woman was far too special to simply use as a body in place of

352

another. "You know I cannot."

Ann chuckled softly. "I know."

"I love her." The simple words told clearly that any hope she harbored was impossible, that any attraction would amount to nothing.

"And no other will ever cause your eyes to stray?"

Anthony grinned. "I cannot promise not to look, but that's all it will ever come to."

"She's a very lucky woman."

"The opposite is true, I think."

"Spoken like a true gentleman." Ann smiled. "You'll be leaving soon." It was more a statement than a question.

He nodded. "By the end of the week, I think. Jasmine is nearly well."

"There will be no further chance for us to say goodbye. Can we say it now?"

Anthony nodded and leaned down as she lifted her face for a kiss.

Their mouths joined, his in a brotherly fashion, hers in bittersweet farewell to a love that could never be.

Jasmine heard the murmuring outside her window and came stiffly to her feet. Who in the world could be outside at this hour? The ache in her leg was greatly lessened, almost totally gone in fact, and she walked with hardly a limp. But the weakness from the loss of blood persisted and she wobbled, reaching out and almost falling against the wall as a wave of dizziness assailed.

At first she couldn't understand what she was seeing, so amazed was she at the sight of the entwined couple. The window was closed. She could hear nothing, but the stars gave off enough light for her to see. His head lowered to hers. Their lips touched. There was a great roar in Jasmine's ears as her heart silently died.

She watched them move together toward the door.

His arm was around her waist, her head against his chest. Amid the pounding rage that nearly obliterated all sound, Jasmine heard the front door close. And then another door. The bed in the next room squeaked softly and then silence.

"There are others, there are others." Again and again the words reverberated through her mind. She'd thought he'd spoken in anger. She'd thought he never meant his words. Her hands came to cover her ears, but to no avail, for the sound came from within. Why wouldn't they stop? Lord, was she to forever hear this haunting chant?

The mere thought of food was nearly enough to send her flying to the chamber pot, but Jasmine forced the sickness aside. She needed the nourishment. She needed it desperately if she was going to make good her escape. Jeb brought her her usual morning tray. Jasmine forced a cheery smile and prayed he noticed nothing amiss.

He did.

"Lord almighty, girl, what have you been doing to yourself?"

"What do you mean?"

"You got circles under your eyes the size of horseshoes. Ain't you been sleepin'."

Jasmine shrugged. "I'm not very tired at night. If you'd let me get out of this bed, maybe then I would sleep better."

Jeb came toward her. The tray in his hand was placed upon the bedside table as he reached for her forehead.

"I'm fine," she lied, for she'd never felt worse in her life. "If I could get up . . ."

"You'll have to look a lot better before getting out that bed. I sure hope you ain't coming down with the fever again."

Jasmine shot him a look of annoyance. "There's nothing like compliments to boost a lady's spirit."

"It ain't your spirit I'm worried about." Jeb eyed her for a long moment. "Something eatin' at you?"

"Not a thing." Jasmine smiled cheerfully. "I'm fine." And at his doubting look, she insisted, "I promise."

Anthony came in to see her. Actuallly he had come four times during that day, no doubt after receiving Jeb's worried report. Thankfully, Jasmine heard his footsteps moments before the door opened and she was able to feign sleep. She didn't want to witness his false concern. She didn't want to see him. With a little planning and God's help she'd never see him again.

Something was wrong. Her forehead felt cool to the touch, but she was so obviously tired, and even though he felt an almost desperate need to talk to her, he didn't have the heart to awaken her. Four times he had come into the room and four times she had been sleeping. Anthony forced down the panic that rose like bile to his throat. Something was terribly wrong. He could feel it in his bones. Was she feeling that unwell, that tired? Anthony felt a wave of despair. She couldn't get sick again. God, he couldn't live through a repeat of the fear and helplessness he had known.

It was late. The house had been quiet for hours. Jasmine strained to hear a sound but heard only Jeb's irregular snores.

All were obviously asleep. And if Anthony chose the Widow Frame as a snuggling partner, Jasmine swore she didn't care. Still, she chanced not to venture into the main room of the house. If he was sleeping out there, he'd surely awaken. No he wasn't going to catch her in the midst of escape. If ever they saw each other again, it would be only to talk of dissolving this pretense of a marriage.

Jasmine gave a wry smile. Having searched out her clothes earlier, she began to dress. There was a time when she believed it possible to live with the knowledge of her husband's infidelity. But that was before she'd grown to love him. Jasmine shrugged. It mattered not her feeling for the man. She could not tolerate his wandering eye. The beast had gone to another while she lay sick in bed. She couldn't trust him, and without trust, this love she felt would soon grow to hate. Pity she didn't hate him already, for it would have saved her so much pain.

She pushed her feet into her boots and pocketed her stockings, to be put on when she could spare the time. Anthony's coat lay over a chair where he had left it earlier, after coming directly to her room from outside. She had watched it most of the day, hoping he'd forgotten about it. Apparently he had. Jasmine sighed with no little relief, for the heavy coat would go far toward warding off the night chill.

Rolled blanket in hand, his coat under her arm, she crept on silent feet toward the window while thanking God with each movement that she was plagued with only the merest sign of her former weakness. Had she been forced by illness to stay, she would no doubt have had it out with the beast. That he would have lied was a forgone conclusion in her mind. He played well the role he'd chosen. He'd touched her gently in her supposed sleep. He'd whispered endearments and acted in all ways like a concerned husband but had spent his nights in another's arms.

The window made hardly a sound as she opened it. The soft thud of her boots hitting upon the earth was lost among the many sounds of the night. An owl asked a ghostly question in the shadowy darkness, the musical sound of crickets filled the night, along with the mournful moaning of some distant nocturnal animal.

Jasmine had to search out the exact location of the barn. Even though she'd spent nearly two weeks at the farm, she'd spent them inside and had yet to become acquainted with its many buildings. The first building she approached was apparently only a large tool shed, for when she opened the door no sounds had come out of the blackness to greet her.

To her relief, for she was tiring already from even this minimum energy spent, the next building was the barn. Jasmine sighed happily at hearing the soft, whinnying sound of a horse. Inside it was as dark as pitch. She dared not light a lantern, even had she known where she might find one. Blinded by darkness she felt her way along the wall and smiled as she came up against a lower wall, obviously a stall.

With whispered soft, soothing words, meant to calm the nervously prancing horse inside, she eased herself toward the opening. Jasmine breathed a silent thanks as her fingers found the bridle hung over the low wall. She cooed gentle sounds as she slipped the reins over the horse's head. There wasn't time to find a saddle. She had pressed her luck far enough on this night. What she had to do was get away. Now!

Jasmine mounted the horse with little difficulty. She had ridden since a child and, whether saddled or bareback, had no problem gaining her seat or controlling a horse. A moment later she was galloping out of the yard, heading blindly into the night. When she finally came across a dirt road, she turned left. She couldn't read the stars, though they sparkled brightly in the sky, and could only pray she was headed in a southerly direction. Granted, this effort would delay her return home, but if Anthony decided to follow, he'd believe her headed north and that was exactly what she wanted him to believe.

Jasmine came across many a farm, but dared not

ask for shelter. If Anthony followed, it was at these small houses he'd make his inquiries. It wasn't until the next night that Jasmine came across the inn. The road was more heavily populated now. She knew she was nearing a town. She had smelled the salty, clean scent of seawater since early that afternoon and prayed this town was situated near the coast. Her one and only thought was to find someone with a boat. The idea grew more appealing as her energy waned. She'd sell the horse and pay her passage home.

It was dark and Jasmine felt exhaustion unlike anything she'd ever known as she dismounted outside the inn's front door. She wasn't hungry, for she had stashed her pockets with cheese and fruit, secreted from the trays of food brought to her room. But she was thirsty. God, she couldn't remember ever being more so. The only stream she'd come across had been green and still. Gnats and mosquitoes had played along its surface. She dared not drink from it, for she'd not chance coming down with fever again.

Inside the inn a cheery fire blazed in the hearth to ward off the evening's dampness. Jasmine walked through the mostly male clientele toward the man who wore an almost-white apron and stood behind the roughly hewn bar. She could feel inquisitive eyes boring into her back, but she forced her feet forward.

"Might I a moment of your time, sir?" she asked softly, but in the sudden silence of the low-ceilinged dark room her voice rang out clear and sweet.

The innkeeper, Charlie, called by all, was impressed that a lady, and there was no doubt in his mind she was a lady, should visit his establishment. He knew, of course, ladies didn't visit his kind of place unescorted. Ladies didn't come bedraggled, late at night and wearing a man's coat that dragged nearly to the floor. A lady's face and clothes weren't smeared with the dust of travel. And yet he couldn't deny her manner of speech, the way she held her head, and the delicate way she moved.

Charlie nodded. "You be wantin' somethin', miss?"

"A room and a hot meal, if you'd be so kind."

Charlie nodded again as her words reaffirmed his first impression. She was a lady all right. Maybe she was one of those eccentrics who got their pleasure out of seein' how the other half lived. He nodded again. "Right away."

"I have one problem Mr. . . ." Jasmine hesitated, waiting for him to offer his name.

"Charlie."

"I seem to be temporarily without funds, Mr. Charlie. If you could advance me the . . ."

Charlie interrupted. "Sorry," he motioned with his head to the sign that hung over the bar. It read in big letters, "No tabs, no owing. You want your drink, I'll see your coin."

"Oh, dear," Jasmine murmured, obviously distressed. "You couldn't see your way clear to . . ." she began hopefully.

"Not a chance," he interrupted again.

"I promise I will . . ."

"Lady, if I had a shilling for all the times I heard . . ."

It was her turn to interrupt. "Well, thank you for your time, Mr. Charlie." She nodded as she reached across the counter and offered her hand.

"Wait a minute," he said as an idea took hold. "If you need a place to stay, you could work off the room and board."

Jasmine's eyes narrowed ever so slightly with suspicion as she studied the heavyset man opposite her. "What do you have in mind?"

"My wife ain't feelin' none too good. What with her bein' big with the baby and all. If you want, you could wait tables and clean up after everyone's gone. I'll give you a room and . . ." He looked at her closely and finally shrugged. She didn't look the type to eat too much. "And three meals a day."

Jasmine sighed with relief. There had been no telling from his hard look what he was going to say.

"Might I have a drink of water before I start?"

Jasmine's original intent was to sell the horse and buy passage to New York. The problem was there were fishing boats aplenty in this small seashore town, but not a one that was large enough to make such a journey north. In order to find one she'd have to travel farther south. Jasmine figured she'd pushed her luck far enough and elected instead to write her mother explaining her situation. No doubt someone would be sent to bring her home.

Two weeks went by and Charlie couldn't believe his good fortune. He'd expected Jasmine to leave within a day or so. He knew this was no work for a lady, but amazingly she had stayed on. She cleaned the rooms upstairs. She emptied slop pots. She changed sheets, even if they'd only been slept on once. He couldn't figure that, since it only made her work harder, 'cause it was her job to do laundry. She was so good and so thorough, he was almost tempted to give her a coin or two. Almost.

Lucky for him Becky was almost always in bed, 'cause she would have insisted he give up a few of his hard-earned coins.

Poor Becky. She could hardly walk, never mind work anymore, and he hated to clean. He had to admit he'd been doing a pretty sorry job of it ever since his swollen wife had taken to her bed.

He was a good man, if a bit tight-fisted as his wife liked to point out. Charlie shrugged a meaty shoulder, having no option but to agree with his wife's remarks. Still, Becky ought to be thankful for his frugal ways, for as his wife, she'd never know the pangs of hunger that assaulted some.

All he'd ever wanted was to own an inn. He loved

to cook. He loved to eat—obvious to everyone by the size of his belly!—and he loved to sit behind his bar and talk with his patrons. Sometimes the sun came up in the mornings before he stopped talking.

Jasmine didn't seem to mind the work. She had no sooner finished one chore before she'd start another. And he didn't even have to tell her, either. He only prayed she'd stay until Becky got back on her feet again.

Charlie watched her now as she cleaned off a table and turned to a customer to get his order. Charlie didn't know what he'd done to deserve such good fortune, but God had surely smiled on him the moment she entered his place.

"Jesus Christ!" came the customer's voice. "I thought it was you, but I figured I must be imagining things. What the hell are you doing here? Where is Anthony?" he asked, his voice almost a roar. He never noticed the chair he had just overturned as he jumped to his feet.

Jasmine blinked her astonishment to find the tall, dark man standing before her. Her mouth turned into a huge grin as she cried, "Joseph!" and lunged into his arms.

"Jasmine?" he asked more softly now that he had calmed down. He sat her opposite him at the small table. "What are you doing here? Where is Anthony?"

"In New York, probably. And I work here."

Joseph shook his head. "What are you talking about?"

Jasmine shrugged as if the thought of her husband didn't bring a knifelike pain to her breast. "Anthony and I have gone our separate ways."

"What in hell do you mean? He left you?"

"I left him."

"Jesus," Joseph muttered as he ran his fingers through his hair. "Where, when, why?"

Jasmine grinned at his obvious bewilderment.

"About two days north of here. Two weeks ago. None of your business."

Joseph's eyes widened and his lips twisted into a grin when he realized she'd answered all his questions. "And that's it? Am I supposed to give you my order now?"

Jasmine laughed. "I imagine I can find a moment to talk with you. Charlie there," she nodded over her shoulder at the innkeeper, "hardly talks that he isn't bellowing, but underneath he's as gentle as a kitten."

Joseph shot the innkeeper a hard look. "He'd better be."

"What are you doing here?"

"I had to drop off some provisions down the coast aways. I thought I'd drop in on a few friends while I was in the area."

Jasmine nodded. "Where's Deborah?"

"Home."

"In New York?"

"My home. Saint Martin."

"The West Indies? You didn't tell me you had a home there. Are you . . . Are you and she . . . ?"

Joseph grinned and gave a great sigh. "Someday, when I have a year or so free, I'll tell you the things she did to me. Do you know she believed me to be José Gaspirilla? Jesus," he shuddered, "when I think of what she put me through."

Jasmine laughed. "And all no doubt well deserved." They were both silent for a moment. "Have you told her you love her yet?"

Joseph grinned. "Think you're pretty smart, don't you?"

Jasmine shrugged. "Smart enough. But it doesn't take intelligence to read your eyes when you talk about her."

Joseph changed the subject. "I was in New York last week. Your letter came and your mother sent Richard to get you." He grinned. "I don't mind telling you she chastised me severely for taking you off like I did."

"Good. Had I any sense I'd have done the same. Where is he? Did you bring him with you?"

"No. He'd left a day or so before I arrived. Besides, she didn't mention exactly where you were."

Jasmine nodded.

"She doesn't know you've left him?"

Jasmine shook her head. "I didn't tell her. They like Anthony. It's not going to be easy."

Joseph looked around the room. "So you'll work here till your father comes for you?"

"I thought you said *Richard* was com—" A long moment of silence went by before she continued. "How did you know?"

"I knew the moment I saw him. I'd have to be half blind not to."

Jasmine nodded, her eyes downcast. "Anthony saw it, too. It took me a while before I believed it."

"I'd have thought you'd jump at the chance. The man's a decent sort, not like . . ."

Jasmine smiled. "I know."

Anthony reasoned correctly her fears for her mother's reputation if others found out.

"She's old enough, Jasmine, not to care who knows."

"You're right, but . . ." Jasmine gave a long sigh. "What does that make me?"

Joseph grinned. "A very lovely, stubborn lady. Tell me why you left my brother."

It wasn't two hours after she waved goodbye to her brother-in-law that she saw the cloud of dust. She was outside rinsing the dishes in a huge pot of hot water when the sound of a racing horse brought her gaze to the road. She almost didn't recognize him for the sneer of fury that had twisted his handsome features when he had spied her. But when she knew for sure it was Anthony, she ran blindly across the yard. By the time she made the steps he was pulling his horse to a stop. Curses rained over her head. She was inside, halfway to her room, when the inn's door nearly shattered as it smashed against the wall. As he bellowed her name, she nearly flew up the remaining steps and slammed her bedroom door. She tried to push the huge armoire in front of it, but the piece weighed a ton and wouldn't budge an inch, no matter how she strained.

She might not have bothered, for she doubted even that heavy piece could have withstood Anthony's kick. Her door was hanging by one hinge as he walked inside. Without a word he turned and replaced it, shutting it softly.

Anthony's face was a hard mask of fury as they stood facing each other for a long, silent moment. If he was honest he'd have to admit she'd given him clear warning. She'd told him from the beginning she would run at every opportunity. Why had he believed she'd changed? Why had he believed she'd come to love him? *Because you're the worst kind of fool*, he silently ranted.

God, he grunted, his lips twisted into a sneer as he remembered the pain and fear at finding her gone. He wouldn't make that mistake again.

There was a loud pounding at her door and a louder voice bellowed beyond the fragmented wood. "Jasmine? Are you in there? Is everything all right?"

Anthony's eyes widened, his lips twisted with scorn. "A new protector?"

"Charlie," she muttered, totally mortified, for she'd just realized the scene they'd made and the many patrons who had witnessed their race through the inn. "He owns the inn."

"Are you so important to him that he's come to your aid?"

"Leave it to you to think such vile thoughts," Jasmine snapped, her anger shining in her eyes, her disgust clear in every word. "The man is my employer. What did you expect the way you came roaring in here?"

Anthony turned and wrenched the door open with a force that nearly pulled it from its only hinge. "You have a problem?"

"Jasmine . . ." Charlie began.

". . . is my wife," Anthony interrupted. "I trust that information sits well with you."

Now Charlie was never one to back down from a fight, but even with his enormous size he dared not object too strongly to the man's remarks. This one was bent on murder. He could see it clearly in his eyes. Still, he couldn't simply walk away and leave Jasmine in his hands. He had to find out if the man spoke the truth. Charlie called into the room, "You all right, Jasmine?"

"I'm fine, Charlie."

"Is it like he says? Is he your husband?"

Jasmine nearly choked, but managed to force the words at last. "He is."

Charlie nodded to an enraged Anthony. A moment later the door was slammed in his face.

They faced each other for a long moment before Jasmine finally managed, "How did you find me?"

Anthony's smile was so evil she felt a chill run up her spine. "What are you going to do?"

Anthony's lips formed a grotesque semblance of a smile. His hands itched to close around her throat. For two weeks he'd searched the roads for her body. He was tormented by the thought that Indians had taken her or that she had come upon some madman and was lying dead in some ditch. Finally he forced a long, calming breath. "What would you have me do, wife? Shall I beat you like any self-respecting husband would?"

Jasmine ignored his words. No matter his anger, she knew she had nothing in the way of violence to fear. What she couldn't understand was why he had gone to the trouble to search her out? He'd found another to warm his bed, hadn't he? Why did he find it necessary to continue on with this sham. What did he want with her? A shiver of revulsion slid up her spine. Did he want them both? Of course he did. He had no idea she'd seen him in his lover's arms, didn't know she was aware of his cheating.

"We've got something to settle between us, don't you think?" he said when the silence dragged out.

"Do we?"

Anthony frowned. "I believe an explanation is in order. Why, Jasmine?"

"Why what?"

"Shall we forgo the games this once? Why did you sneak off like a thief in the night?"

Jasmine took a deep breath and faced him with a sneer. "Is that what I did?"

He ignored her obvious, building anger. "Why?" he continued to insist.

"What difference does it make?" She'd be damned if she'd tell him. She'd be damned if she'd allow him to know the pain he caused.

"I want to know."

"Let's just say I no longer wish to be married to you."

"And you've just now decided this?"

She shrugged. "If you like."

"What I'd like is the truth."

"Is it so hard for you to believe? Can you not bear the thought that a woman, any woman, finds you not in the least irresistible?"

Anthony blinked his astonishment at the sudden fury that shone in her eyes. How in God's name had she imagined him in this light? When had he ever given her cause? Anthony felt his anger subside in measurable degrees, confusion growing in its place. "What in hell is the matter with you? What

366

are you implying?''

Jasmine took a deep, steadying breath, trying desperately to remain calm. "Far be it for me to imply anything, Mr. Montgomery, so I will tell you clear out. So clear, in fact, that even you will understand. I find you all too resistible. I always have.''

Anthony laughed, knowing her statement for the out-and-out lie it was. No one, not even this complicated, willful, stubborn woman could have pretended such eagerness when in his arms. She had enjoyed those moments well. She might be shallow of spirit and a conniving, lying bitch as well, but that she was a passionate creature could not be denied. "*Always?* Surely you exaggerate.''

"I'm afraid not.''

Anthony shrugged. "It wouldn't matter, then, what happened? Nothing will change your mind?''

"Correct.''

"Then take off your clothes.''

Jasmine blinked, unable for a moment to fathom this sudden turn in conversation. "What?''

"Have you suffered an injury to your hearing since last we met? Do it!''

Jasmine read all too clearly the flickering flames of desire her daring statement had brought to life. "And you suppose that to be an answer to all problems?'' She laughed with false bravado, while a pulse ticked at the base of her throat. "Mr. Montgomery, I do believe you have a serious flaw in your makeup.''

"No doubt," he easily agreed. "Still, you will do as I say.''

"Not likely.''

"You will unless you prefer to wear torn rags out of this inn.''

"Will you tear the clothes from my back?''

"If need be.''

"Why?''

"Let's say I want you to prove to me just how

367

resistible I am," he remarked as his fingers moved to the buttons of his shirt.

Jasmine silently cursed her foolish tongue, knowing her hastily spoken words had brought about his ire. His eyes were as cold as ice. He wouldn't be gentle. She should have told him her reasons for leaving. She should have thrown his infidelity in his face. Why hadn't she done it? Jasmine suddenly realized the reason behind her lies. Surely it would hurt more to never know. And Jasmine, filled with spite and anger, wanted nothing more than to hurt this man. She sneered her hatred. "How easily you confirm my lowest esteem."

"I care little for your esteem, Jasmine," he lied. "Right now it is action I want. Prove to me you're not the liar I believe you to be."

"It will mean nothing," she grunted as he flung aside his boots and pulled her resisting form into his arms. "Animals do as much."

Anthony's mouth lowered to hers. She turned her head aside so that his lips brushed only against her cheek. Anthony chuckled and taunted in a voice lazy with sexual promise, "Afraid?"

"Of you?" she returned with scorn. "Not likely."

Anthony chuckled as he pulled her closer. "Perhaps that's been my problem from the first. No doubt I should have roused your fear. Maybe then you would have been a dutiful wife."

"You disgust me."

Anthony's one hand wrapped tightly around her kept her stiff form against him, while the other dug painfully into the thickness of her hair and forced her head back, her face lifted to his. "Do I?" he taunted, refusing to acknowledge the pain her words brought to his chest. His teeth clamped together, never parting as he dared her to deny the passion that existed between them. "Do I?" he asked again as he pulled at her hair with ruthless insistence until she had no choice but to cry out her torment, a torment that could never match the pain in his soul.

His mouth closed over hers then, hot and wet, his tongue demanding entrance, an entrance she was determined never to willingly grant.

Jasmine knew her weakness all too well. She knew what would happen if she allowed the kiss. Her defenses would crumble as would the protective wall of hate she'd erected around her heart. She wouldn't, couldn't, give in to this need. No matter how her body might tremble, no matter how she might long for the feel of him against her. No matter how she might hunger for his mouth, the taste of him, the delight of his tongue piercingly sweet as it entered her mouth.

God, how she hated him!

He pulled her hair again. Careless of the pain he inflicted, he wrapped his hand further into the black, silken cloud. "Open your mouth," he grated with a vicious sneer. "If I disgust you, I might as well do it with full force."

She meant to slap his face, but he easily secured her arms behind her back. She winced when he only pulled harder. Tears smarted her eyes, causing them to grow luminous and so damn bewitching Anthony almost gave up the fight. Had she not broken free of his hold and struck him, this time catching the corner of his eye with the tip of her nail, he might have done just that.

"Bitch!" he grunted, squinting as his eye began to water.

For her part, Jasmine choked back a sob, positive, if he pulled any harder, she'd soon see the last of her hair. Her hands reached behind her head, fumbling as they sought to extradite his hand, searching for a dearly needed measure of relief. The movement caused her back to arch, her hips to press more firmly to his, and her shirt to grow tight across her breasts.

Anthony hadn't missed the movement. His mouth swooped down and unexpectedly captured the soft tip in his mouth. Through her clothes, his teeth caught at it with little gentleness and he grunted with satisfaction as he felt her body stiffen in reaction. He heard the hissing, startled intake of breath and felt her press reflexively against him.

A second later his mouth was at hers again, taking full advantage of softened, pliant lips. His mouth muffled the low groan of despair as she gave up her defiant struggles at last.

Anthony had never before known a need to match this. He never thought to use gentle persuasion. He was wild, nearly crazed with but one purpose. He'd have this woman. No matter the lies she so easily spouted. No matter his anger or her reluctance, he'd have her forever. His lips bruised her mouth, his tongue raped as it speared deep inside, uncaring that he might cause pain. He meant to show his mastery of her body. He meant for her to admit to her need of him.

His hands moved roughly over her, but neither seemed to take notice, for the pressure seemed only to further entice. He tore her shirt open and her thin chemise ripped away from her breasts with one tug.

Her cry of pleasure mingled with his low groan as the heat of his hands seared her flesh. And Jasmine knew all was lost. The picture of him and Ann Frame together faded from her mind. Never would there be a time when she would be able to resist this man. No matter what he did, she'd always give in to this need.

Her hands reached for his face, her fingers slid hungrily into his hair, cupping his head, pressing him closer to the heat of her mouth. She groaned as he sucked wildly, demanding all she could give, taking all that he could, as if this one kiss might have to last him a lifetime.

His mouth never parted from hers as he took her up against him. She was lying on the blanket, her underthings torn away, his body poised above her.

Jasmine heard the cry, never knowing it was she who had uttered the low, aching, animalistic sound as he entered her body with nary a gentle stroke. His fierceness took the last of her breath. He moved with near violence as he sought to absorb her body into his and keep her there forever.

He had lost all control. His near vicious entrance and violent movements would have shocked him had he the power to think on his actions. But thinking was the last thing he was capable of doing. All his mind knew was this woman and the terrible need only she could instill, only she could ease.

His sex grew thicker, harder, inflamed with sensation, pounding with blood as he drove deep, deeper into an inferno of roaring heat until he knew there was no chance of ever coming back, until he prayed he never would. A thunder came to his ears, blotting out all but the racing of his heart, his shattered, gasping breathing.

He stiffened against her, his body shuddering, his breathing nonexistent, his face flushed as with fever, his brow contorted with the pain of this ecstasy, greedily absorbing her cries into his mouth.

He lay still for countless moments. Anthony was still gasping for breath as rational thought slowly came upon him. He stiffened with shock at the horror of his actions. No! his mind screamed. He hadn't done this! He hadn't lost all control and raped his own wife!

God in heaven, let it be a lie, a dream, a nightmare, for how else was he to bear the truth? He'd taken her like the animal he was, the animal she'd accused him of being.

Anthony rolled off her, his mind filled with the agony of remorse. He heard the deep, gasping sound of her breathing and glanced at the woman he loved more than his own life. His eyes narrowed as he watched her lick her lips as if savoring the taste.

Had he truly taken her against her will? Hadn't she responded? How had she inflamed him to madness, to the point where he couldn't remember? How had he become so crazed with this need?

Vaguely came the picture of her groping for him, her hands in his hair pressing his mouth closer to hers. There had been no resistance in that mouth, no resistance as she eagerly wrapped her legs around his hips. Now, as the veil of crazed desire began to drift away, he remembered.

He hadn't ripped into her flesh. She'd been warm and wet. Thank God he had somehow managed to stir her that much. He remembered her responses now. Slow in coming, but responses nevertheless.

Anthony breathed a sigh that mingled relief with the deepest despair he'd ever known. How had they come to this? What had happened that they should have lost the magic they'd once known?

He forced back a low groan. Perhaps he hadn't forced her, but he'd certainly given her no choice but to do his will. Anthony watched as she adjusted her skirt and rolled silently to her side. God, but he wanted to pull her into his arms. His entire body fairly shook with the need to give comfort, to cuddle, to soothe. His mind almost screamed with the need to talk, to laugh. It wasn't enough this coming together. He wanted more than her body. Her wanted her soul.

His heart ached with the unbearable pain of rejection that she should turn her back on him. Why? What had he done? Why wouldn't she tell him?

Did she truly hate him? Did she blame him for the loss of the child?

Jasmine sat, her back to him, as she repaired as best she could the damage done to her shirt. Her movements were slow and jerky as if she were battered and bruised almost beyond endurance. Anthony saw the movement and knew if ever there was a chance for them, he'd just killed it.

In truth, neither Jasmine's body nor spirit had taken the punishment he imagined. If her movements weren't as smooth and graceful as usual, it was simply because she hadn't quite recovered from an experience that might never be matched for pleasure.

She shivered with exquisite remembrance. Why didn't he say something? Why didn't he touch her? Why did he brood in silence? Had she only imagined *his* pleasure? Could it be she was so lost in the throes of passion not to have realized he felt none of her joy?

God, how was she to face him? How could she bear him to witness her shame? His silence only proved he cared nothing for her. He'd simply done what he'd set out to do. He'd proven her a liar and been merciless in his attempt. He'd offered no quarter. He'd demanded and received total submission. Her lips tightened in anger. But if the bastard dared to gloat, she might very well do him bodily harm.

Anthony thought his heart might break as he watched her struggle to her feet. He dared not reach out a helping hand, knowing well enough her reaction should he show belated concern. He adjusted his clothes and left the bed. "Are you all right?"

"Just fine, thank you," she returned coolly, her back to him still.

"Jasmine . . ." he began, but his words were brought up short as she turned to face him. Her eyes were flat and expressionless. She wouldn't acknowledge what had happened between them. He could call her liar from now till the end of time and she'd still deny her need. "Nothing," he muttered, and then cursed at his own helpless fury. He'd made a fine mess of things and he hadn't an inkling of what to do about it.

Jasmine rolled the blanket she'd brought with her into a tight ball and retrieved his coat. "Let's go," he nodded over his shoulder, his eyes betraying not a trace of his torturous emotions.

Anthony paid the innkeeper for the damage done to his door. Jasmine had barely the time to thank him for all he'd done when they were outside. The horse she'd taken was brought from the barn, but Jasmine was halted as he took her arm and guided her to his own horse. "You'll be riding with me."

"Why?"

Besieged with guilt, Anthony felt only frustrating anger, which he unthinkingly directed at her. His lips tightened to a thin line. "I need give you no explanation. I've made my wishes clear."

Jasmine's teeth gnashed together in her silent anger.

Their long ride back to the farm was nothing less than torture. Anthony wondered at the depth of his stupidity. Why had he insisted she ride with him? Hadn't he known the softness of her bottom against his thighs would drive him mad with renewed longing? Hadn't he realized his wrists would often brush her breasts as he held the reins? Hadn't he known even the most casual touch would set his blood to flame, that he would tremble against the force of such need? Why, in God's name, did he feel this particular need to suffer?

He had to clear his mind of the passion she so easily stirred to life. He had to think. There had to be a way for them to regain the closeness, for he yearned to know again that special connection, a oneness that had nothing to do with the flesh, but with the joining of spirits.

It mattered not his pride. He'd beg if need be. He

had to break through this block of ice that surrounded her heart. He longed to know a time when she'd smile and lean into him to whisper a tender word, when she'd offer her mouth to his without thought, when no shadows of pain hindered her sweet smile.

He knew it was there. He'd glimpsed at her sweetness once but foolishly cast it aside, unable to face the fear—the fear of how easily she could destroy his life. It was that fear, that need for self-preservation, that had prevented his admitting she'd saved his life. It was easier by far to believe her a would-be murderess rather than recognize the terrifying depth of his love. He had feared that should he succumb to her charms, allow himself drawn under her spell, he'd find himself less than a man. He realized now—and please God let it not be too late—that he lost nothing of himself in her arms, but only became more a man by loving her.

Anthony dared not speak his thoughts. Surely she'd believe less of him if she knew the confusion that had plagued him. Was it possible for him to make things right between them at last? Was it possible that with some tender persuasion, he might convince her to begin again? Was there a chance that her heart still held even the slightest tenderness for him? Would it be enough to build on? Would it grow to match the love that raged in his breast?

Anthony breathed a long sigh, his arms around her middle pressed her close to his chest. "Jasmine."

"Umm?" she responded, almost half asleep, totally exhausted from the wild encounter she'd shared less than an hour ago.

"I'm sorry," he nearly choked out, knowing there was no way to wipe the slate clean if he didn't say the words. Love was a tender and delicate emotion at best and it could never hope to survive endless abuse.

Jasmine breathed a long, deep sigh that belied the

sudden pounding as gladness filled her heart to overflowing. She'd never expected an apology. She never dared to hope he'd worry of her feelings. She nodded in silence, for she didn't trust the steadiness of her voice.

Anthony took heart at her silent nod for he felt the sudden beating in her chest. He held her tighter to him and whispered close to her ear, "Would you be willing to forgive me the things I've done?"

The corners of Jasmine's mouth lifted in a smile. She could hear his hope, his hesitation, his fear. She knew how hard it must have been for him to say this. A man's pride allowed only so much. She would be a fool not to take his sweet offering. "Shall we forgive each other?"

Anthony's heart did a flip-flop in his chest. He could hardly breathe for the joy that filled him. He wanted to crush her against him, to take her mouth in a kiss that bespoke the depth of his feelings. It took some effort, but he finally managed to control the urge. "And begin again?" he suggested almost shyly.

Shy? Jasmine's eyes widened with surprise. She hadn't mistaken that note in his voice. Anthony felt shy with her. Good God, would wonders never cease? She turned slightly so she might see for herself this phenomenon. She smiled as her eyes took in the slight flush that darkened his complexion and the sheepish, hopeful expression in his eyes. Her heart nearly melted at the sight. "And begin again," she whispered in return.

Chapter Twenty-One

Anthony's eyes sparkled with promise, a devilish gleam dancing in their blue centers. He grinned with growing confidence at her answer. "Shall we seal our bargain with a kiss, then?"

Jasmine returned his grin with one of her own and gave a gentle shake of her head. Demurely she offered him her hand. "For now a handshake, I think."

"Do you think that sufficient?" he chuckled as he took her hand and pressed it to his chest, holding it in place with his own, "for something this momentous?"

She was unable to keep her smile from bubbling over into laughter and Anthony groaned aloud his pain at the soft, husky sound. His lips were against her neck when he spoke. "Do you realize what the sound of your laughter does to me, has done to me since first I heard it?"

Jasmine felt a definite stirring press against her backside as he deliberately shifted his hips. Her eyes widened with clear amazement. "My laughing caused that?"

"Your laughter combined with your present position, I suspect."

"Shall I ride Jeb's horse? I'd not wish to cause you undue discomfort."

His arms tightened around her, and neither professed it an accident that his fingers grazed the underside of her breast, particularly since they appeared to linger overlong on that delectable softness. "Nay," he sighed with no little exaggeration. "Holding you is a taxing chore, but one I expect I'm up to."

Jasmine, feeling very much at ease in their newfound relationship, gave an almost imperceptible wiggle and then remarked with an outrageous blink of innocence, "Indeed, I'd say you're definitely up to something."

He laughed. "You wouldn't be hinting at deliciously naughty things, would you, my love?"

Jasmine laughed that same throaty, sultry sound that never failed to send tingling sensations down his spine and into certain lower regions of his body. "I've no doubt that is your most fervent wish, but I'm afraid I wouldn't know how to go about such a thing."

Anthony felt no need of a horse. There wasn't a doubt in his mind he could have floated back to the farm, so light was he in spirit. His heart felt as if to burst with pure happiness and he wondered if he'd the ability to contain himself should the emotion grow in strength.

There was a chance, a real chance. She hadn't said the exact words but he knew by her offer of a handshake that she wanted to take the time to learn each other before they committed to a love that would last beyond the end of time.

"Tell me why you kissed her," she asked, suddenly breaking the easy, silent camaraderie between them. She bit at her lip unable to keep the question at bay. "I have to know why you turned to her."

"*What?*" Anthony couldn't imagine what she was talking about, for he had kissed no one since first they met. "Who?"

"I saw you kiss her, Anthony," Jasmine calmly insisted.

"Jasmine, I swear I've not kissed another since . . ."

"Ann," she interrupted his would-be pledge.

"Ann?" he asked, clearly amazed. He almost asked "Ann who?" when he realized who it was she was talking about. "When did I . . . ? Oh."

"Indeed 'oh,'" she repeated. "Tell me why?"

Anthony began to laugh. "Did you run away because you saw that kiss?" He should have been angry knowing the needless pain she'd put him through, but he couldn't seem to summon the emotion. All he knew was a joy not to be equalled. God, he was so damn happy. He shook his head, almost afraid to believe happiness of this magnitude existed, and he laughed again.

"I'm delighted to be the cause of such hilarity," she responded dryly, finding herself hard put to keep her annoyance at bay.

Anthony thought for a moment to tease her, but instantly discarded the notion. This closeness between them was too new, too fragile. He dared not endanger it with careless words. He smiled, but his voice lowered to a growl. "I should take you over my knee and beat you soundly for that. "Do you know the terror I felt when I found you gone? What do you mean running off because of one meaningless kiss?"

Jasmine uttered a word no lady had any business knowing, never mind repeating. "If it was meaningless, why did you do it?"

Anthony grinned at her use of profanity. "It appears we are more alike than either first imagined, for we have both jumped to erroneous conclusions and in each case have not seen fit to allow the other to explain their actions."

"I believe I'm offering you ample opportunity to explain now."

Anthony groaned as he hugged her tighter. "I

kissed her goodbye, as I would any friend. I was thanking her for all she'd done for us, and especially for you." Anthony stuck to the truth, the truth regarding his actions at least. He imagined it best not to remark upon Ann's motives behind that kiss. "Jesus, I didn't even remember it until you mentioned it."

"And then you accompanied her to her bedroom," she remarked snidely as the pain of that night returned again to squeeze her chest in a breathless hold. "Do you remember that? Lord, how appreciative of her you must have felt!"

"Jasmine," he breathed on a patient sigh. "The truth is that I was worried half to death over you. God, I couldn't sleep for fear you were taking the fever again. The idea of accompanying her to her bedroom never entered my mind."

"I lay awake for hours."

"Did you?" he asked softly, his tone filled with concern. "And what did you hear?"

"What did I hear? Nothing. Why?"

Anthony shook his head. "That alone should have told you the truth of the matter. How could we have done as you supposed without your hearing? Ann's room was next to yours, in a house with walls so thin Jeb's snores would keep us awake most of the night. Remember? God, you are the most stubborn woman." He snuggled his face in the sweetness of her neck, trying desperately to hide his smile of happiness, for this was definitely not the moment to take her feelings lightly. She had been jealous. Jealous and angry enough to have run away. Surely that proved her feelings for him ran deeper than he dared hope.

In slow, almost hesitant degrees, he felt her slender body relax against him. Anthony breathed at last a sigh of relief. She believed him. Secretly delighted that her feelings ran so deep, Anthony nevertheless swore jealousy would play no future role in their

380

relationship and he vowed silently to never give her cause.

It was dusk on the second day by the time they neared the farm. They smelled it long before their eyes took in the dark, billowing clouds of smoke that circled lazily above the treetops. Neither wanted to believe the obvious, but the closer they came to their destination, the harder it became to deny the truth.

Anthony increased his pace, his heart pounding with dread. He'd told her! Damn it, he'd told her. Why hadn't she listened to his warnings?

Anthony stopped just outside the clearing and cursed as his gaze took in and affirmed his worst suspicions. "Sonofabitch! I told her. Jesus, I told her it wasn't safe." Carefully he surveyed the destruction, his eyes ever watchful for the perpetrators of this dastardly act, for he'd not ride heedlessly in and chance Jasmine's safety.

"Wait here," he said as he began to dismount.

"No!" she cried, her heart racing in fear that he would walk into such obvious danger.

"Jasmine, they might not have left," he reasoned correctly.

Jasmine shivered as she imagined Anthony facing alone whoever was responsible for setting fire to the house and barn. She couldn't allow it. She couldn't sit here and watch him walk away, perhaps never to return. "It's no safer here," she reasoned. "Whoever did this might still lurk in these woods."

Anthony had to admit there was a chance she was right, a chance he dared not take.

He nodded and then urged his horse forward with a slight movement of his thighs. He rounded the burned-out shell of the house and came in from behind. Jasmine cried out and buried her face in her hands at the gruesome sight that greeted them. Jeb and Hopeful's bodies hung from adjoining trees, swaying upon the gentlest of breezes. Ann was sitting on the ground, in an apparent daze, almost at the tips of their lifeless feet.

Her head lifted at the sound of the horse. Blank eyes stared out of a face that seemed to have aged years in mere hours.

Anthony helped Jasmine from his horse and quickly cut the two men down, while Jasmine knelt before the silent woman.

"Are you all right?" she asked as she took Ann's icy hand in hers.

Ann nodded just before the tears came in an almost explosive rush.

It took some time before the bodies were buried and Ann calmed enough to release her stranglehold on Jasmine's neck. The horror she had witnessed on this day was more than most any could bear. In the course of one afternoon, she had been forced to watch her home burn to the ground and stood helplessly by while a cruel band of desperados took the lives of the two men who would have come to her defense. It was more than an hour before exhaustion finally overcame her horror and she slept.

"Tories," Jasmine remarked as she imparted Ann's words.

Anthony cursed this useless loss of life and destruction. It wasn't enough these people had been made to suffer the terror of Indian attacks, the abuse of the English as they commandeered anything and everything needed in the way of supplies. Now the Tories chose to make clear their opinion of any they suspected against their cause in a last-ditch attempt for victory.

He gave a weary sigh. It mattered not this horror, nor all the horrors that were yet to come. The end was most certainly in sight. No doubt the Tories realized this as well, for what else explained their clearly desperate actions?

There was no choice in the matter. Anthony could not leave Ann behind. No matter her state of shock they had to leave immediately for the next settlement and safety.

There was nothing to gather in the way of supplies, for all had been lost in the blaze. Ann sat upon Jeb's horse as it slowly picked its way through the forest, hardly aware of her surroundings so lost was she in the horror that replayed itself again and again in her mind's eye.

They had only the one blanket Jasmine had taken to protect against the cool dampness of night and Anthony's coat. Jasmine struggled but managed at last to gather a silent and subdued Ann into the warm confines of the coat. Later, under the warm cover of the blanket, Anthony cuddled his wife tightly in his arms to ward off a chill.

They did not stop that night, for Anthony was desperate to bring them as far from this danger as possible. The next morning they rested for a short time by the shore of a river.

"You should sleep, darling," Anthony said, knowing she had only dozed, and then fitfully, in his arms as they rode the night before. He held her against him beneath the shade of a giant oak. Ann lay wrapped in the heavy folds of his coat sleeping some three yards away.

"I cannot," she confessed. "When I close my eyes I see Jeb and Hopeful. If it hadn't been for me they'd still be alive."

"Jasmine, don't . . ."

"It's true," she interrupted. "I killed them as surely had I strung the rope myself."

"Jasmine, please. It accomplishes nothing for you to take this guilt upon yourself."

"Perhaps, but the guilt is there nonetheless. It is something that will stay with me for as long as I live." She gave a shaky sigh as she forced back threatening tears. "If I hadn't left Morgan's camp . . . If I hadn't stumbled across their campfire . . . If they hadn't taken me under their wing . . ."

"If they hadn't accompanied us after I found you," Anthony put in correctly. "Darling, they took it upon themselves to come along. You cannot accept the blame for their deaths. It was through no fault of yours that the Tories banded together to wreak destruction."

"But if . . ."

"If they hadn't died today, it might have been tomorrow. How can we know what the future holds? It accomplishes nothing but needless suffering to allow a guilt not deserved. You could have done nothing to prevent what happened."

"If I hadn't left you . . ."

"I'd no doubt be dead as well."

Jasmine shuddered as she realized the truth of his words. He lived only because he had come for her. Her arms tightened around his waist and she held on for dear life at the horror his words brought to mind.

There was no help for it. Anthony hated to force them on, knowing the women, most especially Ann, who still appeared to be in a state of shock, needed to rest, but he wouldn't feel safe until they were no longer alone.

They were a haggard lot by the end of the second day when they came at last across a small village that appeared at first to be deserted. In truth, the farmers had gone off to fight their cause and had, for safety's sake, brought their families to town, leaving their homes and fields abandoned.

At the opposite end of the boarded-up buildings in town, stood a field hospital. Men in varying stages of recuperation lazed away the evening in conversation with their comrades, their backs resting upon the wooden buildings.

The weary travelers had not rested but for a few minutes at a time and had eaten only once in nearly three days, the night before when Anthony had spied and killed a rabbit. It was here he'd leave Ann, hopefully in the care of a kindly, sympathetic family, and for a day or two allow his wife to recover from the hardship of their ride before they'd set out to find Morgan again.

On the edge of town Anthony found a deserted building, clearly once used by a seamstress, for it held still a quantity of needles and threads although all bolts of cloth apparently had been carted off earlier. The house, bare of furniture, nevertheless offered protection against the night and he thus commandeered it for the women. It took some doing but he finally managed to beg enough blankets and bedding. And so they settled in to this their temporary home.

There was little conversation as the three bone-weary travelers prepared for some much needed sleep, the first Anthony knew in three nights.

It was late when they awoke. Anthony smiled to find his wife leaning over him, her warm gaze searching his face. "What are you doing, watching me as I sleep?"

Jasmine's eyes were softened with a look of love. Instantly she lowered her eyes and grinned, not yet ready to bare her soul by telling him how beautiful he was and how difficult it was to keep her eyes off his face and her hands from his body. "Indeed not," she quickly denied. "There was a fly buzzing around your head."

The corners of Anthony's eyes crinkled with pleasure, knowing the truth of her soft look, no matter her denial. "Has it disappeared because I awoke?"

"You swallowed it in one of your snores," she lied shamelessly, a grin tugging at the corners of her mouth.

Anthony chuckled and rolled their bodies so his loomed over hers. "Odd, but I didn't taste a thing."

"You were sleeping," she answered with only the slightest hesitation, her expression telling clearly she had just thought up the answer and considered it quite remarkable upon such short notice.

"Ah, that accounts for it then."

"Accounts for what?"

"For thinking my wife was giving me soft, inviting looks when I awoke. No doubt my mind was befuddled with sleep."

"No doubt," she agreed on a shaky laugh.

"Do you think you might spare a good morning kiss?"

Jasmine shrugged. "I imagine that wouldn't be so great a chore." She pecked a tiny kiss upon his cheek.

"What was that?" he asked as she made to roll from his arms.

"What?" she asked, her momentary confusion apparent.

"That little something you did with your mouth on my cheek."

Jasmine giggled. "That was a kiss, of course."

"Woman, that litle peck did not by any stretch of the imagination resemble a kiss."

"Didn't it?" She laughed happily at the teasing look in his eyes. "Perhaps this is more to your way of thinking, a kiss." Jasmine lifted her head and smacked a hard loud kiss on his lips.

Anthony had a time of it trying to keep his laughter at bay. "A bit noisy, don't you think?"

"You want it quieter?"

He nodded. "Quieter and longer."

"Perhaps tomorrow?"

"Tomorrow? What's wrong with now?"

Jasmine's lips did not crack a smile, although the effort took some doing. Her expression was as prim and proper as if she presided over a formal tea, but a wicked gleam in the depths of shimmering silver eyes belied her cool expression. "You must understand. There is a quota on my kisses, Mr. Montgomery. I'm afraid you've used up all that was reserved for today."

Anthony chuckled as he buried his face in the sweet, delicious warmth of her neck. "And just when they were about to get interesting. What a shame." He raised his head, his eyes twinkling with humor as he allowed a long, weary sigh. "I have no choice then but to take this chore upon my own weakened shoulders."

"And should Ann return? What then?"

Anthony had completely forgotten the other woman's existence, an easy enough happening, for when his wife was snuggled in his arms, there was little room for thoughts of another. His forehead rested against hers as he breathed, "Damn."

Jasmine smiled. "Do you suppose there will come a time when we might live a simple, ordinary life? I've been wondering of late what it would be like to awaken in my own bed." *With you at my side.* She finished in silence, but she might have said the words aloud, for Anthony read correctly her thoughts and smiled as he forced aside the erotic thoughts of her in his bed, sleepy and warm and most definitely naked. "I imagine it not to be all that long in coming. From what I've heard last night, Washington is on the move with an army of five thousand. The French fleet has left Rhode Island and is making its way south. A total of seventy-five hundred troops are heading north from Jamestown and Williamsburg.

"I imagine a confrontation is in the offing."

Jasmine bit her lip. Her eyes darted nervously about, for the moment not daring to look at him. "Will you go?" she asked, her voice filled with dread, for she knew the answer before she spoke.

"I will."

"Anthony," she pleaded. "Haven't you done enough?"

"What have I done that a thousand others have not?"

"You risked your life while working in New York. If they'd have caught you it would have meant almost instant death."

Anthony's smile was gentle as his blue eyes took in her fear. Jasmine seemed to have forgotten it was only she who had posed a danger. It was she who had turned him in. "I won't be spying. No doubt I'll be doing as before, securing supplies, for nary a tot of rum and spare bolt of cloth can be found among the whole of the rebel forces.

"They are a sorry lot indeed. Tired, dirty, sick. They have barely the means to do more than tread one step after another and fire their weapons."

"Anthony, I . . ."

"You need not worry overmuch, Jasmine. I chance little bringing supplies to those who are in such need."

"If you think to bamboozle me with pretty words, think again. I know the means to which you'll go. Tell me you won't attack the English and steal those supplies. Tell me again there is no danger."

Anthony grinned. "There is little I can tell you that you don't already know," he responded, knowing the futility of lying.

Jasmine gave an angry grunt as she pushed him aside and came to her feet. Her hands were on her hips as she glared down at him. "You are a selfish man, Anthony. Swaggering about this countryside bent on playing soldier without a care to others."

Anthony's brow rose with surprise. "How so? Because I feel I must do my duty?"

"Duty, is it? And what of your duty to me? Do you realize how much I love you?" Jasmine snorted her disgust and added, her voice holding just a trace of the terror that filled her being, "Can you imagine what it will do to me if you were killed?"

There was a long moment of almost deafening silence. In her anger, Jasmine had spoken aloud her fears and hadn't as yet realized her words.

"Do you?" he asked, his heart pumping furiously at her admission.

"What?" she asked, her eyes rounding as she realized what she had blurted out.

"Love me?" he repeated, straining for a calmness he was far from feeling.

Jasmine gave him a mutinous stare. She lifted her chin in defiance and then spun around, turning her back to him.

Anthony came to her, standing behind her, so close she could feel the heat of his body through her clothes. And yet he didn't touch her. His breath disturbed the hairs that curled near her ears and sent chills down her back. "Do you love me, Jasmine?"

She turned to glare at him, angrier than she could ever remember. He had no right to feel this much pleasure, not when she suffered this almost strangling fear. Her mouth thinned to a slash of pink, furious that he should chance their future for a ridiculous sense of duty. What if something happened to him? What if he were killed? How was she supposed to live without this dominating, obnoxiously arrogant man? Impatiently she swiped at the tears in her eyes. "And if I did? Would it make a bit of difference?"

Anthony chuckled softly as he pulled her into his arms. His laughter was low and silky-smooth. Jasmine felt her stomach quiver at the low, sensual sound. "Don't laugh at me, Anthony," she whispered, her voice breaking as she pressed her face into his shoulder.

Anthony took a huge breath, wondering if he had the strength to contain the joy that filled his being. Surely he would burst, for he doubted if anyone

389

could withstand happiness so great.

His head lowered. "Jasmine," he whispered against her neck as his warm lips nuzzled her sweet flesh. His voice broke with emotion. "My God, how I love you."

Tears ran unchecked down her face. "Do you?" Her voice quivered as she fought for control. "Do you love me enough to leave this insanity behind and come home?"

Anthony's smile was tender, his hands gentle as they wiped away her tears. "I love you enough to stay. I love you enough to long for a better life, for a future that holds the luxury of freedom."

"Damn you!" she snapped as she tore herself from his warm embrace. "What do I care for freedom? What good is freedom if you're dead? Will you then enjoy it? Will *I*?" Jasmine gave a long sigh. Her eyes pleaded as she choked back burning tears. "Anthony, please. I don't want to be free and alone."

He gathered her to him again. "You won't be alone."

"Can you promise me that? Will you swear on it?" He felt her body soften and lean into his as she begged for reassurance.

"Jasmine, I can only promise to love you for as long as God permits. None of us know the future. None of us are guaranteed more than this moment."

Jasmine sighed, knowing the uselessness of continuing on in this vein. The man was stubborn beyond belief. And she, it seemed, had no choice in the matter. She loved him to desperation and would, no matter her reluctance, accept his decision. "Will you promise me this? Will you be careful? Very, very careful?"

Anthony grinned. "You have no need to worry on that score. I will indeed, for nothing pleasures me more than the thought of growing old with you at my side."

Anthony nuzzled his face into the warmth of her neck and groaned. "Do you know how long I've loved you? Do you know how long I've waited to hear you say those words?"

"How long?" Jasmine smiled.

"Since almost the first."

Jasmine shot him a dark look. "I've yet to forgive you for that subterfuge. Do you realize how terribly I suffered? Can you imagine my despair, my guilt?"

"Your guilt was as nothing compared to the pain I would have endured had I kept myself from your bed."

"You were a beast."

Anthony chuckled and snuggled her closer. "And you were the picture of temptation. Do you realize how I suffered watching you, knowing I dared not touch you lest you realize the effeminate man you married was in truth naught but a lusty male with but one thought and that to bed his wife?"

"Did you suffer?" she asked, her eyes wide with surprise.

"Lord," he groaned as he remembered back. "I can imagine torture no worse were I put upon the rack."

Jasmine laughed softly. She pushed herself from his arms, her eyes shining with triumph. "Good."

"Good?" he grinned, his eyes alight with devilment. His hands reached for her, his clear intent to tickle her into submission, when a soft voice interrupted the teasing moment.

"I'm sorry," Ann said as she entered the room. "I didn't mean to intrude."

Both Anthony and Jasmine smiled as he gathered her into his arms and held her possessively at his side.

"I wanted to tell you I've been offered a home. Letty Sherman, an old friend of mine, has lost her husband. She has five children and not much else. She offered me a place to stay in exchange for helping her out." She smiled. "I'll be staying here a while."

Ann didn't mention the doctor who had been administering care to this small community for the last year or so, nor his obvious interest in her.

It was enough for now that she had found a place to stay. The future would take care of itself.

It was after dinner. Anthony and Jasmine had just returned from Letty Sherman's farm after depositing Ann in the older woman's care. Anthony was just now entertaining some particularly delicious thoughts on how an evening spent in the intimate company of his wife would no doubt result, when they were met by three of his men as they came into town. Sent by Morgan, his squad had split into two factions, both scouting out the areas for some weeks in search of their captain.

The three—Boggs, Cooper, and Billings—bore no startling change of itinerary. As always the rebel force were in desperate need of supplies. Anthony was delivered of his orders to find these supplies and hurry them to the general, who was steadily pursuing Cornwallis as the English Army retreated to the north.

Anthony was torn with indecision. It was imperative he be about his duties and yet he dared not chance his wife's delicate health. Still, he was loath to leave her behind, for he trusted no one but himself with her care.

There was no help for it. He'd never be able to perform his duties while worrying of her safety. Perhaps she could stay with Ann for a time. Anthony told her of his decision.

Jasmine shook her head, dismissing his words as if never spoken. "You won't be leaving me behind, Anthony."

"I'm afraid I have no choice. I dare not risk your health. You have yet to recover from the loss of the child. I know you are weaker than you admit."

"My ass," she snapped. Her silver eyes narrowed to slits of bright fury. "What you want is to play and a wife would encumber you."

Anthony grinned at her choice of words. "Play?" he asked, his dark brows lifting, his eyes aglow with laughter. "Indeed, if my intention were to play, your ass would be my very first consideration."

She waved away his laughter with a delicate hand. "Do not think to soften my heart with teasing remarks and beguiling smiles. I am going with you."

Anthony smiled, his heart filling with joy at her response. "Jasmine, you know well enough the hardship and danger involved."

"Do you believe me so weak in spirit as to remain behind? Can you imagine the fear I would know, wondering whether or not you lived?" She shook her head. "I'm sorry, Anthony. If disaster should befall, I'd best be at your side, and know the whole of it."

"So you can save my life again?" he teased.

"If need be," she answered in all seriousness.

Anthony shook his head. His blue eyes softened with love, his lips smiling tenderly. "I cannot allow it."

Jasmine's chin rose a fraction higher. "I'm afraid you have no choice."

"Meaning?"

"Meaning, I'll follow if I must."

Anthony groaned as he took her against him. "Jasmine, you know the danger."

"Exactly. And you'll not face it alone."

"Damn you, woman," he muttered, knowing he hadn't the strength to refuse her insistence. "Is this a sampling of what the future holds? Will I one day grow so weak in spirit that I must ask my wife's permission to come to her bed?"

Jasmine giggled at the absurd thought, knowing the years ahead held many an argument with this strong-willed man, but never one that would keep him from her bed. "Since I expect we'll be sharing the same bed, I doubt if that issue will come about."

The picture of her warm and willing in his bed was almost more than he could bear. "God," he groaned as he pressed his hips against hers, telling her clearly of the endless ache he suffered. "When am I going to get you alone?"

Jasmine smiled, knowing this tiny building not to be their private abode, for Boggs, Cooper, and Billings had made themselves at home and might at any time burst upon their private moments. "Just think of this time as a test to your strength."

"Jesus, woman," Anthony sighed as he ground his hips into her softness, his face into her hair. "Should I grow stronger, all hereabouts might retire for home, for I could no doubt whip these redcoats single-handed."

Chapter Twenty-Two

Jasmine was tired, bone-weary tired. Sitting her saddle daily caused her back a constant ache, but she stubbornly refused to give in to the discomfort. She'd made her decision to accompany her husband and here, in the midst of nowhere, deep in the woods of North Carolina, she'd not likely find a comfortable place to rest.

They had been traveling for two weeks, up early every morning, late in bed each night. In truth, rest seemed to be the last thing these men had in mind.

Jasmine knew she had made a serious error in judgment. No matter her concern for her husband, she never should have come. It was obvious she slowed the men down, for they surely would have covered more ground without her.

The hours spent working at the inn hadn't brought this measure of exhaustion, perhaps because she had worked at her own pace and then rested comfortably at night. Jasmine gave a disgusted grunt. She was weak, much weaker than she had first supposed.

Anthony's hand reached out to touch her leg as he rode his horse alongside hers. "Tired?" he asked, his voice filled with concern.

Jasmine glanced up at his worried expression and

smiled. "No more than you, I suspect."

Anthony stretched his back and groaned at the stiffness between his shoulders. "We'll be stopping for the night soon. What would you say if we managed to find a bed this time?"

Jasmine laughed. "I'd say you excelled among mere mortal men to conjure up a bed amid this wilderness."

"But if we should come upon a farmhouse?"

"Is one close by?"

"According to this map," he remarked as he strained in the near dark to read the paper held in his hands, "the Bowler place should be just up the road."

"Are the Bowlers sympathetic to your cause?"

Anthony shrugged. "It matters not."

"Anthony, I'd much prefer to sleep on the ground. It poses no great hardship," she said. No matter her disgust of things that might crawl in the night, she preferred the hardship rather than risk a confrontation between her husband and one of the many Tories who lived in this area.

Disregarding her fears, he promised, "You'll sleep in a bed tonight."

Jasmine opened her mouth to protest, but the sound of a lone, galloping horse postponed her ready argument.

A young boy, tall and thin, perhaps fourteen years of age, came suddenly racing out of the near dark. Despite his tender years, his expertise showed clearly as he quickly reined the animal to a prancing stop upon spying the small group blocking his way. His eyes widened as he realized four guns were drawn and aimed at his belly.

"State your name and business, boy," Anthony demanded.

"Andrew Jackson, sir. I ride from Colonel Davies with a message for General Greene."

Anthony nodded. "Is the way clear ahead?"

Andrew grinned. "It is, sir, but for the supply train about five miles back."

"A supply train, you say?"

"I do indeed, sir. Armed to the teeth with lobsterbacks." Andrew grinned as he remembered how he had sped past the lot, already out of range before any weapons could be lifted to his retreating back.

Anthony cursed. He had four men, including himself. How in hell was he supposed to commandeer supplies, guarded by so many, with so few? He nodded, his lips grim. "You'd best be on your way lad. Godspeed."

Andrew was off with a lighthearted laugh and a jaunty wave. A moment later he disappeared around a curve in the road, and then even the pounding sounds of his horse faded into the musical sounds of a forest bathed in dark shadows.

Anthony thought for a long moment. Finally he raised his head and grinned. "We'll be taking the supplies, of course."

The three men muttered their agreement. Jasmine remained silent, her teeth worrying her bottom lip.

"The trick to it will be to create a diversion."

One or two ideas were bantered about but negated by Anthony as being too dangerous. He needed these men and more. As it stood, they'd only be able to take four wagons. Should any of them suffer serious injury, he'd be forced to leave still more wagons behind.

"What you need is someone to occupy their attention for a time, am I right?"

Anthony nodded as he turned to his wife. His lips parted the words, for he knew her thoughts simply by looking at her face. "No, you cannot," he said before she had a chance to go on.

"Anthony," she continued, careless of his refusal. "I will be perfectly safe."

"Out of the question!" His voice was rising.

"All I have to do is walk into their campfire. I'll pretend to be in need of assistance. I'll tell them I've lost my way."

"Damn you, woman. I said no!"

"Capt'n," Boggs said, knowing Jasmine's plan to be the logical answer to their dilemma, "she might be our only chance."

"Boggs," Anthony hissed, his eyes narrowing to slits, his voice holding a clear threat.

"Them redcoats won't hurt a lady. And even had they a mind, we'd be awatchin' their every move."

"Listen to him, Anthony. We need the supplies. There is no other way."

Anthony shot her a look of fury. He knew they were right, but every protective instinct rebelled at the mere thought of allowing her to walk into danger. He shook his head again, knowing the futility of objecting.

"If questioned, what will you say?" he asked. "What reason can you give for being out here at this time of night?"

Jasmine's eyes widened with surprise. When he shook his head, she expected to hear yet another refusal. "I'll tell them I'm Mrs. Bowler's cousin." She shot him a victorious grin, remembering the name of the farm they were heading toward. "I'm here for a visit. I was out riding and my horse threw me. I can't find my way back."

Anthony groaned and shook his head again. "You will be careful."

Jasmine smiled with tender affection. She'd never seen someone agree to anything by shaking his head in the negative. "You need not worry overmuch. I've no doubt that they will be perfect gentlemen."

He shook his head yet again, obviously unhappy with this plan, but a few minutes later he had worked out the details and they were once again making their way down the road.

Jasmine watched the four men spread out and move to their designated positions. Her heart was thumping with trepidation as she mentally prepared herself. Nothing would happen. No one would come to harm, she silently repeated again and again and again, until the words became a prayerful chant.

She straightened her back, calling on all her courage as she stepped into the circle of campfire light. Three men jumped to their feet, guns at the ready as she approached the fire. All told, there were ten. Jasmine prayed no others stood guard, hidden from sight in the dark. "Good evening, gentlemen," Jasmine said, her voice betraying none of the fear that trembled her belly. "I wonder if I might impose upon your kindness? It seems I've lost my way. Could you, do you think, direct me to the Bowler farm?"

All ten men, most sitting, others still bent in a half crouch were flabbergasted as they stared with open fascination at this beautiful woman who had wandered upon them. A moment later, those sitting seemed to remember their manners and, sputtering disjointed greetings, they came quickly to their feet.

Jasmine held up her hand, her voice whispery soft causing more than one to notice the tingling sensations thickening in their pants. "Please do not stand. I know how weary you must be after a long day spent in the saddle. I imagine routing out those traitors to the Crown a most trying task."

She bit her lip and prayed she hadn't ruined everything with her rush of compliments and felt a flicker of surprise when no one attempted to discount her flattery.

Jasmine smiled as chests became a bit more broad and legs spread into cocky stances while answering smiles flashed. "Please sit down," she remarked, her voice still softly feminine. And when no one seemed disposed to move, she pulled a gun from the pocket of her skirt, aimed it at the only officer among them, and said all too sweetly, "Gentlemen, please."

She smiled again as Anthony slipped from the darkness to stand suddenly at her side. From the corner of her eye she saw Boggs pushing the eleventh man forward, while Cooper and Billings, guns drawn, had circled the suddenly hostile group.

In small groups of twos and threes the now disarmed, bootless men were led away from the guarded circle and tied securely to each other and then to trees. Wagons were quickly explored. Some of the more necessary items moved. Supplies that couldn't be taken, including the six wagons that would remain behind, were set afire.

While his men were about the task of tying all the horses to the back of each wagon, Anthony clasped Jasmine's arm in his hand and directed her outside the circle of light. The moment they were beyond curious eyes, he turned her into his body and held her tightly against him. "God but I near died when I saw them scramble to their feet with guns ready to fire." His body refused to stop its trembling now that the danger had passed, and he realized correctly how easily he could have lost her this night.

Jasmine smiled. "You needn't have worried. I was never in danger," she promised as she snuggled her face to his shoulder and neck, breathing deeply his scent into her lungs.

"And how did you come to that conclusion?"

"I knew my husband was watching." She grinned up into his shadowy face, unable to see clearly, for the moon had yet to rise. "He is most protective, you know."

"Is he?" Anthony asked, his mouth spreading into a grin, happy to join her in teasing, for he needed this

400

moment to dispel the terror that yet plagued. "I wonder then, what he would say if he found you in my arms?"

"I suspect his anger a force you'd not wish to reckon with," she said, her voice a low whisper as if she were imparting a closely guarded secret.

"But since the temptation is well worth the risk, I believe I'll take my chances."

Jasmine gave a soft, husky laugh as she leaned her mouth into him and trailed warm lips over his neck. "A rogue. I suspected as much from the first." She sighed as she pulled her head back. "I imagine stealing a kiss from a lady, even a married lady, would pose no tremors of conscience?"

"I'm afraid not. If memory serves, I once happened across a lady in a general's library and did just that."

Jasmine grinned as his words brought to mind that particular episode.

He shrugged. "Of course it would matter greatly on the lady herself. If she were so bold as to give the kiss, there'd be no question of stealing, would there?"

"I suppose not."

"Do you think she might be willing?"

"To give a kiss?"

"Just this once?"

"I imagine she might." Jasmine smiled as she leaned forward again, her mouth reaching his throat. "Sir, you'll find no shy maiden here, but, even so, I cannot accomplish this task without your assistance."

"How so?" Anthony grinned, his mind hazy with desire as her body grew noticeably soft and pliant in his arms.

"Lean down so I might reach your mouth."

"Ah, now that might prove to be a great mistake."

"Indeed?"

"You see, if I gave in to this tender plea, my men

401

would surely wonder of the delay."

"How long do you imagine a kiss to take?" she asked reasonably.

"Two or three hours."

"For a kiss?"

"Ah, madam, you underrate your charms, for one kiss would never be enough. I'm afraid once begun, I'll never find the strength to stop."

Jasmine smiled and patted his chest as if a child. "You need not fear. I will be strong for both of us."

Anthony chuckled as he leaned his head down and, with a sigh of pure enjoyment, felt the last of his terror disappear as he greedily accepted the touch of her mouth.

A quarter of an hour later, four heavily laden, slowly creeping wagons were heading north toward Morgan in Virginia.

Jasmine sighed with pleasure as she eased her aching back against a soft bundle of clothing. A smile lingered at her lips. She couldn't deny the sweet victory that caused silver eyes to gleam with illuminating radiance in the moonlight.

"Mite proud of yourself, wouldn't you say?" Anthony remarked correctly interpreting her glowing smile.

"I've every reason to be, wouldn't you say?"

"What I'd say is my wife is about the most stubborn creature I've ever come across."

"No doubt a characteristic acquired from her husband," she returned.

Anthony nodded and grinned. "I hope you know I have every intention of keeping you forever with child. We'll see how many adventures you wander into with a full belly and a child on each arm while three others pull at your skirts."

Jasmine grinned with happiness, for she couldn't imagine a more lovely adventure. "Six? Lord, you

402

expect to be busy, don't you?"

The gleam in Anthony's eyes belied his weary words, "It won't be without some effort, but I expect I'll manage the chore."

They didn't make camp that night, nor the next. Despite the constant thumping and jangling of the wagon, Jasmine did manage a few moments of restless sleep. Her head was propped upon Anthony's knee, her body restrained by his arm to guard against slipping from the seat every time a wheel took a sharp bump or hollow in the road.

But no matter her short naps, she was exhausted. Her body hummed and trembled with a tiredness she could never have imagined.

Anthony deemed it safe enough to make camp on the third night. Jasmine hadn't the strength to care at that point. She knew nothing but the whispery sensation of strong arms as he took her from the seat and settled her upon a soft mat of blankets. And then she knew nothing but the blessed dark comfort of sleep.

The next morning Jasmine awoke to the usual sounds of early-morning camp. Pans rattled as they were set upon heated rocks. Men cursed without thought as they went about their chores. Horses whinnied, their hooves muffled against the soft earth as they waited impatiently for their feed.

Jasmine moaned with discomfort. Her back ached as did nearly every muscle and joint in her body, since she'd slept so heavily she'd hardly moved throughout the night. With a grunt of the effort it took to move her stiff arm, she brought the blanket over her head as a shaft of sunshine penetrated the heavily laden branches under which she lay. An instant later, even the blanket proved no help, for she detected the scent of coffee and bacon grease.

Jasmine grimaced as the scent brought about the not unusual and most uncomfortable wave of nausea. She detested the smell and taste of the bitter brew, more so these last few months as her pregnancy progressed and the thought of anything cooked in bacon drippings was simply not to be borne.

If she remained perfectly still, she knew the sensation would pass, for this was not her first experience with the discomfort.

Jasmine suddenly stiffened. She wasn't pregnant. Not any longer. Why then should she suffer this discomfort?

Could it be? Had their one encounter since their reunion proven fruitful?

Jasmine grinned. Her heart fluttered wildly as her hand crept beneath the blanket to the soft hollow of her stomach. Silently she prayed for her suspicions to be so.

She dared not tell Anthony, even though she felt near to bursting with excitement, for she hadn't a doubt he'd be wild with fear for her. No, she wouldn't put him through that terror. There was nothing either of them could do about it in any case. Not here in the wilderness. Not now.

Oh for a cup of tea, she silently lamented. She dared to move, snuggling deeper into the cushiony softness of her pallet, trying to concentrate on the new knowledge she had gained rather than the scent that permeated the air.

"Are you awake?"

"No," she muttered. Having conquered the urge to fly into the woods and empty her stomach, she had almost drifted back to sleep.

"In that case, I expect I should give someone else this cup of tea."

"Tea!" she responded with wholehearted en-

404

thusiasm, forgetting her ailment as she swung the covers aside and came to a sitting position. Jasmine swayed dizzily at the abrupt movement, but the sensation passed as quickly as it had come.

She never asked how he had come across the much favored brew, but reached out for the aromatic cup. "I've heard tell the English hold great store in these dark leaves. 'Tis a shame most of the colonists have stubbornly forgone this pleasure for the duration."

Jasmine shot him a sharp look, but otherwise ignored his gentle censure, for they both knew she was not one of those of whom he spoke. She felt no need for sacrifice here, especially since her cause was not that of most of the colonists. Jasmine took a sip and sighed with almost lusty satisfaction at the pure luxury.

"Good?" he asked as he smiled at her clear and obvious enjoyment.

Jasmine shot him a look of annoyance at finding him in his usual cheery mood. Her brows lowered and her mouth thinned into a threatening scowl. "Anthony, I truly don't mind a murmured 'good morning.' Indeed, it is a most correct and proper salutation. But this tendency you display toward laughter upon awakening will have to undergo some control."

Anthony fought back the urge to laugh at her grumpy scowl. "Would you have me as unhappy as my wife?"

"I'm not in the least unhappy," she corrected. "I simply understand there is a time and a place for boundless cheer."

"And morning is not one of them, I take it."

"It most certainly is not."

Anthony bit his lip trying to prevent his smile, which was not an easy task to be sure, for he most always felt so disposed at the mere sight of his lady,

405

particularly so when as now, she was thus deliciously disheveled. "I suppose with some effort, I could restrain myself in the mornings."

"It would be most appreciated, I assure you."

Anthony grinned, a devilish light dancing in his eyes. "There are methods you might entertain to keep my mouth busy. No doubt I'd then find little time for laughter. Even a smile might prove too great a chore." He shrugged almost nonchalantly as he leaned a bit closer. "In truth, the effort might also serve to improve your mood."

Jasmine smiled, despite herself. "I'm beginning to believe my husband has but one train of thought."

"Beginning?!" he remarked, his brows lifting with no little amazement. "You mean you've just now noticed?"

"Go away, Anthony. I'm not yet awake and am no match for your wit."

Anthony chuckled as he leaned back. "Is it all right if I laugh now?"

"Lord but you are annoying." Jasmine finished the last of her tea, placed the cup on the ground, and once again snuggled beneath the covers. "Go away."

A hearty slap to her rear brought her back to a sitting position in seconds. "If you want a bath, I suggest you not waste time lying about."

The sneer that had already formed instantly disappeared. The unspoken words she was about to rain down upon his head at his daring froze on her parted lips as her mind suddenly realized his words. "Bath?"

"Only if you hurry," he nodded.

Jasmine sighed, her eyes half closed with pleasure as cool water ran over her flesh. For weeks her daily ablutions had consisted of the most meager washings, for she was rarely offered a moment of privacy, never mind the time to enjoy a thorough cleaning. Lord, she couldn't remember the last time she'd bathed. And although it stretched the imagination to consider this a real bath, it was close enough for her to greedily enjoy the pleasure of the rushing water.

Anthony had taken her to a small curve in the river. She was protected on both sides by outgrowth. Her desire to be clean, really clean, had left her brave enough to enter the water, despite the fact that anyone on the opposite shore could see her.

Jasmine had opted to leave her one and only shift on, despite its ragged condition and the fact that once wet it would prove no obstacle in the way of protection from her husband's hungry gaze. She simply couldn't disrobe completely, not out here, no matter Anthony's obvious disappointment.

Jasmine glanced over her shoulder. He was sitting upon the shore, his rifle at his side, his eyes drawn with undisguised hunger to the slender line of her back. Her heart leaped as she read his look of longing. She almost called out, inviting him to join her, but knew he'd refuse. Someone had to keep guard, he'd earlier pointed out when she'd given him an inquiring look as he perched on a rock and watched her undress.

Jasmine kept her back to him. Her heart was suddenly pounding and her hands shook as she went about the task of soaping her body and hair. She forced his presence from her mind with difficulty. Knowing he watched her every move brought a tingling sensation up her spine. Purposely she concentrated on her actions and sighed. It was heaven to wash away days of choking dust and the sweat born of suffocating heat. And if she appeared somewhat lusty in her enjoyment, she gave it not a thought.

Thick suds covered her hair and dribbled down over her shoulders as she scrubbed enthusiastically. Jasmine cared little that the offered soap was harsher than she would have liked. It got her clean and for that she was indeed grateful. A moment later she dipped beneath the surface and rinsed away the suds. She spent a few more minutes diving beneath the river's surface, and came at last, and with some reluctance, from the water.

Jasmine looked at the clothes she'd worn for almost a month with pure disgust. Lord but she hated the thought of putting on the same dirty clothes again.

Anthony came to stand before her, straining for breath as his eyes took in the sight of her body clearly visible beneath the wet, clinging chemise. His arm outstretched, his hand held a bundle of folded cloth. "I've found some things among the supplies. They might be a little big, but I think they'll suffice."

Jasmine gave a dazzling smile as she watched him shake out a clean pair of trousers and a shirt. She smiled as she reached for them, only to have them snatched from her grasp.

"I've something else to give you first," he remarked as he took her hand and led the way toward a thicket of forest. He didn't stop until they were engulfed in the absolute privacy of thick woods and heavy undergrowth.

Jasmine's eyes widened with surprise as she read his intent correctly. "Anthony, I don't think . . ." she began, hoping, no matter the yearning that suddenly throbbed to life deep inside, to delay this moment, for Jasmine was not so long married that to make love in open and most especially in broad daylight brought no reluctance.

He shook his head. His gentle smile would have been reassuring, but her cheeks grew red knowing he could see her as if she stood naked, for the wet cloth offered no protection. "A kiss, Jasmine, no more."

Jasmine looked up with some surprise and smiled happily. "Is that all you want?" she teased.

Anthony groaned as he pulled her tightly to him. His mouth and nose nuzzled the sweet flesh of her neck. "What I want is to make you wet."

Jasmine sucked in her breath, knowing well his meaning. "Oh, God," she groaned breathlessly, feeling her knees weaken and her insides melt at the heated look in his eyes.

"Hot and wet," he murmured into her hair, "and ready for me. I want to lick you everywhere, suck you everywhere. But there's no time." He closed his eyes for just a moment, relishing the picture of their coming together. In his mind's eye he could see her slumberous expression, feel her wild passion build. God, he wanted to love her for hours, to watch her writhe with pleasure, to feel her body strain toward his, hungry with need, to lick at the sweat that would film her silken skin, to listen to her cries of ecstasy, to bury himself deep in her warmth, so deep his entire world would become only her. "But we have a few minutes. Enough for this," he murmured as he pulled her close against him and lowered his lips to her mouth.

The touch of his mouth was at first tender as it brushed lightly over her lips, asking nothing of her but the sweet pleasure of this delicate tasting. He meant only to sample her nearness, to delight for an ecstatic moment pressed against the soft lushness of her body. He never meant for the kiss to grow in strength, in longing, in depth.

His tongue slid lightly over her lips, absorbing the taste that was solely her own, delighting in the delicate, silken texture. He groaned as he felt her lips part and knew himself almost instantly lost, for he couldn't stop himself from deepening the kiss. His tongue slid inside her lips, teasing the sensitive, moist flesh found there. His mouth sipped at her taste, taking her breath and leaving her dizzy with his own.

Her lips parted further and she breathed a welcoming sigh as she greedily sought the silken, heated exploration. Her lips closed and hugged his darting tongue.

Anthony gasped at the sensation, his mind reeling at her eager response. Her scent and taste filled his being until his world was nothing but her. Again and again his tongue imitated the movements of his hips as his body pressed against her.

They were gasping for breath, the world about them forgotten by the time he tore his mouth from hers.

Jasmine's head was spinning, her voice barely a husky murmur as she leaned heavily against him. "No one should be allowed to kiss like that," she moaned dizzily as she forced her knees to hold her weight and then moaned again as his hands on the fullness of her backside pushed her toward him. "It must be against the law."

Anthony chuckled at her breathless remark. "I'm afraid not, but there are other things that definitely are. You won't report me if I show you what I've in mind?"

Jasmine laughed as she answered the seductive pressure of his hips with her own and then pulled away. Her voice was a sultry taunt, her shyness at making love in the open forgotten. "If you kept me busy enough, I doubt I'd find the strength or the time."

"Meaning the thought holds some interest?"

Jasmine groaned as he licked at the sensitive flesh beneath her ear. "Meaning I'd know the workings of

410

your mind."

Anthony smiled at the hard shudder that wracked her body as his hands slid down her back, cupped her hips and brought her body against his obvious need. "There was a time when you thought my kisses most objectionable, especially since I dared to use my tongue, and now you dare to know all the evil workings of my mind?"

Jasmine gave a slight shake of her head, a smile touching sweetly curved lips. "Anthony, you mustn't listen to the ramblings of an innocent."

"And now? Shall I listen now that you are no longer an innocent?"

Silver eyes, still slightly dazed, sparkled with merriment as her gaze rose to meet his. "Only if you prefer a life of peace and harmony," she stated sensibly.

Anthony laughed. "A dire threat if ever I've heard one." He sighed as he buried his face in her hair and breathed deeply her deliciously clean scent. "Still, I imagine we should grow quite bored with all that peace and harmony after a time."

Jasmine grinned. "You've no need to worry on that score. I somehow doubt peace and harmony to be our mainstay."

"You mean we'll have differences of opinion?" he asked, feigning astonishment.

"I think it safe to count on it." She grinned and then sighed as his mouth nuzzled the curve of her neck.

"What do you propose we should do about that?"

Jasmine shrugged. "You don't suppose we should reconsider this marriage and separate."

Anthony instantly pulled his mouth from her throat, his eyes narrowed, his look fierce.

"I thought not." She grinned, delighted that her words had the power to wipe the smile from his lips.

411

It seemed he couldn't even tease about such a happening.

"Well then, I expect you'll have no choice but to cater to my every need."

Anthony chuckled. "Is that the way you see it?"

Her eyes widened and she blinked with all innocence. "Is there another way?" she asked, her lips twitching with suppressed humor.

"None that I can think of at the moment."

She nodded. "As I rightly suspected."

"Might there be a need you'd be wanting me to cater to right now?"

Jasmine's eyes narrowed and she bit at her lower lip while pretending to ponder his words. She responded at last with a small shrug, her hands lifting with a helpless gesture. "I'm afraid nothing comes to mind."

"You wouldn't be needing me to touch you or anything?"

Jasmine laughed. *"Anything?* Now that sounds interesting, doesn't it? What exactly did you have in mind?"

Anthony shrugged. "Well, I thought, and this is just a thought, mind you, you might need my mouth about here."

Jasmine took a startled breath as his fingers grazed the tip of her breast. "Do you often think things of this sort?" she asked, her voice holding a clear tremor.

"More often than not, I'm afraid."

"You're very good, aren't you?"

"Actually I was hoping you'd think me very bad."

Jasmine laughed. "Indeed I do, but I meant you're very good in thinking of my needs."

"Oh, that," he shrugged. "I could always get better," there was a short hesitation before he finished, "with practice."

"And you haven't practiced enough?"

"God," he groaned, his mouth at her temple, her cheek, her jaw, her throat. "Not nearly enough."

"Shouldn't we go back?" she asked weakly.

He groaned as if in pain, his arms tightening their hold. "I can't," he whispered as his teeth and tongue ate hungrily with growing desperation at her neck and shoulder. "Not until I've touched you, discovered your taste."

Jasmine chuckled a low, erotic sound that nearly pushed him over the edge of his control as she nuzzled her lips to his ear. "But you already know what I taste like."

"I'm afraid I keep forgetting. You don't mind if I refresh my memory?"

Jasmine moaned as he pressed his mouth to her shoulder, his teeth grazing her flesh as they tugged the lacy straps of her chemise aside, his mouth burning moist kisses to the upper curve of her breasts. "Oh, Anthony, we shouldn't." She gasped, never finishing her thought, for the wet material lowered as if by magic and the heat of his mouth brought blinding pleasure as it drew her nipple deep into scorching flame and erased every word she was about to say.

"I know you'd rather wait for more privacy. And we will. Just let me bring you this small pleasure."

Jasmine groaned, unable to fight the need that grew to life in the pit of her belly as he suckled. She knew she should stop him, but right now she couldn't remember why. In any case, she couldn't seem to find the words. His hands moved to her hip. He followed the smooth line to her leg and under her wet chemise.

Her knees wobbled and yet another gasp escaped slackened lips as he slid warm fingers up her leg, never stopping until they reached the moist, lush heat they instinctively sought. Gently he laid her upon the clean clothes he'd brought for her and slid further down the length of her until his mouth joined his hands in a blissful, mind-boggling massage of tongue, teeth, and lips.

Jasmine was helpless under the onslaught of sensation he aroused. She couldn't gather her thoughts, never mind speak an articulate objection. Capable now only of low groans and broken sounds that might have been words, she raised her hips to his hungry mouth.

Fighting against the need to drown in her scent, her feel, her touch, Anthony kept an ear to any sound of interruption. He dared not lose himself in her sweetness, for he chanced much should another come unexpectedly upon them. Still, it was beyond his power to resist this small, wondrous sampling, no matter the havoc it brought to his senses.

His hands cupped the silky fullness of her breasts, his fingers worrying the tips to hard buds as his mouth sank with a sigh of delight into the warm moistness of her. God but she was beautiful. He smiled, listening to the choking, helpless sounds that came unwittingly from her throat. Her response to his touch was wild and uninhibited. Her submission forgotten, she demanded everything he could give. It boggled his mind to realize she was anything and everything he could desire in a woman.

Her hands clutched at his hair, pressing him closer to her heat, and Anthony groaned, knowing the tension built within. Not for a moment did he grant her quarter from the ecstasy of what would come, but continued his loving assault until Jasmine was naught but a wild, straining being, hungry for the release his mouth promised.

Beyond thought, broken words escaped her throat, garbled and incoherent words she never realized she'd uttered. All she knew was feeling and the need to sample even more of this wonder. Pleasure, pain, it mingled as one as a breathless ache tightened her abdomen. Her hips rose from the bed of leaves and clothing, silently urging him on, wordlessly imploring he end this delicious suffering.

Her breathing grew almost nonexistent as her whole being strained toward the coming exquisite torture. And then it was there at last. She sobbed with relief, a choked broken sound muffled behind her fist as she strained forward, hungry for the sensations that would rock her to the core.

Anthony felt the tremors begin. His mind swam with delight as his mouth greedily absorbed the smooth rhythmic waves of pleasure. He groaned against the painful ache to take her despite their surroundings. If he didn't end this soon there was no telling what he might do.

He was ready to explode by the time he felt the throbbings ease in strength. Never in his life had he wanted a woman like this. Never could he remember being so unselfish in his loving. He took her at last in a gentle embrace and held her close to his still aching body. Curiously he found a measure of joy in this simple act, even if his arms did shake with the effort it took to merely keep her beside him.

Jasmine snuggled her face into his neck. "Small pleasure, eh? You have a talent, sir, for stating with restraint."

Anthony grinned as he brushed strands of black damp hair from her cheeks. "Be careful. I think you're close to giving me a compliment."

Jasmine chuckled, the sound low and throaty. "Oh, dear, I wouldn't want to do that."

"Indeed not. Why, there's no telling what might happen if you bestowed a compliment. Miserly though it would no doubt be, I might believe you enjoyed the times spent in my arms. And if I thought that, I might even . . ." Deliberately hiding the grin that threatened, he allowed his sentence to falter.

"Even what?" she asked with sudden interest as she pressed him to his back and leaned over him.

"What?" he grinned, reading the inquisitive light in her eyes.

"You might what?" she laughed as she swatted his shoulder.

Anthony shrugged. "Well, if I thought you enjoyed our lovemaking, I might go so far as to show you a thing or two that could drive you mad with lust."

"Good Lord, no!" she remarked in mock horror. Suddenly she shot him a sly look and asked, "More than I've already . . . ?"

"Hmm." He grinned. "I see that's piqued your interest."

Jasmine laughed. "You didn't answer me."

"Madam, I'm not about to share all my secrets. Not unless I know I'm appreciated."

Jasmine breathed a sigh as she played with the thick lock of golden brown hair that curled over his forehead. "There's no hope for it then, I'll simply have to tell you the truth of it." She grinned. "After all, I wouldn't want to miss anything."

Anthony nodded solemnly. "A very wise decision, I would say."

"Do you suppose this one telling will suffice?"

"I doubt it."

"You mean I'm to rave of your mastery at every encounter?"

"Would that be asking too much?"

"Probably, since I'm usually incapable of speaking after . . . after . . ."

"Making love?" he offered.

Jasmine nodded. "After making love. But I suppose I could do it this time with no effort, since I'm already talking."

Anthony growled as he reversed their positions. He

loomed above her, his expression fierce. "Are you going to say it or not?"

Jasmine giggled. "I would, but I don't know what to say."

"You could tell me I'm the most passionate, skillful lover you've ever known."

She shot him a look of reproach. "You're the *only* lover I've ever known."

He glared at her. "That makes no difference. You could tell me I make you wild when I love you."

Her eyes widened. "Anthony, you know you do. I can't deny it."

Anthony shook his head. "You could tell me you love my touch."

Her brow furrowed, digesting his words. "Well, I guess I do. I never gave it much thought before."

A grin tugged at his lips. "Woman, you're sure to turn my head at these flowery compliments."

Jasmine giggled as she looked up into his warm gaze. "Suppose I tell you I've never been happier or more content than when in your arms."

"And?" he waited.

"And! You want more?"

His mouth lowered to her smiling lips as he whispered, "I want everything I can get from you."

Chapter Twenty-Three

Indian meal, fried in bacon grease and dried beef! Lord, if she never again saw what had come to be the staple of the colonists' diet, she'd count herself as smiled upon by God.

Jasmine forced another mouthful past her objecting taste buds and down her throat. She needed the nourishment and, although she might prefer the bark from the trees to the flavor, this fare would fill her belly and give her the energy needed to face each grueling day of travel.

After their meal, a jug of rum taken from the confiscated supplies was passed around the campfire. Jasmine watched as each in turn took healthy swipes from the earthen vessel and then wiped their mouths on the backs of their hands. It was obvious from their lusty sighs that the brew did not go unappreciated, for nary a drop had dampened the tongues of these men for months on end.

Jasmine had cause to consider their obvious delight when the jug came around to her. It was clear the men considered her one of them as they offered her a turn. With a shrug Jasmine lifted the container to her mouth and took a healthy swallow.

Jasmine had often sampled drink and she enjoyed a sherry after the evening meal. She'd tasted port and once, when she had a sore throat, had sipped at a snifter of brandy. But nothing had ever prepared her for the bitter taste and searing heat that now assaulted her mouth and throat.

Her eyes widened first in amazement and then shock as the harsh liquid burned its fiery path down her throat and heated her stomach to a roaring inferno. Her eyes watered, tears ran unchecked over her cheeks, and her mouth hung open. She sat suddenly stiff, as still as a statue, for she could neither breathe in or out.

All four men knew well enough her shock, for her expression couldn't have made her suffering clearer. Boggs sat at her right, Anthony to her left. Every eye was turned in her direction, all conversation ceased, mouths smiling as each watched her reaction closely.

Suddenly from her right came a huge hand and a mighty slap to her back. Jasmine gasped. Cool air brought blessed relief from the fire that burned as it rushed down her throat and into starved lungs. She took another breath, this time to steady herself, but coughed instead. She wiped her mouth on the back of her hand and then, bravely, with only the smallest of shudders, took another sip.

Conversation continued as if it had never ceased as Jasmine silently passed the jug to her husband.

Anthony sat quietly, barely listening to the idle talk as the men relaxed around the fire. His attention focused almost solely upon the lady at his side and he wondered what had become of the spoiled, haughty woman she'd once been. Surely the young bride who had most reluctantly come to meet her husband in the Carolina woods would have turned up her nose rather than partake in this community drink. And had she by chance sipped at the brew she would have undoubtedly made loud and clear her distaste.

Anthony could hardly equate this woman to the one who would have wept over a broken nail. Now all of her nails were ragged, hands that were once well cared for were now calloused, her face, neck, and arms were tanned to a deep bronze, and her formerly elaborately dressed hair streamed in heavy, silken waves down her back. Anthony smiled with pride, knowing she'd never looked more beautiful.

It was obvious the others realized her beauty as well, although out of respect to their captain, they did their best to control their impulse to stare. Anthony forced aside a threatening grin as he remembered their expressions upon seeing Jasmine dressed in britches for the first time. Her rounded hips and bottom could not be easily disguised without the aid of petticoats. And the trousers he had thought to be a bit large were in fact only so at her waist.

Anthony had decided the view a remarkably beautiful sight as he followed her back to camp. Once among his men again, it became increasingly obvious that he wasn't alone in this judgment, for his men's eyes nearly bulged from their sockets at the sensual, unusual sight of a lady in trousers.

As soon as possible he managed to get her alone. When Jasmine rejoined the men, her shirt was outside the trousers, disguising a goodly portion of her curves.

Anthony knew the Jasmine he'd first known would not have been half so conciliatory. Enraged at her forced position, she might have purposely flaunted her garb and silently dared the men to do more than stare. No, the stubborn, spoiled lady he had first desired was gone, replaced by this woman of soft humor, of sweet character, of gentle strength.

She might not as yet have taken his cause as her own. Perhaps she never would. But she had put aside her own beliefs and grown into a woman loyal to her husband, no matter their differences. Silently he marveled that he should have been given such a woman to love. All he could hope was to be worthy of this sweetest of gifts.

The sound of more than a dozen men charging into their camp brought him from his silent reverie.

Guns always at the ready, he reached to his side for his weapon, only to find the effort too late, for the hard barrel of a rifle was already pressed sharply to all four backs. There was no alternative. Guns were dropped, hands raised in surrender.

It took Jasmine a full minute to realize she was being addressed, so stunned was she at the unexpected sight of these easily recognizable British soldiers. "Captain Remmings at your service, ma'am." His mouth grew into a hard line, his voice hardly more than a sneer. "My men tell me you were a major factor in the loss of their supplies, madam."

Jasmine came to her feet, forcing aside the shiver of dread that raced down her spine as she faced the cruel glare of the officer in charge. She didn't answer his remark, but faced him squarely with a bravery he was at a loss but to admire. In truth, Jasmine felt not a moment's bravery, but was so frightened she dared not speak, lest all know, from her quivering voice, her terror.

The officer nodded at her silent look, his gaze warming as he took in the full extent of her beauty. "In truth, I can see now their dilemma," he remarked, his eyes widening with surprise as his gaze took in her unusual style of dress.

Still Jasmine said not a word.

"You will come with me," the officer remarked, his head nodding in the direction he wished her to take.

"No!" Anthony shouted, knowing full well by the direction of his gleaming eyes, resting even now upon the lush curve of Jasmine's breasts, the man's intent. An instant later he gave a silent curse as he watched his adversary's mouth grow into a vicious smile of victory. Anthony groaned and damned his thoughtless remark for showing he cared. Now the bastard would take particular delight in Jasmine's abuse just knowing of his suffering.

"Who is he to you?" he asked, his gaze resting for a minute on Anthony's now expressionless face.

Jasmine glanced at Anthony's closed expression and then back to the leering grin of her captor. "He kidnapped me, sir. I was visiting my cousin. She is about to deliver her sixth child, when he and his men attacked the farmhouse. For weeks he's dragged me through these godforsaken forests. How can I ever thank you for rescuing me from these barbaric colonials?"

Anthony fought back the groan at her words, knowing the officer would discount her story, for the telling of it was weak at best. Would the man believe the lie? Did he, too, hear the tremor in her voice? Would he recognize the lady in the rags and treat her kindly? Or would he take the opportunity at finding a woman in this wilderness and bring her to his bed? Anthony could only pray the man was more stupid than he looked.

He was not.

Jasmine's eyes widened as she dared to look behind the man in charge, confirming the truth of her first glance. The men Captain Remmings led were the very same Anthony's small group had relieved of their supplies, not one week past. How he had come upon his comrades, Jasmine had no idea, but she knew they must have marched day and night to have caught up. A quick glance at still-bootless feet confirmed her suspicions, for even wrapped as they were, many had left dark markings of blood upon the dirt.

Captain Remmings looked less than convinced. "If it's true he forced you to accompany him, how was it you were instrumental in his thievery?" he asked while nodding toward the four surviving wagons that stood only partly hidden amid the tall grass.

Jasmine gave an elaborate sigh and prayed he'd believe the helpless flutter of her hands. "I am but a poor woman, sir. What choice had I when a gun was put to my back?" Jasmine shot Anthony what she hoped was a look of hate. "He thought a pretty face would distract your men."

Captain Remmings grinned, feeling a definite stirring in his trousers. Jesus, it had been months since he'd had a woman. Years maybe since he had one who looked like her. "I can see well his reasoning." For a moment Jasmine imagined him satisfied with her answers, but at the growing gleam of hunger in his eyes she knew the futility of such a hope. "You will come with me now."

Anthony's mind was not working with its usual cool competence. He was far too much in love with his wife to keep a rational thought. All he knew was he had to take action now. The thought of this bastard's hands on her was enough to make him lose the last of his reason.

It happened so fast that Jasmine knew she was destined to see the next few moments as a dizzying, speeding blur ending with the sickening pumping of blood for as long as she could remember. Anthony lunged at the man behind him, effectively relieving him of his gun, while hitting him in the jaw with the butt of his own rifle. In an instant he faced Captain Remmings again, the gun aimed with deadly menace at the man's belly. It might have ended there, for Anthony clearly had the upper hand, but for the startling shot that rang out before Anthony had a chance to pull the trigger.

Jasmine jumped at the unexpected sound. A deathly silent pall spread over the camp as the gun slid limply from Anthony's hands. Before this slow movement, she thought the ball had gone wide of its mark, but almost immediately knew the truth of the matter. Anthony's head snapped back and she watched with mounting disbelief as a gush of blood spouted from the side of his head to splash upon his shoulder like a sickening thick red fountain.

Anthony's knees buckled. In dazed amazement she watched his struggle to stand, but the effort proved beyond him. His eyes, already glazed, rolled back until only the whites showed. A moment later his low groan mingled with the sounds of her screams. It was the last thing he remembered as he landed on his face in a small puff of choking dust.

Jasmine tried to take in the scene, tried to make sense of what had just happened. But she couldn't think, for all she could see was the blood. He was dead. She knew it as surely as she would take her next breath. She waited for the pain to crash upon her, the aching breathless agony of her loss that would surely come. But nothing touched her, nothing but a stunned sense of disbelief. She had to go to him. She had to make her feet move, but they wouldn't obey the directives of her mind. And then she gave up trying and, like her husband, knew nothing but the miraculous relief only blackness can bring.

Jasmine awoke to a moment's confusion. She looked around, her eyes widening at finding herself lying upon a cot inside a tent. How had she gotten here? Had Anthony found a tent among the supplies? Why couldn't she remember? There was something important she must remember. Something very, very important. Why couldn't she remember?

Jasmine gave a low groan of breathless anguish as the happenings of the evening flooded her mind. She remembered. Fool that she was, why wasn't she content to forget?

She turned her face into the small pillow lest she let go the wail of agony that begged for release. She

424

dared not give in to the need, for to do so would mean the last of her control. And without control, she'd flee like one possessed, screaming like a banshee into the night, never to stop till she breathed her last.

No, she wouldn't scream, no matter the pain that lodged in her throat and chest, but she should cry. She willed the tears to come then, knowing the action would wash away the sharper edges of her despair. But her eyes remained dry and had she looked into a mirror she knew they'd appear flat and lifeless, for she could not imagine a reason why she should continue to live.

And then it came to her. Out of a night gone insane, out of an anguish that threatened to tear her insides apart, she suddenly knew. She would right this terrible wrong. Only then would she allow herself to dwell on her loss. Only then would she welcome the luxury of tears. Only then would she pray for the sweet relief of death, for to live without him was to not live at all.

The pain, suffocating in its intensity, cut into her chest not unlike a knife and stole the very air from her lungs. The horrifying weight of it lodged heavily upon her chest. Eyes dry, she stared at the white canvas overhead and smiled. No matter the longings of her mind, her body demanded what it would. And she found herself helplessly cursing each involuntary, gasping breath. Idly she wondered if her body refused to die, mightn't she find relief in madness, for the pain was growing to horrifying proportions and she had not the will or the strength to see this agony to its end.

Jasmine lay for long moments, her mind filled with a longing to hold him once more. It mattered not that his life was gone from his body. She needed to touch him, to hold him in her arms one more time. Surely they'd not deny her this one small request.

Deliberately she put aside the unbearable suffering, knowing there'd be time aplenty, years, if she was cursed to live that long, to succumb. Right now she needed to think. She'd accomplish nothing unless she could think. For out of the horror that filled her mind came a surprising revelation. She knew a building rage, a rage that rivaled even her suffering in its intensity. She wanted revenge.

A hatred unlike anything she'd ever before suffered came upon her. She slid long legs over the side of the cot and came to her feet. She couldn't rest. Even now Anthony's murderers were outside the tent laughing as they sat around the campfire, laughing as if they had not on this night destroyed her life. They couldn't be allowed. Not after taking him from her. No, they wouldn't laugh, not on this mournful night. Her mouth tightened. Not ever again.

"I see you are quite recovered, madam. I do apologize for what must seem to you a most barbaric act."

Jasmine's spine stiffened with loathing at the hated sound of his voice. Wisely she knew she'd gain little should this man know the depth of her feelings, less, if she resorted to violence. No, she needed to bide her time. Only then would her chance to inflict equal suffering come.

Jasmine schooled her features to reveal none of her raging emotions. She smiled her most charming smile as she turned to face her enemy. Her voice was softer and sweeter than even she had expected. "Worry not, Captain," she remarked with a slight wave of long, delicate fingers. "It is I who should apologize." She smiled again and allowed a helpless look to enter her eyes. "You must excuse my weakness. I'm afraid I've never before witnessed such violence," she lied, somewhat amazed at the steadiness in both voice and manner, for she was almost wild with the need to run this man through.

Captain Remmings seemed taken aback. He never

426

thought to remind her of her own words, knowing she'd had to have seen her share of violence if her story about being kidnapped was true. The truth of it was he hadn't expected this reaction. He'd thought her to come tearing at him, raining every curse she knew upon his head, for, judging by her expression of horror and blood-curdling scream, she had indeed felt something for the leader of this ragtag group. But if Captain Remmings was amazed at her sweet speech, he was nothing less than astonished at his next words. "You must rest. You will, of course, take my tent for the night."

"Thank you, Captain," she remarked, forcing another smile to her lips and a softness she was far from feeling to her eyes. "You are very kind."

Captain Remmings gave a silent curse as he bowed and left his tent, all the while damning himself to hell for a fool. Why did he feel this need to treat her in so civilized a manner? Certainly he believed none of her lies. What lady, no matter her circumstances, would dress in so disgraceful a fashion? She was obviously a camp follower at best and, at worst, equal to the scum he'd found her with. He'd heard stories of women taking up guns to fight alongside their men. Could she be one of those oddities? He wished to hell he knew. He wished just as fervently he wasn't the gentleman, for he wanted nothing more than to bed the wench.

What he needed right now was a healthy portion of rum. If he partook in enough of the brew, maybe then he wouldn't notice her ladylike mannerisms and speech. Or maybe he would, but just wouldn't care. Captain Remmings grinned as he approached the fire. If he was lucky he might yet convince the wench to share his bed. Remmings laughed aloud, ridiculing his own thoughts, for luck had little to do with it. He was the officer in charge and she had little recourse but to accede to his demands. A smile

427

lingered at his lips as he imagined the delightful night that lay ahead, his pleasure to end only with the dawning of a new day.

Jasmine held to no misplaced illusions. She knew the captain did not believe her story. In truth, she doubted she'd believe the tale herself. She knew as well his original purpose upon entering his tent. The man wanted her. Of that she had no doubt, for his desire shone clearly in his eyes. What she couldn't understand was why she wasn't even now fighting off his advances. Jasmine shrugged. Having no knowledge of the man, she might never know his reasons for leaving her in peace, nor did she care, for all that concerned her now was to devise a plan to get out of the tent. She had to find the others. And if they still lived, she had to set them free.

Jasmine searched through the captain's meager belongings and despaired upon finding not a weapon, not even a knife, among his things. It was with a groan of disgust that she pocketed his straight razor.

A quick look around the tent and her shoulders slumped with defeat. Nothing. All the weapons were outside. She had to get to them, but how?

Jasmine stuck her head out the tent's opening and almost screamed as she came face-to-face with a soldier standing silently on guard. "Oh, my God," she gasped. "You gave me a terrible fright."

Apparently the young man was every bit as shaken as she, for he took a startled step back. It was obvious he hadn't expected to see her, believing her already asleep. Immediately he realized his duty and stepped forward to block her path. "You be wanting something, ma'am?"

"I . . . ah . . ." Jasmine desperately searched for a reason to leave the tent. A reason he'd believe. "I have a need to go into the woods. Would you let me pass?" Jasmine could feel the blush creeping up her cheeks, even as she spoke the lie.

She didn't realize it, but her embarrassment only matched his. His face flamed, for this subject was never mentioned among mixed company. "I . . . I should ask the captain," he stuttered.

"Oh, please don't," she said before thinking, and then prayed he'd take her words for proof of her shyness. "There's no need. I . . . you see, I don't want everyone . . ." She let the sentence falter, giving a helpless wave of her hand.

The young man, all of seventeen, was loath to bring the lady further mortification. He glanced behind him at the campfire and shrugged. "I guess it would be all right. I'll have to go with you, though," he added as Jasmine made to move by him.

Jasmine looked at him as if he'd clearly lost his mind.

"The captain would . . ." His expression told of the helpless situation he found himself in. "I can't let you go alone."

In the end it was Jasmine who took pity on the boy. "Of course. I quite understand," she said, forcing a sweet smile as they moved together into the darkness. She should have known she'd never be able to simply walk out of the tent and free the men. Captain Remmings knew she lied. He would have stationed a guard, of course, and she knew she needed to find a way to get rid of him.

A sideways glance told her the impossibility of winning out against his strength, for the boy might be young, but he stood a good head taller than she. Jasmine shook her head. No, she wouldn't win with strength, but perhaps weakness would make her the victor.

Jasmine stumbled, deliberately making more of the motion than was necessary. Her shoulder hit his chest and a soft cry of alarm escaped her throat. She smiled as he reached out, his intent to steady her.

Jasmine leaned against him for one moment, one arm circling his waist. In her other hand she held the razor, pressing it theateningly against his belly. "Don't move," she whispered and pressed just a bit harder.

The soldier was clearly amazed. It took him a full moment to realize what she was doing, for the feel of a woman as full-bodied as Jasmine leaning against his chest had befuddled his senses.

His hands dropped suddenly to his sides and he made to step back. Jasmine's arm tightened at his waist. She couldn't chance his seeing what she held in her hand lest he simply laugh at her clumsy attempt. He must believe she held a gun to his stomach. Everything depended on his believing it.

"Drop your rifle to the ground and turn around," she ordered, praying her voice held the menace it needed for him to accede to her will.

"You have no gun. You were searched." The boy's voice trembled. Clearly he prayed his words the truth.

Jasmine pressed the blunt end of the razor harder into him. "Are you fool enough to find out?"

"If you shoot me, all will come running."

"What matter is that to you? You will already be dead."

Relief in the extreme rolled over her, causing her hands to shake and her knees to wobble as the soldier did exactly as he was told. "Move," she whispered as she snatched the gun from the ground and pressed its bayoneted end to his back.

Silently, at her direction, they skirted the camp. It seemed to Jasmine to take forever before they reached the three men tied together at the near edge of the tall grass. Jasmine groaned at the sight before her, for they had not been left alone. Two British soldiers stood guard only a few feet to each side.

They didn't have a chance, not any chance at all. Even if she managed to free them, they were four

430

against more than a dozen. What was she to do?

Jasmine's mind worked madly toward a solution. She rejected one hastily formed plan after another when the opportunity miraculously presented itself.

All in camp came suddenly to their feet as one, for their captain was screaming every wild curse word he knew, staggering from the tent with a mighty roar of "She's gone!"

Orders were called out to find the wench. The men, rifles in hand, were running in every direction. A moment later all was quiet but for the murmured voices of the two remaining guards.

Jasmine then made her presence known and indicated the soldier was to go forward by a not-too-gentle prodding at his back. "Drop your weapons," she ordered, her voice barely above a whisper. "I wouldn't," she remarked as the two turned to face her, their rifles ready to fire. She nodded toward her captive. "He'll be the first to go."

There was a moment's hesitation before she repeated her order. "Drop your guns."

With muttered curses, the two men reluctantly did as they were told. "Untie them," she nodded toward the three men staring, eyes agog, at this amazing turn of events.

Moments later, Boggs, Cooper, and Billings were tying and gagging the guards. "We ain't got much time. They'll be awonderin' back when they find no sign of you."

Jasmine nodded, knowing Boggs spoke the truth. "Where is he?" she asked.

It wasn't necessary for any of the three to ask of whom she spoke. By the determined set of her chin they knew as well that to try to talk her out of seeing him this one last time would be a waste of breath.

"Over there," Billings nodded into the darkness, opposite the campfire.

"Get him and let's go."

All three stared in amazement at her easily spoken and to their minds ridiculous order. Did she mean for them to carry a dead man with them? Drag a lifeless body through these woods? Didn't she realize the chances of escaping would be next to impossible if she insisted on this madness? Surely she didn't mean it. No doubt she was suffering some quiet form of hysteria.

"Now, missus," Boggs began.

Jasmine instantly recognized the placating tone of his voice. "Boggs, we've no time for arguing. I'm not leaving without him." She gave them a long look and then shrugged. "If you won't help me, I'll . . ."

The vivid curses would have no doubt singed her ears had Jasmine been more in her right mind. But of this moment, all she could think was of him lying alone in the darkness with no one to care for him. It mattered not what they thought, said, or did as long as they brought Anthony to her. It was her reason for escaping, her reason for living. She had to touch him. She had to hold him just one more time. And if it meant endangering their safety, so be it.

She followed their reluctant steps as they searched out the darkness for Anthony's body. It was Cooper who stumbled across him. Jasmine was immediately at his side almost before the startled curses left the man's throat.

On her knees she pulled Anthony's lifeless, heavy body to her, hugging his bloodied face against her breast. The tears came then with surprisingly sudden and aching force. She couldn't stop the sobs as she rocked back and forth. She forgot their need to be gone. Her only wish was to hold him forever.

She couldn't see, for the night was starless and they were beyond the glow of the campfire. All she knew was the wet warmth of his face. Again and again her hands roamed over the loving surface of his still features. She brushed away the blood and her tears

432

bathed his skin.

"We have to go," one of the three said, taking her arm and trying to pull her to her feet.

"I'm not leaving him," she said as she snapped her arm from his hold.

"I know how you feel. But he's dead. He'll never know . . ."

"I'm not leaving," she insisted, her voice gaining in volume. "If you won't help me, I'll take him myself."

"Get the horses," Boggs suggested, knowing the uselessness of arguing. "All of them," he added, realizing correctly the greater their chances if the Brits had to follow on foot.

Suddenly all sound came to an abrupt halt as they very clearly heard Anthony's low moan. Jasmine stiffened, hardly daring to hope, unable to think, to pray, finding it impossible to even breathe.

He moaned again and Jasmine succumbed to another bout of crying, only this time her tears were of hope, of love, of joy.

"Sonofabitch," Cooper growled. "He ain't dead. Jesus Christ, he ain't dead!"

Chapter Twenty-Four

"I'm afraid it makes little difference. He will be momentarily." Captain Remmings's menacing whisper came from out of the darkness.

The three men dove for cover, rolling wildly upon the ground as they strained to see the exact location of their enemy in the black night. The guns taken from the guards were pointed with deadly accuracy. Shots were fired.

Jasmine lay full length upon her husband, instinctively using her body as a protective shield, but her action was already too late. She never saw the sudden jerking of his body as a ball caught the fleshy part of his thigh nor would she realize this second injury for some time to come.

Jasmine's heart thundered with fright at this newest obstacle. She'd thought they had more time. She'd hoped they might be long gone before the searching men ever returned to camp.

"You might as well give it up. You haven't a chance of escaping," Captain Remmings called out.

But he might as well not have bothered, or perhaps it was well he did, for the sound of his voice gave clearly away his position. Three guns fired simultaneously. They heard the startled sound, a gasp of relating pain, and then a soft thud as a body fell upon

434

the earth.

The next few seconds would forever remain a muddled haze of sounds and movement. Running footsteps. Startled shrieks. More shots fired. And then agonizing cries of pain filled the night as she and Anthony were being dragged deeper into the cover of underbrush.

It seemed to her that the fighting went on forever. Jasmine was anxious to be gone. How much longer would she have to wait until they could make good their escape? Low, unconscious, desperate sounds of fear mingled with prayer as Jasmine cuddled her husband's face tightly to her breast.

She almost laughed in wild relief as Cooper crept up behind her at last. Miraculously he had managed to secure the horses. A moment later she watched as Anthony was yanked none too gently from her arms and settled roughly over the saddle of a horse. She meant to cry out her objection to his careless treatment but forgot her intentions as Cooper mounted the horse behind him. A moment later she, too, was swung up upon the back of yet another horse and the small group was dashing wildly through the underbrush. Twice she was almost knocked from the saddle as tree limbs smacked hard against her. Ebony hair blended well into the dark night but was yanked from her head as if clearly seen and the wildly flowing ends caught upon many greedy branches and vines. A hundred scratches burned her arms and face and yet she never even winced, for she noticed not the discomfort. All she knew was the pounding of her heart as she urged her horse to race forward.

Suddenly they were on the road, the horses' hooves pounding almost as loud as the blood in her ears as they raced down a dangerously dark, uneven dirt road.

They didn't stop, never even slackened their pace until the first rays of dawn slid slowly over the horizon. Jasmine wondered if Anthony hadn't died after all, no matter their attempt to rescue him, for she doubted his weakened state would stand this grueling pace.

They stopped to rest the horses for a time. Her first and only thought being of Anthony and his welfare, she rushed to his side and breathed a sigh of relief to find him breathing still. Silently she blessed his unconscious state, for at least he suffered no pain. How much longer could he take this mode of travel? How much longer before they reached safety?

Thankfully, Jasmine had not long to wait. Her eyes blurred with tears of relief, for before the sun rose to its highest point they came across an inn, a welcome sight indeed to this weary, ragtag group.

The owner was, thank God, a patriot, although Jasmine doubted it would have made much difference to these determined men, for they would see to Anthony's care and comfort before they went on to join Morgan. It had taken a bit of persuasion on their part to induce the innkeeper to spare a room for their injured captain, but in their present anxious state, it mattered not.

Jasmine leaned over and examined the sickly gray tone of Anthony's skin and swayed as a wave of nearly debilitating weakness overcame her. Her heart thundered with something close to panic. How much blood had he lost? Even now the wound bled. How could a man survive such an injury? *Would* he survive? "You will," she muttered. "You'll live or I'll . . ." Jasmine had the sense to grin at her useless threats.

Her back ached. She knew she should rest, but she had no time to cater to her own needs, not when Anthony lay so still upon the bed.

Someone had to see to his care and she trusted no one but herself.

She was shaking with exhaustion by the time she had seen to his comfort. Thank the Lord Mrs. Kelly, the innkeeper's wife, was on hand to assist and lacked nothing in the way of muscle. A white bandage and padding covered a goodly portion of his head, while another his thigh. It wasn't until she'd rid him of the blood-soaked clothes that she'd noticed the second less serious injury. She cursed in frustration, realizing at last he'd been struck again in the short, intense battle just before their escape. But the injury was merely a flesh wound. It bled itself clean and, as far as she could tell, held no bullet.

Three days had gone by, three days that crawled by with incredible slowness as Jasmine sat and watched her husband in helpless frustration. Morning became night and night morning again, but Jasmine barely noticed. All she could do was watch the shallow movement of his chest. All she could think was to pray the movement would never cease. Would he ever awaken? Was she, after all her care, destined to suffer the horror of his death for yet a second time, only this time in truth?

A knock sounded softly upon the door. Jasmine's smile was hardly a smile at all as she greeted the lady innkeeper. "Has his condition worsened?" Mrs. Kelly asked, her voice sharp with alarm.

"Nay, he remains the same." Jasmine shook her head wearily, her slender shoulders slumped with fatigue and worry.

"You should rest."

She shook her head again. "I cannot."

Mrs. Kelly nodded her understanding. "A group of men have quartered themselves for a time upon the grounds. There is a doctor among them. He's promised to take a look at your man the moment he's able."

Jasmine's spirits lifted some at the news. Even so, she held little hope, knowing there was little anyone could do. Doctors, mere mortals, held no magic cures.

Nay, if Anthony was to live through this it would be God's doing.

Jasmine's sigh was filled with frustration as she saw the doctor out. It was much as she'd thought. The doctor could do nothing with his implements or medicine to speed Anthony's recovery, merely suggesting she should talk to him, knowing the longer Anthony remained unconscious, the less his chances for recovery.

Jasmine began following the doctor's advice the moment the door closed behind him. She invented stories. She related incidents from her childhood, describing the horse she had in England, the girls she had attended finishing school with. She talked until her throat was dry, until her voice was little more than a whisper. And when she imagined she couldn't go on, she began again.

It was another two days before she saw the results of her efforts. She was just finishing Anthony's daily bath when she heard, "How is it I never realized before how talkative my wife can be? Haven't you imagined it a bit more merciful to allow your husband a few moments of peace and quiet? Don't you realize you've an injured man on your hands?" Jasmine's head snapped up, her eyes swung to his face, her mouth hung open with shock.

When it became apparent he had silenced her at last he grunted crankily, "That's better." And then, "I'm thirsty."

Jasmine's smile was slow in coming, but when it did it nearly dazzled him with its brilliance. Her soft, silky laughter filled the room as her silver eyes showed clear the love and relief that filled her being. "Are you injured? Indeed, sir, it's well you've awakened in time to tell me."

Jasmine managed to lift his shoulders from the bed

438

as she held a glass to his mouth.

Anthony hadn't the strength of either body or mind to comment upon what he perceived as unwarranted sarcasm. He groaned as she once again placed his head upon the pillow. "Where are my men?"

"They've gone on to find Morgan."

"Sonofabitch! And left me behind?"

"I'm afraid you would have been of little use to them in your present condition."

"How long?"

Jasmine shrugged as she sat beside him again. "About four days ago."

He eyed her suspiciously. "You aren't going to tell me you've been caring for me alone for four days."

Jasmine laughed. "Would you rather Mrs. Kelly saw to your needs? I promise you she'd not be half so gentle as I."

"Who the hell is Mrs. Kelly?"

"She and her husband own this inn."

Anthony's gaze moved about the strange room. He nodded with a tired sigh. His eyes drooped as he struggled to remain awake. He wanted to ask a hundred questions, not the least of which was how they managed to escape the English, but he couldn't seem to summon the strength. "I won't have you tiring yourself. You look awful. You need rest," he murmured, his voice growing noticeably weaker with every word spoken.

Jasmine shook her head with a wry grin. "Can't say much for how you look either, beast that you are." He'd been asleep for five days, and what did he do the moment he awakened? Did he tell her how much he loved her? Did he thank her for saving his life? Jasmine's grin threatened to burst into wild laughter, so great was the happiness that filled her soul. In truth, she didn't care what he did or said, as long as he lived.

Jasmine laughed softly to see him sleeping again,

only this time she knew it was truly sleep and not some horrifying form of unconsciousness. "If you know what's good for you, you'd better apologize the minute you wake up." And for the first time in five days she was confident he would.

Jasmine stood in the ale room, her eyes wide with surprise. She had been just about to lift the tray and take it upstairs when through the large windows she saw the rider dismount and tie his horse to the hitching post outside. Her heart fluttered with pleasure as she moved to welcome him. How had he found her? How long must he have searched?

"Richard!" she said as she opened the door and pulled him inside.

"Jasmine!" Richard gasped, momentarily stunned. Suddenly he took her in a bearhug and swung her off her feet, spinning her in a circle. He almost growled, "Jesus, I can't believe I've found you at last. Your mother's been half out of her mind with worry. Are you all right?"

"As you can see I'm fine. You needn't have worried."

Richard shook his head. "When we got your note . . ." He left the sentence hanging as if he couldn't relate the terror they'd known. He breathed a long sigh. "It took me some time, but I finally found the inn where you claimed to be and they told me you had been taken off by some madman. Not that they believed him, but he claimed to be your husband."

Jasmine giggled. "Anthony and I had a bit of a disagreement."

Richard shook his head. "I suspected as much. Where is he?"

"Upstairs. He's been seriously injured." And at Richard's look of concern she added, "He's weak, but he's healing nicely."

"I don't suppose you'll be leaving soon?"

Jasmine shook her head. "Anthony won't be ready to travel for some time."

Richard sighed unhappily, for he wanted nothing more than to return to New York and Elizabeth. "I'd best send off a note to your mother and get myself a room then. She will kill me if I come back without you."

They met again that evening in the ale room and shared a leisurely evening meal. "I've convinced Mr. Kelly to part with his coach. Now I have to rustle up some horses. Damn, supplies are nearly non-existent what with Washington commandeering anything that can move. The only reason Kelly still has his coach is that the damn thing is so old and heavy, it would take too many horses to pull it.

"How is Anthony coming along?"

"Just fine." Jasmine chuckled. "When he wakes up he's as grouchy as a bear."

Richard grinned. "I know. He didn't appear thrilled to see me this afternoon."

Jasmine nodded. "He's not the type to stay in bed. It frustrates him. But he has no choice. He's lost a lot of blood. No matter his anger, he hasn't the strength of a baby."

Richard nodded in understanding. "Would you like to take a walk before bed?"

"I'd like that very much," she agreed. Jasmine hadn't been outside since she'd arrived more than a week ago and greatly appreciated the offer. They moved toward the edge of the clearing, beyond the company of rebel soldiers who had camped on the grounds of the inn. The top floor of the inn had been taken over for the care of those seriously injured soldiers, while others sat around a dozen or more fires, awaiting their orders to march again.

"Jasmine . . ." Richard spoke, his hesitation clear.

"I've been wanting to tell you something for a long time. I don't want you to think any less of your mother because of what I say. It was not her fault. She was only a young girl, a confused and unhappy young girl."

Jasmine shot him an inquisitive look and noticed his worried expression. She smiled. "I'm sure Mother would not agree with you. As far as I know, she's never done anything she hasn't wanted to do. I imagine that includes loving you."

"Yes, but . . ."

"I already know you are my father."

Jasmine heard his startled breath and smiled. "And the knowledge doesn't upset you?"

"I think you are a very nice man, Richard Townsend. My mother's never been happier. It's not up to me, I think, to pass judgment on anyone."

"You are a very wise young lady. I expect your mother will want to explain the circumstances."

Jasmine's smile froze on her lips as she heard the sound of drums and spotted the movement. She spun on her heel, her intent to race back toward the inn, but Richard grabbed her arm and knocked her to the ground. "No!" he grunted as she fought him fiercely, for the men at the campfires had been caught unawares and were now scrambling to find some sort of cover from the hundreds of uniformed British soldiers who surrounded the inn.

The sounds of gunfire filled the night. She had to get to Anthony. He couldn't be left unprotected. He wouldn't have a chance if those men broke through the lines and entered the inn.

Jasmine needn't have worried, for the British were not at all interested in entering the inn. Indeed, their intent was to burn it to the ground as a reminder to any who would aid the enemy.

Jasmine screamed a blood-curdling sound of pure horror as she saw the torches and realized their intent. When the building caught fire, she watched as those able to ran from the flames. She clawed at Richard. She kicked and screamed like someone possessed, but he held on, refusing to allow her to run into certain death. It might have been better if he allowed her to go.

Jasmine walked along the busy streets of Manhattan. No longer did the British hold the city, for on the very night the inn had been torched, Cornwallis had surrendered to Washington at Yorktown. Jasmine gave a small, sad smile. It had all been for nothing. Anthony had died not for the freedom he held so dear, but because of some British officer's revenge.

She had lost her sense of reason on that day. For weeks she had drifted on the edges of insanity. Greedily she'd hungered for oblivion. She didn't want to think. She didn't want to know.

After she had screamed her throat raw, Richard had returned her to her mother in a close to comatose state. There was nothing she could do to relieve her mother's worry. She couldn't seem to help herself, for she'd felt no will to respond, no will to live.

It was five months to the day. Five months of sitting in her room. Five months of wishing she, too, was dead and cursing every morning that found her alive and healthy. Until this morning. This morning she had felt her baby kick for the first time. She'd felt movement before, but not anything to equal this strength. Suddenly the knowledge had come upon her. Anthony wasn't dead. She was carrying the proof that he indeed lived on.

Jasmine spent most of the morning shopping for material. There was little enough to be found in this huge city, since the shortages of war had yet to right itself, but a bolt of flannel was finally found, and with it a yard of ribbon had been sent to her house. With her mother's help, Jasmine would make the baby's clothes. She felt another kick and grinned. If she was wise, she'd hurry her loving chore, for she doubted this child had any more patience than had his father.

Before she returned home, Jasmine stopped by the stable to check on Hercules. It had been ages since she'd ridden him last and months before she'd be able to do it again.

The stable gave her a bit of a twinge, for this was where it had all begun. For a long time she stood beside the animal, lost in the memories of a daring young man and his even more daring treatment of a certain young lady. Jasmine smiled as she remembered Anthony's supposed fumblings. How he had grabbed at her. How he had *accidentally* touched her. She gave a soft laugh. She had thought him simple-minded, and the beast, the wonderful, darling beast had taken full advantage. Jasmine's memories were disturbed by the sound of a rider bringing his horse back.

With a wistful smile of sweet remembrance, Jasmine left Hercules's stall. The horse had been well cared for. Mr. Cramby had seen to his brushing, but she needed to talk to the man. Perhaps he could find someone to ride Hercules occasionally. The horse needed exercise.

"Mr. Cramby?" she called out.

At the sound of her voice he flattened himself against the wall. His heart pounded in his chest. His hands began to sweat.

Suddenly she was standing before him. Her back was to him. She didn't suspect his presence. He didn't want to scare her. Her mother had told him of her condition when he stopped by the house. How in hell was he going to break the news to her without causing her a fit of hysterics?

"Don't be afraid." His hands had come around her thickening waist to rest on her small but swelling

444

stomach as his low voice whispered close to her ear. His face twisted as sweet joyous pain came to flood his entire being. He hadn't known it would hurt like this. He'd wanted her for so long, he hadn't imagined his joy to bring this exquisite agony of need.

Jasmine gasped and stiffened. She hadn't expected anyone might be lying in wait for her. Where was Mr. Cramby? Would he hear her if she screamed for help?

Jasmine opened her mouth, having every intent on finding out, when a hand quickly covered her mouth. She was being dragged back. He was saying something, but the words wouldn't penetrate the fog of terror that had suddenly taken hold of her mind. He was dragging her toward the tack room. God, she had to break free. If he hurt her . . . If he hurt the baby . . .

She kicked him. He cursed. She jabbed him in his belly with her elbow. She heard his breathless grunt and yet still he held her against him, his hand over her mouth.

Jasmine sank her teeth into a finger and grunted with some satisfaction as she heard a string of curses. Suddenly, with a small shove Jasmine was flung free of his hold. The door to the tack room slammed ominously behind her. Every nerve tingled with dread. She wanted to run, she wanted to hide, but Jasmine would face her attacker. She turned in slow, almost measured degrees, trying to prepare herself for a monster who would take a woman against her will, for Jasmine had no doubt the man meant to rape her. The room was silent but for her soft gasp. Her eyes grew wide with amazement. Her lips began to form an almost haunted smile but never quite made it before the blackness descended and she crumbled into a boneless heap.

Anthony caught her a second before she would have hit the floor. He was cursing wildly. This was exactly what he hadn't wanted to do. Jesus, if he'd

445

hurt her or the baby, he'd never forgive himself.

Jasmine came awake with a soft moan to find herself cuddled in someone's arms. For a long moment she couldn't imagine who held her. He was sitting on a low stool, his back against the stable wall. They were still in the tack room.

She gasped as she remembered. Her head snapped back butting hard against his jaw. "Damn it!" he grunted as he began to rub the injury.

"Damn *you*, don't you mean?" Jasmine returned as an anger unlike anything she'd ever known filled her being. "You son of a bitch. You bloody bastard. You . . ."

"Jasmine," Anthony interrupted her tirade. "Why are you cursing me?"

Jasmine jerked herself from his arms. On wobbly legs and fighting the dizziness that assailed, she clung to the room's only table. "Why did you let me think you were dead? I hate you for how I suffered. I hate you."

Anthony came to his feet, muttering a stream of disgusted curses. "It just so happened after I stumbled out of the fire, I lay in the woods for days. A young boy eventually found me and dragged me home to his mother. I was feverish for months, maybe more. I don't remember. It was a long time after that before I was strong enough to travel." Anthony looked down at his snarling wife with equal fury. "Here I was expecting a joyous reunion. I should have known better. No sweet-tempered wife for me."

Jasmine muttered another curse and pushed by him. The door was open and she was almost through it before she came to an abrupt stop. What was she doing? Was she out of her mind? God, she'd suffered the ravages of hell for five months, believing him dead. Somehow he had miraculously escaped the fire. He stood here now and what did she do? She cursed him and screamed as if she had totally lost her reason.

Jasmine smiled, knowing it was the shock of seeing him again that had brought on her unreasonable, almost hysterical behavior. Well, she could rectify that.

Slowly, silently, she moved back into the room and shut the door. Anthony's back was to her. His shoulders were slumped as though exhausted. He thought she had gone. Jasmine's eyes moved hungrily over his form. He was thinner than last she'd seen him. Now that she thought on it, his face seemed gaunt and almost gray with fatigue. Jasmine closed her eyes with a silent prayer of thanks that God had brought him back to her.

Jasmine settled the bar to the door in place and smiled as the sound brought Anthony's attention to her.

"What are you doing?" he asked after a long moment of silence, his breath coming in short almost gasping puffs as his eyes took in the movement of her hands.

"I'm taking my clothes off. You don't mind, do you?" Her dress was dropped carelessly to the floor.

Anthony gave her a long, lazy grin. He leaned his hip against the table and crossed his arms over his chest. His warm gaze watched with avid interest as she pulled her chemise over her head. Never in his life would he have imagined their meeting in a barn again. "Not angry anymore?"

Jasmine's eyes were soft, half closed with building desire. "Was I angry?" Her grin sent his blood to pounding and she shrugged and then smiled at his sharp intake of breath, her breasts swinging free with the motion of stepping out of her petticoats and frilly drawers. She was standing there completely naked and never more at ease. "Would you rather we wait until we get home?"

Anthony shook his head, unable to take his eyes from the delicious sight of her. His mouth grew dry.

A pulse ticked in his throat. She was more beautiful than he'd ever dreamed possible. Her belly was rounded with child, but she didn't look the least matronly. She was a bold temptation, a temptation he'd never have the power to resist. Her waist was thicker, but her hips lushly round, her breasts fuller, heavier. And if he didn't touch her soon, he might just die of this longing.

It didn't seem at all incongruous to find his wife naked in this roughly hewn room. In truth, the primitive surroundings only seemed to emphasize her silken loveliness. "What would you have done if I'd come across you in the street?"

Jasmine smiled and shrugged. "A hackney, perhaps? Actually, since this is where it began, it's only right for us to . . ." She was walking toward him, her hands eager to help him disrobe.

"Finish it?" he offered, his voice tight.

"Well," she shrugged, allowing her breasts to rub enticingly over his chest and belly as she helped him off with his trousers. "Finish isn't exactly what I had in mind."

"Isn't it?" Anthony almost choked, his breath no more than a rasping sound, for the touch of her bordered on agony. "What exactly did you have in mind?"

"I love you," she whispered so softly he had to strain to hear. Her voice was low and throaty, her eyes were shining with unshed tears. "I'll always love you. What I had in mind was to show you how much."

"Ahh, God, Jasmine," he groaned as his arms moved around her. He closed his eyes with the exquisite pleasure of her softness against him. His face was pressed into her hair. His voice shook with longing, but neither noticed as he asked, "Forever, Jasmine?"

"Forever, my love."